An Arranged Marriage

"I know what I have said in the past, Allie. And I know how I feel about you. I cannot promise that I will make you the best of husbands, but I will promise to try. By my troth, lass, I *can* tell you that I want you... more, I think, than I have ever wanted anything in my life."

With that, he put gentle hands to her shoulders, drew her closer, and when she continued to gaze up at him, he kissed her softly on the lips.

Heat rushed through her, and her arms slid around him, drawing him tightly to her. She felt his body move against hers. Then one of his hands clutched her hair, lacing fingers through it and cradling her head while he kissed her thoroughly.

RAVES FOR THE NOVELS OF AMANDA SCOTT

HIGHLAND HERO

"4½ stars! Scott's story is a tautly written, fast-paced tale of political intrigue and treachery that's beautifully interwoven with history. Strong characters with deep emotions and a high degree of sensuality make this a story to relish."

—*RT Book Reviews*

"[Scott's] colorful characters and their relationships will absorb readers, while her plotting, dialogue, and narration are also excellent. She's a true master of the Scottish historical romance... We can all look forward to Wolf's tale in HIGHLAND LOVER. Judging by the first two (and other of Ms. Scott's fine series), I'm confident enough to highly recommend all three books." —RomRevToday.com

"[A] deep early fifteenth century Scottish romance starring a strong cast. As always in an Amanda Scott historical the inclusion of real persona and facts enhances the romance... Readers will enjoy the historical romance between Ivor and Marsi as they escort and protect the future king of the Scots while falling in love."

—GenreGoRoundReviews.blogspot.com

"[A] well-written and a really enjoyable read. It's one of my favorite types of historical—it's set in medieval times and interwoven with actual historical figures. Without a doubt, Amanda Scott knows her history... If you enjoy a rich historical romance set in the Highlands, this is a book to savor."

—NightOwlRomance.com

"[A] gifted author... a fast-paced, passion-filled historical romance that kept me so engrossed I stayed up all night to finish it. The settings are so realistic that the story is brought to life right before your eyes... This story is sure to be a favorite... It can be read as a standalone, but for additional enjoyment, do not miss the first book in this series, *Highland Master*. I look forward to reading Ms. Scott's next addition... In the meantime, do not miss *Highland Hero*!"

—RomanceJunkiesReview.com

"A highly enjoyable read with some surprising twists and turns."

—FreshFiction.com

HIGHLAND MASTER

"Highly recommended! Marvelous Scottish tale of a time in history when various plays for power were held... a powerful story and a piece of history as well as a great tale. Amanda Scott does it again with another fascinating part of Scottish history."

—*Romance Reviews Magazine*

"Scott, known and respected for her Scottish tales, has once again written a gripping romance that seamlessly interweaves history, a complex plot, and strong characters with deep emotions and a high degree of sensuality."

—*RT Reviews*

"If you like conflicted heroes and the feisty heroine who adds to their conflict, you will love Fin of the Battles and the Mackintosh Wildcat." —*Romance Reviewers Today*

"Great with sensual scenes, Scott escapes the cliché of a masterful male taming a 'wildcat' woman; instead, Fin and Catriona learn to communicate and compromise in this solid romantic adventure." —*Publishers Weekly*

"Ms. Scott is a master of the Scottish romance. Her heroes are strong men with an admirable honor code. Her heroines are strong-willed...This was an entertaining romance with enjoyable characters. Recommended."

—FreshFiction.com

"One of the more accomplished and honored romance novelists writing today...If you are one of Scott's fans, you'll want to make sure you don't miss this...If you haven't read Scott before, you'll be pleasantly surprised to see how she uses her knowledge of Scottish history to weave an engrossing and sexy story."

—TheCalifornian.com

"Deliciously sexy...a rare treat of a read...*Highland Master* is an entertaining adventure for lovers of historical romance." —RomanceJunkies.com

"Passion, swordplay, and exemplary research of the era."

—*Sacramento Bee*

"Fast-paced...dynamic...Amanda Scott proves once again she is the Highland Master when it comes to a thrilling tale starring Scottish Knights."

—*Midwest Book Review*

"Hot...There's plenty of action and adventure...Amanda Scott has an excellent command of the history of medieval Scotland—she knows her clan battles and border wars, and she's not afraid to use detail to add realism to her story." —All About Romance

TEMPTED BY A WARRIOR

"4½ Stars! TOP PICK! Scott demonstrates her incredible skills by crafting an exciting story replete with adventure and realistic, passionate characters who reach out and grab you...Historical romance doesn't get much better than this!" —*RT Book Reviews*

"A descriptive and intriguing novel...Scott's characters are most definitely memorable." —Rundpinne.com

"Captivates the reader from the first page...Another brilliant story filled with romance and intrigue that will leave readers thrilled until the very end."

—SingleTitles.com

SEDUCED BY A ROGUE

"4½ Stars! TOP PICK! Tautly written...passionate...Scott's wonderful book is steeped in Scottish Border history and populated by characters who jump off the pages and grab your attention...Captivating!"

—*RT Book Reviews*

"Another excellent novel from Amanda Scott, who just keeps producing one fine story after another."

—RomanceReviewsMag.com

"Readers fascinated with history...will love Ms. Scott's newest tale...leaves readers clamoring for the story of Mairi's sister in *Tempted by a Warrior.*"

—FreshFiction.com

TAMED BY A LAIRD

"4½ Stars! TOP PICK! Scott has crafted another phenomenal story. The characters jump off the page and the politics and treachery inherent in the plot suck you into life on the Borders from page one. This is the finest in historical romance."

—*RT Book Reviews*

"[Scott] instills life and passion in her memorable characters...Few writers have come close to equaling her highly creative and entertaining stories."

—ClanMalcolm.com

"Fascinating...fourteenth-century Scotland's rich history comes alive in this romantic novel full of intrigue."

—FreshFiction.com

"Scott creates a lovely, complex cast."

—*Publishers Weekly*

Other Books by Amanda Scott

HIGHLAND HERO
HIGHLAND MASTER
TEMPTED BY A WARRIOR
SEDUCED BY A ROGUE
TAMED BY A LAIRD
BORDER MOONLIGHT
BORDER LASS
BORDER WEDDING
KING OF STORMS
KNIGHT'S TREASURE
LADY'S CHOICE
PRINCE OF DANGER
LORD OF THE ISLES
HIGHLAND PRINCESS
THE SECRET CLAN: REIVER'S BRIDE
THE SECRET CLAN: HIGHLAND BRIDE
THE SECRET CLAN: HIDDEN HEIRESS
THE SECRET CLAN: ABDUCTED HEIRESS
BORDER FIRE
BORDER STORM
BORDER BRIDE
HIGHLAND FLING
HIGHLAND SECRETS
HIGHLAND TREASURE
HIGHLAND SPIRITS
THE BAWDY BRIDE
DANGEROUS ILLUSIONS
DANGEROUS ANGELS
DANGEROUS GAMES
DANGEROUS LADY
THE ROSE AT TWILIGHT

AMANDA SCOTT

Highland Lover

Book 3 Scottish Knights Trilogy

FOREVER

NEW YORK BOSTON

Forever
Hachette Book Group
237 Park Avenue
New York, NY 10017

www.HachetteBookGroup.com

Printed in the United States of America

First Edition: April 2012
10 9 8 7 6 5 4 3 2 1

Forever is an imprint of Grand Central Publishing.
The Forever name and logo are trademarks of Hachette Book Group, Inc.

To Debi Allen, Jody Allen, Rosemary Murray &
the many other readers who have become members
of the Aid Amanda's Research Society,
I thank you all most sincerely!

Rothiemurchus
CAIRNGORMS
Balmoral
HIGHLANDS
Dundee
Cargill
Perth
St. Andrews
Lindores
River Earn
FIFE
MENTEITH
Kincardine
Aberfoyle
Doune
Falkland
Dunblane
Firth of Forth
Drymen
Stirling
Balloch
Dumbarton
Milton
Edinburgh
Glasgow
Firth of Clyde
Ayr
Turnberry Castle
SCOTLAND 1403
- - Highland Line

Author's Note

For the reader's convenience, the author offers the following guide:

Ciara = SHAR-a

Clachan = village

Fain = eager

Forbye = besides, furthermore, however

Gangplank = the board or ramp that provides access from dock to galley

Gangway = the walkway between the rows of oarsmen's benches on a Highland galley, birlinn (a large galley designed to carry cargo), or a hybrid

Ivor = EE-ver

Owf = not crazy but "off," not normal

Rothesay = ROSS-y

Shoogle = roil, shake up

Strath = valley, usually a river valley

. . . the noo = now

Highland Lover

Prologue

Falkland Castle, Scotland, 27 March 1402

The man she saw lying awkwardly on the dirt floor was unnaturally thin, little more than skin and bones. Even so, she could sense his pain. She sensed, too, that his parched, dry skin felt too tight for his body. His once silky, fair, shoulder-length hair was straw stiff and dull from grime and lack of nutrients.

He lay curled on one side, as if he had sought to return to his mother's womb or felt pain in his stomach. One thin arm stretched outward, palm open, to catch cornmeal drifting down on pale beams of light that slipped through narrow spaces between planks of the mill floor high above him. The meal looked like ordinary dust motes dancing in ordinary moonbeams.

Since her view of the scene seemed to emerge from a surrounding black cloud, she was unsure of how she knew about the mill. But she was certain of its presence and certain that the drifting motes were cornmeal, not dust.

Even as that thought passed through her mind, she recognized a stronger perception that could not be hers and must be the man's own vague awareness of meal in his open palm that he lacked strength to bring to his mouth.

His frustration seemed to add force to his thoughts, making them easier for her to discern. He was as good as telling her that he lacked even strength or will enough to lick his lips, which also bore a coating of meal. It had kept him alive for what he reckoned must be more than a fortnight now. His guards had given him water only twice. But he had known better than to trust those who had imprisoned him, and made each drop last as long as he could.

Almost wryly, he told himself that if he survived this ordeal—if a friend learned of his peril and summoned aid to him before it was too late—right after he hanged his fiendish uncle and the Douglas, he would order the royal dungeons altered. To see sunlight and moonlight only when filtered through corn dust and wood planking was more torturous than never to see light at all.

She knew that it was already too late. He lacked even the strength to acknowledge the pain in his shrunken gut anymore.

As that thought drifted through his mind…or hers… or both together…blackness followed. The last of his pain disappeared, and she felt tears streaming down her cheeks.

Sitting bolt upright to find herself alone and shaking in the familiar darkness of her bedchamber in St. John's Town of Perth, her tears still streaming, she knew that what she had seen was no nightmare but a truth that she dared speak to no one.

Davy Stewart, the heir to Scotland's throne, had just died.

Chapter 1

Stirling Castle, late February 1403

The English ambassador disapproved of his mission and had from the instant he'd understood its goal. However, it was no business of his to express his opinions to heads of state, not to his own and certainly not to Scotland's Duke of Albany, who eyed him now across the large table Albany used as a desk in his audience chamber.

Clad elegantly in black, the sixty-two-year-old duke stood second in line for Scotland's throne. He had, in fact, due to one cause or another, ruled Scotland as regent—or Governor, as the Scots called it—for many years, occasionally even when, as now, he lacked any titular right to do so.

Although his still-dark hair contained increasingly more silver, Albany was as politically astute as ever, and as ruthless.

Having long negotiated secretly with him for Henry IV of England, the ambassador knew that the duke possessed a quick, intelligent mind and was cold-blooded, unpredictable, and skilled in wielding his authority. His usual tone was chilly, but he could be affable if it served his purpose. Above all, he was a man with a deep understanding of power who did all he could to increase his own.

"You will need a royal safe-conduct for your return," Albany said abruptly.

Reflecting on the fact that the duke had already kept him kicking his heels for a fortnight, the ambassador wondered if his safe-conduct had become an issue.

Warily, he said, "Although our countries enjoy a rare truce, my lord, one does feel safer passing through your Borders *with* a safe-conduct than without one. However... Pray forgive me, sir. But as his grace, the King, is away..."

When Albany frowned, the ambassador paused again, hoping he'd made his point. After Davy Stewart's death, many having suspected Albany's hand in it, the Scottish King and Parliament had refused to name him Governor again.

Albany had waited barely two months before demanding that the King summon his lords again and order them to do so. His grace had submitted, as usual, to Albany's stronger will and ordered Parliament to meet directly after Easter. But would its ever-unpredictable lords submit as easily to the duke's demands?

"No one will dare doubt the validity of a safe-conduct bearing my signature," Albany said flatly. "Now, I'm sure you've arranged the details of that matter we discussed before and have everything in train."

"Yes, my lord," the ambassador said. "As I said when last we met, we require only the name of the—"

"I received that information yestereve," Albany interjected curtly, reminding him that the duke also had a passion for secrecy. "Recall that *you* must not act as intermediary."

"Indeed, my lord. I shall employ the courier who acted for his . . . um . . . for us before. One assumes that the promises we made about the cargo . . ."

Again, diplomatically, he paused.

"I care only about matters on which your master and *I* have agreed and not a whit about promises to his minions or about the cargo," Albany said. "So, unless you have more we must discuss, our business is done. Collect your safe-conduct from my steward as you leave."

"With respect, my lord, you still have not given me the name I require."

Albany did.

The Firth of Forth, Friday, March 16

Nineteen-year-old Lady Alyson MacGillivray grasped the urgent fingers clutching her arm and tried to pry them loose, saying, "Prithee, calm yourself, Ciara. If this ship sinks, clinging to me will avail you naught."

"Mayhap it will not, m'lady," her middle-aged attire woman said, still gripping her hard enough to leave bruises. "But if this horrid ship drops off another o' these giant waves as it did afore, mayhap neither o' us will fly into yon wall again."

Alyson did not reply at once, having noted that, although the huge vessel still rocked on the heaving waters of the firth, the noises it made had changed. The wind still howled. However, the awful creaks and screeches that had made Ciara fear aloud—and Alyson silently—that the ship would shake itself apart had eased.

"We're slowing," Alyson said.

The cabin door opened without warning, and Niall Clyne, Alyson's husband of two and a half months, filled the opening. He was a handsome, fair-haired, blue-eyed man of mild temperament, whom she'd known for most of her life. He ducked as he entered, to avoid banging his head against the low lintel.

Alyson saw at once that he looked wary.

"Put out that lantern, Allie," he said. "We must show no light aboard now."

"Who would see it?" Alyson asked reasonably. "That tiny window—"

"Porthole," Niall said.

"—is shuttered," she continued. "Little light would show through it in any event. Surely, on such a dark night—"

"Just put it out," he said. "It isn't safe to keep a flame here in such weather."

Ciara protested, "Sir, please, it be scarifying enough in this place *with* light! Forbye, in such weather, we ought never tae ha' left Leith Harbor! Men did say—"

"An overturned lantern would quickly start a fire," Niall interjected. "And, with no way to escape, a fire at sea would be even more terrifying than one on land."

"But—"

"Hush, Ciara," Alyson said, watching Niall. Although the order he'd given was sensible, she was as sure as she could be that he was relaying it from someone else. Without moving to put out the lantern, and glad that Ciara had released her arm when the door opened, she said to Niall, "We have stopped, have we not?"

"Aye, or nearly, for we've dropped two of our anchors," he said. "But you must put out that light, lass. Even the storm lights on deck are dark now."

"So we don't want to be seen," Alyson said. "But who would see us?"

"That is not for you to know."

"Do *you* know?" she asked. "Or is your friend Sir Mungo keeping secrets from you as well as from us?"

With audible strain in his voice, Niall said, "You must call him 'Sir Kentigern,' Alyson. His friends call him Mungo, because that's what friends often do call a man named Kentigern. But he is not *Sir* Mungo to anyone."

"I keep forgetting," she said calmly. "Sir Kentigern is such a lot to say. But you do not answer my question. Do you know why we have stopped?"

"I do not," he said. "I ken only that they've sent a coble ashore with six oarsmen to row it. Now, will you put out that light, or must I?"

"I'll do it. Good night, Niall."

"Good night, my lady." Evidently, he trusted her, because he left then and shut the door.

Ciara waited only until he had done so to say with panic in her voice, "Ye'll no put that light out, m'lady, I prithee! 'Twould be dark as a tomb in here!"

"Do you want Sir Kentigern to come down here?" Alyson asked.

"Nay, I do not," Ciara said. "For all that he may be the master's friend, I dinna like him."

"Nor do I," Alyson said, careful not to reveal the understatement of those three words in her tone. "Lie down on yon shelf bed now and try to sleep when I put out the light. I shan't need you to undress me."

"I ken fine that I shouldna sleep in your bed," Ciara said. "But I'll take it and thank ye, because get in that hammock and let this storm-tossed ship fling me about with every motion, I *will not*!"

"Hush now, Ciara. Take advantage of this respite and try to sleep."

Why, though, Alyson wondered, were they stopping?

They had left Edinburgh's Leith Harbor at dusk, Sir Kentigern "Mungo" Lyle having insisted they could wait no longer. Mungo was secretary to the Earl of Orkney, whom Niall also served. It was on business of Orkney's that the men were sailing to France, and since they could be away for months, Niall had agreed to take Alyson with him. Mungo had not concealed his disapproval when they'd met him at the harbor. But Niall's insistence that he could not send Alyson all the way home to Perth, alone, had been enough. Whether it would satisfy Orkney when he learned that she was with them remained to be seen.

Alyson had met the earl, who was a few years her senior, several times. As the wealthiest nobleman in Scotland, and one of the most powerful, Orkney knew his worth. But he was not nearly as puffed up in his own esteem as Mungo was in his.

But Mungo had doubtless meant only to please the earl by hastening their departure. Storms had delayed and battered their ship, the *Maryenknyght*, on her voyage from France with her cargo of French wines. Then men had to load the return cargo, and the ship's captain took two more days to make hasty repairs.

But now, whatever was occurring on deck...

"I am going up to see what's happening," Alyson told Ciara. "Prithee, do not argue or fling yourself into a fret, because you won't dissuade me. We are where we are, but I want to know where that is and what they're doing on deck."

"Prithee, m'lady—"

"We can judge our danger better if we have information, Ciara. So just be patient and try to sleep. I'll hold this lantern until you are safe on that bed but no longer, lest Mungo come down and dare to look in on us."

If he did come down, he would likely run into *her* on her way up. But Alyson doubted that Ciara would think of that. Ciara was concerned with her own safety, which was reasonable but irrelevant when one could do naught to ensure it.

Ciara eyed her mistress measuringly. Although she had served Alyson only since her wedding, she evidently knew her well enough to see that further debate was useless, because she quickly unlaced and doffed her kirtle. Then, lying on the narrow bed in her flannel shift, she pulled the quilt over her, gritted her teeth, shut her eyes, and nodded for Alyson to put out the light.

Alyson donned her fur-lined, hooded cloak and snugly fitting gloves, then blew out the lantern and found its hook on the wall. Hanging the lantern carefully, she felt for the door latch and raised it, hoping she would not be so unfortunate as to meet anyone before seeing what there was to see.

The cabin door opened onto a narrow, damp passageway ending at a ladder that stretched to the deck. The ship's hold lay below, no longer containing wine casks but roped piles of untanned hides and bales of sheared wool going to France. That cargo was noisome enough already to fill the passageway with pungent odors.

Wrinkling her nose but relieved to see faint light coming through the open hatchway, Alyson raised her skirts with her left hand, touched one wall with her right for balance, and moved toward the ladder.

Its rungs were flat on top and the ladder just seven feet or so to the hatchway, but ascending it in skirts was awkward. A wooden rail aided her when she climbed high enough to reach it, and she emerged in an area between the shipmaster's forecastle cabin and a second, smaller one.

The wind was thunderous. But the hatchway, recessed between the two cabins, sheltered Alyson from the worst of it. The hatch cover was up, strapped against the cabin on her left as she faced the stern.

She wondered if it had been so all along or if Niall had opened the hatch and left it so. Surely, it should stay shut to keep the angry sea from spilling into the passageway, the two tiny lower cabins, and the vast hold below.

Above her, black clouds scudded across the night sky. Gaps between them briefly revealed twinkling stars overhead and a crescent moon rising above the open sea to her right amidst flying clouds. Those clouds seemed to whip above, across, and below the moon in a wild, erratic dance.

Since Edinburgh was behind her, she knew she must be facing east. The ship's prow therefore pointed southward, so they were at the mouth of the Firth of Forth.

Looking aft but still to her right, she saw moonlight playing on glossy black mountains of ocean. To her left, she discerned the firth's south coast where dots of light twinkled in the distance—perhaps the lights of North Berwick.

When she stepped forward to look due south past the master's cabin, she had to hold her hood against the whipping wind. But the view astonished her.

At no great distance beyond the ship's rail, sporadic moonlight revealed a precipitous rock formation looming above tumultuous waves that broke around it in frothy, silver-laced skirts wherever the moonlight touched them.

She could hear that crashing surf despite the howling wind.

Surely, she thought, no boat could land there. But why stop if not to send one ashore or wait for one coming to them? Stepping back into the deep shadows of the alcove between the two cabins, she continued to watch.

Shadowy figures moved on deck, but no one challenged her.

Not long afterward, through the darkness, she saw a boat, a coble, plunging toward them through the waves. In a patch of moonlight, she saw that it was full of people. At least two were small enough to be children.

Not far away, unbeknownst to anyone aboard the *Maryenknyght*, a smaller ship more nearly akin to a Highland galley than to the merchantman rode the heaving seas. Sir Jacob Maxwell, the *Sea Wolf*'s captain, kept his gaze fixed on the much larger ship. When its sail had come down as it passed North Berwick, he'd suspected the ship was the one he sought. When it dropped anchors off the massive, nearly unapproachable formation known as the Bass Rock, he was sure of it.

The wind blew from the northeast quarter. The merchantman had anchored well away from the rock and with its prow facing southeastward. Thus its leeward length sheltered its steerboard side when it lowered a boat.

"Be that our quarry, sir?" his helmsman, Coll, asked in Gaelic.

"It must be, aye," Jake replied in that language.

Although born in Nithsdale, near the Borders, Jake had spent two-thirds of his life on ships. Much of it he'd spent in the Isles, so he believed he was nearly as much a Highlander as his helmsman was. Moreover, most of his men spoke only Gaelic, so most conversation aboard was in that language.

"I cannot make out her flag in this darkness," Coll said.

"She is the *Maryenknyght* out of Danzig," Jake said. "She was flying a French flag when she entered Leith Harbor, and I'd wager she flew that flag when she departed. However, it could be some other flag now."

He did not add that the *Maryenknyght* belonged to young Henry Sinclair, second Earl of Orkney. Nor did he mention that Henry had ordered the ship to Edinburgh for this particular, hopefully secret, purpose.

Orkney owned more ships than anyone else in Scotland. But he had not wanted to use one that others would easily recognize as his. Thus had the *Maryenknyght* made what Jake knew was her first voyage to Scotland.

For a fortnight, he'd kept a man posted at Leith to watch for the ship, harboring his *Sea Wolf* at a smaller, less frequented site on the firth's north coast. However, he had learned the *Maryenknyght's* name and intended time of departure only that afternoon. Glancing at his helmsman, he knew that Coll was bursting with curiosity, although his expression revealed none.

Looking back at the *Maryenknyght*, Jake said, "The coble's returning."

"I don't envy them climbing up that hulk in these seas," Coll muttered.

Jake realized he was holding his breath as he watched

the first of the coble's occupants, clearly its steersman, prepare to climb a rope ladder to the ship's deck.

Exhaling, Jake forced himself to breathe normally.

One of the six oarsmen caught the ladder's end while his two comrades on that side did their best to keep the coble from banging against the ship. Meanwhile, fierce winds and incoming waves tried to push ship and coble back to Edinburgh.

"By my soul," Coll muttered when the steersman had reached the deck and a second, much smaller passenger gripped the ladder. "That be a bairn, Cap'n Jake! What madness goes on here?"

Jake did not answer. His attention riveted to the lad, he felt his pulse hammering in his neck, as if his heart had leaped into his throat.

"Sakes, look at him," Coll breathed. "He's going up that ladder as deftly as ye might yourself, sir."

"I suspect that after being lowered in a basket to a plunging boat from halfway up the sheerest face of Bass Rock, as I heard they would be, climbing a rope ladder must seem easy," Jake said.

"On a night like this?" Coll exclaimed. "Who the devil would be crazy enough to order such a thing?"

"His grace, the King," Jake replied.

Aware of Coll's stunned silence, Jake watched the second lad climb the ladder as lithely as the first. Returning his gaze to the coble to see a tall, slender man grab the ladder next, he felt his jaw tighten again.

Having counted the men in the boat, he knew that this one had to be Henry of Orkney. Jake had known him almost from Henry's birth and liked him. He did not want the wicked weather to plunge the earl into the ice-cold sea, where he might drown before others could reach him.

However, Henry could swim. And Henry was not Jake's first priority.

"Am I to know who those lads be, sir?" Coll asked.

Jake hesitated. But he had known Coll for over a decade and trusted him. Moreover, they'd be following the *Maryenknyght* to her destination. And accidents happened, even to men who had lived their lives aboard ships. If aught happened to him, Coll should understand the exact nature of their mission.

Knowing that the wind would blow his words away before they reached ears other than Coll's, and that the men were heeding their oars, Jake leaned nearer and said, "Wardlaw said nowt to me in St. Andrews about any second lad, Coll. But one of those two lads will inherit the Scottish Crown."

In the uncertain moonlight, he saw Coll's eyes widen. "Jamie Stewart?"

"Aye, sure, for since Davy Stewart's death—"

"Sakes, sir, that were a year ago!"

"It was, aye. But whilst Davy's death was still new, James was safe at St. Andrews Castle under Bishop Wardlaw's guardianship. Forbye, after Parliament proclaimed Davy's death an accident instead of the murder we all know it was, his grace began to fear for Jamie's life, too."

"That explains why the lad has been missing these two months and more," Coll said. "But how could they have survived so long atop that rock?"

"There is an ancient castle built into it about halfway up."

"Ye be jesting, sir. Nae one could build a castle there."

"Believe it," Jake said. "Sithee, Coll, when his grace recognized the threat to Jamie, he decided to send him to our ally, the King of France, for safety."

"Aye, well, ye need not tell me who his grace fears might harm the lad," Coll said with a grunt. "Only one man can be sure to benefit from such, and that be his murderous uncle, the Duke of Albany. But if aught happened to the laddie, would not the country rise in fury against Albany afore he could seize the throne?"

"Likely they would have, had Jamie died last year soon after Davy," Jake agreed. "But he did not. Recall, too, that folks expected Parliament to declare Albany responsible for Davy's death. Instead, the early winter prevented many of the Highland lords from reaching Perth, allowing Albany's allies in Parliament to declare Davy's death an accident. They could not, however, vote to make Albany Governor again, because the King was too distraught to agree."

Coll nodded. "But Parliament will meet again afore Easter, and Albany has had time to persuade his grace. What be our place in this business, sir?"

"We are merely to report back to Wardlaw when Jamie gets safely to France," Jake said. "And perhaps to do what we can to aid that ship if aught goes amiss."

After watching men rush to help the first child aboard and wrap him in blankets, Alyson went back down to her tiny cabin. Since the country had been speculating for months about the fate of their eight-year-old prince, she immediately suspected who one of the two children might be.

The business that Mungo and her husband, and doubtless the Earl of Orkney himself, had in France was likewise more understandable. Was Henry not head of the wealthy and powerful Sinclair family, which had long supported kings of Scots even when many Sinclairs had disagreed with them?

Indeed, from the outset, she had wondered why, when they were on Henry's business, they were sailing on a storm-battered merchantman. Henry owned dozens if not hundreds of finer ships. She also knew that if she was right and James Stewart *was* their primary passenger, she dared not linger to see who else was with him.

She would be wiser to proceed with caution until she learned more.

When they raised anchor and headed south with the wind behind them, it was less thunderous, and she slept well on Ciara's swaying hammock until morning.

Alyson wasted no time after waking before going on deck, where with overcast skies and rain threatening, one of the first things she saw was Henry's tall figure emerging from the master's cabin. He showed neither surprise nor delight at seeing her but greeted her cordially.

"Good morrow, my lord," Alyson replied.

"In troth, 'tis a dismal day," he said with a wry smile. "Forbye, I must tell you how sorry I was to miss your wedding to Niall."

"And are even sorrier to see me here now," she said. " 'Tis true, is it not?"

With a rueful look, he said, "It is, aye, though in courtesy I should not say it."

"With respect, sir, you may always speak the truth to me. I admire candor. What others call tact or cosseting often results in misunderstanding of one sort or another. Do you not agree?"

His blue eyes twinkled. "*I* might, but others would disagree, madam. Most people, in my experience, don't appreciate honesty as they should."

She smiled but said, "That *was* young Jamie Stewart I saw come aboard from the coble last night, was it not?"

"You saw that, did you?"

"I did, aye," she said. "In troth, Niall ought not to have let me come."

"Niall didn't know," Orkney said. "Very few people do. I sent my secretary to Danzig to arrange quietly for this ship simply because it had not sailed in Scottish waters before and was unlikely to be known as one of mine."

"I see. Am I right to deduce that we are taking James to France? Or have you another destination in mind?"

He glanced around before replying in a lower tone than before, "We do sail to France, Lady Alyson. But this ship's captain and crew are Prussian. So, although we'll address both boys by their given names, we'll say little about them to others."

"Doubtless that is an excellent notion, sir. However, I trust that you won't keep two such lively lads cooped up below, in that wee cabin opposite mine."

"They slept on pallets in the master's cabin last night, with me, and are still asleep," he said. "Likely, I'll turn Mungo and your husband out of the cabin next to mine and order *them* into that smaller cabin below. I did not do so last night for fear of waking you and your woman."

"I see," she said. "But if you want no undue attention drawn to the boys..."

Henry frowned, saying, "I thought that as Jamie has been living rough these past months, I could at least give him the more comfortable cabin. But I should not. Still, one dislikes . . ." He paused thoughtfully.

"In troth, I have been trying to imagine how Ciara and I might earn our place on this ship, sir. Since you are unhappy to have us . . ."

"Not unhappy, my lady, nor is it of use to repine now if I were."

"I was thinking that whilst we travel, we might help look after the boys."

His relief was visible. "I'll accept that offer," he said. "After more than three months on that rock, my ability to devise new entertainments has abandoned me."

Satisfied that she had eased his concerns, Alyson went to tell Ciara that their voyage would no longer be as tedious as it had so quickly begun to seem. What Niall or Mungo might say to it all, she did not trouble herself to consider.

When a seaman brought food to her cabin so she and Ciara could break their fast, he told them that Orkney had also ordered food for the boys and had ordered their belongings moved to the cabin across the way. Alyson assumed that the earl would soon shoo the boys out of his cabin and summon his secretaries to see to what business they could as they sailed.

When the seaman returned to collect the remains of their meal, he affirmed that assumption. "Them two lads be on deck now, m'lady," he added. "It be still blowing a gale, but they dinna seem tae mind."

Alyson gave the boys time to acquaint themselves with the ship before she donned her cloak and went up to find them at the railing, peering down at the sea.

Addressing James, whose current title was Earl of

Carrick, she said, "I am Alyson MacGillivray, my lord Carrick. Orkney has suggested that, if you do not object, we might devise ways of entertaining ourselves together whilst we sail. My husband, Niall Clyne, serves as one of Orkney's secretaries. My woman, Ciara, is with me, and our cabin is across from the one that you and your friend will occupy."

"We decided that people should call me James whilst we are all on this ship," he replied, looking her up and down as if he were assessing her but without any sign of impertinence. Then, he added matter-of-factly, "Orkney said ye were beautiful, my lady. I believe he understated that fact considerably."

His seriousness invested his words with charm that surpassed that of most adult males she had met and drew a smile from her as she thanked him.

He was a sturdy-looking lad with a mop of dark auburn curls, doubtless inherited from his Drummond mother, since most Stewarts were fair and blue-eyed. His were dark brown, with long, thick eyelashes. He would be nine at the end of July, but he had spoken with solemn dignity far beyond his years. When she smiled at his compliment, he smiled back rather wistfully.

Then, as if recalling his duty, he gestured toward his companion and said, "This be my friend, Will Fletcher. He isna used tae the Fletcher bit yet, though. We began calling him so on Bass Rock, 'cause they had three other Wills there. Sithee, Will's da was a fletcher, so calling him Will Fletcher seemed a good notion."

"It sounds wise to me," Alyson said, smiling at Will, who bobbed a bow in return. He looked a year or two older than Jamie, had darker, curlier hair, and a demeanor nearly as solemn. "Your father made arrows, did he, Will?"

"He did, aye, m'lady."

"A cousin of mine is a highly skilled archer, so I know about fletchers. How did you come to be friends with James?"

"Me mam were dead, and when me da fell out o' an apple tree, he died, too. I didna like the tanner we worked for in Doune, so I joined up wi' Jamie instead. D'ye ken how long we'll be aboard this ship, m'lady?"

"That likely depends on the weather," she replied. "The winds have been unpredictable, so we cannot count on their goodwill. Would you two like to go below with me and see your cabin and mine?" When they nodded, she said, "Did you bring aught with you to occupy yourselves?"

"I have a chessboard and pieces tae play chess or dames," Jamie said. "Orkney and I taught Will tae play, too. So if you know how..."

Alyson grimaced. "I know the moves, but I fear that either of you will beat me easily. Still, it will be good for me to learn more."

"Aye, well, I can teach ye, m'lady," Jamie said. "Mayhap Orkney will, too, or your husband, Master Clyne."

Alyson nodded as she passed them to go down the ladder. In truth, she had barely spoken with Niall since they'd arrived at Leith Harbor to meet Mungo. And now that Orkney was aboard, she doubted she would see much of Niall at all. Orkney's business would keep him and Mungo busy, as it usually did.

Unstable weather continued as they traveled south. By Tuesday, their fifth day at sea, the wind had picked up again, and Jake thought the merchantman's captain was letting it push the ship dangerously near the English north coast.

Although England, France, and Scotland were enjoying a rare truce, he had no faith in truces. Moreover, he had heard men say that pirates prowled that coast.

Chapter 2

By Thursday, Alyson had still seen little of her husband, because other than brief encounters, the only times she saw him were when they took their midday dinners with the boys, Mungo, and Orkney in the earl's cabin. The three men spent the rest of their days and evenings together, while Alyson, Ciara, and the boys occupied themselves below or walking on deck when they could.

Seamen brought down trays each morning for them to break their fast and again at night for supper. Meantime, they played chess or dames, or walked, and talked about any number of things, including the boys' time on the Bass Rock.

Alyson found it hard if not impossible to imagine how any business of Orkney's could consume so much of three men's time. But so it was, and it was no business of hers to question the earl. Her husband was another matter. At midday, during their meal, she asked if she might have a private word with him afterward.

Niall nodded, but when Mungo asked him to spare him just a moment first, Alyson went on out with Ciara and the boys. Sending Ciara below, Alyson watched the boys run about on deck while she waited for Niall…and waited.

Because it was unlike him to break his word, she believed that Mungo had intervened. Growing chilly, she rapped at the master-cabin door. When Mungo opened it, she did little to conceal her displeasure beneath her courteous request to have a word with her husband.

"Sorry, lass," Mungo said quietly. "His lordship has commanded that we get right to work. If this is important, I can relay your message to Niall."

"I would liefer speak to him," Alyson said. "If Orkney can spare you to answer the door, surely he can spare Niall more easily."

To her surprise, Mungo smiled and said, "Aye, sure, but be quick. His lordship may *seem* always to be charming, but he does have a temper. And we have much still to discuss before we reach France."

He shut the door, making her wonder if he meant to leave her waiting again. But it opened moments later, and Niall said, "I thought you saw that I had work to do. What is so important that you could not wait to discuss it later, at supper?"

"I apologize if I have vexed you," she said. "You did agree to talk with me, though. Surely you will not count brief discourse at this open door as such."

"Nay, but if you are irked that I did not tell you about young James..."

"I know that you were unaware that he'd be on the ship," she said when he paused. "But I am your wife, Niall, and we have scarcely enjoyed an hour together since leaving Perth. Nor had I seen you for weeks before then. Come to that, sir, other than the two days you spent with my family last summer to ask for my hand and the few days you spent at MacGillivray House for our wedding,

I've seen you only occasionally since our childhood. We did agree that this voyage would give us time to know each other better as husband and wife."

His cheeks reddened, but he said with his familiar twinkle, "Allie, I did not know Orkney would be traveling with us, either. Mungo told me only to look after our usual tasks whilst he was away and to meet him at Leith. But, as you just said, *we've* known each other since childhood. I doubt that we have much more to learn."

"Aye, sure, we do," she said. "As children, we learned only as much about each other as children *can* learn with parents and families about. You ken fine how much my family demands of me now. You saw that for yourself when you stayed with us those few days after our wedding. We'd both be so tired by the end of a day that we could scarcely stay awake to bid each other goodnight."

"True," he agreed. "We kept busy at Leith whilst we waited for Mungo and the ship to arrive, but I'll admit I'd hoped for more time now to relax. We have work to do, though, before we reach France. This matter of James is delicate, lass. His grace trusts the French king to guard him. But Orkney must be able to make his grace's expectations clear without offending the French king or his court. We've only begun to plan our strategy. In troth, I dare not linger now. Mayhap we can stroll on deck tonight and talk."

"If it's too cold, Ciara could stay with the boys for an hour," Alyson said.

"Aye, she could. But I likewise expect that, after spending the whole afternoon below, as you will unless you and Ciara brave the winds up here, and mayhap rain this afternoon, you will be chafing to breathe fresh air."

Looking at the dark sky, she knew he was right. "Just

do not forget, sir. A gentleman should not neglect his lady wife as wickedly as you have neglected me."

Kissing her cheek, he said, "I'll try to do better in future."

She heard Mungo's voice in the background.

"I must go," Niall said, already turning away.

When he shut the door, she called to the boys and heard Jamie shout that they'd be along straightaway. Realizing that Ciara was likely growing impatient in the cabin, and would either carp or complain, Alyson went below.

The boys did not come immediately, but they did eventually, and Jamie brought his chessboard and pieces. When Ciara complained that the cabin was too small for four people, Alyson, weary of her grievances, said, "Mayhap you would liefer enjoy a nap in the boys' cabin, where you can rest undisturbed."

With an injured look, Ciara said, "Mayhap I'll seek some fresh air."

Alyson knew that the woman did not enjoy the voyage and could scarcely blame her. Thanks to the unfortunate weather and Niall's preoccupation with his duties, Alyson would not have enjoyed it either had it not been for the boys.

Jake was watching the skies. The weather had grown worse, and they were still dangerously close to the English coast. By midafternoon, besides the incessant heavy wind, the air was so damp and clouds so dark that a downpour was imminent.

So far, they had had no difficulty following the *Maryenknyght*, because the galley was faster and more maneuverable than the larger ship, and in the Isles, his lads often worked in heavy seas. But if the weather closed in, it would become much harder to see the merchantman.

Feeling the first sprinkles of rain, he went to the top of the forecastle cabin to view the sea around them. A squall line had formed in the northeast.

Turning, he saw five ships emerge from behind a massive outcropping to the west and head for the *Maryenknyght.*

In her cabin, by the light of two oil lanterns swinging overhead, Alyson was playing dames with Will, supervised by Jamie, when Ciara burst into the cabin.

"My lady—!" The ship lurched unexpectedly, making Ciara break off to grab the door jamb and Alyson fear for the lanterns as she and Will scrambled to grab and replace pieces sliding out of place and off the board.

"My lady," Ciara repeated as she latched the door, "a flotilla o' ships be coming toward us! They must be some o' them pirates we heard of in Leith. Ye'll recall that the captain o' this very ship warned that such villains plunder vessels along this coast."

"What I recall is that Captain Bereholt said the *Maryenknyght* would easily evade any pirates," Alyson said. She watched the board to be sure that she and Will were putting the pieces back in their rightful places.

Jamie said, "We heard talk o' pirates, too. Aye, Will?"

"Aye," Will said, catching one of his pieces when the ship's wretched rolling slid it off the board again. "Lord Orkney did ask that Mungo chap if he'd heard aught o' them lately. But Mungo said he'd heard nowt."

"But he must have, because he traveled to France to arrange for this ship and back again," Alyson said, looking from one lad to the other. "Sithee, Ciara is right. Captain Bereholt did talk of pirates. He told us, too, that we would be keeping at least ten miles off the coast to avoid running into them."

"We're none so far off the coast now, though," Jamie said. "Will and I could see it from the rail today after our midday meal. The clouds were hanging low, but we could make out the coastline."

Ciara stood nervously near the door, shifting from one foot to the other.

Abruptly, Jamie said, "I'm going up on deck. I want tae see those ships."

"I'll wager that they are just traders or merchantmen like this one," Alyson said. "Doubtless, they are setting out for some European or Hanseatic port and travel together to deter the pirates."

"Likely, ye're right," Jamie said. "But I want tae see them. Come, Will."

Since she had no true authority over either boy, she warned them only to keep out of mischief, and won a grin over his shoulder from Jamie.

When they had gone, Ciara said, "I dinna think them ships be friends, m'lady. Sight o' them sent a sailor running for the master's cabin. I hied m'self down here, so I dinna ken what happened after that."

"Whatever happens, the boys should be safe," Alyson said. "No one will let harm come to them."

"I ken who that Jamie is as well as ye do," Ciara said. "I should think that with him on this ship, we'd have a flotilla along to protect him."

"Well, we don't," Alyson said.

She did not want to try explaining to Ciara that Orkney and others who had arranged the voyage, including the King, must have hoped to transport Jamie in the deep secrecy that had cloaked his whereabouts before Christmas. According to her cousin Ivor Mackintosh, such a scheme had worked the year before to convey Jamie to St. Andrews, where he had lived under the bishop's watchful eye. But then, shortly before Christmas, Albany had summoned the lords of Parliament to meet at Easter.

Doubtless, aware that Albany meant to retake the Governorship he had lost to Davy Stewart on Davy's coming of age—and wanting to protect Davy's little brother now that Davy was dead—the King had decided to move Jamie again.

Ciara had grimaced at Alyson's brief reply but said nothing more, and Alyson retained her customary composure until they heard a distant boom.

Frowning, she said, "I don't think that was thunder."

"Nay," Ciara said. "Mayhap we should go up and—"

"Hark!" Alyson interjected, hearing pounding feet in the passageway.

The door burst open, and Jamie, entering with Will on his heels, exclaimed, "They have cannon aboard the biggest o' those ships! It's shooting at *us*!"

~

Hearing cannon fire, Jake saw the merchantman heave to and watched in dismay as the English ships surrounded it. The two largest ones, using grappling irons, flanked it.

Although he climbed the mast to watch the confrontation, he could do naught to aid the *Maryenknyght*. The much smaller *Sea Wolf* carried no artillery and was heavily outnumbered. Nor had it been anyone's intent that he do more than witness the prince's safe arrival in France and report back to Bishop Wardlaw.

If the pirates took captives, Jake would follow them and hope to create an opportunity to rescue Jamie and Orkney, at least.

~

Alyson jumped up, steadying herself against the roll of the ship as she headed toward the door. Chessboard and pieces lay forgotten on the table.

Pulling the door open, she stepped into the passageway just as a crash and instant darkness told her someone had slammed the hatchway shut.

As she struggled to collect her wits, Jamie said in a carefully calm voice, "Do you think those pirates will capture us?"

"Whether they will or not remains to be seen," she said. Knowing that the boys had explored the ship, she added, "It may be wise for us to hide, in case they do, though. Do you know of a place where you and Will might conceal yourselves?"

"We *could* go into the hold," Jamie said, frowning. "Orkney did say that we were no tae go down there, because there will likely be rats. And the captain said we'd no see anything anyway, 'cause he has strict rules against lanterns unless someone else goes along wi' water tae douse any fire. But with all this wind—"

"Aye," Will said, nodding. "The way the sea be a-tossing o' this ship, even a grown man would ha' trouble staying upright down there wi' a lantern in hand."

Eyeing them both, Alyson suspected that the only way either would descend to the hold would be if she and Ciara went with them. Recalling the older woman's terror of the dark, the possibility of the ship's sinking if a cannonball struck it, and the way that Ciara's eyes had widened at Jamie's mention of rats, Alyson knew she'd have trouble persuading any of them to seek refuge in the hold.

Her usual common sense stirred sharply then.

"I expect that the hold is the first place the pirates would go," she said. "Whatever else they may do, they'll surely take what stores we carry and our cargo of hides and wool. Can you think of anywhere else to hide?"

"We've a big kist in our cabin like them two yonder," Will said, pointing to two wooden chests by the wall opposite the shelf bed. "If we climbed in and ye threw a dress or two over us—I've me doots any pirate would touch a dress."

"Aye, sure," Jamie said. "We might both fit inside ours if we take our things out and scatter them about."

"Go and do that, then," Alyson said. "Do you need help?"

"Nay, we'll do it," Jamie said, dashing out with Will right behind him.

"Ciara will throw clothing over you and latch the kist," Alyson shouted.

"I'll be right along," Ciara added. She had opened one of Alyson's kists and was flinging clothing from it onto the bed. As she did, the whole ship shuddered.

"What was that?" Alyson said.

"I been hearing more o' them booms. Mayhap a cannonball hit the ship."

"I doubt they'd risk damaging the ship," Alyson said.

"They must want its cargo, after all. Why else would pirates attack us?"

Ciara glanced toward the door that the boys had gone through.

Following her thoughts, Alyson felt a shiver. Nevertheless, she said firmly, "Don't be daft, Ciara. English pirates could not possibly know who is aboard this ship. I would remind you that it sailed to Edinburgh from France and that we are still flying a French flag. Moreover, England and France are enjoying a truce."

"France is our ally, m'lady. But for most o' my life and surely all o' yours, the French have been at war with England. We should never have got so close to shore."

"In such awful weather as we've had, the captain surely thought it safer," Alyson said. "You know as well as I do that he could arrange only hasty repairs after the great storm that damaged this ship on its journey to Scotland. He dared not fight the force of the heavy winds and inflowing tides any more than necessary."

"Get into this kist, m'lady," Ciara said. "I've left a few things at the bottom so ye'll no be lying on hard wood, and I'll drape summat over ye. Then I'll see to the two lads afore I climb into that other kist."

Alyson nearly protested. But, again, common sense intervened. She and Ciara would be no safer than the boys were if enemies boarded the ship.

Thanks to the *Sea Wolf*'s rutter, the invaluable record in which Jake noted details learned from experience or from other seamen about every mile of coastline that he or they had sailed, he had identified the outcropping from behind which the five ships had come as Flamborough Head. It jutted from England's Yorkshire coast some twenty miles south of Scarborough.

He wished he could know what was happening aboard the *Maryenknyght*. That the merchantman had submitted after the lead English ship fired its cannon told him only that the merchantman was as unarmed as the *Sea Wolf* was.

He knew Henry of Orkney well enough to be certain that the young earl was reacting strongly to this turn of events. But Henry was no fool and would do nowt to endanger his charge. He and Jamie would be traveling as ordinary passengers, not as a great nobleman and a prince of the Scottish realm.

Even if Henry should so far forget himself as to think of declaring his identity, he would surely realize before he did so that even the powerful Earl of Orkney could not fight off five shiploads of greedy pirates, if that's what they were. Henry would also understand that identifying himself would suggest to pirates or anyone else that the Almighty had sent them a wealthy earl they could hold for ransom.

Jake also wished he could be sure that the English attackers *were* just pirates. No one would care for the loss of hides and wool, least of all Henry. Nor would he care if pirates stole the ship's stores or anything else aboard, as long as they left the young prince alone and the ship seaworthy. And why should they not?

To pirates, Jamie would be just another child—a nuisance to themselves if they took him aboard. The only real danger then would be if they seized the *Maryenknyght* and decided that its captain, crew, and passengers were expendable.

A sense of unease stirred as these thoughts sped through his mind. He was certain that no other ship had followed the *Maryenknyght*. But he could not be as certain that the reason for its journey to Edinburgh and back had remained a secret.

A year ago, almost to the day, Jamie's older brother Davy had died. If the King of Scots died today, Jamie would succeed him, thus setting off a power struggle to determine who would control the throne. The Scots were tired of governors—or regents, as other countries called them—ruling in place of their rightful King.

Many believed that a full-grown man, a strong one, should rule.

Jamie's uncle, the Duke of Albany, believed *he* was that man. And Albany stood next after Jamie to inherit the crown. Worse, Albany had a long history of learning things that others did not want him to know.

"May God curse him if he's arranged this!" Jake growled.

When the five English ships finally disengaged themselves, leaving the *Maryenknyght* to pitch about in the angry waves, apparently uncontrolled, Jake ordered the *Sea Wolf* closer. He wondered why the pirates had not sailed their prize into harbor and, more important, if they had left anyone alive aboard.

Having shut the lid of the kist into which Alyson had curled herself, Ciara had run across the passageway to drape clothing over the boys. Meantime, Alyson listened intently but heard only great crashing sounds that made the whole ship tremble. Trying to ignore both sounds and fury, she heard Ciara return at last and begin flinging things from the second kist to the shelf bed.

"Did both boys fit in the one kist, Ciara?"

"Aye, m'lady. But I doubt they are comfortable or that such a hiding place will serve if them villains come down here."

"Pirates will think only about our cargo," Alyson said, praying that she was right. "They'll want to offload it to their ships and won't spare a thought for these two wee cabins before they do that."

"I'm none so sure o' that," Ciara said. "What if they seize this ship?"

Alyson sighed. "I'd hoped that that dreadful thought would not occur to you. You did not share it with the boys, I trust."

"Nay, nor would I," Ciara said "But if they do board—"

"If they do, they do, and we'll cope as well as we can," Alyson said.

Another crash rattled the ship. "Do hurry, Ciara. These bangs and shudders grow worrisome, because it feels as if other ships are banging into ours. If the pirates are boarding, you *don't* want them to find you!"

"I should bolt the door. Not that it will keep them—"

"Don't," Alyson said urgently. "If you bolt it and someone comes, he will know that someone is here. A bolt cannot shoot itself home."

No reply other than a rustling sound came to her ears, but it told her that Ciara was climbing into the kist. As Alyson waited to hear the thud of its lid closing, another crashing shudder diverted her.

Heavy footsteps thundered in the passageway.

Yearning to tell Ciara to hurry, she dared not make a

sound, lest it carry into the passage. As the thought flitted through her mind, she heard the door bang back on its hinges, followed by a cry of alarm from Ciara.

"Here now, what's this?" a deep voice demanded. "What be a female doing aboard this ship?"

"Get ye gone from here," Ciara snapped. "Ye've nae business troubling a decent woman."

"To me, lads," the man shouted. "Come see what I've found."

Ciara screamed, and more feet pounded in the passageway.

Alyson tried to push the lid of her kist open but could not. Evidently, Ciara had slipped the steel pin into the hasp that secured the lid in place.

Alyson bit her lip to keep silent, praying they would not hurt Ciara.

Ciara screamed again. Then Alyson heard the last thing she wanted to hear, when Jamie shouted, "Leave her be, ye gallous beast!"

Sounds of more struggle ensued, and she heard Will's voice along with Jamie's and Ciara's. Other masculine voices joined in, followed by more cries and conflict as captors shoved their captives out the door and along the passageway.

Alyson reached to try the lid of her kist again, only to tense every muscle when a footstep sounded right beside her.

The metallic sound of a pin being slowly drawn from its hasp followed.

She held her breath, afraid to let it out.

A voice, clearly English, shouted from the passageway, "Stir your stumps, Geordie. This devilish tub be a-sinking!"

"God-a-mercy," the man murmured. Then he was gone.

Pushing against the lid as hard as she could, Alyson realized the effort was useless. Ciara had put the pin in, and the villain had not got it all the way out!

Jake saw long before the *Sea Wolf* neared it that the *Maryenknyght* was listing. "Nay, then," he muttered, amending the thought. "She's going to go under!"

Beside him, Coll nodded. "She is, aye, sir. But likely they've taken all aboard her onto them other ships." Looking up, he added with a frown, "I think it be starting to rain, but with this wind whipping up the sea as it is, a man cannot be sure."

"Get us closer," Jake said. To one of the lads resting nearby, he added, "Fetch my sword from my cabin. I want to see if anyone's still aboard."

"She's like to go under afore ye could search her," Coll said. "And if we be alongside, she'll take us down with her."

"Just get me close enough to see for myself that those villains have not left anyone behind. They'll have been interested only in her cargo of wool and hides."

"I doubt they thought of aught but their *own* hides, sir."

"If Orkney knew the ship was sinking, he'd have done everything possible to get his young charge out of danger," Jake reminded him. "Sakes, what the devil...Coll, do you see that? There *is* someone aboard, and if my eyes do not—"

"Your vision be as good as ever," Coll said grimly. "That be a female, and by the way she moves, a young one."

"Bring us alongside the ship," Jake said in a tone that

would brook no argument. He was already scanning the ship's side, seeking a way up.

The man he had sent for his sword returned with it, and Jake slung it on.

"Someone's cast a rope over the side yonder near the stern," Coll said. "But she's sinking fast. I'd wager that their cannon shot farther and more accurately than they expected, or them villains damaged her when they grappled onto her."

"The latter, I think," Jake said, pointing. "That gash there dips below the waterline. But we'll climb up here. 'Tis a shorter climb, and in this wind and these seas, we've no time to try aught else."

"Sir, with respect, she's like to go under afore ye can get back to us."

"We'll just have to move faster than she does," Jake said. "Mace, to me!" he shouted. "Bring your sword!"

A fair-haired oarsman on the first bench, nearest the stern, relinquished his oar to another man. Grabbing his sword and sling from under his bench, he stepped to the gangway down the middle of the deck between the two banks of oarsmen, and moved swiftly along it to Jake.

"Aye, Cap'n?" he said as he slung his own longsword across his back.

"You and I are going to board her. At least one person is still on her. But there may be others, and the ship is sinking. Coll, get us near enough to catch that rope. Wait only to see us aboard, and then haul off a safe distance. It is indeed beginning to rain and may soon come down in buckets. Whether it does or not, in the increasing darkness, you'll likely lose sight of us. If you do, turn back to Filey Bay."

"Northward, sir? Won't we be a-following them villains then?"

"We'll certainly try to learn where they're going if they take Orkney and his charge with them," Jake said. "But even if they do, they'll likely have a lair nearby. They turned back toward Flamborough Head, that great promontory you can still make out yonder to the northwest. I'm thinking they'll seek shelter until they can sort things out for themselves. I doubt they'll keep innocent men and boys aboard. Nor are they likely to risk killing them."

"Sakes, why not?" Coll demanded.

"Because Orkney will identify himself if he must, to protect his charge. He will doubtless say that James is his son and claim that returning them alive will fetch those villains an enormous ransom from the Sinclair family."

"If he thinks of that," Coll said.

Mace was silent, eyeing the dangerously listing merchantman narrowly as the *Sea Wolf* sped toward it, and Jake didn't blame him.

"Don't fret," Jake said. "That rope may have been a wee bit short for us before. Now it's well within our reach. You go first."

"Aye, sir," Mace said.

Jake saw something else. Chuckling, he said, "We'll be safe enough, Coll. They've left their coble on the deck. And with the ship at the angle it is now, Mace and I should be able to launch it ourselves. Then we'll be fine. Mind you don't go too far north if we lose you," he added. "Filey Bay has a long reef at its north end. Check the rutter. Seek a barren patch of sand midway, and we'll find you in a day or two."

"Aye," Coll said, shaking his head at them, indicating—

and not for the first time—his firm belief that his master was daft and took too many risks.

They were close enough now for Mace to grab the rope. He went up it without hesitation and hauled himself over the railing.

Jake followed and saw that Mace had gone straight to the coble. He saw no sign of the lass. Then he heard her voice: "Help us! Over here!"

He saw her, half in and half out of a hatchway between the forecastle cabins. Praying that "us" included the prince, he shouted to Mace and ran toward her.

Chapter 3

Minutes earlier

Having forced herself to ignore the unknown pirate's opinion that the ship was sinking, Alyson focused her mind on finding a way out of the locked kist. Since he had begun to pull the pin from the hasp, mayhap she could rattle it loose.

Curled in the kist as she was, she could not exert her full strength against the resistant lid. However, after painful maneuvering, she managed to twist at the waist enough to press her shoulder blades flat against the bottom.

By pushing hard and banging on the lid, she managed only to bruise the heels of her hands. Even so, angry, frustrated, and frightened out of her wits, she continued to hit the unrelenting lid with the sides of her fists.

The ship went on tossing throughout. But she realized after a time that her body pressed harder against the kist wall to her right, as if the *Maryenknyght* were listing that way. Remembering the cannon fire, the ship's shuddering, and the awful crashing sounds, she feared that while the pirates boarded the *Maryenknyght*, their flanking ships had crashed hard against her.

How much damage they might have done to the storm-battered ship, she did not want to imagine. What if it *was* sinking? What if everyone else had got off?

Sakes, but where was Niall? Surely, Mungo or no Mungo, pirates or no pirates, he would come and find her.

Feeling utterly abandoned, she called herself sharply to order. *Think; listen for footsteps so you can shout. You are where you are; do what you can.*

Time crept as if hours were passing instead of minutes.

At last, with profound relief, she heard running feet, then Will's voice surprisingly near, shouting, "Lady Alyson, be ye still in one o' them kists?"

"In this one, aye, Will! Pull the pin from the hasp."

Moments later, the lid opened to admit faint light, and she gratefully drew a deep breath. The air in the cabin still reeked of untanned hides and damp wool.

"We must hie ourselves tae the deck," the boy said, trying to pull her out. "Near everyone's got off and them other four ships be already away. Only the lead boat stays, but I had tae hide m'self whilst the last 'uns were a-boarding it, and I waited till I could hope nae one might see me. But they've taken our Jamie on the biggest ship, m'lady! I should be wi' him. Can ye no get yourself out the noo?"

"I can, aye," Alyson said, trying awkwardly to do so and finding it harder than it had been to get in. "But surely the pirates won't abandon this ship."

"One side o' her got crunched, and they say she be a-sinking," Will said as she managed to hoist herself and get her feet under her. Grabbing her near arm to steady her against a lurching movement of the ship, he added, "We must run!"

Needing no more encouragement, she caught up her skirts and stepped out.

The boy turned and ran, his dark figure outlined in the grayer light of the doorway. In the darkness, he tripped over the raised threshold, tried wildly to catch himself, and crashed to the floor of the passageway. Trying to get to his feet, he let out a cry of pain, stumbled forward, and fell to his knees.

"Ay-de-mi," he muttered as Alyson bent anxiously over him. "I've done summat tae me ankle, m'lady. Ye must run ahead. If ye canna stop 'em afore they cast off, we'll be stuck here tae drown!"

"I'll stop them, Will. Then I'll come for you."

"I'm too big for ye tae carry," he said. "Getting me up yon ladder—"

She waited to hear no more but snatched up her skirts, ran to the ladder, and climbed swiftly. But she was not quick enough. Nor would they have been had Will not fallen, for as she emerged into gale-force winds, she saw that the lead ship must have cast off before or just when the boy had hurried below. It was well away, its sails full, swiftly distancing itself from the *Maryenknyght*.

Alyson shouted and waved. But the wind whipped her words away, and she knew that no one on the departing ship could have heard her. The sky had grown darker, full of lowering black clouds more ominous than ever. Doubtless, the English pirates thought only of getting themselves and their captives to shelter.

As she turned to go back down, she remembered Will's mentioning four other ships and wondered if they had all headed in, too. The pirates must have hoped to collect the *Maryenknyght*'s valuable cargo before the ship sank, but despite her earlier sense that time had crept at a snail's pace and the fact that the villains would have entered the hold through the stern hatch, they'd not had time enough yet to offload hundreds of bales of hides and wool.

Shouting to Will that she would return shortly, she ran to the portside railing and scanned the open sea, seeing nothing akin to a sail. The roiling, cloud-filled sky hid any distant prospect. And a line of darker, more thunderous-looking low clouds loomed not far away, in the direction that she thought must be eastward.

As she crossed the deck to the steerboard side, she realized that the ship was listing more. She kept sliding awkwardly downhill even as waves made the ship rise. Catching herself at the railing, she discerned a sail at last, moving toward her.

When she was sure that the other ship was approaching the *Maryenknyght*, she rushed back to the hatchway to shout to Will that rescue was at hand. Praying desperately that whoever it was was not of a murderous nature, she waited at the top of the ladder to see what happened next.

Seeing first one man and then a second climb over the railing, she shouted. When she knew they had seen her, she scrambled down the ladder. With the light behind her, she could scarcely make out Will's shape in the passageway.

"The last ship has gone, but two men boarded this ship from a much smaller one, and they don't look like pirates," she told him hastily when she reached him. "Their ship has oars as well as sails—like an Isles galley, only larger. It also has stepped sides rising at each end to a high prow and an equally high stern."

"I ken what ye mean, for I ha' seen a ship like that,"

Will muttered. Then, with a sigh, he said, "Me falling were a daft thing tae do, m'lady. I'm no usually sae clumsy. It hurts like fire, but I dinna think anything's broke."

"Try to stand," she said, reaching to take his hand.

From well behind her, a masculine voice called, "Lass, where are you?"

"Here in the passage," she shouted, knowing he would barely hear her over the screeching wind whipping around the hatchway above him. "I've a lad here who cannot walk. He rescued me but fell when we were running to get to the deck."

"Is anyone else aboard?"

"I don't think so," Alyson said as Will said, "I saw nae one else."

She could see only two large, silent, dark shapes moving toward her against the faint light through the hatchway. But her fear had ebbed.

The leader had very broad shoulders and was taller and lankier than the heavier-looking man behind him. Both had swords slung across their backs.

"How badly are you hurt, lad?" the nearer one asked in a pleasantly deep, definitely Scottish voice. Hearing his accent, Alyson felt the last of her fear vanish. As he stepped past her to take a knee by the boy, the man seemed very tall.

Will said, "I ha' me doots I did more than twist me ankle. Gave it a good sharp twist and nae mistake, though, tripping over yon devilish threshold piece." Grimly, he added, "I hope ye dinna be more o' them wicked pirates."

"We're not."

The second man remained silent but hovered near

Alyson. She wished he would speak and mayhap give her a better idea of who they were. But a more important question still teased her mind.

"Are we sinking?" she asked. "I know the ship is listing. It also feels as if it is shaking apart."

"We'll talk later, lass," the first man said as he rose. He was at least a foot taller than she was. "We must get you both topside straightaway."

Although she still could not see much, she could tell that he was helping Will to his feet. Since she could imagine no other reason for not answering her question, she decided he did not want to terrify them.

"Try putting weight on that foot, lad," he said. "I won't let you fall."

"She were a-going tae try taking me up herself," Will told him, obeying the command only to lurch into him as he did and stifle another cry. "I—I'm near as big as she is," the boy added determinedly. "So I didna think she could carry me. But I dinna think I can walk much yet either."

Alyson said, "If you will help him, sir, I can see to my own needs. But prithee, be frank with us. *Is* this ship sinking?"

He said, "It is, aye, lass, so we must make haste. Mace and I can sling the ship's coble over the side and then—"

"*Our* coble? But what happened to your ship?"

"Nary a thing," he said. "But when this one goes under, she is going to create a wide vortex that will suck anything nearby right down with her. My ship must not be within range when that happens, nor should *we* be if we can prevent it. These devilish winds will aid us, though, if we can but get beyond the ship's immediate vicinity. Hence, our haste now."

"I'll need things from my cabin," she said.

"Nay, lass, we must go straightaway," he said.

"I don't want to be left with only the clothes I stand in, sir. I'm a sennight or more away from home, so I'll need at least a change of garments. And if I'm not to freeze before we reach shelter, I'll also need my cloak."

"Where's your cabin?"

"Just behind you, to your right," she said.

"Take the lad up, Mace," he said. "And uncover they coble."

"Aye, Cap'n," the other man said, stepping nearer.

Startled to learn that the leader was the smaller ship's captain but realizing that he meant to give her at least a minute or two, she slipped past them into her dark cabin. Feeling for her fur-lined cloak on its hook, she flung it over her shoulders, then felt her way to the shelf bed, hoping to recognize her garments by touch.

"I'm behind you, mistress," the leader said quietly.

Whirling, but able to see no more than his denser shadow blocking most of the dim light at the open doorway, she said, "I'm coming, but my woman and I threw our clothing over here to make room for ourselves in the two kists."

"Your woman?"

"Aye, Ciara. They captured her as she was getting into her kist. She had latched mine, and I couldn't get out. One of the men rattled the pin, but someone called him away. Had it not been for Will—"

"Just grab a kirtle or something and come on," he interjected. "Whatever you take will get soaked before we reach my ship, or, more likely, the shore."

"Dare we seek refuge in England?" she asked, grabbing what felt like her blue kirtle and a bit of softer fabric beneath it that she hoped was a shift.

"We may have to," he said, urging her toward the doorway. "If I am not mistaken, that squall line I saw bearing down on us will shortly engulf us. And my lads are likely somewhere between us and the squall."

"Will it swamp them…or us?" she asked him as they moved to the ladder.

"Nay, but since we'll be safer sailing with the wind than against it, we'll likely let the waves and weather carry us ashore."

Earlier, his voice had echoed at first, melding with the noises of the storm above and the crashing of waves against the ship. But as close as he was to her now, she'd detected a familiar note in it and wondered if he was someone she'd met or just a man accustomed to telling others what to do. Her older brothers had been such men before their deaths, and her cousins James and Ivor Mackintosh were as well.

"Now, lass, up you go!" he said.

Telling herself that it did not matter who the Scotsman was if he could get her and Will safely off the sinking ship, Alyson hurried up the ladder.

~

Watching her go, Jake wished he could see her face. His night vision was excellent, but it had been too dark below for him to see her features, although he had easily sensed her slipping past them into the cabin, and had followed her.

When he'd paused at the cabin threshold, his senses attuned themselves more to sounds and movements of the ship than to her. Even then, the echo of her voice lingered, stirring a vague if unidentifiable memory of laughter, pleasant people, and good food. He knew that he had startled her by announcing his presence behind her. But she had remained calm and determined, despite the danger, to find her clothing.

A sudden lurch of the ship made him say, "Hurry, mistress. If she rolls..."

"I'm hurrying!" She swept up her skirts with her left hand, thrust the small bundle she carried under her left arm, and went up the ladder now using only her right hand for balance. Her calmness impressed him. He had not met many women who would act with such assurance on a storm-ridden ship.

Her speech had informed him that she was of gentle birth. Her thickly lined cloak and immediate resistance to following orders strongly suggested a noble one.

Going up after her, he saw that Mace and the lad stood by the sturdy-looking coble, which rested on the deck devoid of its canvas cover. Its mast would go up easily, and stout cables and ropes led from bow and stern rings to pulleys above.

"Hey, that's *our* boat!" The shout came from three rough-looking men in leather breastplates who erupted from the stern hatchway, waving swords.

Snatching his own from its sling, Jake saw Mace grab his sword with one hand and thrust the boy aside with the other.

"Stay here, lass!"

Without awaiting a reply, Jake dashed down the slanted, rain-slick deck with a shout to divert the second and third men from their onslaught. Both turned toward him, allowing Mace time to dispatch his challenger. Jake engaged the nearer man. As he did, he said, "Be ye a seaman o' the *Maryenknyght* or a gallous Englishman?"

"I'm English, damn your Scottish hide," the man said, lunging.

Flicking the Englishman's sword aside with a deft stroke, fighting to keep footing on the slippery deck but damned if he'd let his opponent see him fall, Jake said, "Ye've missed your ship, laddie."

The man, breathing hard, had already slipped twice. "They said there be treasure here," he said. "Tell me where it be or I'll spit ye t' hell!"

Deflecting another wild swing of the sword, Jake snapped, "*Who* told you?"

"Aye, ye'd like t' know." Raising his sword again, murder in his eyes, the man drove his sword toward Jake.

Stepping aside, Jake finished him and looked to see how Mace did with the third man just as the chap darted around him, waving his sword like a madman.

Mace ducked under the blade and when the man rushed him, the burly oarsman heaved him up and straight overboard.

Glancing about as if seeking further opponents, Mace said as if naught had happened, "All's ready tae hoist yon coble, sir. She'll clear that railing easy."

Glancing over his shoulder, Jake saw the lass hurrying toward them, holding her hood with one hand and her wee bundle in the other.

The lad had managed to get himself to the railing just behind the coble.

Before hoisting the boat, Jake said over his shoulder loudly enough to carry despite the howling winds sweeping down across the deck from its higher port side to where they stood near the steerboard railing, "We'll put you and the boy in the coble before we lower it, mistress."

"Aye, sure, I ken who ye be now," the lad said abruptly. "It ha' been a-tugging at me memory since ye called tae us down in yon passage."

Looking right at him for the first time, Jake smiled. "I remember you, too, now that I see you. Your name is Will, is it not?" When the boy nodded, Jake said, "We met on another ship, a year ago, on the Firth of Tay."

Saying the words sharpened his earlier vague memory of pleasant people into who they had been. Knowing now why the lass's voice had triggered the memory earlier, he remembered with some dismay just who she was.

"Lady Alyson, I trust you remember me, too," he said, taking her bundle from her. Her beautiful, widening gray eyes told him that she did.

"Mercy," she exclaimed. "Jake…that is, Sir Jacob Maxwell!"

" 'Tis m'self, aye. And 'Jake' is enough, my lady, since your cousin Ivor and I are closer than most brothers. In troth, though, I'd never have expected to find you on this ship. When last we met, you were about to marry."

"I was, and I did. My husband, Niall Clyne, is one of Orkney's aides, which is why you find me here. But, as you said yourself, sir, we must make haste."

"We must, aye," Jake agreed. Stifling the unexpected disappointment that rippled through him at learning that she had indeed married, he added, "When we reach shore, I hope you won't object if we address one another informally. I think it will be safer to do so until we know more."

"If you can get us to safety, sir, you may call me whatever you like."

Jake chuckled, but Mace said, "Cap'n Jake can sail aught that floats, m'lady."

"Sir Ivor said the same, aye," Will said, nodding, as Mace scooped him up and put him into the coble. As the boy made his way to sit on the midthwart beside the lowered mast, he said urgently, "Them pirates took Jamie, Cap'n Jake!"

"I know," Jake said, handing him Lady Alyson's bundle. "Sithee, lad, we've been following the *Maryenknyght*. Now, my lady," he added, scooping her up much as Mace had done with the boy, "in you go."

"Can you lower this boat safely?" she asked.

"Aye, sure," he said, steadying the coble while she moved to sit by Will.

"After you do, how will you and your man get into it?"

"You'll see," he said. "You need only sit still whilst we do it."

When she and Will were safe and gripping the mast, he helped Mace hoist the bow enough to clear the railing. Then they raised the stern. The tricky bit came next, but both men had done similar tasks many times. Using the pulleys and tie bars, moving with well-accustomed dexterity, they let the coble swing out over the railing and into position to lower.

Roping it off once more and standing on the railing, Jake got in first, then Mace. They raised the mast, then untied the ropes, watching each other as they slowly began to lower the boat. The increasing list of the ship made their task easier, but Jake knew that they remained in dire peril. The next giant wave might make the ship turn turtle, and that would be that for all of them.

At the last minute, a wave nearly undid them, but he and Mace released the ropes and grabbed oars to steady the boat as it slid down the offside of the wave.

"Row from where you are, Mace," Jake shouted. "I'll get the sail up and set whilst we're protected by the ship. That wind will hit us hard in the open."

Alyson watched intently, looking from one man to the other, and feeling as if her heart were seeking a home away from her chest. Although she believed that one should cope with life as it came, seeing her rescuers face three swordsmen and then having to descend from the ship in this small boat... She shuddered.

Surely, the pounding in her head and throat were but echoes of her pounding heart, but she could not recall a time when she had been more terrified. And Jake Maxwell's saying that the *Maryenknyght* could roll at any time kept repeating itself in her mind. That didn't help, but try as she might to stifle the thought, it lingered.

She and Will both bent over, trying to protect themselves from seawater that sloshed over the sides and rain driven by the errant gusts of wind that whipped and howled around the *Maryenknyght* as Mace, rowing in the bow, pulled the coble away from the ship. Jake stood right between Will and Alyson, unfurling the sail.

Will hauled himself up to help as well as he could, and Jake did not object. Alyson wished he would order the boy to sit down again but held her peace, having all she could do to keep her hood in place with one hand and her free arm wrapped around the mast. When wind caught the sail, Will sat down with a bump and bent swiftly away from a spray of seawater, so their faces were close together.

Jake moved sternward to take the tiller.

"Are you frightened?" she asked the boy.

"Not if I can keep me eye on summat tae do," he said. "When they was a-lowering us doon tae the water, I near lost what I ate earlier. But, after coming doon from the Bass Rock in that great basket wi' Jamie, even that were nowt."

Remembering the graphic description that the boys had given Ciara and her of their departure from the three-hundred-foot rock at the mouth of the Firth of Forth, Alyson managed a smile for Will. "The two of you are so brave," she said. "I'd have swooned away at having to sit in a basket whilst someone above lowered me into heaving seas like those raging that night around the Bass Rock."

"Aye, well, where they lowered us were no sae wild as what they rowed us through tae get tae the ship. In troth, I were more scared a-climbing up that rope ladder than in the basket. Lord Orkney said most folks prefer the basket tae walking over tae the leeward shore, though. We couldna go that way, 'cause it were too close tae where Tantallon Castle sits on the opposite shore. Since only Douglases live there, and most Douglases were a-looking for us fierce…" He shrugged.

"Why did people otherwise prefer the basket to the leeward shore?"

"'Cause flocks o' gannets fly forever round that great rock and leave a middeny mess," the boy said, his nose wrinkling at the memory. "Me shoes stuck wherever we'd go. I'd wager Orkney hisself preferred the basket tae them gannets."

Alyson smiled. "I think you are right, Will. Orkney pays great heed to how he looks. *And* he likes silken shoes. Such shoes would *not* like gannets' messes."

"Does he truly wear silk ones?" Will asked. "I ha' seen him only in boots. Will they be safe, d'ye think, him and Jamie?" he added with a worried frown.

Tempted though she was to assure him that they would, and hoping that Ciara was safe, too, Alyson said, "We must pray that all of our people are safe, Will. But their safety will depend on why the pirates took them."

Will's face crumpled and he looked away.

A strong gust ripped Alyson's hood from her grasp, and she realized they had moved beyond the shelter of the ship. Looking back as she readjusted her hood, she gasped to see the *Maryenknyght* slowly, inexorably tilting nearer the sea. Abruptly, her railing and masts dipped beneath the surface and her keel turned upward.

"Coo," Will muttered beside her. "All them smelly hides and bales of wool be a-going tae the bottom o' the sea. Them pirates got nowt o' them."

The pirates had taken a much more valuable cargo, though, Alyson thought.

Mist and rain closed off their view. Ahead, she could see only more rain-filled mist on endless gray sea. Hoping that Mace's—and Will's—trust in Jake was well deserved, she wondered if they were even heading the right way. And, if they were, she hoped the sea and the rain would not swamp them before they reached shore.

So focused was she on concealing her fears that Will's voice startled her when he said, "When did *ye* meet him, then—Cap'n Jake?"

"It must have been just after you did," she said. "He

was with my cousin, Sir Ivor, and another man called Fin Cameron. Fin is married to Ivor's sister, Catriona."

"Aye, I met Sir Ivor and Sir Fin, too," Will said, pushing dripping hair from his eyes. "I were wi' Sir Fin just a short time, though. I ken Sir Ivor better."

"Captain Jake came with Ivor and Fin when they visited us in St. John's Town of Perth last year," Alyson said. "My Highland cousins visit us at MacGillivray House at least once a year and whenever the lords of Parliament meet. Sithee, Parliament meets in Perth more often than elsewhere."

"I'd forgot ye was married till Cap'n Jake mentioned it," Will said. "We saw little o' your husband, ye ken. And now, them pirates..." He frowned.

"What about them?" Alyson prompted when he did not continue.

Clearly reluctant, the boy said, "They... they put some folks overboard when they didna move quick enough tae suit them. The captain o' the *Maryenknyght* just stopped the ship when the cannon fired. I think he ought tae ha' fought."

Gently, she said, "He had to think of Jamie's safety, Will."

"Well, I dinna think he'll be safe wi' them pirates," Will said gruffly.

More gently yet, Alyson said, "I am exceedingly grateful that you stayed to rescue me. In troth, I believe Jamie must be glad of it, too. Our prince may be young, Will. But he has an old head on his shoulders, and he will not be thinking of himself alone. He will be very glad that *you* are safe."

Will's frown eased, but his lips tightened before he

said, "Ye've the right of it about Jamie, m'lady, 'cause he *told* me tae find ye. And I'm no going tae say that I wish I hadna done it, 'cause that isna so. But, in troth, I'm nigh tae grieving, too, that I canna be wi' him the noo. I *should* be, ye ken."

"I do know what you mean, Will. I have had exactly those feelings—"

Breaking off with a cry when the boat topped a giant wave and careened wildly down into the trough between it and the next one with a huge splash, soaking her with icy water, Alyson tightened her grip on the mast and began to wonder if she might freeze to death before they drowned.

Chapter 4

To gain speed, Jake had let the wind and waves carry them southwestward away from the *Maryenknyght*. But, nearly certain that the pirates had headed back to Flamborough Head, he hoped to beach the coble nearby.

That meant they had to turn north. Shouting to Mace to take the tiller, he noted the *Maryenknyght*'s fate with only a brief glance. Having expected it, he did not let it trouble him but fixed his attention on what lay ahead.

According to his rutter, both sides of the great headland had harbors. With winds from the northeast, the pirates would make for the primary harbor on the south side of the headland in Bridlington Bay. That harbor would offer more shelter than the one on the headland's north side, in Filey Bay.

Sheltering from wind as one made landfall was always good. But it would matter more to large ships than to the oared coble. The lead ship of the group that had captured Jamie was as big as the *Maryenknyght* if not bigger.

The smaller harbor on the north side of the headland would do for the coble. Just to get that far would tax it enough. Trying to make it any farther in the fifteen-mile, wide-mouthed Filey Bay would be foolhardy against the winds and seas that they were experiencing. As it was, every time he tacked into the wind or turned away from it, he risked swamping the coble or rolling it.

Plowing over waves and plunging down as they were while he fought the sail to tack northward, and tied it off, he knew they'd be safe enough even if wind ripped the sail. The journey would take time in any event. But if the sail ripped, they'd have to land wherever the waves took them, because he and Mace would not be able to row long against such weather. However, barring a reef they failed to see or some unexpected freak of nature, he was confident that they would not sink.

He was soaked. But so were the others, and from where he stood, he could quickly ease strain on the sail if need be. He was also blocking some of the wind and rain from the two sitting low in front of the mast. He saw that they had their heads together and hoped they were managing to keep warm.

He did his best to watch the waves around them through the increasing murk, paying special heed to waves rolling landward. The course he had set was holding, and if he had not mistaken their current location, he ought soon to make out the shape of the two-hundred-foot-high headland.

He had mixed feelings about the increasing darkness, recalling that his rutter warned that the north harbor lay deep in a small inlet. However, he knew that folks ashore would soon light candles and lamps, which would make it easier for him to judge distance and discern the inner curve of the bay. Continuing his vigil, he tried to imagine all that might go wrong. On the positive side, the mast was sound, the sail held strong against the wind, Mace was skilled at the tiller, and the two of them had sailed cobles together in rough seas before.

Alyson and Will held an oar across them that Mace had given her in passing, to hold in case Jake needed it. Mace kept another near himself. Chiefly, what threatened them were the unknown factors. A dangerous reef shot out from Filey, so what if there were others unknown to the rutter? Or lone, unnoted boulders?

Aware of a continued murmur of voices from the lad and Alyson, Jake's thoughts shifted to what he knew about her. Although he had met her only once before, his memory of her slender, curvaceous body; smooth, almost silvery blonde hair; and a certain mysterious faraway look in her eyes was clear.

His memory of her cousin Ivor was even clearer.

He had known Ivor Mackintosh and Fin Cameron from their boyhood days together at St. Andrews Castle, where they had studied under the tutelage of Bishop Wardlaw's predecessor, Bishop Traill.

Jake had stayed at MacGillivray House only one night before going home to Duncraig, on the west coast of Kintail. The news of Traill's death reached him a month later, and his grief had been almost as great as if he'd lost his father.

Captain Wat Maxwell, Giff MacLennan, and others had taught Jake all he knew about sailing. But Traill had taught him things that were just as important, if not more so, primarily the value of strong friendships.

Although the wind still howled around them, Jake had reached that familiar state of sensing the movements of a boat without thought and recognizing intervals needed before resetting the sail. He hoped to be north of the headland before it came into view and thus avoid anyone's seeing them from the south harbor or town.

However, the chalky whalelike shape of Flamborough Head loomed out of the murk ahead portside with some distance still to go. He was sailing as near to the wind as he dared, but the coble was out far enough for them to pass the head safely. Also, the murk had thickened in Bridlington Bay. He could not see the harbor, which meant that no one in the harbor could see them.

Adjusting course slightly to give himself more room to turn inland, he heard Will wonder aloud how much longer it would be. Jake realized that sitting as low as the two in front of the mast now were, they could not see what lay ahead. In the driving rain, they had probably stopped paying heed in any event.

Alyson glanced up, smiled, and his memory flitted back to the crackling fire in the comfortable hall and a distant clatter of some menial dropping a tray on the dais. The charming lass with whom he had been enjoying pleasant discourse had looked up from a more demure posture and smiled at him just so.

He had been flirting shamelessly with her at the time, and her smile had encouraged him. Then Ivor had joined them long enough to let him know that she was soon to marry, thus taking the wind from Jake's sails.

Smiling at the memory, he recalled how Lady Alyson had seemed to be aware of what everyone in the room was doing and saying, even as she carried on her conversation with him. Twice, she had briefly disengaged to answer a question he had not heard and to inject a comment into another conversation. He had been astonished at how deftly she did such things without losing the thread of what he—or, for that matter, she—had been saying at the time.

Once, when a dispute arose, the two most involved had soon drawn others into the argument. He had nearly grown dizzy looking from one person to another. But a quiet observation of Alyson's had settled the matter in a trice.

He saw that she had returned her attention to Will. Her cloak was soaked, and she was still clutching her hood to keep it up. He knew few women who would not complain bitterly at finding themselves in such a situation.

"Do you know where we are, sir?" she asked, raising her voice in the apparent belief that he would not otherwise hear it over the wind.

"We're approaching Flamborough Head," he said. "'Tis the place from whence the pirates sailed. They appeared from behind the headland when we were north of it, so they had harbored in Bridlington Bay. I'm nearly certain they've returned to shelter there."

"Then should we not head inland, to see where they go next?"

Will declared, "Aye, we should. We need tae see where they take Jamie."

"If Mace and I were alone, I might risk that," Jake said. "No one aboard those ships but Orkney would recognize us easily. He and Jamie are the only ones likely to recognize Will, Mace, or me. And they both have sense enough to say nowt. But everyone who was on the *Maryenknyght* would know you, my lady."

"But Ciara—" She broke off, biting her lip. Then she said, "Nay, you are right, sir. Ciara would shout out my name the instant she clapped eyes on me."

"Nay, she—" But Will, too, broke off whatever he had been about to say.

"What is it, lad?" Jake asked. "You may say what you like to us."

Looking down, Will muttered, "Nay, sir. It were nowt."

"Speak louder, Will," Alyson said. "I doubt he could hear you."

Sensing that the boy had thought better of what he had nearly said, and realizing that his silence might have something to do with Alyson, Jake said, "He can tell us later. Meantime, my plan is to find the north-side harbor, beach this coble, and seek shelter for the night."

"Where?"

"Flamborough must be that clutch of lights atop the headland, and it looks big enough for an alehouse. Also, it lies too far from Bridlington to draw anyone from there in this weather. Still, I'll wager that if we can find an alehouse there or nearby, we'll soon hear news of those five ships."

Giving him a searching look, her demeanor as serene as if she were sitting by her own hearth fire, she said, "I want to learn what they've done with my husband, sir. Will said the pirates threw men overboard if they did not obey fast enough. Niall is a complaisant man, so I doubt that he would be one of those. Even so..."

"I understand, my lady. Forbye, you must not show yourself anywhere near those ships. When we make landfall and get our bearings, we'll learn what we can. You should know, though, that if those pirates discover what prizes they hold in Orkney and Jamie, they'll guard them well."

Will looked up at him, clearly about to speak again.

Then, tightening his lips, the boy looked away. They had rounded the headland, so although his behavior made Jake more curious than ever, he resisted the urge to question him and fixed his attention on finding the harbor.

The wind now behind them, they sailed parallel to the headland's looming chalk cliffs. With their tall columns, arches, and caves, they made an impressive sight even at dusk. As Jake had expected, pinpricks of light showed in cottages atop the headland and here and there around the bay, marking its shoreline. Shifting his attention back to the headland, he saw the opening in the cliffs.

"There, Mace!" he shouted. "Just off the port bow. See it?"

"Aye, Cap'n," Mace shouted from the stern. "D'ye think it might harbor ships as big as them others?"

"According to the *Sea Wolf*'s rutter, it can take one or two large ones. I doubt they'd risk trying to take five such into it, though."

Will said, "What if there be rocks?"

"If we keep to the center of the opening, we'll have good clearance, lad."

"What of the tide?" Alyson asked. "Is it going in or coming out?"

"Coming out," Jake said. "These rollers will make any landing a challenge, but that beach is said to be safe in all but the highest spring tides. I doubt we'll need the coble again, in any event."

~

His last statement stunned Alyson. "But what if we do?"

"We won't. As you see, this wide-mouthed bay provides little protection against the wind. We're nobbut eight miles from our meeting place and can walk it faster and safer than we could sail it against such fierce winds as these."

"Doubtless, you're right," she said, thinking in truth that after their wild ride, once she was out of the tossing coble, she would be grateful to walk.

Looking up at the high, cave-ridden headland above them and seeing no sign of any inlet from where she sat, she hoped again that Jake knew what he was doing.

"Coo, them cliffs reach tae the sky," Will said. "If there do be a beach in amongst them somewheres, how will we get up from it tae yon village?"

"Where there is a harbor, there will be a path," Jake said.

"Most often, aye," Will agreed. "But I'll believe in it when I can see it."

Nearly agreeing with that earnest declaration, Alyson noted that Jake had fixed his gaze on a point ahead of them, doubtless the opening of the harbor that he had mentioned to his man. She would have liked to see where they were going. But she could not even see the shore there over the prow of the coble, and she was not about to stand to do so.

For one thing, she was uncertain that she would be able to perform either movement, as cold as she was. She also knew that she would stay calm only if she continued to place her trust in the coble and in the two men sailing it.

Jake had lost his hat, and his dark hair had plastered itself to his head. Strands of it stuck to his face. It had been windblown when she recognized him on the deck of the *Maryenknyght*. But she remembered his dark soft curls from his visit to MacGillivray House. That evening had been a pleasant one, and as far as she could tell, he had not altered in the year that had followed it.

Since he was Ivor's friend, she knew she could trust him to look after her until they found Niall or learned what had become of him, because Ivor would take a dim view of anyone who betrayed her trust. And people never liked it when Ivor took a dim view. But what, she wondered, would they do next?

Will wanted to rejoin Jamie Stewart. But what if the pirates had *not* returned to Bridlington's harbor? If they had gone elsewhere, how would anyone find them? And if the four of them did find the pirates, what then?

"The *Maryenknyght* be nae more the noo," Will said, as if his thoughts had followed a similar track. "How will we get Jamie tae France if we *do* find him?"

"Orkney is wealthy and powerful," she said. "If the pirates don't know that, if they took them aboard only because the *Maryenknyght* was sinking and have released them hereabouts..." She stopped, seeing tears in Will's eyes. "What is it?"

"Nowt," he muttered. "I just ha' a gey bad feeling about all o' this."

A tingling sensation touched her as he spoke. And the shudder that ran from her nape to her shoulders and rippled through her body had naught to do with the chilly wind. She recognized its meaning. Will was right, more so than he knew.

Jake's thoughts followed a similar track as he considered what lay ahead. He had to discover what had happened to Orkney and James.

His two passengers would be devilishly in the way, and he could not do a thing about that. He itched for a few minutes with her ladyship's husband to tell him what a fool he was for having brought her on such a voyage.

In any event, he couldn't abandon her or Will. And rejoining the *Sea Wolf* quickly might not be an option while the wicked weather continued. Still, Coll would aim for the coast near the center of Filey Bay, as Jake had ordered him to do.

So the first order of business was to learn what he could and decide what his options were. The next would be to see to Lady Alyson's safety.

They would have to walk north along the cliffs lining the bay to meet the *Sea Wolf.* Since that would take them away from Bridlington, he might have to depend on what news he could glean from folks on the headland or along the cliffs.

Unless the pirates left James and Orkney in Bridlington, he suspected that the Fates had seriously limited his options.

The harbor mouth looked larger as they neared it, and the coble passed with ease between the flanking chalk cliffs. Ahead, he saw a long jetty and a deep sandy beach at the base of the cliffs. Besides sand, though, there were scattered rocks and boulders. On any normal day, beaching safely would be easy. However, the heaving seas were driving huge waves inland despite the ebbing tide. In such an inlet, one rarely expected to find such powerful rollers.

Swiftly scanning the shore as he dropped the sail, he saw a pathway leading uphill from the jetty. It looked steep, but he would be glad to exert himself. The exercise would warm them all. He was sure that both of his passengers must be freezing in their wet clothing. He was none so warm himself.

The effects of the wind were less powerful in the harbor than on the bay. He saw two boats larger than the coble tied on the leeward side of the jetty, dancing wildly on the waves. He would keep his passengers safer by beaching the coble. However, their speed had increased on the rollers. They were going too fast to depend solely on the tiller for a safe landing.

"Mace, lock that tiller and grab an oar," Jake shouted, grabbing for himself the oar that Alyson still held. "Face the beach, Mace, and row steerboard!"

Standing on the midthwart, steadying himself at the mast, Jake stepped over the two sitting in front of it to the bow thwart, used the oar as a third leg when he sat, then shoved it into the portside rowlock and snapped the lock into place.

"Pull hard," he shouted. "We'll aim between those two boulders dead ahead. You two stay put and hold on," he added over his shoulder to Alyson and Will.

Fixing his gaze on his chosen landing place, he plied his oar, adjusting his pull as needed to keep them on course. The next moments went quickly. Then the boat soared atop a huge roller and plunged toward the beach. He saw smaller rocks, half-buried in the sand, too late to avoid them. The coble landed hard, right where he'd wanted it, and shot wildly up onto the rain-and-wave-soaked sand.

He heard rocks scraping the hull. Then came a loud crack, and their forward momentum abruptly stopped.

Since he and Mace had experienced hard beach landings

before, Jake barely spared him a glance but turned his attention to their passengers.

Will looked relieved and shot him a grin. "We made it!"

"Aye, we did," Jake said. "How did you fare, my lady?"

"My legs are numb," she said with surprise. "I don't think I can stand."

When it became apparent that both of their passengers would require help to get out, Jake lifted Alyson out without ceremony and let Mace see to young Will.

As he carried Alyson above the reach of incoming waves, he saw a shallow cave in the looming cliff face and carried her there. "Try to stand now," he said, setting her on her feet. "I'll hold you steady until the numbness wears off."

"My legs feel all tingly," she admitted, shivering. "I got colder than I knew. But I need only stamp about to get warm. At least we are out of the rain here."

He kept hold of her until he was sure she was not exaggerating her ability to see to herself. Then, seeing Will also stamping one foot and waving his arms about, he said, "How is that ankle of yours, lad?"

"Better," Will said. "I can stand on it now."

Nodding, Jake went to help Mace drag the coble above the high-water mark. It would be unusable until repaired, but someone would be glad to attend to it.

They had not seen another living creature.

Gesturing toward the path up the cliff, Jake said, "They seem to have carved steps right into a declivity there. Are you ready to go up and find proper shelter?"

Although Alyson was ready, she kept her opinion of the rough-hewn steps to herself. At least she was not taking a few steps up only to slip back, as she would have done on such a slope without steps. Even so, she could not be sure that she was seeing the top end of them when she tilted her head back as far as it would go.

Mace went first, then Will, with Alyson behind him and Jake behind her.

The rain continued but was lighter than it had been, and the wind barely caressed them on the steps. When they had found their rhythm, climbing them, Jake said casually, "What did you see, Will, before you went to help the lady Alyson? Did you see the pirates board the ship?"

"Aye, some o' them," Will said, glancing over his shoulder at Alyson.

"When Ciara said ships were approaching the *Maryenknyght*, Will and Jamie ran up on deck," Alyson said, speaking loudly enough for Mace to hear her, too.

"We wanted tae see what were what," Will said. "But when they fired their cannon and yon fool, Cap'n Bear-dolt—"

"Bereholt," Alyson corrected.

"Him, aye," Will said nodding. "When he stopped the ship, Orkney said we should go below. Jamie said he wanted tae watch, but Orkney spoke tae him sharp. So we went doon and told Lady Alyson and Ciara that the pirates was a-boarding. Then we hid. But some o' them villains came and found Ciara. When she screamed, Jamie ran tae help her. I did, too. But we shouldna had done that."

"I'd wager you had few choices, lad," Jake said. "Had you stayed where you were, they'd likely have found you in any event."

"They must have come down to the lower cabins straightaway," Alyson said. "I'd expected them to head for the hold, but evidently only a few of them did, as we saw. Ciara had just fastened the lid of my kist and was getting into hers when they burst in on her. Then the boys ran in, and the men hustled all three of them away. That's when I discovered that I was locked in."

"A good thing you were," Jake said. "Had the kist not been locked, that chap who rattled the hasp-pin would have opened it and seen you straightaway."

Alyson grimaced, knowing he was right.

"What did you see topside, Will?" Jake asked next.

"Men all a-shouting and a-cursing," Will said. "Some was still a-jumping aboard from the two ships hooked tae the *Maryenknyght*. Others herded our lads sternward like sheep. Someone shouted about us taking on water, and Cap'n—" He glanced at Alyson. "The captain said he'd feared all along that the oakum they'd caulked seams with at Leith hadna had time tae dry proper and wouldna hold. Them fools a-banging their ships against ours as they did must ha' finished her."

"You told me that the pirates threw men overboard," Alyson prompted. "But you did not see them fling anyone we know, did you?"

"No tae say 'fling,'" Will said slowly and with audible reluctance.

"Did someone else *fall* in?" she asked, tensing, fearing for Niall.

Will was silent.

Behind her, Jake said with firmness that she had not heard from him before, "Tell us what you saw, Will. If it was dreadful, 'tis better for us to know."

"It...it were Ciara," the boy said, turning at last to look at Alyson, his misery plain to see. "She...she did fall, I think. Sithee, the ship they wanted her on were no the one that they'd said *we* should board. I think she were afeard tae get on t'other one by herself and afeard for ye, too, m'lady."

Alyson swallowed hard and pressed her fingernails into the heels of her hands to give herself something else to think about. She did not want to lose her composure before Will and the men.

"Did she fall between those two ships?" Jake asked the boy.

"Aye, she did," Will said, nodding. "The pirate ship were lower than what the *Maryenknyght* were. And they'd put a plank from railing tae railing. I'd no ha' wanted tae walk across it m'self, and ye could see she were scarified. Them louts wouldna help her, neither. They just laughed and told her tae go. Then one o' them gave her a wee push. No tae make her fall in, I think, only tae make her get a move on. But wi' the down-slope and all, she lost her balance."

Jake said quietly, "They could not have done much to save her after she fell, my lady. Likely, had they tried to lower a rope and pull her up, the two ships would have crushed her between them. Drowning was a better way to go."

She knew that he meant to ease her distress. Instead, his words drew horrible images in her mind that seemed to loom and recede, each fighting others to inflict itself on her: One was of poor Ciara sinking, terrified, beneath the waves; the other of Ciara with two great ships flinging themselves at her from either side.

Bile rose in Alyson's throat. Shutting her eyes after placing each foot on the next step, as if she could thereby banish the gruesome images, she concentrated on breathing deeply in and out, then opened her eyes and continued upward, still breathing deeply, until she could trust herself to think properly again.

"What about Niall, Will?" she asked at last, knowing that she had to learn all that she could. Otherwise, her imagination would exhaust itself, and her, suggesting increasingly horrible answers to her questions. "Did you see him or Sir Kentigern?"

"Aye," the boy replied. "We saw them straightaway when them louts what captured us in your cabin took us topside. Niall and Mungo boarded the lead ship—the biggest one—with Orkney. He were a-talking tae the captain o' that ship when them louts hustled me and Jamie on tae the deck from the ladder. They pushed us right tae that ship. And when their captain saw us..."

He paused and glanced back at Alyson.

Jake said, "What did the captain do, Will?"

In the brief second before Will replied, Alyson felt the tingling shiver again.

Will said, "Their captain said..." Clearing his throat, he added in a gruffer voice, "'Nah then, what ha' ye got there, lads? Be that no the young heir tae the Scottish crown? Ye do be Jamie Stewart, d'ye no, laddie?'" Looking back again but past Alyson at Jake this time, the boy added in his customary voice, "Ye dinna think Orkney told him about our Jamie, do ye, sir?"

"I do not," Jake said grimly.

Alyson agreed. No Sinclair Earl of Orkney would betray his prince.

Jake knew that he had spoken harshly, but Will seemed to accept his words as assurance. And so they were where Orkney was concerned. Jake was certain that while the young earl might identify himself as one who could gain the pirates an enormous ransom, he would not identify James for any reason other than to save the boy's life. If the captain of that so-called pirate fleet had known Jamie on sight, then that captain must have *expected* to find Scotland's prince aboard the *Maryenknyght.*

Silence prevailed until they reached the top of the harbor path and as they followed it up a gentler slope in the deepening darkness. The wind had eased, but when they reached the crest, Jake saw from the village lights that Flamborough was larger than he'd expected. He recalled another detail from his rutter that he'd barely heeded at the time but which now seemed much more important.

"Mace," he said, "the Danes dug a dyke hereabouts to divide this headland from the mainland. It is west of the village and runs all the way across the headland north to south, and boasts only two crossings. One lies nearby. I want to know where it is before full darkness and before we risk entering the village."

"It looks as if there may be a crossroad o' sorts ahead," Mace replied.

It proved to be no more than a cart path, but they followed it. Although Jake feared they might find themselves without light before they found the dyke, they soon saw widely scattered lights in the distance. Shortly afterward, they came to a wooden bridge over a chasm of a depth that astonished him. The thing was at least fifteen or twenty feet deep, its sides far too steep to scale easily.

"That looks to me like an alehouse across the way, sir," Mace said. "I'm thinking we'd be wiser tae stop there than tae turn back tae the village from here. I can hear her ladyship's teeth a-chattering."

Jake said, "'Tis a good notion, Mace. It does occur to me, though, that anyone inside is likely to know us for Scots straightaway from our speech if nowt else. Truce or no truce, I distrust the English."

"Aye, sir, but if them pirates release the *Maryenknyght*'s crew or her passengers in Bridlington and they try to head back toward Scotland, they'll likely pass by on the other side o' this dyke, will they no?"

"They will, aye," Jake agreed.

"Then nae one in that alehouse now be likely tae know us or do us harm."

Alyson said quietly, "If I might add something, sir..."

"Aye, sure, lass."

"I've heard that Borderers' accents are similar whether English or Scots."

"That is also true," he said, feeling his usual confidence surge back.

Accordingly, they crossed the bridge and entered the alehouse through a door flanked by burning torches that lit up a sign overhead, in the shape of a blue pig.

Inside, the air smelled of good food and burning peat, with an added tang of unwashed men. A man stepped forward, saying, "Ah be t' taverner, Sam Metlow, and Ah bid tha welcome t' Blue Boar," he said. "Coom by yon fire and be warm."

To Jake's astonishment, Alyson said in the same accent

and cadence as the alemaster, or taverner, as he called himself, "We thank tha, good man, for tha kindness. We would ken if tha hast two rooms we might tak' for the night."

"Ah do, mistress. All o' these lads be local. From whence dost tha coom?"

Chapter 5

Alyson hesitated. Unsure of what to say, she glanced at Jake.

With a self-deprecating smile, he said, "Sakes, man, can ye no tell by the look o' us that the sea swept us in tae yon wee harbor t'other side o' that great ditch o' yours? The waves shoved our coble over some rocks, so she'll need new strakes and caulking afore she's worth aught tae anyone. We canna linger, so mayhap ye'd consider taking her in place o' our reckoning here. Sithee, I misjudged yon squall earlier and got separated from me ship out yonder somewheres, lost it in the storm."

"Wi' your *woman* and the bairn by ye?"

"She's nae me woman but me widowed sister, Allie," Jake said, revealing a gift for prevarication that delighted Alyson. "Married a chap from a place just north o' Scarborough," he added. "The poor mon dropped dead a month ago and left nowt for her, so I were a-fetching her home again. We'd headed north when yon squall hit us and fair shoogled our innards tae bits. Carried us past Filey when we tried tae avoid their reef, and we ended up here. 'Twas by God's grace that we found that wee harbor, I can tell ye. I thought we'd be sped down tae the devil in

Hell. Ha' ye a tub then, and a maidservant wha' can help our Allie warm herself?"

"Ah'll send me daughter up t' her straightaway," the taverner promised. "Tha'll be wanting dry clothes tha'self then, too. If tha dinna be choosy, some o' me lads your size will share their things till yours be dry."

"Ye're a kind man, Sam Metlow," Jake told him. "Me sister will likely tak' her supper in her chamber. The lad, me man there, and I will sup down here. We'll share that second room o' yours, too, if ye've pallets for me man and the lad."

These arrangements being agreeable, the man's wife soon bustled in. They followed her up a narrow stairway to two small chambers under the eaves.

"I'll wait here wi' me sister, Mistress Metlow, whilst ye hurry whoever be bringing yon tub and hot water for her," Jake said, ushering the stout woman out.

Then, without so much as a by-your-leave, he shut himself in with Alyson.

She shook her head at him. "You, Jake Maxwell, are an outrageous liar."

"Outrageous? I thought I told a fine tale."

"You did, aye. But you should *not* be in here, sir."

"I ken that fine," he said more soberly. "But I want to know where the devil you picked up that Yorkshire accent you laid on Taverner Metlow."

"From him. I've entertained myself since childhood by mimicking my elders and our servants. You must agree, 'tis a useful skill to have cultivated."

He grinned, and his dark eyes danced as he said, "A devilish useful one. Will you have any trouble carrying on with it if we have to stay more than a day?"

"I've a good ear. It got me into trouble more oft than not when I was a bairn. I could ha' said I coom fra' the Borders had I heard ye speak so afore," she added.

"Is that how I sound? I'd no notion I had such a high-pitched voice."

"Now you are mocking me, and in troth, you should not. I can do it in French and Gaelic, as well. I might fail to use the correct words, because people of different regions call things by different names. But I can imitate whatever I hear."

"You did seem to do so easily," he agreed.

Deciding to take advantage of his agreeable mood, she said, "I did see two women in the common room, sir. I would liefer sup down there where it is warmer. Perhaps you might arrange to use that table in the nook by the fireplace. We should be able to talk quietly there without being overheard. I'd like to know what else Will saw whilst he was on deck."

Having thought he'd insist she stay safely in her chamber, she had planned her arguments as they'd come up the stairs. To her astonishment, he said, "I doubt that you would freeze here with the heat rising from below. In troth, I thought you'd dislike supping in company with some of those louts in the common room."

"I am confident that you and Mace can protect me," she said. Recalling Will's behavior earlier, she added, "Sakes, I'd not be astonished to find that Will could protect me by himself. He seems to be a most resourceful boy."

"So is Jamie Stewart," Jake said.

"He is," she agreed. "Both of them are wise beyond their years."

"Aye," Jake said. "Jamie talks as if he were a man of

forty with years of experience in all things behind him. He is as different from his late brother, Davy, as flint is from tinder."

"Before I met Jamie on the ship, I'd not met him before," she said. "But, living in St. John's Town, I knew Davy well. 'Twas a travesty, what happened to him! For the lords of Parliament to call *that* an accident—"

"His death was a shock to me, too," Jake said, "especially coming on the heels of his mother's death and that of Bishop Traill, as it did." He put a finger quickly to his lips then, silencing the words that leaped to her tongue.

A rattle of the latch heralded the entrance of a young woman so like in appearance to the taverner's wife that Alyson knew she had to be their daughter. She carried a colorful bundle of things under one arm.

"Ah be Lizzie Thornwick, mistress," she said. "Me mum and da own this place, and Da said Ah should look after thee. I'll set yon screen so tha canst get thy wet clathes off," she added, moving to do so. "I've brung a robe and towels t' dry tha some afore tha gets into t' tub our lads be bringing up."

"I thank thee," Alyson said, following her to the screen and accepting a towel. "Tha shouldst go, brother. Tha must ha' dry clathes thyself, as weel."

"Aye, me da put some in yon room across the way," Lizzie said.

Two men hefting a tin tub and two others carrying pails of steaming water came in as Jake went out. When Jake cast Alyson a look of concern just before he shut the door, she gave him a sober wink in response.

She was relieved to see him go, though. She had come too close to sharing her opinion of the villains who had insisted that Davy Stewart had died of natural causes, rather than the way he had. She had no reason to distrust Jake and good reason to trust any friend of Ivor's. But some opinions were safer unshared.

She greeted the tub men confidently, although she began to suspect that maintaining the Yorkshire accent would be harder than she had thought.

Wondering how Lady Alyson could be so bedraggled and remain so beautiful, Jake had been unable to resist that last glance at her as he left. When she caught his eye and winked just before he shut the door, he knew she was just expressing confidence in her ability to deal with Lizzie. He also noted a dimple below the left corner of her mouth that he had not noticed before.

Putting the image with the dimple firmly out of mind, he crossed the landing to their second room, where he found Mace and Will changing out of their wet clothes. Will wore a dry but threadbare shirt that fell to his knees, and was reaching for a thick, knitted, moss-green jersey that looked as if it might fit him better.

Mace said, "They ha' been gey kind to us, sir."

"They have, aye," Jake agreed. "I was going to send you into Flamborough to learn what you could about those other ships. But, as full as this inn's common room is, I'm thinking we'll do better to chat with men here. When you've dressed, go down and ask Metlow if we may use that round table in the nook by the fire. If he says aye, tell him 'Mistress Allie' will sup with us."

Mace raised his eyebrows. "D'ye think that be wise? Some o' them lads…"

"I agree," Jake said. "But she believes that the three of us can protect her. Forbye, she wants to hear more of what Will can tell us about what happened."

Mace's lips twitched in a near smile. But he said only, "I agree that it be better for me tae stay here. Most o' them chaps below ha' drink enow in them the noo tae forget what they say or how I sound when I talk."

"If anyone questions you too closely, confide that your mother was a damned Scot afore she married. After our years together your Scots is gey like mine."

Mace did smile then. "Happen she *were* a Scotswoman, coom tae that."

Will watched them, saying nothing. But when Mace was ready to go downstairs, the boy eyed Jake quizzically.

"You stay with me, lad. No one has asked who you are, but they must think you are my son or Mistress Allie's."

"Is that what I should call her ladyship, too, then, sir?"

"Aye, and refrain from saying 'sir' and 'm'lady' until we reach my ship. Can you remember that?"

"Aye, sure," Will said.

"That is a fine sweater you are wearing," Jake said.

"Aye, well, the man said it be one his son outgrew," Will said earnestly. "He said I could keep it, but he didna ha' any o' his outgrown shirts, so I'm a-wearing one he brung up for ye or Mace. I didna think ye'd mind."

"I don't, nor would Mace," Jake assured him.

"D'ye think Jamie will ha' dry clothes? Mayhap we should keep some for when we find him."

Hesitating only a moment, Jake said, "We may not be able to rescue him, Will. We are only four people, after all. Even with the *Sea Wolf*'s crew, we'd be too few to take on that pirate fleet. Our job is to tell people at home what happened. But first," he added, "Mistress Allie wants to hear about all that you saw on deck."

"Aye, sure, but mayhap I should tell ye first that—"

"You need not tell it twice," Jake said. "We must talk whilst we eat if only to look normal, so we might as well talk about that as anything else. It should be safe enough as long as we take heed of anyone coming near us. It wouldn't do to let others hear aught we say about the *Maryenknyght*."

"I didna want tae tell her about Ciara," Will said glumly.

"I ken that fine, lad. So does she. But you were right to tell her. Shall we see if she is ready yet to go downstairs?"

They had their answer when he opened the door, because Lizzie opened their door at the same time, and Alyson was peering over Lizzie's shoulder. Clearly ready, she wore a plain white veil over her hair, which hung in loose, silky-looking flaxen plaits, one lying forward over her left shoulder and breast.

"Lizzie thinks Ah should dry me hair by t' fire downstairs," Alyson said. "So Ah plaited it as it were afore. I can brush it later, for it'll dry quick."

He nodded, having no idea how long it took a woman to dry her hair. At Duncraig, he and his father lived with Giff MacLennan and his lady, and Lady Sidony often plaited her hair. Alyson's looked fine to him.

Downstairs they found Mace seated at the nook table near the fire with a jug and a mug before him. As the two women of the alehouse darted around them, setting hot food on the table, Jake pulled out the stool nearest the hearth for Alyson.

She accepted it, shifting the errant plait to her back.

Motioning for Will to take the stool on the hearth side of the table between Alyson's stool and the bench under the window where Mace sat, Jake sat opposite Will. From there, he and Mace could both watch the common room.

"They been a-talking o' them ships," Mace muttered when the alewife and Lizzie left them to their supper. "They say all five ha' harbored at Bridlington this past fortnight or longer. They harbored there although their leader hails from a village called Cley, much farther south, in a shire called Norfolk."

"Have these pirates attacked others?" Jake asked him.

"Nae one mentioned other attacks. The men a-talking did *call* them pirates, and said they'd been a-prowling the seas as long as they've been here."

Alyson's forehead creased slightly before she said, "Surely they must have seen other merchantmen, even ones from… from the north."

"Aye, that be so," Mace agreed. "One lad did say they ha' stopped near every ship from the north. But nae one seems tae ken nowt about seizing any cargoes."

"Which means they did not," Jake said. "A single merchantman's cargo would fill the hold in the largest of those ships. They'd have no need to stop every ship coming south. Moreover, Will said most of the attackers did not even look for the *Maryenknyght*'s hold. Is that not so, lad?"

"Aye, it is… least I didna see anyone near that stern hatch, but them three did come out o' there, later. Them wha' Jamie and I saw a-boarding her did just herd our lads about, though, and took… um… them others wha' they did take." He glanced at Jake as if to ask if he had been clear.

Giving him a reassuring nod, Jake said, "Their leader identified our youngest friend with astonishing, even suspicious, ease. Tell us what else you observed, lad."

"What if one o' these others can hear?" Will asked. "I canna talk and watch."

Jake rested his left hand on the table and wiggled its forefinger. "I'll keep watch for anyone coming near. If I lift my finger so, stop talking."

Nodding, Will glanced at Alyson and then looked back, fixing his gaze on Jake's left forefinger. "Ye asked earlier did I see Mungo and Niall." Raising his gaze to Jake's face, he said, "I should call them so, aye?"

"Aye."

"Well, we did see them when we got topside, like I told ye. But I saw 'em again later, too." He grimaced uneasily.

Alyson understood that Will did not want to tell her the rest. She said gently, "Tell us, Will. Were they no longer aboard that lead ship?"

"Nay . . . I mean we were all aboard her by then. Jamie and me kent fine that ye were still below, so I watched them. I thought one o' them would ask about ye—Mungo or Niall, that is, no the captain or the louts. But nae one did till they was turning away wi' the captain. Then that Niall said summat about going back tae find ye"—he glanced at Alyson—"but Mungo said he'd sent someone tae fetch ye and that Niall should go below wi' him and Orkney. I kent fine that Mungo had sent nae one, and Jamie did, too. Ye should ken that all were disorder, wi' planks stretched ship tae ship all along where they was hooked together. Nae one paid me heed. I think they were too busy fleeing the *Maryenknyght* tae heed one lad slipping back tae her. I were near enough the forecastle tae slip into Orkney's cabin. It were gey easy from there tae get back down the hatchway. I thought Jamie would tell your Niall, and they'd wait for us."

"But they didn't," Alyson said. "And it is as well that they did not, Will. Whatever happens, we know where they are right now. We may be the only ones other than their captors who do."

"Aye, well, I dinna ken what they be a-doing wi' Jamie," Will said. "Ye should ha' heard Orkney a-telling that Englishman that he'd nae right tae touch our prince or tae interfere wi' his journey, let alone tae damage his ship as they had. Orkney said he should arrange tae find them proper transport tae go on forthwith."

"What did the captain say to that?" Jake asked dryly.

"He said there'd been a change o' plans, that we had entered King Harry's waters without his royal permission. That were when someone shouted that the *Maryenknyght* were a-sinking, and men began scrambling tae get from our ship tae them two other ones. That's when I slipped away."

"You saved my life," Alyson said. "I'll never forget that, Will."

Raising his left forefinger, Jake said in his Borderer's accent, "Will ye tak' some o' this fine bread the noo, Allie-lass?"

"Ah will," she said, as Lizzie passed behind her and bent to refill Jake's mug from a fresh jug of ale. "Ah'll ha' the butter as weel."

Passing her the butter crock, Jake thanked Lizzie and took the jug from her, handing it to Mace.

"Will ye ha' some, too, laddie?" Mace asked Will.

"Aye, sure," Will said.

"Ye've barely touched yours," Jake murmured to Alyson.

"I am not fond of ale, I fear," she replied.

"Ah, nae doot ye'd liefer ha' whisky."

With a wistful smile, she said, "We do have gey fine whisky at home."

"I remember it, aye. Near as potent as Isles brogac, as I recall it."

They all fell silent, making the most of the tasty fish stew.

Then, abruptly, Jake said, "How came you to be on the *Maryenknyght*, lass? You said it was because your husband serves Orkney, but I'd have thought the trip was all men's business—Orkney's and his grace, the King's, in fact."

"That may, in fact, have been the case," she said. "But Orkney himself told me that very few people knew the true purpose of the journey and that Niall was not one of them. I think Mungo must have known, because he is chief secretary and had been traveling much on Orkney's business. Niall stayed at Roslyn Castle, Orkney's primary seat, to tend to business there. Since we had been so briefly married—"

"Briefly?" He gave her a sharp look. "But you must be married nigh a year by now. I distinctly recall Ivor's saying that you were to marry in June."

"Doubtless, he did, sir," she said, amused to think of just what Ivor might have said to Jake, who had been amusing himself at the time by flirting with her. "From one cause or another, we postponed our wedding until December. So we had been married little over a month when Niall learned about this journey. He told me only that he and Mungo would be leaving the first of March for France. I said I'd like to go if I could, as it would give us a chance to know each other better."

"Ivor said you had known your intended since childhood."

"Aye, but not as a husband to live with."

"So, you thought such a journey would let you spend time together."

"Aye, for I'd barely seen Niall since our wedding day."

"And didna see much o' the man on the ship, neither," Will said darkly.

~

Seeing her blush, Jake said evenly, "That will do, Will. You are speaking now of things that are no concern of yours."

Will met his gaze with a direct one of his own but kept silent.

Turning to Alyson, Jake said, "Ships do not lend themselves to romance, I'm afraid. Few have room for comfort. I saw that you'd shared that tiny cabin with your woman. I expect the men all shared Orkney's cabin, did they not?"

"Nay, for he was playing ship's master. The *Maryenknyght was* his. He wanted to put Jamie and Will in the smaller forecastle cabin and Niall and Mungo—Sir Kentigern Lyle, that is—in the one opposite mine. But when I suggested that that might be a mistake—"

"Aye, sure, it would," he agreed. "Every man aboard that ship would have wondered why two lads were sharing such quarters, whilst a knight and a gentleman slept in hammocks below."

She nodded, and as she did, Jake heard an echo of her words in his mind. "*You* told Orkney not to put the boys in the deck cabin?"

Her long-lashed, gray eyes twinkling now, she said, "I believe I said that I'd *suggested* as much. I do know him, sir. I am well aware that one is wiser not to sound as if one is flinging orders at him."

Jake laughed. "You may well say so. I've known him since we were bairns, and I knew his father even better. I can tell you, too, that the first earl was nothing like as impressed with his august position as Henry can seem to be." Still smiling, he added, "I can just imagine him puffing off to that English captain. In fairness, though, I must say that Henry is a gey good friend and an expert swordsman."

She nodded. "Will told me that he took an aversion to the gannets that fly around the Bass Rock."

Laughing again, Jake noted that the level of noise in the room had diminished enough so that his laughter was drawing attention. Nodding to a man whose gaze met his, he turned to Mace and said quietly, "Finish your ale. And if there is more in that pot, share it out to the rest of us. We'll drink up, and then Will and I will see Alyson to her chamber. When the alewife returns, suggest that she send Lizzie back up to see if 'my sister' requires assistance. Then, refill that jug and see what more you can learn about our friends in Bridlington harbor."

Mace nodded and poured the ale.

Alyson shot Jake a speaking glance when Mace poured more into her mug.

"You need not drink it if you loathe the stuff. But look as if you're tasting it."

~

Alyson obeyed, although she thought the English ale worse than any she had tasted and decided she need only pretend to drink some.

She was glad that Jake did not linger over his but soon stood and extended a hand for her to rise. Gesturing then for her to precede him upstairs, he followed.

Aware that others in the common room were watching, she waited until they reached her chamber before she said, "Those men below will quiz Mace about us, won't they?"

"Aye, sure, but he will tell them nobbut the tale we devised earlier," Jake said. "You may have noticed that Mace does not talk much. He does, however, have a rare gift for listening, so people tell him more than they think they do."

Lizzie came upstairs then, so Jake said goodnight, and Alyson greeted her.

As they entered the chamber, Lizzie said, "Ah hope tha be comfortable here, mistress. This room be smaller than t'other and overlooks the yard. But it bain't as if we was in Flamborough where tha'd be hearing folks coming and going all night. The road t' Filey runs past here, but nae one will likely be on it t'night."

"It'd no trouble me, any road," Alyson said. "Me eyelids be drooping already. But Ah wonder if tha wouldst mind brushing out me hair afore Ah sleep t' be sure it be dry. It does dry gey quick, but—"

"Och, tha mustna sleep wi' a wet head. Tha wouldst catch thy death!"

"Ah ha' me doots it would be that bad," Alyson said.

Then, realizing that she would likely give herself away if she tried imitating Lizzie at length, she encouraged the girl to talk about herself instead.

Learning that the young woman was a widow, her husband having "drooned off a fishing boat through his ain foolishness" the previous year, Alyson expressed her sympathy with a look and a few words, then asked if Lizzie had children.

"Nay, for we were wedded just a short while afore the accident. But me cousin Mae near Filey kens a lad as is looking for a wife, and Mae thinks Ah might do. Me da says it be too soon, but me ma says time doesna stand still and if Ah'm nae careful, Ah'll soon be as old as dirt."

She chattered blithely on until Alyson knew more about Lizzie's family than she knew about some of her own cousins.

She climbed into bed at last and fell asleep at once, waking only to the gray light of dawn and thudding hooves below her window.

Getting up, she snatched up the kirtle she had worn the previous night and stepped into it, lacing it up the front and then moving to look outside. The rain had stopped, and as Lizzie had said, the window overlooked the yard. A dozen mounted men were there, their mounts stamping restlessly. A man led one horse away while a second man stood with his back to her, talking to a third still on horseback.

That man nodded and dismounted, tossing his reins to a second rider.

The man with his back to her and the one to whom he'd been talking turned then toward the alehouse. Alyson recognized the first man at once.

Darting to her door, she yanked it open and stepped onto the landing, just as the door opposite opened, and Jake stepped out.

"What's amiss?" he asked her.

"It's Mungo... in the yard. I must go and ask him—"

"Nay, lass, think first. What do you mean, he is in the yard? Are you sure?"

"I am, aye. And he must know what has become of Niall."

"Did you not tell us that Mungo serves Orkney, and did Will not say that Mungo insisted they all board the pirate ship, if in troth it was a pirate ship?"

"What makes you think it was not?" she asked, chafing at the delay. If Mungo left before she could even ask him about Niall—

"The fact that its captain recognized Jamie when he saw him," Jake said, interrupting that thought. "You heard Will. That captain had no doubt who Jamie was. They may be pirates. But if that's all they are, they know more than any pirate *should* know. The fact that Mungo is apparently free again—"

"There were men with him. Mayhap they are his guards."

"Did he act as if he were under guard?"

Gritting her teeth but unable to insist that Mungo had looked anything like a man under guard when he had walked inside the inn with only one person, while others rode out of the yard, Alyson sighed. "Nay, he did not. He is below in the common room now, I think, with one other man. Both of them were smiling."

"If they came from Bridlington, they are traveling north," Jake said.

"We must find out where Niall is," Alyson said more sharply than she had intended. Nevertheless she met his narrowed gaze resolutely.

"Aye, we must," he replied. "But we must also take care not to endanger ourselves whilst we do. I've a notion that the men who took Jamie and Orkney would not be happy to know they'd left witnesses behind."

"But Mungo is no enemy," Alyson said. "I cannot say I like him, for I do not. But he *is* Orkney's chief secretary."

She started to turn away to go downstairs, but he caught her by the shoulders. Gently but firmly, he turned her back to face him.

"Hear me now, lass, and heed what I say. If the captain of that English ship knew Jamie by sight and had been seeking ships from the north for a fortnight, he was *seeking* Jamie. And if that is so, he had knowledge that none save Bishop Wardlaw, the King, and Orkney shared. Therefore..."

When she gasped, he paused but held her gaze, clearly inviting her to finish the sentence.

Dampening dry lips, she said, "Therefore, someone close to one of those men must have shared knowledge that he had no right to share."

Chapter 6

Expelling a sigh of relief, hoping he had persuaded Alyson of the danger that lurked around them, Jake said, "Someone certainly shared the fact that Jamie was leaving Scotland by ship. I'd like to see this Mungo of yours—"

"Please, sir, he is *not* mine. He is merely Henry's secretary."

"And he is apparently riding northward now with a company of armed men. Art sure that your husband was not with them?"

"Had I seen Niall, I would have recognized him at once," she said. "I did not see all the riders. But I'm sure that Niall would not leave this area—not to ride away to the north—without first learning what had become of me."

Gentling his voice, he said, "Someone likely told him the *Maryenknyght* had sunk, lass. Judging by the way the pirates treated anyone who did not obey them quickly whilst she was sinking, I expect they'd have treated anyone else who gave them trouble in a similar manner."

Her face paled. "Do you think they might have thrown Niall overboard? But he cannot swim!"

"Since we cannot know what they did, such speculation

is useless. If you did not see him with Mungo and the other riders, Niall is likely with Orkney and Jamie. The only other choice is that he is dead. You did say earlier, however, that he possesses a complaisant nature, did you not?"

"He seeks to oblige, aye. But if he knew that he had left me to die on a sinking ship, or that Mungo had..." She paused, frowning.

"What is it?"

"I don't know exactly. My words just then felt wrong somehow."

"What do you mean, *felt* wrong? You were just thinking aloud."

"I was. But don't you get feelings sometimes, when what you say does not—rather suddenly—seem to agree with the facts as you know them?"

He opened his mouth to deny it, only to realize that he had experienced such feelings. "I think I do," he said. "The sensation is akin to what often happens when someone asks how long it will take us to reach a destination. I tell that person how long it usually takes from where we are, and sometimes I get an odd feeling when I do. I'll realize, after I think, that I'd unconsciously noted things about the weather that meant a change was likely coming. Such details had simply not added up yet to full awareness. Is that the sort of thing you mean?"

"I don't know. It seems as though it might be similar, but I often get such a feeling and cannot explain it so easily."

"Forbye, we are left with the same possibilities for Clyne's fate."

She nodded. "We must learn where Mungo is going,

but we must also take care and keep an eye on those pirates."

His mouth tightened, but he did not argue with her. He did have to learn all he could, if only to report the details to Wardlaw. But he was experiencing feelings or instincts of his own that did not bode well for the others who'd been aboard the *Maryenknyght*. To her ladyship, he said only, "I suggest that before we do aught else, you finish dressing. Meantime, I'll go downstairs and see what I can learn."

"I *am* dressed," she said.

He smiled. "You might want shoes."

Glancing down, she looked at him ruefully. "You must think me demented."

"Nay, only worried about your husband. Go and put your shoes on. Mace has bespoken our breakfast, so it will be ready when you are. I just rousted Will out of bed, though. I'll tell him to wait for you."

He saw her back into her chamber, spoke to Will, and then went down to the common room. From the turn of the stairway he saw that two strangers sat at a table near the kitchen door, drinking from mugs of what was likely ale. The two talked as equals, and since he did not know which one was Mungo, he studied both closely enough as he continued down the stairs to recognize either man again.

Mace caught his eye when Jake reached the foot of the stairs and gestured toward their table of the previous night. Jake nodded but said nothing, strolling to the front door instead to have a look at the yard.

The two strangers chatted too quietly for even his quick ears to catch all they said, but he heard enough to tell him they were waiting for something.

Outside, the wind was still high, but an azure sky alive with scudding white clouds seemed to belie the storms of the previous week. The air still felt wintry, and the breeze carried more than its usual dampness. Nevertheless, he enjoyed the salty tang in the air as he studied the scene before him.

Away to his left, off the road, a mounted troop waited. Some walked their horses, but most seemed to be talking. He tried to decide if one of the men might be the lass's husband. To him, they all looked like men-at-arms or armed ruffians.

Seeing the taverner crossing the yard toward him, Jake strode to meet him.

"Ye've a fine place, Metlow," he said when he was near enough.

"Suits us," the Yorkshireman said. "Will tha be off t'day?"

" 'Tis true the weather ha' turned for better," Jake said noncommittally. He would not decide until he knew more about what was happening in the area.

"Looks fine, but a man canna trust t' weather beyond his thumb."

Jake nodded. "Aye, that be a fact. I see ye get early custom here. 'Tis a fine site for an alehouse."

"It is, but Ah did tell them louts on horses yonder that Ah'd no ha' their beasts a-fouling me yard whist they wait for their friends, inside."

"What's keeping them?"

"The younger one's horse coom up lame. M' lads be seeing how bad it be, but Ah wager we'll lend him another beast. That 'un cooms fra' Bridlington. Ah'll tend it till we can get it back safe and let t' lad tak' one o' mine."

"How far will he ha' tae take it?"

"Sakes, he be a-going right across t' border. Sithee, he carries a safe-conduct from our own King Harry. Them others will see him to the line, and then they'll bring me beast back in good condition, or I'll ha' summat to say to them. The lad will ha' to find hisself another mount on t'other side o' the line."

"A royal safe-conduct? Be the chap a Scotsman then?"

"Aye, sure, were he English he'd ha' nae need o' one, would 'e?"

"Well, he might ha' been a Frenchman," Jake said. "If he's a Scot, did he come off one o' them ships we heard sae much about last night?"

"He did, aye, and Ah'll tell thee summat more. There be rich prize on them ships, they say. But King Harry hisself will be a-keeping of it, for they say he sent them pirates out to find it. They said 'twas because that ship were a-taking its cargo past England to France without our Harry's say-so."

"Sakes, what manner o' cargo would it be, then, tae need such permission?"

"That would be tellin', that would," Metlow said. "For all, Ah canna say what Ah dinna ken for truth. Nor would it matter an I did."

"Why not?"

"'Cause them ships be gone, is why. Put ashore yestereve long enough for Captain Hugh-atte-Fen t' tak' 'is supper at Bridlington's tavern. Then off again they went without waiting even for t' storm to pass. Men say that Captain Hugh did ha' t' get straightaway t' London t' deliver his prize."

"But we heard he'd let their prize ship sink."

"Aye, 'twas a pity, that. But happen that Hugh and his men dinna care. By time they get home, they'll be tellin' tales o' selling her for a grand price, choose how. A Norfolk man, Hugh, and none too fine in his ways. He had nae pity for the crew from yon merchantman."

A shiver slid up Jake's spine. "What happened tae them?"

"That gent inside be one o' the lucky ones. He told me the captain said o' t'others that any who couldna pay good ransom were nobbut a nuisance. So his lads tossed them all overboard. Some might ha' swum in, even wi' the storm. But if any did, Ah've heard nowt of it. Ah saw t' one Scotsman, is all."

Alyson watched Jake and Metlow from her window but took care to keep to one side. She told herself she did it only so that if Mungo came out, he would not catch sight of her. She knew, though, that if Jake looked up and saw her, she would feel both embarrassed and guilty for watching him.

The two men were clearly in deep discussion. Jake had his back to her until he turned and walked back toward the inn with Metlow, still conversing.

A lad ran from the nearby barn to the taverner, said something to him, and dashed back. Jake and Metlow continued toward the front door.

A rap on her door startled her, but it signaled only Will's readiness to go downstairs. Joining him and remembering that she had not seen Mungo leave the alehouse, she asked Will to go down first and see if there were still two strangers sitting together in the common room.

He was gone for only a minute before he reappeared on the landing at the turn of the stairs and beckoned. The only people in the common room were Jake and Mace. Mungo and the man with him had gone.

Taking the seat she had occupied the night before, Alyson found hot rolls, creamy butter, bramble jam, and a boiled egg awaiting her.

Lizzie soon entered with a jug of ale for the men and warm cider for Alyson. "Ah did see yestereve that tha didna care for ale, mistress. But me da makes the finest cider in t' East Riding."

Thanking her, Alyson tasted the cider and nodded approval. Lizzie hurried away, and Jake looked as if he were about to speak only to pause instead. Then, clearly as an afterthought, he said, "Will, pass me that butter-pot, will ye?"

Sensing motion behind her, Alyson glanced back and saw the alewife approaching them purposefully.

"Good day to thee all," she said. "Ah hope tha slept well." When they assured her that they had slept very well, she said, "Ah ha' thy clathes dry and all. But Ah did wonder if tha means to go on t'day, and if tha do, which way tha be a-heading and if tha wouldst like a bit o' dinner to tak' with thee."

Alyson looked at Jake and saw Mace and Will look to him, too.

He said, "We willna waste this fine weather whilst it lasts, mistress. Sithee, me ship will be a-looking for us soon and a-coming down the coast slow and easy tae find us. We'll ha' better luck meeting wi' her an we walk along the bay, I'm thinking. They'll ken nowt o' that wee harbor below the Head, nor where tae find us an they do make their way in."

"Aye, they'd see thee plain from t' water, though, an tha walk t' cliff path, sir. And tha wouldst see them. Nah, that coble wi' broken strakes in t' harbor..."

"'Tis too damaged for us tae use, and I canna wait," Jake said. "I told your man he might take it in payment for your kindness tae us here, if he will."

"Aye, he did say as much, but he wanted tae see it first. He says it will no take great fixing, sir, although it might take some few days."

"It would, aye. So if he be willing..."

"He is, but Ah ha' been a-thinking on summat else," Mistress Metlow said. "Ah ken that t' young woman here be thy sister, sir. Still, if tha and thy man mean to walk along t' shore wi' her, 'twould be better an she had a female wi' her, too. Folks would talk and make up tales in their heads about her, else, if only to pass time on a winter's eve."

Alyson said, "Ah thank thee for thy concern, mistress. But I am quite safe with me brother and his man, and our Will."

"Nanetheless, mistress, tha wouldst be wise to tak' sensible counsel."

"We would, aye," Jake said as Alyson tried to think of a tactful way to reject what she thought was unnecessary advice. Looking at him in astonishment, she saw that he had made up his mind.

He said, "What would ye ha' us do, mistress?"

"Why, tak' our Lizzie along," Mistress Metlow said. "Sithee, me sister abides on a wee farm near Filey. So if thy ship fails t' meet thee in t' bay, tha wouldst ha' a place to tak' shelter without coming all the way back here. And if thy ship does find thee, Lizzie would ha' only a short walk to their farm. They ha' been after us to send her ever since her man's accident. It would do her good, and she'd be doing thee a good turn, too."

"Then she shall go with us, and welcome," Jake said. "We accept your generous offer tae pack us a meal, as well, mistress."

She nodded, satisfied, and bustled away.

Alyson gave Jake a look, but he met it with a twinkling one of his own. "If you could have said nay to her, you have more grit than I do," he said. "It worries me that our supposed kinship does not impress her. But refusing her offer would likely stir her curiosity if she is *not* wondering about us. Moreover, they have been kind to us, and we *would* be doing them a good turn."

"I don't mind; I like Lizzie," Alyson said. "I have difficulty maintaining a conversation with her, though. I find that I'm dismally ignorant of what to call things here. I can imitate accents, but I cannot pull unknown words out of air."

"They seem to accept us as we are," Jake said. "I do have bad news, though."

Alyson tensed, fearing he had learned that Niall was dead.

~

Jake read her thought as easily as if she had expressed it aloud and hastened to reassure her as much as he could. "I ken nowt of Niall Clyne," he said. "But Metlow did say that the pirates threw all of the *Maryenknyght*'s crew overboard. Some may have swum ashore, he said, but he'd heard nowt of any that had."

Hesitating, Jake decided that he could not keep his own

thoughts on that matter to himself. "Metlow also said that one of the men riding through this morning told him that the captain—a Norfolk man called Hugh-atte-Fen—also disposed of anyone who could not fetch a large ransom. Would Clyne have means for such, or might anyone else pay it on his behalf?"

She swallowed visibly. Then, drawing a breath, she said, "His parents are dead, and his older brother is not fond of Niall. I doubt he has means to pay much in any event. However, Henry *may* have promised that the Sinclairs would pay for Niall and Mungo, as well as for himself."

Jake shook his head, saying, "That would not answer, I'm afraid. The captain would likely say that if Henry's people would pay for two others, they'd pay more for Henry. After all, they'll expect a king's ransom for Jamie. And from what I've heard so far, they won't want to guard or feed more captives than necessary. As for Mungo..." He paused, deciding that he had said enough.

Alyson grimaced. "You need not explain about Mungo, sir. Seeing him out and about as he was, riding as freely as if he were in his own country—"

"Metlow told me that Mungo is riding to the border—apparently with royal safe-conduct. The men with him are nobbut an armed escort to see that he gets across the line safely."

"And Will said the pirates insisted that our ship lacked King Harry's consent to be in English waters," she reminded him. "Do you think Harry might have wanted someone to tell *our* king that the English have captured Jamie, and so the pirates sent Mungo? Because if that is the case," she added, "might they not have kept Niall as a hostage to ensure that Mungo does as they've bidden him?"

"We cannot know what Mungo's purpose is," Jake said. "However, I'd think English Harry would send a well-trusted courier of his own."

"Then why provide Mungo with a safe-conduct?"

"It is possible—sakes, it is likely—that it was part of a previous bargain," he said. "If so, Mungo is not riding to report to his grace but to someone else."

She frowned and then glanced at Mace and Will, each of whom seemed engrossed in his breakfast. Leaning closer, she murmured to Jake, "Then you suspect that Mungo is the one who shared his knowledge that Orkney and Jamie were on the Bass Rock, waiting for the ship. But Mungo could hardly have told English Harry."

"He wouldn't have to if someone else had made secret arrangements with Harry," Jake said. "Someone, perhaps, who has spies throughout our kingdom."

"Albany," she muttered. "But would he truly betray his own nephew so? I know people worried last spring that he might take Jamie into his custody, but what demon could possess him to arrange for the English to capture the poor lad?"

Glancing at Will, Jake lowered his own voice more to say, "Last spring Albany's son, Murdoch, was safe at home. But, in September, the English captured him in battle at Homildon Hill. They still hold him hostage, lass. What better ransom could Albany offer, to retrieve him, than to send English Harry the heir to Scotland's crown to keep in Murdoch's stead?"

"So you think that Mungo told Albany about the *Maryenknyght*, which I find hard to imagine of anyone serving

Orkney. Also, Mungo must know as well as I do that Niall would never be party to any scheme that would endanger Jamie."

"How was the *Maryenknyght* summoned to Leith Harbor?" he asked.

"Mungo sailed to France weeks ago and returned on the *Maryenknyght*. So he knew what ship we'd be on. And the ship needed repairs, so we...we had to wait. Faith, sir, you must be right about him, and if you are, the pirates have *no* reason to keep Niall alive. Only, if Niall *were* dead or in danger of dying, I think I'd—"

She broke off, coloring deeply.

"*What* do you think?" Jake asked her.

" 'Tis naught," she said. "One just has the sense that if someone close to one has died, one would sense the loss. Doubtless, 'tis plain foolishness. I did not think straightaway of Albany, although I do see that I should have," she added in her usual tone. "Everyone knows how long he has coveted the Scottish throne."

Will looked up then, glancing from Jake to Alyson before he said, "Sithee, I ken that Albany chap m'self. He's Jamie's wicked uncle, and I can tell ye Jamie didna trust the man—and nor do I—as far as we could spit. He's a bad man, that 'un. Jamie did say that 'twas because Albany wants the throne that he and the wicked Douglas did kill Jamie's big brother, Davy."

~

Alyson shuddered, barely able to heed Jake's words when he told Will that they would talk of less important matters while they finished breaking their fast.

"I just meant I ken fine about evil men," Will said.

"Them in the kitchen canna hear us, any road." To Alyson, he said, "I'm a-wondering, too, how ye could be so sure o' your man when ye've scarce clapped eyes on him since we boarded the ship. Ciara said that she'd seen nearly nowt o' him since your wedding day."

Alyson stared at the boy as she tried to wrench her thoughts away from Davy Stewart's death and Niall's possible demise. Before she could gather her wits to reply, Jake said sternly, "If you can tell me how someone else's marriage is any concern of yours, my lad, prithee do so at once."

"In troth, sir…" Alyson began, only to pause when he shook his head.

"Aye, well, it isna my business," Will said. "But I can tell ye that when *I've* got a wife, I mean tae treat her better nor he treats her ladysh—"

Speaking over that last word before Will could finish it, Jake said with steel in his voice, "When you marry, it will be your *business* to decide how a man should treat his wife. Until then—"

"Och, aye, then, I'm mum," Will said. But he shot Jake another of his penetratingly direct looks and muttered, "I were just a-saying…"

He fell silent then, which, judging by the look that Jake was giving him, Alyson thought showed wisdom.

"Go fetch what you'll take with you, lad," Jake said, adding, "Mace, we'll leave as soon as everyone's ready. Take a turn around the yard, and find out if anyone kens aught about that troop that rode through earlier. I want to know what route they took, and if possible, how long it will take them to reach the line from here."

"'Tis a pity we canna follow them," Mace said. "Or follow them ships."

"We'd have nowt to gain," Jake said. "The ships sail for London, and we've no way to stop them. The riders aim for the border, and we cannot stop them either. If I could have a chat with Mungo, I might learn what I want to know. But even if we could abandon our charges here, we'd not get close to him whilst he's riding amidst a troop of English men-at-arms."

Nodding, Mace left, and Alyson said quietly, "Don't be too harsh with Will, sir. He is a bit too direct, but I think he takes his ways from Jamie."

"I don't mean to skelp him, if that is what you mean. But he does have a habit of saying what he thinks without counting the cost. He'd be wise to learn to curb his tongue until we're safely aboard the *Sea Wolf.* But come upstairs now. I must talk more with you before we leave, and we can be privy in your chamber."

"Until Lizzie comes looking for me."

"Aye, so let us not dawdle."

Accordingly, she led the way upstairs to her chamber. When he walked right in with her, she knew it would be foolish to object. Moreover, instinct had told her from the start that she was as safe with Jake as with Ivor.

"What is it you want to discuss?" she asked as he shut the door.

"First, I want to say that I accept your opinion of Clyne," he said. "Also, to tell you that although Albany is no friend of mine, I do know him and have learned much about him over the years. He can be ruthless, and he uses people, but he rarely involves more people than he must in any scheme. Nor does he share his plans with underlings.

Moreover, he has spies everywhere, lass. I'd wager all I own that Mungo is involved but is *not* the sole source of whatever information Albany gleaned of Jamie's whereabouts or of his grace, the King's, decision to send Jamie to France."

"He would not have told Niall that he was involved," she said firmly.

"I agree. However, you also said that you didn't think Clyne would be able to fetch a ransom. What if he names your family? Farigaig is wealthy, is he not?"

"I expect he is, but Niall has no claim on Father's wealth," she said. "Most of what he owns will go to my brother, Ranald. My two older brothers, as I think you know, were killed some years ago, so only Ranald remains to inherit."

"And you, surely," Jake said.

"I have my tocher," she said. "When I married, Father gave me two estates. Braehead lies northwest of Perth and Ardloch on the river Findhorn near the Moray Firth. It is also near my grandfather's lands and my cousins' at Rothiemurchus. Niall collects the rents from both, but they are not enough to provide a ransom like those for Jamie and Orkney. Faith, who else *could* command as much as they will?"

"Still, Clyne might have been wise enough to say that he could. Or mayhap Orkney said so on his behalf without suggesting the Sinclairs as its source."

"Perhaps," she said. "Henry is kind enough to promise such a thing and generous enough to do it. But one does wonder if it would occur to him. Sithee, he has a temper, and when he loses it, he does not always think clearly."

"True, but a dire situation can clarify any man's thoughts."

"Perhaps," she said. "But if Niall *is* still alive and a captive, it will likely be a long while before we know his fate. Even captives who fetch high ransoms, on either side, often take years to return home."

Chapter 7

As Lizzie led them along a path that followed the cliffs overlooking Filey Bay, Jake saw that the tide was out, exposing hundreds of rocky pools.

The wind had increased, and atop the cliffs, it was strong enough to blow the women's skirts wildly if they did not take care. When the path drew them near the highest clifftops, Will said, "How high are we?"

"About three hundred feet," Jake said.

"That be what I thought, m'self," Will said. "These be near as high as—"

"Keep away from the edge," Jake warned him hastily, certain that Will had been about to say that the cliffs they were crossing were as high as the Bass Rock.

Gesturing toward several large white birds with visibly black-tipped wings, circling over the bay, Will shouted back, "Coo, them be gannets! Ye've nae need tae fear I'd get too close tae *their* rocks. I'd ken them big devils anywhere."

"Wouldst tha, laddie?" Lizzie asked.

"I would, aye, so mind where ye step! I hope they stay out there," he added, looking up as if he feared to see one directly overhead.

Hearing the birds' distant hoarse cries, Jake watched as one tucked back its wings, much as Highland osprey did, and plunged headlong into the sea after a fish.

"Me da says that ours be the only gannets nesting in all England," Lizzie said to Will. "Hast tha been here afore, then?"

"Nay, but likely the ones I saw was Scottish birds," Will said.

"What can a bairn like thee ken o' Scottish birds?"

Jake shot a glance at Alyson and saw her eyes twinkling. He said, "We live near the Borders, Lizzie. I dinna ken nowt o' birds, but the lad takes an interest. Likely, he's seen Scottish ones cross the line now and now."

"Aye, that would be it," Will murmured, avoiding Jake's gaze. But when Alyson drew Lizzie's attention to a plant a few minutes later, asking if she knew what it was, Will looked ruefully at Jake. "I should ha' kept me mouth shut," the boy said. "Can I run ahead for a bit? I havena had a good run for months."

"Run on then," Jake said. "But stay where I can see you and keep away from the edge. I don't want to have to fish you out of the bay."

"Ye won't." Grinning, Will took off, leaping over hillocks and apparently forgetting any danger of stepping into evidence of the gannets' presence.

Noting that Alyson had drawn Lizzie ahead, Jake seized the opportunity to talk with Mace but learned only that, in the opinion of those to whom Mace had spoken, Mungo and his English escort would at least take four days to reach the border unless they rode more than forty miles each day.

"They'd ha' tae change horses often," Mace said. "And

he'll need two days more from the border tae reach Stirling if that be where he's a-heading."

Jake agreed. "I doubt that Mungo or any of those others are Borderers, who can travel fifty miles on an overnight raid."

"Aye, but most men dinna be as mad as Borderers."

"You'd do well to recall that I was *born* a Borderer, my lad," Jake said.

"I do recall that, aye," Mace replied, grinning. "Be we likely tae see the *Sea Wolf* soon, a-sailing into this bay?"

"Coll won't bring her in until after nightfall," Jake said. "It will be easy enough even then, with the bay's curving shore, to judge where its midpoint is."

"I'll be glad tae see her, and the lads, as well," Mace said.

"I'll be even happier to get shut of England," Jake said.

He was watching Alyson and Lizzie, noting that Alyson did not seem to have any trouble conversing with the taverner's lass.

~

"Me mum said thy man died nobbut a short time ago," Lizzie said abruptly during a pause in their discussion of plant life. "Be that so?"

"I do fear that I am a widow, aye," Alyson said.

"Ah be a widow woman, too," Lizzie said with a sigh. "Me man, Jeb, were a fisherman like most lads hereabouts. Ah miss him sorely, though he's been gone nigh a year now. I expect tha must miss thy man even more."

Alyson realized guiltily that she did not miss Niall. She was concerned about him and feared for him. But Will had been right. She and Niall had spent very little time together since their marriage—or before it, for that matter.

Ruefully, she realized that more than she feared for his safety she feared that she would find herself doomed to live as a married woman whose husband's fate was unknown, trapped in the bosom of her loving family.

Since that very sense of entrapment had spurred her to marry him in the first place, if such a thing *was* happening, it would be an ironic betrayal of Fate.

Apparently mistaking her silence for overwhelming emotion and a resultant inability to talk, Lizzie said, "Ah shouldna ha' brought it up. Me mum would say Ah should no be asking personal questions. But Ah dinna ken anyone else near me age wi' such a loss. Still, if tha wouldst liefer no talk o' thine…"

"Ah dinna mind," Alyson said. "It will be easier with time and doubtless easier each time Ah do talk of it. Doest tha still find it hard?"

"No to say 'hard,'" Lizzie said. "Ah wish the lads hereabouts would stop thinking that Ah be ripe for picking, though. Ah do miss bedding wi' Jeb, but that doesna mean Ah want to leap into bed wi' every Jack that kens me name."

"Good sakes, do other men ask thee to *sleep* wi' them?"

"Och, aye, from a sennight after Jeb drooned. All commiserating like, and telling me they ken fine that Ah miss the bedding, as if Ah must be nigh begging for a boon or such. Ah canna say that Ah *don't* miss the bedding. Tha must miss it, too. 'Tis only natural, that. Och, but Ah kent nowt afore Ah married Jeb, 'cause nae one tells a lass nowt about what to expect, just that she should do like her man says. But Jeb were a *fine* man in bed."

Feeling heat suffuse her cheeks, Alyson said, "In troth, Lizzie, I'd liefer discuss another subject now."

"Aye, sure. Ah can tell thee, though, Ah do miss Jeb touching me doon there. He were no just a fine specimen of a lad wi' a good thick piece on him. The man were skilled wi' his hands, too, a-stroking and a-petting till he'd drive me near to madness. He could mak' me cry out for it, too, any time he'd a mind to. Times, it were like he mistook me for a plaything, wanting to stroke me all over, and nuzzling at me bubs like a wee pup at its mam's tit. But Jeb were nae pup, Ah can tell thee. Sakes, that lad had only to put a finger to one o' me nipples, and—"

"Lizzie, stop!" Alyson exclaimed, aware that her whole body was burning at hearing such intimate talk. What was Lizzie thinking to say such things to her?

Recalling that Lizzie supposed her to be just such a woman as Lizzie was, Alyson called herself to order. That she was a lady born and not someone who discussed her body parts and physical sensations with such careless abandon was not a point to make just then. However, she did find it tantalizing to imagine being such a person and having such stirring memories as Lizzie did.

She tried to imagine doing such things with Niall. Her imagination boggled.

"Will! Come, see what I found!" Jake shouted from right behind her, startling her so that she whirled toward him with a surge of dismay and brief fear that he might somehow know what she'd been thinking.

Swiftly collecting her wits but unsure, from his suddenly quizzical expression, if she had been quick enough, she said, "What did you find?"

Stretching out a hand, he showed her a smooth white

rock with a round hole about an inch in diameter through its center. "One might find a wee stone like this in a riverbed," he said. "Mayhap even on shingle by the sea. But it is odd, I think, to find it up here on these cliffs. It's gey smooth, too. Feel it."

She took it from him, feeling an inexplicable reluctance to do so. The rock felt colder than she'd expected, but it was perfectly smooth, just as he had said.

"Let me see," Will said, running to them. "What is it?"

"A rock," Alyson said, handing it to him. "A rather odd one."

"Coo, it's got a hole clean through it! How'd it get like that?"

"In fast-moving water, most likely," Jake said. "Someone must have found it somewhere else and lost it here. It doesn't look like any other rocks I see."

Alyson recovered her equanimity enough to say, "According to ancient Celtic folklore, if one looks through such a stone, one might see a person's intended bride or groom standing by that person. Seers and bards say that one might even see one's own intended mate."

Will raised the stone to his right eye and peered through it. "I see gannets and more gannets, nowt more," he said, handing it to Jake. "Ye should look, too, though. Ye're at least *old* enough tae take a wife."

Obligingly, Jake put the stone to his eye and turned as if, Alyson thought, he sought an intended bride wherever he might find her. After making a full circle, he lowered the stone and shook his head. "No spouse for me or anyone else I see. 'Tis a good thing for me, though. I'm a man who enjoys his freedom."

"Me, too," Will said, nodding fervently. "Hoots, but I

wish Jamie was here. He'd want tae look through it, too, I'll wager."

Jake put a hand on the boy's shoulder and gave it a squeeze.

Mace asked if he could look through the stone. Jake handed it to him, but Mace had no better luck than he or Will had had and gave it back.

Jake offered it to Alyson. "Have a look, lass."

Taking an involuntary step backward, she said, "Nay, it is too soon. Let Lizzie see what she can see."

Lizzie having no better luck than the others, Jake slipped the stone into a small leather pouch attached to his belt, and they continued on their way. They had passed beyond the highest cliffs by then and were walking downhill.

Cliffs of varying heights ringed the bay from one end to the other. Below them, with the tide low, as it was, Alyson saw areas of smooth-looking sand, rough shingle, and hundreds of rocky outcroppings replete with tidal pools.

"Are there places where one can walk down to the shore?" she asked Lizzie.

"Och, aye. Nane so many o' them, but we'll see some."

"Mace, walk ahead wi' Lizzie and Will for a time," Jake said. "Get Lizzie tae tell ye summat about this area. 'Tis a fine and splendid place, I'm thinking."

Moments later, Alyson was alone with Jake. She could not help but note that he was eyeing her quizzically again. Suspecting that he had noticed her reaction to the rock, she sought for something sensible to explain it.

~

Jake wondered what had disturbed Alyson's peace of mind. As the thought occurred to him, he realized that in the short time they'd been together, he had come to value her equanimity.

During the wind, storm, and chaos of the previous day, he'd found it astonishing that she could remain calm. Today, it disturbed him that she had not.

"What is it, lass?" he asked. When she did not reply, he said, "You seem distressed. Did something about that stone unsettle you?"

"Nay . . . or not the stone at all events."

"Something has," he said.

She looked at him then—measuringly, he thought.

Gazing steadily back, he saw that the angle of the sun was such that her eyes had turned an unusual shade of ice green and appeared to be almost translucent.

They crinkled at the corners. He saw then that she was smiling quizzically and realized that his steady look had turned into a rather rude stare.

"Sorry," he said. "I've never seen eyes with such changeable color as yours have. With the sun shining down as it is from over my shoulder, they are a most unusual light green and so clear that I found it hard to look away."

"I felt as if you were trying to see right to my thoughts," she said.

"I would like to know what they are. Something has upset you."

"I suppose that Lizzie did but by no fault of her own," Alyson said. "Her mother told her that I'm a widow, and Lizzie asked how I felt about certain things. She apologized all the while, though, for asking such personal questions."

"As well she should," he said, raising his eyebrows.

"Now you're doing what I did," she said with a glimmer of amusement. "We are pretending to be people just like Lizzie and her family, after all. She would have no cause to think she should treat me with any formality. But when she began telling me uncomfortably personal things about her husband and . . . and about bedding with him, including things he did that gave her pleasure . . ."

"Her words must have made you miss your husband more than ever," he said then. "I ken fine that this is all gey difficult for you."

"But it isn't," she said, surprising him. "Sithee, although I have known Niall since we were children, we saw each other only on certain holy days and whenever Parliament met in Perth. I have always liked him, but after listening to Lizzie talk about how much she misses her husband a year after his death, I realized that I barely know Niall as a husband. Not being distraught over someone so rarely at home must be only normal. I just did not see, before Lizzie said what she did, that although I'm worried about Niall, worry is *all* that I feel."

"Perhaps," he said. "But shock often delays grief, lass."

"Aye, sure, and I'll admit that when I saw Mungo without him, I did feel a surge of emotion and greater concern for Niall. But not grief, certainly none such as Lizzie feels for her Jeb. I'd just like to know what happened to Niall."

"A gey practical attitude," he said dryly. "I'd commend it if I believed it."

"Truly, I just don't *feel* as if he can be dead." She bit her lip, looked away, and he saw that she had clenched her hands in the folds of her skirt.

Glancing ahead to be sure the others were keeping

each other occupied, he said, "You know, this is the second time you've mentioned such feelings, as if you think you *ought* to be feeling his death."

She stared straight ahead but not as if she watched the others.

Realizing that she was not heeding where she put her feet, Jake cupped a hand gently under her elbow but did not urge her again to share her thoughts.

He had his reward when she said, "Do you believe in…in magical things?"

"What sort?"

"Any sort." Looking at him, she said, "You peered through that stone as if you thought you might see something. Did you do that for Will's sake or because you believed you might actually see a betrothed couple?"

He looked into her unusual eyes long enough to gather his thoughts. Then he said, "I believe in God, and I have experienced things—especially on the sea—that defy logical explanation and thus may be magical. As a child I firmly believed in boggarts and worricows, especially when my da sent me down to tidy up the hold of his ship. It was dark, and he would not let me take a lantern. He said I was apt to set the ship afire and should seek to improve my night vision instead."

"*Did* you ever set a ship afire?" she asked.

"Aye, come to think on it, I did. It burnt right to the water, too. But we need not talk about that. Tell me more about these magical things of yours."

Instead, she said, "In a way, it was your doubting that I might sense Niall's death. Sithee, I've experienced such things before…on occasion."

"I think everyone has such feelings," he said. "In my

experience, most of them turn out to be false. W
asked me about magical things, I thought you me
wee folk, witches casting spells, and the like."

"Do you believe in the Sight?"

"*Second* Sight?"

When she nodded, his impulse was to deny that he did. But her tense expression told him the question was important to her, so he gave it more thought.

"I don't have much experience," he said. "None, unless you count an uncanny sense of direction that serves me almost magically at sea on the stormiest day or darkest night. One doesn't live in the Highlands or Borders, though, without hearing tale after tale of the Sight. However, I've never 'seen' anything, myself."

"I did not want to look through that stone because I'd liefer believe I may still *have* a husband, God willing. But I feared I might see him dead." She spoke quickly, as if overcoming reluctance to make the statement at all.

"But why should—" He broke off, eyeing her speculatively before he said, "Sakes, lass, do you imagine that *you* have the gift?" As the words left his tongue, he regretted his tone and added quickly, "I don't mean to mock you, but—"

"Believe me, sir, I do not think of the Sight as a gift. Nor do I think that anyone else who has experienced it would deem it so. But you asked me what had unsettled me. In troth, I'm not sure. But something about that stone impelled me to give it back to you with*out* looking through it."

"But have you—?"

"I would ask you a question now, if I may," she interjected.

"Aye, sure."

"You once said that Davy Stewart was as different from Jamie as flint from tinder, but did you *know* Davy?"

"I know about him, and I'd met him several times. But that's all."

"What do you know about his death?"

"I know he died at Falkland Castle almost exactly a year ago."

"A year ago Tuesday," she said. "Do you know much about *how* he died?"

"Too much," he said, grimacing. "I won't repeat the details to you, lass."

"Do you think many others know what you know?"

"Not many, I'd warrant. I had what I know from Bishop Wardlaw, and he had it from monks at Lindores Abbey who prepared Davy's body for burial."

"My family will watch the Papal Legate consecrate Bishop Wardlaw as Bishop of St. Andrews and Prelate of Scotland next month at Scone," she said. "But I have not met him. Nor do I know anyone at Lindores."

"Why do you feel obliged to tell me that?"

"My parents and younger brother rarely go anywhere. Since my two older brothers died," she went on, "the only visitors to MacGillivray House are members of our family. Many of them do like to visit Perth, though, and they stay with us. They look to me for many things, sir, but *not* to discuss political matters." With a sigh, she added, "In troth, I'm rather hoping that those who lingered there since Christmas will have returned to their homes before I get back."

"Again, lass, why tell me all this whilst we talk about magic?"

"Because when I describe Davy's death, I don't want you thinking I had the details from someone else. I know of no one who *could* know what I believe I do."

A chill shot up Jake's spine, and he experienced a sudden recurrence of feelings he'd had as a child when his father had sent him into the hold. He did not doubt her word. Something deep inside him acknowledged her integrity. Whatever she was about to tell him, she believed with all her heart.

"Tell me," he said.

"On the day Davy died, he was thin as a rail, and cold. They had starved him. He lay on his side, curled tight against deep pain. He held one hand out with its palm open, hopeful of catching grain that sifted through the floor of what must have been a mill above him. The only light in his dungeon came from beams filled with dustlike bits of meal. But he was too weak to bring them to his mouth.

"He lay there, helpless, and just faded away. But I knew as I watched that he had been in that chamber the whole time he was at Falkland. He felt pain until the end. His hair was mussed and stiff with dirt, and I think that upset me as much as anything, for he was a bonnie lad and always looked princely fine. That Albany and the Earl of Douglas insisted that Davy died of natural causes outraged me. But I could say nowt to anyone of what I'd seen."

Striving for calm, he said, "'Tis as likely you dreamed that, is it not?"

"Is it?" She stopped walking, caught his arm, and turned him to face her. Her penetrating eyes gazed steadily into his. "*Was* it just a dream I had, sir?"

Jake dampened his lips. He could no more lie when she looked at him like that than he could close his eyes and vanish magically from her sight.

"Nay, lass, I don't believe it was a dream. What you describe fits with what Wardlaw told me. Davy was little more than a skeleton under desiccated skin. His clothing, his hair, even his face and lips bore a dusting of meal. Although he'd been a prisoner at Falkland for only eighteen days, he'd lost more than half of his weight. They'd starved him and denied him water. The monks could tell as much from the state of his body."

"Someone must have given him water," she said. "I don't think that anyone could go so long without it."

"I agree, but as Albany's primary seat, Falkland teems with his minions. One of them likely dared to provide water for Davy without daring to do more."

"At all events, sir, you do believe that I saw him. It happened on the very day they say he died. And from what I saw, he did just fade away as if God had taken pity on him, perhaps even taken him by the hand. I also had the sense that I could hear some of his thoughts. I felt his pain."

"I believe you," he said. "Is that the only time such a thing has happened to you, or did you know beforehand that Jamie's ship would be captured?"

"The Sight does not work like that... not for me, at all events," she said. "I did see my brothers die, as well. But I don't believe that I've ever seen an event before it has happened, only when it does. However, I do get odd feelings at other times, which I've come to believe mean that *something* will happen. So far, I have never been able to identify, predict, or prevent the happening. The feelings are not nearly specific enough for that. I did have some such feelings whilst we sailed, but there was naught in them to explain *why* I was having them."

Truly curious now, he said, "What are these feelings like?"

"I don't know if I can describe them well enough for you to understand. I can give you an example, though. I had a cat I loved dearly for nine years. Then, for no apparent reason and at odd times, I began feeling as if I loved him too much. He'd do something to make me smile, or he'd say something... What?"

Jake knew he had failed to conceal his disbelief. "Sorry, lass, but I've never known a cat that could talk."

"Aye, well, wee Pallie did, in cat sounds to be sure, but clearly. Forbye, you divert me from my explanation. If you do not want to hear it—"

"I do, and I apologize for interrupting you. Tell me."

"When Pallie would do something to amuse me, I would smile or laugh, and suddenly, I'd feel a slight pricking sensation—mental, not physical—as if warning me of caring too much. Not long after those feelings began, a dog killed him."

Tears sprang to her eyes at the memory, and Jake wanted to touch her, to comfort her, but also to tell her she had let her imagination run amok. However, he was not sure of that, himself. The fact was that he'd had a similar experience, years before, when such a "feeling" had led him to save a man's life.

He said, "You say that you had such feelings during the voyage?"

"Aye, since the night we collected Jamie, Will, and Orkney at Bass Rock," she said. "Those sensations were more physical, though, more akin to shivers than aught else. I had one when Ciara said ships were approaching the *Maryenknyght*."

"That may have been merely apprehension, don't you think? Surely, when you realized who your traveling companions were, you felt a sense of peril just in knowing that men who wished Jamie ill were searching for him."

"Perhaps. But I had another of those sensations this morning when I saw Mungo striding round the yard. I'm not afraid of him, sir. I have no cause to be. But seeing him free, and apparently caring for naught, chilled me to the core."

Chapter 8

Alyson eyed Jake uncertainly. She had been sure that, just moments before, he had nearly laughed aloud at the thought of wee Pallie talking to her. But Jake had listened to her. And, so far, despite that one moment when he'd stirred her doubt, he had not dismissed anything that she had said.

She had not told him that when she'd "seen" Davy, it seemed dreamlike until she awoke, sitting up with tears running down her cheeks, and knew without a doubt that it had been no dream. She had not meant to tell Jake about the Sight, not until she'd seen how he peered through the circle stone, as if he expected that he might see a scene such as the one she had described to him.

He was a strange man, was Jake Maxwell, a man unlike any in her family. Although he was a friend of Ivor's, he was not like her cousin. She had often been wary of Ivor, especially as a child, because if someone made him angry, one could see it building until it erupted. It was, she thought, like watching sparks in tinder, glowing a little, smoldering, and then bursting into flame.

Jake did not seem temperamental and was certainly not as volatile as Ivor could be. Both of her older brothers had had tempers like Ivor's. Her younger brother, Ranald, was milder, more like their father…in many ways. She sighed.

"I understand why seeing Mungo without Niall would give you chills," Jake said. "You fear for your husband, and seeing Mungo made you expect to see Niall, too. When you did not, your deepest fears stirred, chilling you."

"Perhaps," she said. Knowing that she had no acceptable way to explain why she believed that his explanation was inaccurate, she said no more.

"Is that what you were thinking about when you sighed just now?"

"Nay, my thoughts had shifted to other men in my life," she replied. Then, giving him a look, she shook her head as if that might clear it of such impulsive declarations. "You are too easy to talk to," she said. "I don't usually share my thoughts, and I rarely mention the Sight. Some in my family are aware of it, but even those who are don't understand it. They just think I'm a bit owf."

"I ken *that* term," he said with his quick smile. Sobering, he added, "I don't think you're owf, lass. Your mind seems sounder than my own. So, what do you think of those others that made you frown so?"

"I expect I do frown sometimes when I am trying to sort my thoughts," she said. "I was thinking that you are different from Ivor and my brothers—less volatile. My older brothers were like Ivor; my younger one is not."

"What's this younger one like?"

"Do you have siblings, sir?"

"Nary a one."

"I might have envied you before I knew what a loss

my brothers would be. I cannot tell you how many times, before then, I'd wished I had none."

"They sound like troublesome louts," Jake said.

"Eamon and Artan were just ordinary, domineering Highlanders. They were warriors, both of them, skilled with swords, dirks, lances, and such. But not with words. And both of them were short-tempered men who lacked courtly ways. I was thinking about that, comparing them to Ivor and to you."

"I can understand comparing them to Ivor, because his temper is legendary. At least, it was until he married. But I vow, lass, although I don't think of myself as courtly, I am as mild as bairn's pap in every other way."

"Mild" was *not* a word she would choose to describe him. He radiated too much energy. Often, the air around him seemed to crackle. She had seen him with a sword in hand, and striding thwart to thwart in a boat that tossed on stormy seas as if he did it every day. The twinkle in his eyes told her that he was teasing. Even so...

"Continue, lass," he said. "I diverted you when you were about to describe your younger brother."

"Aye, well, Ranald is as volatile as Eamon and Artan were but is otherwise their exact opposite. Nay, that is wrong, for it would imply that Ranald displays the courtly manners they lacked."

"So Ranald is a lout, too?"

She shook her head. "They weren't as uncomplicated as louts. Ranald is polite, I suppose, but he rarely thinks of anyone save himself. I've seen that in other men who fall youngest in their families. They seem to think that because others cleaned up their messes when they were small, others will go on doing so forever. And we do. We all look after Ranald." She paused, surprised at herself. "I don't know why I tell you all this. It cannot interest you in the least."

"But it does," he said. "Never having had what one might call an ordinary life, I find other people's lives fascinating."

"Did you really grow up on ships?"

"From the time I was small until I was nearly fourteen, I did," he said. "My mam died when I was six, and my da took me aboard his ship. Sithee, I was terrified I'd lose him, too, so he promised not to leave me behind until I was old enough to decide for myself what I wanted to do. He kept his word, too."

"He sounds like a good man."

"He is, aye. When I left for St. Andrews, we had lived at Duncraig Castle in Kintail for about five years. Da served Sir Gifford MacLennan there, and Giff serves the Lord of the Isles. Sithee, one of Giff's good-sisters had married a Sinclair. Thus did I come to know the first earl and later our friend Henry."

They chatted so until Will rejoined them and announced that he was hungry. Mace and Lizzie were close behind, so Jake and Mace sought a place out of the wind where they could eat the meal that Mistress Metlow had packed for them.

"It may take us some time to find a good place," Jake warned them. "These clifftops provide a grand view, but winds have swept them nearly bare of shelter."

Briefly eyeing Alyson and Lizzie, Will dashed off with the men.

Lizzie laughed. "Poor bairn, left wi' the womenfolk and having nowt o' it. Ah do wish that me Jeb had given me a bairn afore he died." Sitting on a nearby rock, she added, "Ah never thought to ask if thy man might ha' left thee wi' child, mistress. 'Twould ease thy loss an he did."

"Nay, Ah canna think when he might," Alyson replied, nearly forgetting to speak as Lizzie had. "Sithee, Niall were gey busy, always off and away."

"So were Jeb, being a fisherman. But, sithee, it only takes once. So happen tha *might* be growin' a bairn. 'Twould be a good thing, that."

Alyson stared at her, wondering how a woman could be with child and not know it. It seemed a daft notion to her. Aware that Lizzie was eyeing her curiously, she said, "I hadna given it much thought."

"Ah can see that. As bonnie as tha be, though, Ah'd wager the man plowed thee whenever he could. Tha's only been wedded a wee while, me mam said."

"Since just after Christmas," Alyson said weakly.

"That explains how tha couldst be unsure. Me mam said she didna ken nowt till she were three months along wi' her first."

Desperate to change the subject, Alyson said, "I think we should follow the men, don't you? They seem to have wandered right out of sight."

Having found a semisheltered declivity with a stream running through it, Jake turned to shout to the women and was glad to see that they had not waited but were coming toward him—at some speed, too.

"Och, 'tis a good place," Alyson said when she and Lizzie joined them. "Those flat rocks will mak' good sitting whilst we eat."

"Aye, but I'll send Mace up tae watch for the *Sea Wolf*," Jake said. "I told Coll that we'd be a day or two, mayhap even three, but here we be."

"If tha lacks a place to sleep," Lizzie said, "me aunt and uncle would be fain to tak' thee in overnight."

Aware that Alyson was intently eyeing him, Jake said, "That be kind o' ye, Mistress Thornwick, but I did order me helmsman tae seek us here. How far be it from this place tae your uncle's farm?"

"Nobbut over yon hill," she said, gesturing vaguely. "'Twill tak' us an hour or such. Sithee, we be halfway to Filey. Tha canst see t' houses near where yon reef juts out, though it do be near covered, wi' the tide a-rising as it be."

Jake nodded. "When we finish eating, I'll send Mace and young Will here tae see ye safely tae their farm."

"Och, but me mam said Ah should stay close by Mistress Allie."

"I ha' me doots that your da would want me tae send ye off alone, lass. Nor would he expect our Allie tae walk tae yon farm and back when she might stay here wi' me," Jake said. "Dinna forget that I'm her brother."

Eyeing him doubtfully, Lizzie evidently decided that further debate would be futile. When Mace handed her a roll and a wedge of cheese, she took them, sat down on a rock, hiked her skirts off the damp ground, and began to eat.

When Mace left to seek higher ground where he could watch the bay, and took his food with him, Will looked uncertainly at Jake.

"What is it, lad?" he asked.

"Could I ha' a privy word wi' ye afore we eat, sir?"

Since, aside from his brief interest in the rock that Jake

had found, the boy had looked glum from the time they'd left the alehouse, Jake said, "Aye, sure. We'll take our food tae yon hillock. Then ye can ha' as many words wi' me as ye like."

Will did not wait until they had reached the grassy hillock but said as soon as they were beyond earshot, "I'm a-going the wrong way, Cap'n Jake, as ye must ken fine. I felt it more strongly yet when ye told Mistress Thornwick I'd go tae yon farm wi' her and Mace. We be a-going north when I should be a-heading south. Jamie needs me, and I feel as if I ha' abandoned him."

"I know how you feel, Will," Jake said. "Sithee, lad, I feel as if I've let Jamie down, too, as if I've somehow failed in my duty to him."

"Aye, and he will be King one day. We...we *should* help him!"

Hearing the sob in the boy's voice, Jake said, "In troth, what we both feel is not failure but helplessness. We both know the pirates sailed last night. They are long gone, lad, with Jamie. And following them would have gained us nowt."

"Aye, but if we had followed them earlier tae the other harbor—"

"They were armed with cannon, and they outnumbered us. The best we might have hoped for was to get ourselves captured with the others."

"Aye, well, at least we'd ken where Jamie is."

"Or we'd be dead, Will, drowned like those they threw overboard."

Will paled but said doggedly, "Ye might at least ha' sent the *Sea Wolf* on tae see where they were a-going."

Jake hid a smile, recognizing characteristics in Will

that put him forcibly in mind of himself at the same age. He had rarely taken no for an answer either, and had often pushed matters until he'd smarted for his efforts.

"We ken fine where they're going," Jake said. "The captain of the big ship is taking Jamie to London, where the King of England will demand a high ransom for his release. But the King won't harm him, Will. Jamie is too valuable to him."

"Aye, and Lord Orkney, too, I warrant."

"Orkney, too," Jake agreed. "We must be thankful for that, lad. You and I must also act wisely. Our duty is to report what happened to those who need to know. You can be proud, too, that you rescued Lady Alyson."

Will looked into Jake's eyes, his own welling with tears as he said, "Jamie *said* I was tae go. He said he didna think the lady Alyson could get out o' that kist by herself, so if I didna do summat tae help, she'd sink wi' the ship. Sakes, sir, her husband left the ship and barely looked back for her."

"I thought you said that Mungo told Niall someone was fetching her."

"I did, but when Mungo said it, Niall Clyne just nodded and went along o' him without another thought. That be when I kent Jamie were right. We couldna both go for her, so I slipped away."

Thanking God for the young prince and feeling a rage toward Niall Clyne greater than any he could recall feeling toward anyone since his childhood, Jake said, "You know, Will, Jamie is going to make a fine King of Scots one day."

"An he lives long enough, aye," Will muttered darkly.

"He will," Jake said. "English Harry has much more to gain by indulging him than by mistreating him."

"Aye, and 'tis true that when Orkney told that Cap'n Hugh that Jamie were a-going tae France tae improve his French, Hugh said King Harry would teach him French hisself. But Jamie speaks French gey fine already. D'ye think King Harry will be wroth when he learns that he does?"

"I do not," Jake said firmly. "What I think is that you still believe you can somehow help Jamie."

"He'll be a-missing me summat fierce!"

"Aye, he will, but not as fiercely as he would if those pirates had tossed you overboard. Of that you may be sure. How would you find him, Will?"

The boy was silent for a time, and Jake did not rush him. It was nearly always good to take time to think. He should do more of that himself.

At last, Will said, "Nae one would heed me much, would they? I mean, I might get tae London, 'cause people wouldna think nowt o' a lad walking tae such a great city. But Kings ha' many castles, and getting inside the right one would be as hard as if I'd tried tae walk in tae Castle Doune whilst Murdoch Stewart—him they call Earl o' Fife, now—were still a-living there... afore the English captured *him*."

"You would find it even harder to get inside an English castle," Jake said. "I'd forgotten, though, that you are acquainted with the Duke of Albany's son."

"Aye, sure, 'cause Murdoch lived in Doune like me and me da, only in the castle there. The English took him prisoner, too, but I dinna care about Murdoch."

"No, but the English have looked after him well, lad, and for the same reason that they'll look after Orkney and Jamie... for the great ransom they will fetch."

Will sighed. "So what am I tae do if I'm no tae follow Jamie? I ha' nae family, ye ken. Me mam's been dead a long time, and me da died nearly two years ago. Nor I dinna want tae go back tae the tanner o' Doune. The man liked leathering me too much for my taste. That be why when Sir Ivor and Jamie rode through Doune on their way tae St. Andrews, I joined up wi' their lot."

"So Ivor told me," Jake said. "We'll have to think about what you might do next, but you can stay with me as long as you like. If shipboard life suits you, I'll make a sailor out of you. If you dislike the sea, I'd wager Bishop Wardlaw will have some ideas. At all events, we'll sail to St. Andrews straightaway. Not only must we get Lady Alyson back to her family, but we must also tell Wardlaw about Jamie's capture. I'm not looking forward to that, I can tell you."

"Coo, I hadna thought about ye being in trouble wi' the bishop," Will said.

Jake nearly smiled at the boy's visible concern. Then, remembering Ivor, he said, "The bishop does not worry me as much as your good friend Sir Ivor does. Sithee, the lady Alyson is his cousin, which is the real reason I encouraged Mistress Thornwick to accompany us today. I had me doots that Ivor would accept one lad and two men as respectable protection for her ladyship."

"Hoots awa'," Will said, his eyes widening. "Ye dinna want tae make Sir Ivor angry. *I* can tell ye that!"

Alyson was trying to watch Jake and Will while listening with half an ear to Lizzie's chatter about her aunt and uncle. The taverner's daughter was clearly on good terms with her kinsmen, enjoyed talking about them, and required only an occasional murmur from Alyson as encouragement to continue.

Jake had his back to them, so Alyson saw only Will's face. However, since Will had initiated the conversation and, by turns, looked worried or as if he listened hard to what Jake said, she could sense the tenor if not the topic of their discussion.

Will had a problem—likely, his concern for Jamie, which she shared. And Jake was not only listening to him but also encouraging the boy to confide in him.

Watching them gave her an unfamiliar sense of comfort, although until then, she had not thought about needing comfort. The situation was what it was. But it was better with Jake as a part of it than it would have been if he were not.

Confidence radiated from the man. But his self-confidence was not the boastful sort that her older brothers had often displayed. He seemed to know himself and be sure of himself without any need to puff off his abilities so that everyone might be aware of them.

A twinge of guilt struck her. Niall had probably died a horrible death, and here she was, thinking about Jake. She realized, too, that Lizzie had stopped talking.

Ruefully, Alyson said, "I beg your pardon. My wits had gone a-begging."

"'Tis how it were for me, too," Lizzie said sympathetically. "Days would go by as if nowt were amiss, and then a memory would strike like a clout on me lug. Ah'd be awash in tears afore Ah kent Ah were sad."

Alyson nodded. She could sympathize, although she could not honestly say she understood, because she did not share Lizzie's feelings. She had no reason to mourn for Niall's probable death other than logic. Instinct said that he lived, and curiosity kept shifting her thoughts back to Jake. That Jake listened to people as if naught else were of importance fascinated her. The discussion she'd enjoyed with him earlier had stimulated her mind, because Jake accepted what she said and considered her opinions more seriously than other men she knew ever had.

Niall had been a good friend and a kind one. She had been able to count on him when she needed a partner at a social gathering or court function. But she had never discussed the Sight with Niall or considered doing so.

He was not a man to whom one confided such personal details. The sad fact was that although Niall usually gave the impression of listening to her, he often did not seem afterward to have listened at all.

She realized when that thought lingered that she had expected Niall to dismiss her Sight—whether he believed in it or not—as something that one ought never to talk about, lest others think one were daft. In troth, he too often concerned himself with what others might think of him, or of her.

Most people did fret over such things at times. But, to Niall, other people's opinions were of much greater importance than they were to Alyson. She would dislike creating a spectacle that others would discuss for their own entertainment, but she would not fret over what they thought of her every word and action.

Things were what they were, and talking with Jake was more interesting.

Still, Niall was her husband as well as her friend, and she wanted to believe he was alive. Perhaps, she mused, she might find him as interesting as Jake if she could get to know him as well as she had hoped she would on the ship.

That thought hovered as if inviting contradiction. But she told herself firmly that it was the thought of his still being *able* to spend time with her that caused the mental struggle. Surely, if he were alive, she would have a sense of *that* and not just a lack of any sense that he was dead. She felt nothing when she thought of Niall.

"But I ought to," she murmured to herself.

"What's that tha say, mistress? Ah couldna hear thee."

Starting, recalling that she was not alone—although Lizzie must have been silent long enough to let her fall into such a reverie—Alyson said, "I beg your pardon, Lizzie! I'm being horridly rude to you. And in troth, I should not!"

"Och, but Ah did the same. Me mum said it were like havin' a ghost in the hoose. But thy brother and t' lad be a-coming back. How fast the time went!"

Jake whistled for Mace, and shortly afterward the oarsman, Will, and Lizzie walked off together toward the more distant cliff road, while Jake sat atop the hillock with Alyson and watched until they were out of sight.

The silence between them felt comfortable, if one could call it silence with gulls and gannets shrieking overhead, the pleasant sound of waves rolling in and out on the shore below, and the wind whistling by.

"Jake?"

"Aye," he said, facing her.

"Why did you send them both with Lizzie? I don't mind; I just wondered."

"If your cousin Ivor asks me that question, I hope he just wonders, too," he admitted. "But I could not see another course that would serve our needs."

When her response was only a tilt of her head, inviting further explanation, he said, "We are indebted to the Metlows, and although Lizzie is a widow and not a maiden, I ken fine that her father would disapprove of sending Mace alone with her. Beyond a clachan or two, there are few people on this moor. No father would like his young daughter being alone with—"

"I see why you thought of Ivor, rather than *my* father," she interjected dryly. "I assure you, though, Ivor does not trouble himself about me, either."

"So you may think," Jake said. "But when you and I met last year at MacGillivray House, that lad told me straightaway after he saw us talking together that you were betrothed and would marry in June. His meaning was clear."

"Was it?"

"It was, aye. And although you may not have experienced his temper, I have. Sithee, we spent much time together as lads at St. Andrews. No one crossed Ivor on purpose, believe me. The man may seem perfectly pleasant one moment, but then... Well, it isn't pleasant when he erupts."

"So I've heard," she said. "Will you *tell* him that we were alone today?"

"Not unless he asks me. I value my hide. But, what did you mean about your father? In troth, with Ivor about, I scarcely heeded Farigaig."

"Few people do," she said. "Before my brothers died, Father was much like my uncle Shaw MacGillivray, dividing his time between Perth and Farigaig in the Highlands. Afterward, he seemed to die inside. My mother was always a gentle soul, who agreed with whatever he said and followed his lead in everything. After Eamon and Artan died, lacking Father's direction, she seemed to fold inward."

"Sakes, then who runs Farigaig's estates? Your younger brother?"

"Nay, for Ranald prefers other pursuits. My father's stewards look after Farigaig, which is in the hills west of Loch Ness. If we lack company at home, Ranald takes himself to visit cousins or friends."

"Then you...?"

"Not to make a song about it, sir, but I have run the household in Perth for nearly five years. With the help of my father's stewards, I've run the estates, as well."

"I see. I expect, then, that you'll miss your husband even more sorely."

Amusement tinged her voice as she said, "Niall did not interest himself in such things. Recall that he served Orkney, whose affairs—or Mungo's demands—frequently required Niall's presence. He never asked me to go with him. And in troth, I'd have felt uncomfortable leaving my family."

"What changed?"

"I learned about the voyage. Believing that it was my duty to know him better, I conferred with my father's steward, who said he could see to everything whilst I was gone if I could persuade one of my aunts to manage the household. My great-aunt Beatha agreed with alacrity, as I knew she would. She had been with us since October, was in no hurry to leave, and loves to give advice. She won't trouble herself more than that, though, so our people will go on as they have. In troth, I was tired of them all and *did* want to know Niall better as a husband."

Jake shuddered at the picture she'd portrayed. Shaking his head as if the motion could clear away the images she'd stirred, he said, "You reinforce my belief that life ashore is *not* the life for me. Give me the freedom of the seas over the chains of estates, households, extensive family, and the like."

"Living on your father's boat and at St. Andrews, then earning your knighthood, and shipboard life again... You seem to have spent most of your life with men, sir. Does that not grow tedious?"

He grinned. "Duncraig Castle and its vicinity are not bereft of womenfolk, lass. Nor am I a saint. When I want feminine company, I can find it."

"I don't doubt that," she said, looking out at the sea again.

A new thought struck him. "Art worried about what I might do whilst we're alone here? You need not be."

"I know."

"Still, it might be wise for us to walk," he said. "I want to look at that trail down to the beach, because it will be dark when the *Sea Wolf* comes in."

"Surely, we'll light torches."

"I'd liefer draw no attention," he said, extending a hand.

Accepting it, she let him help her to her feet but withdrew her hand from his when she was upright.

Sensing that she remained uneasy, he waited until they reached the top of the path to the shore before he said, "What were you thinking about earlier, whilst I was talking with Will... before he and Mace left with Lizzie?"

Gazing at the wide, curving bay below, she said almost casually, "You must have seen that I was talking with her."

"What I saw," he said bluntly, "was Lizzie talking and then looking quizzical and *not* talking, just watching a companion who'd clearly stopped listening to her."

"I fell into a reverie, aye, but Lizzie said she understood," Alyson said. "Sithee, since her mother told her that Niall is dead, Lizzie thinks my feelings must match her own from last year when her Jeb died."

"Do you fear they won't if Niall *is* dead?"

She looked at him, clearly startled. A frown wrinkled the skin between her eyebrows. "I don't know what I'll feel," she said. "I cannot know that until someone reports his death or his capture."

"But . . . ?" He let the single word drift as he led the way down the path.

"Niall *is* my husband," she said as she followed. "I cannot help but think that since I saw Eamon's death and Artan's—aye, *and* Davy Stewart's—I must surely have seen Niall's *if* he were truly dead."

Jake said over his shoulder, "But you said the Sight does not follow rules, did you not?"

"I don't think I said it exactly that way, but it does not follow a set pattern."

He sensed that she did not want to talk about her gift just then, and he was as sure as he could be that she would not welcome a suggestion that such feelings were usually false. So he fell silent, wondering if she'd offer another topic for discussion.

Instead, a warning rattle of rocks made him turn just as she slipped, tried to catch herself, and stumbled toward him.

Catching her at the waist, holding her steady, and looking into her eyes as he did, he felt an immediate, overwhelming urge to kiss her.

Her hands clamped tightly to his upper arms, and she pushed herself away.

Primal instinct urged him to pull her back.

His good sense, sadly, warned him to do no such thing.

Chapter 9

Nerves atingle, Alyson stared into Jake's face, trying to read his expression but aware only of the sensations raging through her body. She had felt that odd tingle again earlier, the moment his hand touched hers to help her to her feet.

When she slipped, she'd tried to catch herself. But her other foot clipped a rock as she shifted it to stop her slide, and she had flown right into Jake's arms.

The path was steep enough to be dangerous to anyone who stumbled. Her first thought had been that she might take them both down when she crashed into Jake, but he'd reacted so swiftly that he had easily stopped her fall.

She had never expected the slight tingle she felt each time he touched her, or brushed against her as they passed, to turn so suddenly into a full-blown nerve storm.

But when he caught and held her as he did, that is exactly what happened.

Her impulsive reaction had been to shove herself away as if she had got too close to a fire that might consume her.

Briefly, she had seen a hungry look in his eyes that she had seen before in other men's eyes. Such men were usually strangers who had either not bothered to request proper introduction to her or had simply forgotten themselves. That look at such times had felt intrusive, even intimidating, and most discomfiting.

Once such a man had irritated her throughout an evening at a cousin's house, despite Niall's presence, until her brother Eamon had spoken to the man. The man had gone away then, and Eamon had said curtly that Niall was a fool.

In fairness to Niall, and because she'd had little reason to expect anyone to intervene, she had not mentioned her irritation. Thinking back now, she doubted that Niall would have done more than tell her to avoid the man. Niall was never eager to confront other men, but she had welcomed his gentleness then.

She and Jake reached the shore without further incident. When he suggested that they walk along the shingle to make sure there were suitable places for his men to beach their towboat, she readily agreed.

He said, "We can beach the *Sea Wolf* if it becomes necessary. I'd liefer not do that, though, because we'd have to await the incoming tide to row her out again. Our wee towboat will take the four of us easily."

Feeling a shiver of unease, she said, "How wee is it?"

"We'll be safe," he assured her. "I'd not let it come in otherwise." Looking skyward, he added, "The wind is easing."

They chatted on companionably about many topics until he said they should return to the clifftop to meet Mace and Will.

"We'll build a fire up there, so Coll will know where we are," he added.

"Why don't we just build it down here?"

"People seeing us on the cliff with a small fire will

think nowt of it, lass. The evening is warmer than recent ones have been and may draw others to the cliffs or the shore. They'd notice us on the beach, especially if we stayed after dark and put out our fire without igniting torches to light our way back up. I'd liefer no one wonder about us before we're safely away from here."

"But if we don't light torches, won't that path be dangerous?"

"We'll have to be careful, but I won't let you fall."

She did not argue, and when she wondered at her easy acceptance, she realized that she trusted him as if she'd known him much longer than two days.

Soon after their return to the clifftop, Mace and Will arrived and reported seeing Lizzie safely into the arms of her aunt and uncle.

"Kind people they are, sir," Mace said. "They would have it that we should stay the night." Handing Jake a cloth sack, he added, "I said we had tae meet our lads, so Mistress Thornwick's aunt sent food for us." Having delivered his message, he stretched out on the wind-and-sun-dried ground, clasped his hands under his head, and shut his eyes.

Will, watching him, mimicked Mace's actions.

Chuckling, Jake said, "If you mean to nap, lad, pull your cap over your face or the sun will burn it summat wicked even on a cool day like this."

"If we all sleep," Will murmured, "who will watch for the *Sea Wolf*?"

"Don't you worry," Jake said. "I'll know when my lads arrive."

Although Alyson had seen no sign of a ship or a boat, Jake stood abruptly soon after dark and said, "She's coming." She still saw and heard nothing.

Nevertheless Jake doused their fire, woke Will and Mace, and urged them all toward the path.

Shortly after reaching the shore, she heard the creak of oars. Moments later, two oarsmen beached Jake's boat. It had two sets of oars and no sail.

When Alyson saw how small it was, dread swept over her. She trusted Jake, but shaking now, she realized with shock that she did not trust the sea. It had nearly swallowed her before. She couldn't...

"I...I can't do this," she said gruffly. "The sea...I thought I could—"

"You can," Jake said. "I'm with you now, lass. I won't let the sea have you. My lads are expert oarsmen, and although Mace is a good man at the tiller, I'll take it myself. You and Will can sit right beside me if you like, or hunker down low in front of me as you did in the *Maryenknyght*'s coble. Mace and the oarsmen will easily balance our combined weight in the stern with their own."

"I dinna mind sitting up in the bow if Mace does," Will said. "It be a fine night, and the sea be a-coming in and going out without a fuss."

"The tide is turning, so 'tis is a good time to go," Jake said. "Take my hand now, Allie. I'll see you safely aboard."

Swallowing hard but telling herself that he knew what he was doing and she was being foolish, she gripped his hand. Although she expected to feel the usual unnerving tingle when she did, she felt only its comforting warmth.

Jake urged her toward the boat and introduced her to the oarsmen.

They had beached it bow inward, and when she saw that the men expected her to get in first, she nearly balked. But Jake shifted his hand to her elbow, told the oarsmen and Mace to hold the boat, and stepped into it with her, steadying her as she stepped over the midthwart to stand uncertainly in the tipsy stern.

To her slight annoyance, despite the tilt of the boat on the shingle, and its stern still rocking in water, Jake made his way as steadily as he would on solid ground. Her boots wanted to slip on the polished wooden strakes.

She was wondering if she should sit on the stern seat while the boat remained atilt when, taking her bundle from Mace and handing it to her, Jake said, "Sit down low on this, lass. We'll try to keep you dry this time."

Will and Mace got in, and with Jake and Mace manning oars to help, the other two men shoved the boat into the waves, turned it bow outward, and leaped in. For a time, Alyson expected the waves to fling them right back onto the shingle, but they were soon well away from the shore.

Jake and Mace rowed until they were far enough out to exchange places with the other men. Then Jake took the tiller, and Mace moved forward with Will.

The moon was not up yet, and the sky was a blanket of stars that created a shimmering glaze on the sea. The night air was chilly, but Alyson's cloak was warm and dry and her feet were snug in boots and woolen netherstocks.

The boat rocked up and down on the waves, but her fear was gone. Glancing at Jake, she caught him gazing at her.

"Feeling better?" he murmured.

"Aye, and foolish for showing my fear so readily."

"Recognizing one's fears and expressing them is *not* a bad thing."

She smiled at him, warmed by his understanding. It was, she realized, the first time she had truly felt like smiling since the English ships had appeared. But as that thought flitted through her mind, she felt the unnerving sensation that she had felt so often with her cat, Pallie, shortly before his death.

The sensation vanished then, replaced by a chill that began at the base of her spine and shot upward, radiating through her as it did.

Suddenly frightened, fighting to control her expression so that Jake would not see her fear, and praying that it was too dark for him to note it in any other way, she realized that she was still staring at him and shifted her gaze. The strange sensation could not, she told herself fiercely, mean the same thing for Jake that it had eventually meant for Pallie.

That warning twinge meant nothing where Jake was concerned. It certainly could not mean that she cared too much about him, let alone loved him. That would be daft. She barely knew him, and she was a married woman.

Swallowing, she realized that in such an instance, the sensation might hold some lesser but distinctly similar warning—perhaps that, as a wife uncertain of her husband's fate, she should not be thinking about Jake Maxwell at all, and certainly not in such disturbing ways.

Jake was just a man who had rescued her from a sinking ship. Feeling grateful to him was one thing. Letting her mind dwell on his character, his behavior, and...

and other things about him...might prove to be a grave mistake.

~

Jake wondered what the lass was thinking now. Thanks to the starlight and his excellent night vision, he could see her clearly enough to know something was amiss. Although he'd detected little more than a twitch of her lush lips and the fact that her serenity had not restored itself after her brief rebellion against the sea, he was aware that some new but equally disturbing emotion had surged through her.

Or else, he told himself dryly, he was a fool, trying to imagine he possessed that gift of hers himself. He wondered if it had occurred to her that what she thought was Second Sight might be no more than keener insight than most people had.

Her description of Davy Stewart's death argued strongly against that, though. She had described it as if she *had* been there to watch—even, chillingly, as if Davy had spoken to her or she'd overheard his dying thoughts.

Likely, more news had escaped Lindores Abbey than he knew. Its Benedictine monks were not loose-lipped, but they were human, as were the people at Falkland. Perhaps she'd heard a whispered rumor here, another there, until her sensitive mind and keen intelligence put everything together to provide her with a nightmare that no innocent maiden should ever have endured.

She had still been a maiden at the time, too, because Davy had died the previous March, and she'd married Clyne after Christmas. To be thinking of her maidenhood struck an odd note, so he dismissed the chain of thoughts as irrelevant.

The primary difficulty for him was that her description was so apt, filling gaps in what the monks had deduced from the state of Davy's body. That she believed she had been aware of Davy's dying thoughts made him shudder.

Her gaze was far away now and had shifted to a point beyond him. An impulse stirred in him to make her look his way again, but common sense intervened sharply to suppress it. It was one thing to do his duty by a lady but quite another to interest himself as much as he seemed to be doing. *That road*, murmured a voice deep inside, *can lead to nobbut trouble*. If, by some miracle of God, her husband *was* still alive, it would be bad enough. But if he were dead…

"Straight ahead, Cap'n," Mace said.

"I see her, aye," Jake said. Instinct or his mind had already noted the shape of the *Sea Wolf* ahead of them against the stars. He had already adjusted his course.

"She's much smaller than the *Maryenknyght*," Alyson said.

"She is," Jake agreed. "But she is a stable craft and unlikely to draw interest from any pirates still lingering along this coast. If necessary, I have a Norse flag we can fly and another from the Hanse. Ships like her are common in the Isles, but most oared ships on this coast come from Norway."

"How long will it take us to reach Perth?"

"We go to St. Andrews first, because I must let Wardlaw know what happened straightway. We're about two hundred miles from there, so if the wind stays strongly behind us, we could do it in three or four days. But with the wind against us and picking up each afternoon, as it has been, it could take a sennight—if it storms, longer still."

"Have you enough provisions?"

"Aye, sure, we had enough to take us to France, after all. Although the *Sea Wolf* looks like a Highland galley, her design is more that of a birlinn."

"I don't know the difference."

"Just that the *Sea Wolf* has a cargo hold. Ordinary Highland galleys don't. Our hold has room to string hammocks for sleeping and for our towboat."

"Will I have a hammock?"

"Nay, I'll put you in the master's cabin. You'll have a bed much like yours on the *Maryenknyght*." Recalling that she'd also had her attire woman on that ship, he added, "You're going to miss Ciara, but young Will can help if you need him."

Jake next remembered sharing with Will earlier his doubts that Ivor would accept one lad and two men as respectable protection for his cousin Alyson.

Nor, he realized now, would Ivor accept thirty-six oarsmen, a helmsman, and their captain as such, especially since Ivor, of all people, would know that Jake's men would lie themselves into Hell for him if he asked them to. However, Ivor might accept the word of one ten-year-old boy whose character he knew. If Will were able to tell him honestly that Lady Alyson's good reputation remained intact...

Jake could only hope. A mere whisper of impropriety could so easily damage or destroy a woman's reputation. Although he'd taken care not to draw censure from anyone in England, simply to avoid unwanted attention, he'd had no way—short of abducting Lizzie Thornwick—to provide Alyson with a respectable female companion for the voyage home.

It occurred to him that his mentor, Giff MacLennan, whose motto was "Reck not!" might well have abducted Lizzie under such circumstances. Jake liked to think that *he* was more practical.

If he could get Alyson quietly back to her family, she would be safe. But that meant he'd have to keep his distance as much as one could on the small ship. They would stop briefly at St. Andrews so he could report to Wardlaw, but there was no need to take her to the castle with him. It was, after all, an all-male establishment. However, if circumstances demanded that he ask Wardlaw to shelter her overnight, no one there would gossip about it.

Alyson watched with interest as the towboat approached the *Sea Wolf.* She had expected to hear men shouting orders, but the small boat skimmed in near silence up to the larger one, and their two oarsmen turned it deftly to bring the two vessels side by side. The *Sea Wolf*'s sail was down. No oars were visible although she could see the oar holes, so she decided the ship must be at anchor.

Rope ladders unfurled, and men climbed down to help secure the towboat. Others lowered ropes that Jake rigged into a net sling around Alyson, saying, "'Tis only a short way. But as they draw you up, sitting in this sling will protect your modesty and assure that you get aboard without falling into the sea. Since the alternative is for me to hoist you to the men on board and let them haul you over the railing, this will be more to your liking, I promise you."

She believed him.

As two men aboard began to hoist her, Jake grabbed hold of a dangling rope and climbed up the side of the ship beside her.

He encouraged her as he did, talking quietly. Curious about his boat, she barely heeded his words, but the sound of his voice was soothing.

The galley's sides stepped steeply upward at stem and stern, and the lower stretch of railing was much nearer the water than any railing on the *Maryenknyght* had been. The line of oar holes was even closer.

In moments, she was looking over the edge to the *Sea Wolf*'s deck.

~

Jake lifted her over the wale and undid the sling he'd created for her. Then he said, "Let me take your bundle from Mace, my lady. Then I'll show you to your cabin. Will, lad, you come with us."

"Aye, sure," the boy replied. "This boat looks like the one ye had in the Firth o' Tay last year. But it isna the same one, I'm thinking."

"Nay, that was one of Orkney's ships. This one's mine."

Moments later, he opened the stern cabin door for Alyson to enter.

"I can't see a thing in there," she said.

"Here, sir," Coll said, stepping to Jake's side with a shaded lantern, only one side of which showed light.

"This is Coll, my lady," Jake said. "He is my helmsman." In Gaelic, he added, "Coll, this is Sir Ivor's cousin Alyson MacGillivray. She and the lad there, Will, are the ones the pirates left aboard the *Maryenknyght*."

"My faith," the older man said in the same language, regarding her with respect. Turning back to Jake, he added, "She's a brave woman to get on another boat after such an experience, sir."

In Gaelic, Alyson said, "I should tell you I speak the Highland tongue."

"Och, m'lady," Coll replied. "I ken fine that I shouldna make comments about ye in a tongue ye might no speak. But I dinna speak Scot verra weel."

"You need never apologize for a compliment, Coll," she said, smiling. "In troth, I disliked getting in the towboat and dreaded the thought of sailing on another ship. But I ken fine that you and Sir Jacob will see me safely to Perth."

"We will, aye," Coll said, nodding earnestly.

"In you go, my lady," Jake said. "Will has your bundle and can show you where to stow it. When we're under way, I'll return to fetch the lantern. We don't keep them alight overnight."

"I mean to go to bed, sir," Alyson said. "But this must be your cabin. Won't you need things from in here?"

"I will, aye," he admitted. "I'll fetch them now."

He slipped past her, taking care not to brush against her. He had enjoyed the pleasure of talking freely with her as they'd walked along the cliffs and the shore. But he wanted to set an example of formality for his lads to follow.

Still curious about the galley, Alyson turned to look the length of it to its front end, or stem. A wide plank ran up the middle between the rows of benches—eight on a side—for the oarsmen. There had been only a few men in sight when she boarded, but they had increased in number, and she realized that what had seemed to be bundles of clothing in the spaces between benches had, in fact, been sleeping oarsmen. Others appeared from elsewhere, doubtless from those hammocks in the hold that Jake had mentioned earlier.

She wondered if she should call him Captain Maxwell now that they were on his ship. She had enjoyed thinking of him as Jake.

He spent little time in the cabin. But he hung the lantern from a hook in the ceiling and opened the lantern's other shutters.

"Might someone not see that light?" she asked.

His smile flashed, and he said, "I don't care if someone does. We're far enough out and low enough to the water here that we won't attract pirates or other English vessels that might be patrolling this coast. Such vessels will be looking for ships of war, or merchantmen to seize. That is one reason Bishop Wardlaw wanted the *Sea Wolf* to follow the *Maryenknyght*."

"You said you'd used one of Orkney's ships before. Would it not have been easier to use that one again?"

"Wardlaw wanted to avoid all things Orkney," he explained. "Recall that by then Henry was on the Bass Rock with Jamie. Wardlaw wanted to be sure we would not inadvertently draw the attention of anyone searching for them. But I must see to my duties, lass. If you need aught, send Will to me."

He left, and the cabin seemed suddenly larger and emptier.

Will was looking around. "'Tis nearly the same," he said, moving to pull up a trapdoor near a cunning little washstand attached to one wall. Above the washstand was a round shuttered window. She saw another in the opposite wall, where an alcove contained a table flanked by two narrow benches.

"We could put things in here," Will added, pointing to the space he had opened. "By daylight, we'll be able tae see what's what wi' just the light through them portholes. Cap'n Jake's clothes must be in them kists by the door."

"I have an extra shift and another kirtle," Alyson said with a smile. "I'll hang them on one of those hooks yonder. But there are two beds in that end wall, Will. If you want to sleep here, too, I'm sure Captain Jake will let you."

"Mace said I could sleep in a hammock below, where he and some others sleep," Will said. "That'll suit me, 'less ye *want* me tae stay wi' ye."

Agreeing that it would be much more exciting for him to sleep below, she soon handed him the shuttered lantern, shooed him out, and went to bed. The lower of the two shelf beds boasted a featherbed below her and a soft, thick quilt above, making it more comfortable than the bed on the *Maryenknyght*.

Snuggling in, realizing that she could tell from the motion of the boat that men were rowing, she was sure she would sleep like a bairn in its cradle.

Jake breathed the fresh sea air, thinking as he had so often over the years how much fresher it seemed away from the coast than when he stood on the shore and breathed it. Since it was the same air, he had always thought it a curious thing. He wondered if the sensation was due only to the added freedom he felt on the sea.

The lads were rowing strongly, and he would keep

them at it until they were well beyond Filey Bay. When he saw the lights of Scarborough in the distance, he'd rest the men and rely solely on the sail. The breeze was stiff and more easterly tonight than northerly. By using the jib, he could maintain a good pace.

The Scottish border lay nearly a hundred and fifty miles north of them. If the wind held as it was—a most unlikely prospect—it would take them four to four and a half days to reach Berwick-on-Tweed. They would travel faster than the men on horseback, though, because he could keep the *Sea Wolf* moving night and day. But the riders did not depend on the wind, and if it dropped altogether—also an unlikely prospect at that time of year—the *Sea Wolf* would depend entirely on its oarsmen. And oarsmen needed frequent rest.

Coll said, "How far off yon coast d'ye want me to keep her?"

"Keep the coast just within sight," Jake said. "I doubt we'll have company in this darkness. But if it becomes overcast, wake me. I'll be sleeping on my old pallet in the forecastle cabin."

"Aye, sir," Coll said with a smile. "Her ladyship seems a pleasant woman."

"She is by nature one of the most unruffled women I've ever met," Jake said, when a piercing scream erupted from the stern cabin.

The first thing Alyson would remember about the dream was feeling warm and safe. Then someone shook her awake with horrible news, the gist of which she would not recall. Then, in the nature of so many dreams…

She found herself outside in the cold, facing a forest full of pikes and lances, wondering where Jake had gone and how soon he might return.

"They're coming," someone shouted. "Make haste, they come!"

Looking around, she saw horses flying toward her through the air, their hooves kicking squares of fresh-cut peat off stacks reaching to the sky. The horses carried hooded men waving swords and axes, who bellowed at her that she had no good cause to be there, that she should leave at once.

As she turned, a polished wood coffin appeared before her. The lid flipped upward, and Niall's waxen face and shrouded body appeared.

Then Mungo leaned from the lead horse, his axe raised high behind him but sweeping down toward her in an arc that would surely send her head flying from her body.

Screaming, Alyson threw a peat square at him. Mungo changed to her cousin Ivor, then abruptly to Jake. She screamed again… and awoke screaming, sitting upright in her shift, looking into Jake's anxious face.

Chapter 10

Aware of Coll behind him with a lantern, Jake caught Alyson by the shoulders and held her firmly, saying, "It's Jake, lass. You're safe. You had a bad dream."

"I... I—" She fell silent, and he felt a shudder ripple through her.

"What was it?" he asked, trying to avoid looking too closely at the heaving soft breasts beneath her thin cambric smock. "What frightened you so?"

When she did not immediately reply, he realized that Coll had hung the lantern on its hook overhead and was offering him the quilt, which had slipped to the cabin floor. Jake took it from him and put it around her.

"You must learn to sleep with everything tucked in," he murmured as he tugged the ends of the quilt together under her chin. "Otherwise, as the *Sea Wolf* rides the waves, quilts and such will slip. Can you tell me about your dream?"

"I—I'm not sure."

Coll said, "I'll leave ye tae talk privily with her ladyship, sir."

"Stay," Jake said. "Coll is as close as an oyster, my lady. He won't repeat aught that you say to me. But I must not be here alone with you."

Swallowing visibly, she looked past him at Coll. The older man moved to the door, shut it firmly, and leaned against it.

"It was horrid," Alyson said then in a low, still-quavering voice. "At first, I thought it was like . . . like the other one I described to you. I don't know why. It just had a similar feeling. I cannot describe it. Faith, sir, I'm not even sure that it felt the same way throughout."

"Tell me what happened."

She told him what she recalled, adding, "It sounds foolish when I put it into words. I don't know *where* I was. I just saw a forest of pikes and lances and . . . and then that horrid coffin. Niall *is* dead, sir."

Jake frowned. "A coffin amidst a battle? Did you see an army or just pikes?"

"It was a real forest, with trees. But amongst the trees were hundreds of pikes and lances. It was too dark to see men. But it seemed as if there were many."

"You could count many weapons, yet not see the men?"

"I told you it sounds foolish, but that *is* what I saw. When I turned, I saw the coffin and Niall's face. A mounted troop flew through the air toward me. Mungo led on a big black horse. He raised a long axe and swung it at me. As he did, his face turned into Ivor's face, and . . . and then into yours."

"I was here by then," Jake said, "because Coll and I were just outside and heard you scream. It is understandable that you mixed me into your dream."

"Perhaps," she agreed. "Nevertheless, for your face to replace Ivor's after his replaced Mungo's . . . Whatever can it all mean?"

"It means you had a nightmare, lass, that's all. I ken

fine what you are thinking. But if you recall, you told me yourself that your...um...dreams"—he lowered his voice to keep his words from Coll's ears—"never foretell events. Since I was in this one and am clearly still alive..."

"Nevertheless, sir, Niall is dead. I'm sure of it now."

Jake was likewise as sure as he could be that Clyne was dead. From all she had told him, the pirates would have had little reason to keep him alive, even if Orkney had promised to arrange his ransom. Since they could demand what they wanted for Orkney and James and had thrown everyone *else* overboard...

But he would not debate that with her now.

Instead, he said, "From what you've said, all the men in your dream other than Clyne were alive at the end of it. What I think is that you have been fretting about Clyne, got cold when the quilt slipped off you, and what began as a pleasant dream faded into an unpleasant one and wakened you."

"But I felt—"

"I don't doubt your feelings, lass. You admit you don't understand the gift yourself. Mayhap it is changing, but to allow what is likely an ordinary nightmare to destroy your serenity this way *is* foolish."

She drew a breath, and something in her expression righted itself. Exhaling, she said, "You're right, sir. I'm sorry to have disturbed everyone's peace in such a way."

He eyed her measuringly. "If you are apologizing because you think you should not have troubled us, I'll have more to say to you when you are on your feet again, in broad daylight. Until then, I'd advise you to sleep."

She bit her lower lip and looked at him from under her

lashes. "I am glad I was not alone," she said. "Whatever it was, it was frightful."

"If you'll lie back and draw that quilt over you, I'll tuck this side in for you," he said. He maintained control of himself, but as he said the words, he wished fiercely that he could take her in his arms and smooth her fears away.

Instead, he waited patiently while she arranged herself, then tucked the quilt in tightly beneath the featherbed and followed Coll back out on deck.

Alyson breathed more easily when they had gone, but her emotions remained in turmoil. Was Jake angry with her for admitting that she had been a nuisance?

Never before had she viewed Ivor's quick temper as a blessing. But, just then, she would have given her finest piece of jewelry to be able to read Jake's temperament as easily as *anyone* could read Ivor's.

The edge in Jake's voice when he had said that he would speak to her in daylight had sent a shiver up her spine. But she did not fear Jake. She liked talking with him. Although they often disagreed, she found his opinions and his ways of expressing them interesting and thought provoking. In fact, his generally easy manner made her hope that...

Jake was standing before her, looking as if he were trying to judge her mood. Then his beautiful smile flashed. It amazed her, as it always did, that he could look so serious one moment and so boyishly delighted the next.

She wished she had known him as a boy.

As she moved toward him, she was conscious of the tingling sensation that had become so familiar to her. But soon the sensation was running amok. It touched nerves here and nerves there until her body seemed to have caught fire. The closer she got to him, the hotter she burned inside.

Now he was only a step away. Without hesitation, she took that step and melted against him. The fiery sensations increased, sending impulses to her nipples and to parts of her body deep inside, where she had never felt anything before.

The area at the juncture of her legs tingled and burned. Muscles clenched tightly there, stirring new feelings.

Jake caught her chin in one hand and tilted her face up.

"I want to kiss you," he said.

"Do you?"

Instead of answering, he captured her lips with his much firmer ones, and his arms went strongly around her, warming her and setting all the fiery nerves inside her leaping like sparks in a greenwood fire.

Everywhere he touched her, she burned. Nevertheless, she wanted him to keep touching her, wanted him to...

Waking as abruptly as she had earlier, Alyson felt nearly the same shock at herself as the nightmare had caused, for dreaming such a thing. Worse was that her body still tingled and burned everywhere it had reacted to Jake's touch in her dream. Worst of all, she wished that she had not wakened.

Her lips and mouth were dry, but the area between her nether lips was hot and felt strangely moist. Recalling her last thought before waking, she wondered what else she'd have wanted him to do.

An image of Lizzie, talking, jumped into her mind along with Lizzie's words as she recalled them: *"I tell ye, I do miss Jeb touching me doon there... The man were that skilled wi' his hands, a-stroking and a-petting till he'd drive me near to madness. He could mak' me cry out for it any time he'd a mind to do it, too. Sakes, that lad had only to put a finger to one o' me nipples..."*

Alyson could still imagine Jake's hands on her breasts, as they had been in her dream, but the fiery tingle had gone. Touching a nipple, she felt a slight sensation but nothing like what he'd made her feel in the dream.

She lay sleepless, her thoughts jumbled, and began to suspect that perhaps her marriage had not been all that a marriage could be. But she slept at last, and when she awoke, a thin golden line of sunlight framed each shuttered porthole.

Standing on deck at the stem end of the *Sea Wolf*'s gangway, near the door to the small forecastle cabin, Jake idly fingered the circle stone he'd found on the cliffs. Rubbing it, he mentally calculated how far the English ships might have sailed since leaving Bridlington's harbor with James and Orkney.

Scudding clouds overhead showed winds steady from the northeast again. Therefore, he had taken the *Sea Wolf* farther from the coast to give them room to tack without drawing undue attention. Unless the winds shifted eastward again, or blessedly southward, it would be a slow day.

It was Sunday morning, and the men were resting, some still breaking their fast. He'd set them to their oars only if he needed extra power while tacking, or if the winds dropped, or if for some reason they had to go ashore.

Having gleaned details of England's coastlines from years of sailing and talking with sailors, he decided that, unless the five English ships had put into port somewhere else, they could be a third of the way, even halfway, to London. A third of the way—a hundred miles—was more likely than 150.

Whichever it was, he could not have stopped them.

Even had the English waited for dawn before leaving Bridlington, Jake knew he could not have abandoned Alyson to follow them, or taken her along.

What he had said to Will remained the truth. The *Sea Wolf* might have followed the English ships all the way south to the Thames Estuary. But following the river Thames fifty miles to London would have been madness, and they'd know no more than they knew now.

He was nearly certain that Albany was responsible for what had happened. Cynically, he wondered if winning his son Murdoch's freedom was Albany's primary reason, or if it was that the most likely man to rule Scotland if the King of Scots died while the English held Jamie was Albany himself.

Some imp at the back of Jake's mind suggested that had "Reck Not!" been his motto, as it was Giff MacLennan's, he'd have managed to steal Jamie and Orkney back from the English. But Jake shook his head at the random thought.

Even Giff would not be so foolish as to set himself against five armed ships from an Isles longship built to carry a small cargo and sixty men at most.

At present, the *Sea Wolf* carried fewer than forty.

As he rubbed the smooth circle stone, Jake saw Mace move to talk to Coll at the helm. Memory stirred of Alyson saying that if one looked through such a stone, one might see a man's intended wife standing next to him.

With a sudden sense of mischief, Jake raised the stone to look through it at the two near the stern. Only Mace knew of the stone, but both men were observant and would see what Jake was doing. When they did, he would explain to Coll and hint that he'd seen a bride for one of them.

He saw nothing unusual. Thinking it might look more persuasive if he shut his other eye and focused more, he did so. Mace stepped away without glancing his way, and Jake was about to lower the stone and return it to his pouch when movement at the stern cabin door caught his eye.

Still looking through the stone, he shifted to see Alyson step outside on the deck. She did not look at him either, did not even glance his way. He suspected then that she'd seen him the minute she had opened the door.

She did look toward Coll, or mayhap Mace. So Jake kept following her with the stone until she stood by the helmsman.

To his shock, he saw not Coll standing beside her but *himself.*

Hastily lowering the stone, Jake shoved it back into the pouch at his belt and stepped inside the forecastle cabin to collect his wits.

~

Alyson had seen Jake, but she was looking for Will.

Breathing the fresh morning air after that of the stuffy little cabin was glorious. Moreover, she was hungry, and she did not immediately see Will. She did see Coll and Mace by the helm, chatting, just before Mace returned to the first bench on that side, where apparently he rowed.

Accordingly, she said in Gaelic to the helmsman, "Good morning, Coll. 'Tis a fine day, is it not?"

"It is, aye, my lady," he replied with a smile. "I trust ye slept well after yon bad dream ye had."

"Like a bairn," she said. "Is young Will nearby? I want to break my fast."

"I'm here, mistress," Will said from behind her.

"Mercy," Alyson exclaimed, turning sharply. "I did not see you at all. But you must have been nearby."

"I was a-sitting yonder in the corner." He gestured toward a bench nestled where her cabin wall met the stepped area on the port side. "I saw ye come out, though, and thought ye might be hungry."

"Starving! I was just telling Coll."

"Cap'n Jake has apples, ale, and water in yon forecastle cabin for ye, if that will do," Will said. "He may even ha' some bread up there, or I can fetch some."

She eyed the gangway askance. The winds were not as fierce as they'd been, but the galley's often unexpected motions played merry havoc with one's balance.

"Mayhap you could go and fetch me some water and an apple," she said.

"Cap'n Jake said he wanted tae talk wi' ye," Will said. "I can get ye there in one piece if ye dinna like tae walk the gangway on your ownsome. It takes a mite o' practice tae walk it without falling off."

"There isn't room for us to walk side by side."

"Nay, I'd go first, and ye'd put a hand on me shoulder tae steady yourself."

It had to have been a trick of his imagination. Surely, people who thought they saw their future through a circle stone were people whose minds simply provided them with the image they wanted to see.

He had not lied in telling Alyson that he believed in magical things. But he had not been including anything akin to seeing a likely wife through a stone. Sakes, he didn't want a wife! He was a man of the sea. The longer the voyage, the better. Moreover, he was a knight of the realm, trained to fight on land or sea, and he enjoyed that, too... the physical effort, at all events.

In truth, he preferred tiltyards and tourneys to battles. Pitting his wits and his strength against others of equal or greater skill was a welcome challenge. But he knew his duty, and he had never turned from a fight or a battle.

The forecastle cabin door opened, and Will said, "I've brought our Allie. She says she's gey hungry."

Jake nearly suggested that Will remember that he ought to address her as Lady Alyson, but something in the lass's expression stopped him.

He said instead, "Thank you, Will. If you will run and fetch a roll for her, I'll give her an apple or two." As the boy turned to leave, Jake added, "Leave the door open when you go. There's a wee rock by it to keep it so until you return."

When the boy had set the stone against the open door and gone, Jake said, "What is it, lass? Another bad dream?"

Alyson felt herself relax and realized that, until then, she had been unaware of her tension. She said, "Will said you wanted to see me. And, last night, I thought…" Pausing to consider *what* she had thought, she recalled only the dream that had wakened her that morning, in which Jake had played such a prominent role. Abruptly, then, she remembered. "You said you would talk to me by daylight, sir, and the way you said it—"

"I remember," he said. "You were fretting about being a nuisance, and I may have sounded curt. I don't want you to feel so about something beyond your control, lass. One simply has nightmares. One does not create them."

His tone was mild, but she detected a difference in him this morning. If she had not come to believe that he lacked ability to fret or to worry, she might think something was disturbing *him.*

Perhaps he did not want to fratch with her. But she needed to know if she was reading him correctly. "I thought perhaps it was my insistence that I might be 'seeing' Niall's death with that dream. Or my thinking that it was a warning of some sort. You did sound a bit…well… irked."

His smile flashed. "Lass, if something angers me, you'll know it. You won't have to guess. I've learned enough about you to believe that, whether it is the Sight or just finely-honed insight, you *can* rely on your instincts in most situations. You won't pretend that I frightened you into thinking you'd face a scolding or worse."

"Nay, not that I—" She paused. "In troth, sir, I don't know what I thought. Although you suggest that I should rely on my instincts, I must tell you that in the past sennight, I've come to doubt them sorely. Faith, but I've come to doubt much about many things, and…and about people that I thought I knew."

He frowned, then glanced past her and said, "Will is coming back with your rolls. I'm going to send him away, because I want to talk about this. We'll leave the door open, though. No one will hear us whilst we stay in here, but I'd liefer give the lads nowt for gossip, so we'll stay in plain sight of anyone who looks this way."

Will entered and handed her two crusty rolls. "I cut ye a bit o' cheese, too, m'lady," he said, shooting a glance at Jake before he added, "I trow I shouldna ha' called ye 'our Allie' afore, as I did. Since we're no wi' that Lizzie and them."

"'Tis a good notion," Jake said. "It was clever of you to think of that."

"Aye, well, ye were a-looking as malagrugrous as me old master when he were a-reaching for his leather, so I thought I'd best talk soft," Will said.

Alyson suppressed a smile but could not resist saying, "Malagrugrous?"

Jake said evenly, "The polite word would be 'grim' or 'forbidding.'"

"I thought 'malagrugrous' *were* the polite one," Will said. "'Tis a *long* enough word and better nor 'peevish,' I'd think."

Alyson laughed, and Will grinned at her.

Jake said sternly, "That, my lad, will be enough from you. The sea is well-behaved today, so 'tis a good time for someone to tidy the hold. You may ask Mace to hang a lantern down there for you."

"Aye, sure," the boy said cheerfully. "I'll see tae it." With another grin for Alyson, he dashed down the gangway to Mace's bench.

Alyson shifted her gaze to Jake. "It is good to see him smile."

"I was just thinking how good it is to hear you laugh."

She sobered. "Will and I have both been worrying about Jamie and Orkney. It is hard to be cheerful when they are both in grave danger."

"The only danger to them would be if Hugh-atte-Fen sinks his ship," Jake said. "And with such prizes aboard, I doubt that he will. Nor will English Harry let harm come to them, because they're even more valuable to him. Now, I want to know what was troubling you," he added. "What did you mean when you said you've come to doubt much about many things? I especially want an explanation for the bit about people you thought you knew."

She hesitated, but she was grateful for the opportunity to talk and determined to learn what she could. Jake would not have been her first choice as confidant, because—rescuer or not, friend of Ivor's or not—he was a man and she barely knew him. Even so, he had been the first one that came to mind when her questions arose. Something about Jake Maxwell kept telling her that she could trust him.

It wasn't just that she liked him or that he listened so intently to whatever she said. It was that something deep inside her rejected the notion that he might share her confidences with anyone else. She knew that about him as clearly as she knew it about herself, although she could not have explained why.

As it was, getting the first words out was almost painful. At last, she said, "In troth, I don't know if I understand the matter well enough to explain it. Sithee, I told you about my conversation with Lizzie but not all of it."

"I doubt that you should worry about anything that Lizzie told you," he said. "She leads a gey different kind of life."

"But she was married," Alyson said.

"As are you."

She grimaced, finding it more than difficult now to explain.

He glanced out the door, then took a step away from her before he said softly and with more gentleness than she had yet heard from him, "Lassie, just spit out the words dancing in your head. I've nae doubt they're there, teasing ye tae spring them free. There's nowt that ye canna say tae me in safety."

Drawing breath, she said before she could stop herself, "Lizzie talked about intimate things she did with her husband. Things just between the two of them."

"D'ye fear ye'd be breaking her confidence to tell me?"

"Nay, I think she would say what she said to nearly anyone who would listen and understand her. But . . . I told her I did not want to discuss such things, and she apologized, saying she ought to have known it would be too painful."

"Wasn't it?"

"Nay, the fact is I did not know what else to say to her." Determinedly, she added, "In troth, I did not understand much of what she was talking about."

~

For the first time in his life, Jake wished that he had a sister. If he'd had one, he might understand women better. It was, however, the first time that he had wanted to understand them better—one of them, at least. Hitherto, his notion of the opposite sex had been that they were interesting, even fascinating, could be entertaining in many ways, particularly in bed, and often had caper-witted notions.

Knowing no way other than with his usual bluntness to manage the one at hand, he said, "What, exactly, did she say?"

Alyson flushed deeply and looked away. But he waited until she looked back again and said, "She talked about how her husband, Jeb, touched her…down there…and she said he had a thick piece. I think I know what she meant by that, because I *have* seen a man naked."

"I should hope so," he said. "You do, or did, have a husband."

"Aye," she said doubtfully. "Niall was usually away after our marriage, though, and…" She spread her hands.

"Don't stop there," he urged her. "What else are you trying to say?"

She nibbled her lower lip. "I don't know what else *to* say."

"See here, Allie, you married Clyne. Surely, he bedded you at every chance, no matter how often he was away."

She did not reply. She just gazed at him, as if she expected him to say more.

"Well, didn't he?"

"We slept together when he was home, aye. But…but from what Lizzie said about her marriage—the bit I told you about and other such things—I suspect that Niall and I did not behave as other married people do. Or perhaps they do such things only in England. I thought you might know more about that than I do."

"I know little about English customs. But when I was a bairn, folks on both sides of the line seemed tae be much of a muchness, as they themselves would have said. Without knowing what other things Lizzie said…"

An absurd and most implausible thought entered his

head just then. To keep it from lingering there, he said, "You coupled, surely."

She looked uncertain but said, "I told you, we slept in the same bed."

"Aye, but... D'ye ken what coupling is? Your mother must have explained what your husband would expect of you."

"My mother does not converse much," she said. "She sits in her solar at her tambour frame and plies her needle. She eats what we put before her and sleeps when her woman says it is time for bed. I meant to ask Cousin Catriona when she came for our wedding, but her second child was born just then, so her husband, Fin, came, but Cat did not. I asked my great-aunt Beatha to tell me what duties my marriage would entail, but she said I should ask my husband, that I was too fond of telling everyone else what to do and should learn to practice wifely obedience."

"Did you ask Niall?"

"Aye, but he said I need do no more than what he asked of me, and he asked only that I welcome his friends and see to his needs. Three days after we married, he left with Mungo. I scarcely saw him again until we boarded the ship."

Jake exerted himself to conceal his shock. Unless he was mistaking the matter, Alyson was still a maiden. His cock stirred at the thought, but a surge of anger struck at the same time. Clyne was—had been—a damned fool!

Chapter 11

Alyson sensed Jake's anger and knew that it arose from something she had said. He did not seem angry with her, though. Wanting to be sure of that, she said, "What is it? If there is more that I should know, I wish you would tell me."

"The issue is likely moot now," he said soberly. "But I suspect that you are right, and your marriage was not all that a marriage might be. One does not like to pry too deeply—"

"Say what you will," she said. "I want to know how it *should* have been."

"Sithee, the time you spent with your husband should have been pleasurable. You must have done *some* things in bed together besides sleeping—things that made you feel closer and gave you both pleasure. Did you not?"

Frustrated, she said, "You will have to be plainer, sir. I will say that it was more pleasurable to sleep *with* Niall in my bed than without him. But I do not know if that is what you mean about its being pleasurable. I think it was likely more *comfortable* to sleep with him than with a husband I had not known since childhood. Other than that..."

She paused when she realized that the feelings in her dream must be the sort of pleasurable things he meant. The thought sent a flush of heat through her cheeks that made it hard to meet his steady, probing gaze. She nearly shut her eyes.

Jake noted her blushes and the way her eyelids drooped. He noticed whenever anything prevented him from gazing into her beautiful eyes. But he also sensed that she was concealing something. As always, such behavior stirred his deepest curiosity.

"What is it?" he demanded. "Don't keep things from me if you want my help with this. Relations between a man and his wife are ever a delicate subject that neither ought to share with a mere acquaintance, or indeed, with *any*one else. I will admit, though, that your current situation is difficult."

Looking remorseful, she said, "I do not mean to be difficult. It is just that I *have* felt things in my dreams that were most pleasurable. But—"

"You cannot be talking about that nightmare you suffered last night. Tell me about these other dreams."

Her gaze dropped, and her flush deepened until it looked painful.

Annoyed with himself for such clumsiness, he said, "Never mind that. You were doubtless dreaming of your husband—"

"But I wasn't. I've never dreamed about Niall." Nibbling her lip in that tantalizing way she often did, she added, "In troth, I rarely recall my dreams. But I am sure..." Pausing, she looked up, and he detected a rueful twinkle in her eyes. "This is much more difficult than I thought it would be. Perhaps we should not—"

"Look here," Jake blurted. "If you want me to explain what married people do in bed, I will. 'Tis plain that, although you may have some small knowledge of how two people couple to create a child, you are trying to discuss something of which you know next to nowt."

"That is exactly how it is," she said, relief strong in her voice.

Wishing one moment that he could shut the door against possible intrusion and hoping fervently the next that neither Ivor Mackintosh nor Fin Cameron would *ever* learn of this conversation…

With a near groan, he blinked away the image he'd stirred of the two teasing him mercilessly and collected his thoughts. Then, taking care to spare her sensibilities as much as he could by speaking frankly and drawing on what little she knew about the behavior of farm animals, he described the act of coupling.

When he finished, she gazed at him thoughtfully but silently until he began to wonder if she had understood.

Alyson was trying to imagine Jake doing the things he had described. Surely, she thought, he must have had more than a little practice to describe such behavior so glibly. He had, however, provided absolute clarity on one point.

"Niall did sometimes put his arm around me and I would lie close to him and rest my head on his shoulder," she said at last. "But I don't think we ever did anything even similar to what you've just described."

"Then you did not," Jake said. Although he did not laugh, she detected a strong note of amusement in his voice. "I'm sure you'd remember."

She could not help smiling at the understatement. "I would, aye."

"Usually, a married couple consummates their union soon after they wed," he said. "In many places, especially where great inheritances are at stake, witnesses watch them to be sure they *have* coupled."

"Mercy, but I'd have disliked that!"

"Even so, I'm surprised that your father did not encourage an immediate consummation."

"But I've told you, sir, neither of my parents takes sufficient interest in the lives of others in the house even to suggest that we behave in a particular way. They have not done so these five years and more."

"Since your brothers' deaths," he said. "I know that you said as much. But in the case of a marriage, consummation is vital. One couples, after all, to produce offspring. Surely, Clyne wants children, and so do you."

"Niall did say that he wanted sons and lots of them," she said. "But he also said he wanted to improve his position with Orkney before we began a family."

"Sakes, Orkney is wealthy beyond most people's dreams, certainly wealthier than anyone in the royal family. He pays his people well, too, and looks after their interests. Your Niall could easily have supported a family."

"Do you *do* things like that?"

"What? Pay my men well and look after them? Aye, sure, I do."

"I...I didn't mean that," she said. "I meant..." She

stopped, blushing again. "I do know, after all, that you have not yet married, sir."

Feeling sudden heat in his own cheeks, Jake said, "When you asked me about women before, I admitted I'm no saint, lass. It is not a bad thing for a man to gain experience before he weds, however."

"I should not have asked you that. I wondered only because you must spend so much time with just men. But I suppose all warriors do that, and I do apologize. Mayhap Niall knew no more about such things than I did."

"Perhaps," Jake said, but he doubted it. Lads talked about lasses and women from the time they first observed differences between the sexes. Moreover, as he had learned the first time his cock reacted to a lass strongly enough to make him want to kiss her, things usually progressed naturally from that point, if only experimentally. The fact was that one experimented until one's partner either took a hand herself or used hers in a good swift slap to deter her would-be swain.

"Did Niall not kiss you often?" he asked.

"Aye, sure, whenever we met. And if he was with me at home, he'd always kiss me goodnight and good morning."

"Did you not feel things then?"

She licked her lips and looked away as if the answer to his question might be floating outside the open door. Then she turned back with renewed determination.

"In troth, I don't recall feeling anything except friendly warmth toward Niall, as I always have. However," she added before he could probe further, "in those dreams I mentioned earlier, I did feel things whilst kissing."

"So, if he kissed you at home, you felt nowt. But, in dreams, you do feel things. What sorts of things?"

"I would call the sensations different forms of tingling," she said. After some thought, she added, "And heat. I felt warm, then hot all over."

"So, he could make you feel— Nay, wait, you said you've never dreamed about Clyne, so who—"

"It was . . . was someone else."

"I see," Jake said. Hearing the edge in his voice, he felt no surprise when she nibbled that kissable lower lip again. He did wish she'd stop doing that. "I won't ask you who it was, lass. 'Tis no business of mine."

Rather than looking relieved, he thought she looked annoyed.

"I will say one thing more," he said. "From what you tell me, I begin to fear that Clyne lacked a passionate nature. I also suspect that you do *not* lack passion. How deeply did you miss him whilst he was away?"

"It was as it always had been," she said with a shrug. "Sithee, with the house full as it has been these past months—since before Christmas until I escaped with Niall to board the *Maryenknyght*—I scarcely had time to miss anyone. But I'm used to seeing him rarely. So it seemed as usual."

Her elusive dimple suddenly appeared, and she added, "I suspect Great-Aunt Beatha was right when she said that I'm fond of telling everyone else what to do. I had a husband who never interfered, but he might have if he had been more often at home. I rarely miss men who persist in telling me what to do, rather than discussing the options that might exist."

Jake grinned. "As I recall, your aunt also recommended learning to practice wifely obedience. Were you disobedient?"

"Nay, how could I be? Niall was the gentlest creature and never the least bit decisive. But I don't want you to think I admired that trait in him, either, for I did not. Although I can be willful about things and may be fond of having my say, I prefer decisive men to indecisive ones. To my sorrow, however, I have found myself of late surrounded by the latter sort. Even when I'd find a chance to request Niall's advice, he would say he was sure that I knew best. My father refuses to make decisions, and Ranald makes poor ones when he makes any."

"That is not surprising," Jake said. "If Farigaig is indecisive, he could scarcely have taught Ranald to be otherwise. Were your older brothers the same?"

"Nay, for before Eamon and Artan died, Father was not indecisive. His ability to order others about seemed to die with them. It was as if he withdrew inside himself. In troth, I think Eamon's death alone would have had that effect."

"He was the elder?"

"Aye." She met his gaze. "Eamon did not like Niall. He said he was a fool."

Jake felt sudden kinship to Eamon and sorrow that the man would never know that his opinion of Niall Clyne matched Jake's own.

How Clyne could have kept his hands off a wife as lovely and desirable as Alyson, Jake could not imagine. Every time she licked or nibbled that lower lip of hers, or met his gaze with her extraordinary black-lashed, changeable eyes, his heart either thudded like a war drum or seemed to stop beating altogether.

She glanced out the open doorway again.

He knew they had stayed longer than they should. And she had not eaten a bite of food. He reached for an apple and handed it to her.

"You should break your fast," he said. "If you'd like to sit at that wee table yonder, you may. I'm going out on deck."

"Thank you, but I'd liefer sit in the sunlight. We've seen so little sun of late that I yearn to bask in it."

"Sit on that bench outside your cabin," he said. "It is sheltered from the wind, and you'll be more comfortable. My lads won't disturb you."

"Your lads, as you call them, don't trouble me at all, sir. I ken fine that I can trust them as much as I trust you."

"You can trust them more than you can trust me," Jake said, knowing that he spoke the truth and that he ought to warn her. He was only human, and the more he saw of her, the more he wanted to do things he had no business doing.

Her eyes smiled then, and he realized that that was exactly the right word for what they did from time to time. It was not that *she* had smiled, nor did she show real amusement. Her eyes twinkled when she was amused. What they did on their own was different. Perhaps it was just that her eyelids curved up at the ends, and her long black lashes exaggerated the curve. Whatever it was, it made her eyes smile.

And whenever they did, his body reacted strongly.

"Why do you think I should put more trust in your men than in you?"

"Because I watch them, and they know better than to anger me. But they would do nowt to make *me* mind *my* manners."

"Now you are jesting, sir," she said. "I have learned

that you are a man who leads by example. I do not believe you would do aught to undermine the influence that such leadership gives you over your men."

"Do you not? Then you do not know the power *you* wield," he said. "Take your apple now and those rolls, and go sit in the sun."

To his infinite relief, she obeyed.

Even so, he took himself to task. How he could have spoken to her so, he could not imagine. Nonetheless, he had felt impelled to warn her that she should not take chances where he was concerned.

In troth, her very presence shoogled his internals, as he had been wont to say as a child. For that reason, if for no other, she was more dangerous to him than any woman he had met before her. And she was utterly forbidden fruit.

Although she now spoke of Clyne in the past tense, Jake could not. He had an uneasy feeling that if he began to accept that Clyne was dead, the damned fool would reappear, insufferably alive, and reclaim his lovely wife.

The voice in his head muttered, *And what if you learn that he* is *dead?*

Stepping onto the deck, Jake drew a deep breath of the wondrous air and let it out again, trying to banish the question from his mind. But it would not go. The fact was that, with Clyne out of the picture, Alyson MacGillivray could pose a greater threat to Jake's continued freedom than he had ever known.

~

All that remained of the past fortnight's turbulent weather was a northeasterly wind and the scattered, scudding white clouds that flew before it. Sitting in the shelter of the stern castle, using the high, stepped, portside wall as her backrest, Alyson realized that the *Sea Wolf*'s heading just then kept the wind at their back and thus sheltered her from it.

The men were rowing, as they often did to increase the ship's speed and keep it on its course when it tacked back and forth against the wind. The oarsmen's rhythm and the warmth of the sun were relaxing. In many ways, the small ship was more enjoyable than the *Maryenknyght* had been.

The wind in the big, square sail remained steady. Gulls screeched overhead, and wiser ones would soon see that she was eating. She had learned that they would follow alongside the ship, hoping to catch scraps.

Her thoughts drifted so for just a short time before they shifted to Jake and what he'd told her about the marriage bed. Such things ought perhaps to have been embarrassing to discuss, but she felt no embarrassment with him. His quick understanding of what she had tried to say had made it easy to talk to him.

If she felt anything beyond a vague satisfaction at learning that what she'd suspected about her marriage was true, it was curiosity to know more.

Recalling Jake's moment of anger and his agreement that her marriage had not been all that it might have been, she considered his reaction for a moment or two. He had also assumed, at first, that Niall must have bedded her often.

When she denied that that was the case, he'd said that Niall must have lacked a passionate nature. She tried to imagine a passionate Niall and failed. He had always been kind and friendly. But even as a child, he'd let her make the decisions about what they would do.

The truth was that Niall had been a comfortable friend. Knowing only what she had about marriage, she had thought he would make her a comfortable husband and provide her escape from the cares of MacGillivray House. She had expected to live with him at Braehead Tower or Ardloch. How wrong she had been!

The ship turned then so that a chilly wind struck her, and the sunny bench lost its appeal. Seeing Will chatting with oarsmen, she asked the boy if he'd like to improve his skill at the game of dames, and he readily agreed.

During the following three days, she began to suspect that Jake was avoiding her. He was polite and informative if she asked him questions, and he saw to her needs by sending Will to inquire about them and to do what he could to serve them. But the few times that she happened to meet Jake on deck, he seemed to take exceptional care to talk only briefly and never to touch her.

She had gained her sea legs, as he called them, although they were naught to match his own. She'd seen him move agilely in a coble tossing wildly on the sea, run from one end to the other of the *Sea Wolf*'s gangway, and to her shock, even walk along the ship's railing as if such feats were of no consequence! Although she was pleased that she no longer needed a steadying hand to move about, she would have preferred to enjoy more of his company.

The next day, Wednesday, passed as others had. But as she lay in bed that night, ready for sleep, she suddenly found herself in a royal audience chamber, watching Mungo talk to Albany. Although both men's lips moved, the scene remained silent, and darkness soon enveloped them... and her.

When she awoke the next morning, she vividly remembered the scene and wondered if she should tell Jake, but decided it had been just an ordinary dream stirred by their suspicion that Albany had arranged Jamie's capture. After all, she had not awakened from it in distress. She had slept soundly until morning.

By Thursday afternoon, they were nearer the coast than usual when Jake came to tell her they were nearing Berwick-on-Tweed. "I expect you know that for much of history, the river Tweed has formed our border with England," he said. "At present, Berwick lies in English hands, but eventually we'll win it back."

"We're near the line, then?"

"Aye, we'll see Scotland before sundown."

As promised, they watched the sunset from Scottish waters. Jake sent men ashore to hunt rabbits for the next day's stew and to fetch fresh water. But although Alyson was elated to be in safe waters again, darker emotions tempered her delight. Had she escaped, she wondered, only to return to the unrewarding family life that she had known before and after her marriage?

That night, even the thick featherbed and quilt were not cozy enough to encourage sleep. Once again, she and Will had spent much of the day playing dames. She had taught him some new tactics, but they had both tired of the game. Although Will was an amusing companion, having so little to do was difficult. Both of them were accustomed to greater activity.

How she was to sleep when she felt so wide awake, Alyson did not know.

At last, when moonlight shining through an open porthole touched her face, she abandoned any thought of sleep, got up, and put on the kirtle she'd taken off earlier. Lacing it up the front, she pulled on her boots, donned her cloak, and stepped out onto the moonlit deck.

Mace stood at the helm. All of the other oarsmen were resting or sleeping, and she realized that the wind was behind them, filling the sail as they sped northward through the water just off the Scottish coast.

The moon was bright, midway between a half-moon and a full one. Hanging well above the eastern horizon to her right, it spilled a wide, silvery path across the shimmering water to the *Sea Wolf.*

Savoring the night's beauty, she nodded to Mace as she went past him to the seaward railing to see if the moonlit path came right to the ship.

Below, all was silvery and white, as if the ship had split the moon's foamy pathway, making it swirl round the *Sea Wolf* fore and aft as it sailed. The sea was beautiful, vital, and vast. She could easily imagine herself far from any land, in a place shimmering just as the sea was, shimmering, wavering, and...

She saw him, lying in the darkness, slumped against a wall. He was not moving, and a chill formed in her chest, radiating outward with a swiftness that terrified her. Although she could not see his face, she knew it was Jake. She would recognize him anywhere, in any light. She could feel his nearness. But when she tried to go to him, her feet refused to move. Then she saw herself gliding toward him, kneeling swiftly, sorrowfully, slipping an arm around him. Only it was too late. She could sense that he wasn't Jake anymore.

~

Atop the stern cabin, leaning lazily against the sternpost, Jake watched Alyson move to the steerboard railing and look over it. Most of the lads were asleep. Two lay on the gangway near the mast, ready to leap up and tend sail or jib if necessary. With the steady wind, it was unlikely they'd have to do so.

Will had gone below and was doubtless asleep in his hammock.

Alyson pushed off her hood, and moonlight gleamed on her hair, turning it as silvery as the light on the water. She looked wraithlike, the sort of specter that some folks insisted they'd seen haunting Stirling and other old castles.

He did not believe in ghosts, so the thought of her as one made him smile. He remembered his boyish terror of boggarts, worricows, and their like. On a night like this, however, he believed only in the mystery and magnificence of the sea, and thanked God again for granting him the freedom to spend his life on it.

So certain was he in that moment that his way of living would never change that when he felt the urge to talk with her, he succumbed to it. Rising, he walked silently to the portside edge of the roof where it met the stepped stem rail, then along the first step, down to the next, and from it to the next.

Long practice made the skill second nature to him. One of the stays for the mast slightly impeded his way. But even that, he negotiated easily.

Stepping down to the bench on which she liked to sit, and then to the deck, he moved toward her in his usual quiet way. When she did not turn, apparently deaf to his approach, he said quietly, "Lass, I don't want to startle—"

She whirled with a shriek and stumbled, catching herself at the rail. In an abnormally high voice, she exclaimed, "Wherever did *you* spring from?"

"Up there," he said, pointing. "Come and I'll show you."

"You must be daft."

"Not I. Just step on your bench yonder, and I'll help you up."

Alyson stared at him, her mouth open to protest. But Jake grinned, and she shut it again. If he said she could do it, she could.

As they crossed the afterdeck to the bench, she cast a glance at Mace. But his face remained expressionless, as if they were invisible.

Jake, too, was silent.

At the bench, she started to gather her skirts.

"I'll take your cloak up first," Jake said. "It will be easier for you not to have to manage it and your skirts as well. I'll put it where it will be safe."

She handed him the cloak and watched in amazement as he stepped onto the bench, then to the solid rail, and up, from one step to the next as if he were on a normal stairway, rather than one with risers over a foot high and the icy sea below.

"Are you sure I can do that?" she asked when he reached the cabin roof.

"Unless you fall in, aye," he said, descending to the first step again. "But I won't let you fall. Give me your hands."

She did as he bade her, and he gripped them firmly in his own warm ones. Then, clearly as a second thought, he said, "Can you kilt up your skirt in front, under your lacing? You'll do better if you can see where you put your feet."

"If I look down to do that, won't I see the sea below me?"

"Afraid of heights, lass?"

"I don't know," she admitted. "I don't fear many things, but I've never stood in such a place as that before. Do you mean to lift me up there?"

"I won't have to. You can step up yourself if you take care. 'Tis not far, the planking is wide, and I'll steady you. Now, give me your hands again."

When she did, he told her to put one foot by his. A moment later, she stood on one foot beside him and saw that the railing was wide enough for her to put her other one down beside it. She glanced down farther, saw waves roiling around the ship, felt a rush of dizziness, and decided not to look down again.

"Your hands are shaking," he said.

"Perhaps I *am* just a trifle afraid of heights," she admitted. "Moreover, I think you are more than daft. You are mad."

His grin flashed again. "You're not the first to say so. Nonetheless, I will see you safely onto yon roof. Then, if you prefer it, I can easily get you back to the deck from there without coming this way."

"I would most sincerely prefer that," she said.

He chuckled, and she found herself smiling in response.

They had to negotiate only three steps, and the mainstay helped. Jake held on to it and guided her to the second step. Then Alyson held on to it while he moved to the third. Soon they stood together on the flat roof of the stern cabin.

He picked up her cloak and draped it around her shoulders.

"Better?" he asked when she reached to tie its strings.

"Aye, but *how* did you learn to do such a thing so easily?"

He shrugged. "I've been running everywhere on ships since I took my first voyage," he said. "To me, it is much like doing the same things on land."

"I do not think it could ever become so for me."

"How do you like it now that you are up here?"

"The view is spectacular," she said. "I'm glad I'm here, but I'll admit, sir, I was terrified that I'd slip and take us both down into the sea."

"Ah, but you told me you can swim."

She laughed then. "And so I can, although I don't recall telling *you* so."

"In troth, you said that Clyne could not, from which I deduced that you can."

His voice changed as he spoke, and his gaze sharpened, holding hers.

Chapter 12

The moonlight was magical, Jake thought. The way it touched Alyson's face and made her eyes sparkle was magical, too, although she didn't need magic. She was enticing enough without it. By moonlight, she was a goddess, a Fate drawing him nearer with the wind dancing round them, singing a siren song.

He would not say so, though, not to her. She already thought he was daft, and mayhap he had been, bringing her to the roof in such a way—sakes, bringing her at all. But he'd wanted to show her how the sea looked from there by moonlight. And more than that, he'd wanted her to share his way of doing things. It had seemed important that she share something that he had shared with no one else, ever.

Mace was below them. They were out of his sight as long as he did not turn to look, but Jake knew that Mace would say nowt of aught his captain did, if he did see them. The other lads were asleep. And Jake had been heedful for days.

But now…

He gazed into her eyes and knew that her power over him was too strong. It was also dangerous. He should not allow himself to succumb.

With a groan, he grasped her upper arms and pulled her close. When she did not object, he put two fingers to her chin, tilted her face up, and kissed her. He'd meant only to steal a taste. But when his lips touched hers, he was lost.

Her lips were cushiony soft, and the little moan she gave was more in the nature of a woman savoring a delicious sweet than one objecting in the least to his kiss. Not that he was personally acquainted with such objections, but he did believe he would recognize their sounds if ever he heard any.

"Oh, lassie," he murmured against those yielding lips. "You taste the way the nectar of the gods ought to taste."

"Do I?"

"You do." Deciding that a mere taste would not suffice, he captured her lips again. He wanted to savor her, but he could not give himself free rein.

There were rules about such things. And if he forgot them with Alyson, her cousin Ivor would remind him of them...painfully. Not that he feared Ivor, for he did not. But he did value Ivor's friendship, and his own honor.

Alyson had shut her eyes when Jake touched his lips to hers. Her body had reacted to his slightest touch from the start. But standing atop her cabin roof in the moonlight with him had stirred a host of new feelings. Moreover, she had known what he'd meant to do from the moment his gaze locked with hers.

And, right or wrong, she'd let him do it.

If God was watching, what must He think? Surely, He would expect her to mourn her husband longer than a sennight. She realized to her shame that the only reason she'd thought of Niall was that Jake had mentioned him when he'd teased her about perhaps having to swim.

As Jake's warm lips brushed enticingly to her cheek and then to her ear, other thoughts fought to intrude. She should feel guilty...and...As she struggled to finish the thought, his breath caressed her neck, stirring a tiny shiver.

She remembered the earlier chill she'd felt. The awful image she had seen as she'd stood by the railing filled her mind again. She stiffened in Jake's arms.

He released her at once. "What is it, lass?"

"You said you were up here before, aye?"

"I did, and I was."

"How? What I mean is, were you standing, sitting, or lying down?"

He cocked his head, either trying to remember or wondering at the question.

"Prithee, sir, it's important."

"I was leaning back against the highest bit there behind us. For a time, I expect I was half dozing, just watching the moonlight play on the sea. Then a beautiful wraith moved across the afterdeck below me and diverted my attention."

"Before that, were you lying with your head turned away from me?"

"Suppose you tell me why you are asking such a question."

She winced, realizing how she must sound to him. Then, remembering how easily he had talked with her about the Sight, she said, "Sithee, I saw you. You lay in dark shadows, slumped awkwardly against a wall."

"I suppose one might describe my posture then in such a way, although I reject the notion that I am ever awkward."

Although he clearly expected her to smile, she could not. She said, "Your head *was* turned away from me."

"Then how did you know that it was I?"

"I knew. I saw myself holding you and feeling sad when you died."

"But I'm not dead, lass. Also, although I may have turned my head away earlier, I did not do so then. I saw you go to the rail and did not look away even whilst I made my way down and crossed the afterdeck to you."

"Did you not? By your troth?"

"Not once. Might you have *seen* me as I was and then shifted to see some other time or place, as one does in a dream?"

She sighed. "Such a thing has not happened before, nor would I like it if that *were* the case. Sakes, I don't understand what I saw unless God is trying to warn me that I must mourn Niall's death in every way for a more seemly length of time."

He was silent, his gaze studying hers. Then he said, "Do you think of the Sight as a gift from God?"

The question startled her. "I've never questioned its source," she said. "I just know that it exists and that it has caused me strife more often than not. But if it comes not from God . . . then from whence *could* it come?"

He shook his head. "I know nowt of it but what you've told me. It does occur to me, though, that bards say the Sight has existed since the dawn of time."

"So has God."

His lips twitched. "Aye, but d'ye think the poor Man

looks down here and strives to guide our every step? I don't. I think He allots certain gifts to certain folks and expects them to get on with their lives without troubling Him to look after them as closely as that. Sakes, but the Man would go daft from us all."

"He is all-powerful. He would *not* go daft."

"You make my point, lass. If He'd meant to make a perfect world, He'd never let anyone take a misstep. All-powerful as He is, He'd have less obscure ways to show us the right path. I think He gives us each a brain to use and innate wisdom, as well as certain talents—and perhaps certain powers, such as the Sight. Then the Man lets us get on with it—choose how, as a Yorkshireman might say."

"You may be right," she said. "In troth, I hope so. But I do not know how to explain what I saw or how I felt when I saw it, except to say that it felt like a warning. You'd mentioned Niall, and I do think of him with guilt. He has been gone just a sennight. Yet here am I, his wife, enjoying the kisses of another man."

"You enjoyed them then."

"You ken fine that I did," she said.

"I do, and I shouldna tease ye." He stroked her cheek with a finger. "You said you could not see the shadowy man's face. Could you see his clothing?"

Grasping his hand, she pressed its palm to her cheek. "I saw his shape," she said quietly. "Would you know mine if you saw me in a similar way?"

He grimaced. "I would, aye. But if you are thinking you saw me as I was at the time, I'd remind you that the moon was shining down on me and I could see you clearly from where I sat. Had you turned and looked, you'd have seen me. You can see the top of Mace's head from here now. Beyond it, the railing where you stood is as visible as it was to me then."

"I don't know what to say then," she said.

"Use that wisdom of yours, lass. You told me that you see things only as and when they happen. Yet nowt was happening to me."

"But if it was a warning about *my* behavior—to make me heed the warning—mayhap it revealed a moment in the future."

"So you fear that something dreadful will happen to me in the future, because of something *you* are doing now. That is what you said, is it not?"

"When you put it that way..."

"Aye, it makes God sound like a gey vindictive chap, not to mention a most unfair one, does it not? That is not the God I know, lass. Nor, from what you've told me, do I believe your Sight works in such a complex way."

"Perhaps not," she said. "But the Fates often do unfair things. Do not forget the odd warnings I felt before my cat, Pallie, died. I felt them when I was small, too. They were especially strong before Grandmother MacGillivray died."

"But you did not see the cat or your grandame lying in darkness. Nor did you dream about your grandame's death before it happened, did you?"

"I did dream about her being dead before they *told* me she had died. Forbye, we'd heard that she was sick, and I don't know that I saw it happen as it did. I *had* worried about her for some time."

"Then this, tonight, was not the same," he said flatly. "That dream about your grandame's death sounds much like the one where you saw Clyne's. At St. Andrews,

Bishop Traill used to say that the value of things lies not in possessing them but in understanding their use. I'd look on your gift that way if I were you."

"But how can I understand it when I cannot control it?"

"We learn best from experience, lass. My da used to say that trying to understand summat of which one kens nowt be right daft. If what you saw pertains to the future, you'll learn more about it soon enough. Meantime, you'd be wise to exercise patience and go on as if you'd seen nowt tonight."

She bit her lip. *As if she could forget that she had seen him!*

"Don't do that," he said with an odd note in his voice.

"Don't do what?"

"Nibble your lip like that." His grin flashed but looked rueful. "Sithee, I do try to behave. But I *cannot* watch you do that without wanting to do it for you."

"You would bite my lip?"

"Nay, just nibble it, taste it... like this." He reached for her, and a chaos of sensation rushed through her before he even touched her. Despite knowing that she should not let him do such things, she banished sense and let instinct rule.

Jake felt her melt against him as he teased her lower lip with his teeth and tongue. When she moaned again softly, he slipped his tongue into the moist softness of her mouth. She responded at once, pressing harder against him, and he stroked her back and waist, holding her close. When his cock responded eagerly to her body's touch, one hand drifted to cup the curve of her bottom.

Although he had deftly moved her out of the moonlight

to the darkest area of the roof, it was as well, he thought, that they were outside and atop her cabin.

Had they been anywhere more private, with a bed, his self-control would vanish. He wanted nothing more *now* than to scoop her into his arms and take her to his bed. That that bed was a narrow straw pallet on the forecastle cabin floor would not matter a whit to him. Her shelf bed would be worse.

His lads would keep their mouths shut. But he knew that their silence would be as great a condemnation of the example he'd be setting as his guilty conscience could produce. Come to that, the case would be the same if any of them should chance to look his way while he trifled with the lass.

Almost as if she could hear his thoughts, Alyson put both hands on his chest and pressed firmly.

Letting go of her, he said, "What now? Is summat more amiss?"

"Aye, this is, and you know it."

He nearly reminded her that she had enjoyed it, but she was no alehouse wench for teasing. Instead, he said, "It may not be wise. But in troth, I've wanted to kiss you for so long that I seized the opportunity when it presented itself. And then, when a second opportunity arose..."

"I did not stop you. I ken that fine. Also," she added, "since we're being truthful with each other, I enjoyed it. I even felt much of the pleasure that you and Lizzie described. However, this is not only wrong because I should more properly be mourning my husband. It is also wrong because naught of good can come of it. You did say, did you not, that you never intend to marry, that your freedom is too important for you to risk losing it so?"

"I did say that," he agreed. "And I meant it." *At the time*, the irksome mutterer in his head added. Jake ignored it. He'd meant what he'd said, so she was right. To take advantage of her as he had was wrong, in more ways than one.

So why did the thought of not doing it again seem worse?

~

Alyson felt a sense of righteousness at having expressed her feelings. But when he released her and did not move to touch her again, the feeling died.

"You did say that I would not have to go down by way of those steps," she reminded him with a small sigh. "How will I get down otherwise?"

"I can lower you or get down first and lift you down," he said with a twinkle. "Your cabin is just eight feet high, after all. The reason I did not jump down before was that I knew I'd wake the lads if I did."

"*And* you like to show off your agility."

"In troth, lass, I wanted to share that view with you. I wanted you to share my way of getting up there, too. I haven't done that with anyone else before."

"I'll never forget going up as we did," she said sincerely.

"Were you terrified?"

"Not with you. I felt dizzy when I looked down, but the feeling passed." She did not mention that she took care not to make the mistake again. The truth, though, was that she had not given the sea a second thought until she was on the roof with him and gazing out on its moonlit splendor.

"I'll go down the way we came up," he said. "I still

don't want to wake the lads. They need their sleep. Also, I like my route best."

She moved to the edge of the roof to wait and saw Mace at the helm, apparently still oblivious to her and to Jake. Watching Jake descend, she marveled again at how easy he made it look and hoped that Will never saw him do it. The way the boy aped and admired the men on the *Sea Wolf*, she was sure he would try to emulate anything that he saw them do.

Jake spoke quietly to Mace before turning back toward her. Then he came to stand beneath her and said, "You'll have to sit at the edge, lass. Then, if you lean forward, I'll be able to reach you. Take care as you lean toward me that your cloak does not catch on anything."

"I'll drop it down to you first," she said. She could almost feel his hands on her just by thinking about them.

He took her cloak, glanced around, then opened the cabin door and put the cloak inside before turning back. He reached up, and when she leaned, he caught her at the waist and eased her down until she could put her hands on his shoulders. Then, he took his time before letting her feet touch the deck.

She told herself that he lowered her slowly only so she could avoid snagging her skirt. But when her gaze met his and she saw how his eyes sparkled, she knew that he meant to tease her.

With a guilty notion that her eyes were sparkling, too, she hoped Mace would continue to ignore them.

"What did you say to Mace?" she murmured when her feet finally touched solid decking.

"You need not speak so softly, lass. I just told him that I think it will be light enough for us to see the Bass Rock when we pass it in the morning. He agrees, and I thought you might like to see it by daylight. I'll wager young Will has not yet seen it so before, either."

"Would he not have seen it when he, Jamie, and Orkney first got there?"

"Nay, because they'll have approached it as they left, in darkness. They'd not have wanted anyone seeing a boat so near Bass Rock. Douglases at Tantallon can see what goes on there by daylight. Doubtless Albany had men along the coast seeking any sign of them, too. So they'd have anchored on the windward side of the Rock and kept their lanterns dark, as the *Maryenknyght* did when it collected them."

"We did, aye," she said. She realized she still had her hands on his shoulders. His face was near enough for her to see the desire in his eyes.

Sobering, he said, "Get you in, lass. It is too chilly to be out without a cloak. Also, if we are to see the Rock in the morning, we both need sleep now."

"Aye, sure," she murmured. "Thank you for showing me your view, Jake. I'll remember it forever as one of the wonders I have seen."

She turned then and went into the cabin. When she had shut the door, she leaned against it, remembering the sensations he'd stirred in her and hoping she could enjoy such feelings again. Mayhap someday, somewhere, she would meet someone else who could make her feel those things, someone who did not know and love the freedom Jake Maxwell found on the open sea.

She envied him that love. Faith, she envied him that freedom! But she feared that his desire for her, however strong, could never overcome his yearning for the freedom of the sea. She knew, thanks to Niall, that she would not stay in love with a man whose love for her was not strong enough to keep him home with her.

Friday morning, Jake sent Will from the foredeck to rap on Alyson's door in time for her to dress and enjoy a good long view of the Bass Rock.

When she emerged from her cabin, Jake noticed that she had plaited her hair in one long braid that draped over her left shoulder. It was long enough to fall across her left breast and extend past her waist. The sight stirred a strong desire in him to see it hanging free. He thought it might reach to her knees.

Reluctantly shifting his gaze, he saw the Bass Rock looming out of the thin morning mist ahead. Catching her eye, he gestured toward it. Will was already standing near the first portside bench, eyeing his erstwhile home.

Alyson joined the lad, and the two of them gazed at the Rock. Will glanced back at Jake moments later, his expression set and sorrowful.

Jake crooked a finger, and saw the lad speak to Alyson before he turned to the gangway and ran along it to Jake.

"Aye, sir? Ye said I could look at yon rock. But if ye want me for summat, I'll see tae it straightaway."

"I thought you looked sad," Jake said. "Art missing Jamie, lad?"

Will grimaced. "He'll be a-missing *me.* Be ye sure they willna hurt him?"

"I'm sure. English Harry thinks highly of himself, and he is no fool. By now he has realized that he cannot conquer all of Scotland. We will never bow to his notion that Scotland is but a northern shire of England."

"That's a right daft notion, that is," Will said fiercely.

"It is, aye. So my thinking on the matter is that English Harry will exert himself to influence us in every other way he can. Although he pretends to a truce now, he may still send armies to attack us. But he is also likely to try to persuade our Jamie that England has only good intentions toward us. If Harry can do that whilst Jamie is young, then when Jamie becomes King of Scots, Harry will wield much influence over the Scottish Crown."

"Jamie is too smart for that. But he will return. Ye're sure about that?"

"As sure as I can be," Jake said. "Sithee, laddie, if Harry hurt or killed a child...and Jamie *is* still a child, although he talks as if he were grown..."

"Aye, he does that," Will agreed with a wry smile.

"He does, but if Harry were to harm him, it would stir the wrath and disgust of the Scottish people and inflame their enmity. He would thus lose any chance of influencing Scotland to benefit himself."

"Aye, perhaps," Will said. "But men said the same about the wicked Duke o' Albany afore this happened. And *my* thinking is that Albany must ha' told that old Harry in England that our Jamie were on that ship."

"We agree in our thinking, lad," Jake said. "You make me realize, too, that you've a head as good as Jamie's on your own shoulders. You are also wise enough to know that we should keep our opinion to ourselves. Albany has long ears, and he will not want such opinions flying around Scotland."

"But he'll become King now when his grace dies, won't he?"

"Not as long as Jamie lives. When his grace dies,

Jamie will be King of Scots until *he* dies, which we must pray does not happen for many a long year. But Albany will likely be Governor of the Realm again, and gey soon now."

"'Tis much the same, tae my thinking."

"Not the same but close enough to satisfy him for a while, I hope."

Hearing the boy's deep sigh, Jake gently ruffled his hair.

Will looked up again. "How long till Jamie comes home then?"

"I wish I knew." Pondering the question, he considered what he knew about Albany. "It may be a long time."

"Mayhap until Albany be dead hisself?"

Jake closed his eyes. "We will hope it is not *that* long," he said.

"Aye, but he's a rare villain, that 'un, so it may be," Will muttered.

After learning of the *Maryenknyght*'s capture, Albany had wasted no time. Early Thursday morning he rode from Stirling to Rothesay Castle on the Isle of Bute, near Glasgow, where the King had resided since his son Davy Stewart, Duke of Rothesay, had died. There, as gently as Albany's chilly nature allowed, he informed his grace of the disaster that had befallen young James.

As expected, the King took the news badly. Albany thought the shock might kill his grace. Briefly, he thought the King suspected that he, Albany, had arranged James's capture. But when Albany dulcetly suggested that his grace might harbor such suspicion, the King assured him of his certainty that no uncle could betray a beloved nephew so, Albany least of all.

Had it been anyone else, the duke might have suspected cynicism, a parsing of words, even mockery. But Robert III was incapable of such duplicity. He *was* capable, however, of persuading himself that what he *wanted* to believe was the truth. Without a qualm, Albany assured him that it was.

The King had invited him to stay longer than overnight, but Albany found his grace's anguished grief tedious. Scotland had lacked a firm hand for too long, and the duke had much to do. He'd left for Stirling at dawn.

Alyson stared at the enormous rock and thought it a horrid place for the boys to have spent three months of their young lives. If the pirates, or whoever they were, had taken Jamie and Orkney to London, the English king would surely provide better housing than a gannet-ridden rock in the sea.

Men said that London was the finest city in Christendom. Edinburgh and Stirling castles were grand places, so surely their counterparts in London would be grander. Nevertheless, she knew that Jamie would hate being a captive, wherever they housed him. He would also be furious and dreadfully homesick.

If Albany had arranged for the young prince's capture, he was even more evil than Ivor had deemed him. She hoped no one ever presented her to the duke, because if she had to speak to him, she would surely let her disgust of his actions show.

The sun rose as the ship sailed across the mouth of

the Firth of Forth. The day was mild, with a promise of spring, so Alyson strolled back and forth for a time on the afterdeck. The breeze was not strong enough to call a wind, but it kept the sail full and nudged them slowly along.

When Will brought food for her to break her fast, Mace followed him along the gangway to the steerboard bench nearest the helm.

Alyson asked him how long it would take to reach St. Andrews at such a speed and learned that Jake expected them to arrive by nightfall.

"Truly?"

"Aye, sure, 'tis nigh the same distance from the Bass Rock as the Bass Rock be from Leith," Mace said.

If she had hoped for more discourse with Jake in the meantime, she was disappointed. She caught his eye several times and felt the warmth of his gaze, but although he was friendly if she spoke to him, he did not linger to talk.

By midday, she was uncertain of which she desired more, to shout her increasing frustration at him or feel his arms wrap around her. The thought of those powerful arms brought a flush to her cheeks and an equal rush of heat into other parts of her body.

Chapter 13

Jake sensed Alyson's gaze on him now and again throughout the morning and thought gratefully that, unless the wind began blowing from due north, pushing them backward, they'd reach St. Andrews Bay by nightfall. It occurred to him that he'd likely be wiser to take the lass straight home to MacGillivray House.

The impracticable notion was still teasing him when Mace brought him a mug of hot stew in the forecastle cabin for his midday meal. In the calmer weather, the lads had set up firepots to stew the rabbits they'd shot the day before, along with some roots and berries. That idea of taking the lass home before he met with the bishop had more appeal than leaving her on the *Sea Wolf* in St. Andrews harbor. Not that he could do that either, since they would arrive after dark.

As much as he would have liked to leave her aboard the *Sea Wolf*, the royal burgh of St. Andrews lay in Albany's shire of Fife, just fifteen miles from his seat at Falkland Castle. Although the duke was unlikely to send a patrol through the burgh after dark unless he suspected mischief afoot there—and Wardlaw had shown little interest in mischief—Jake knew he dared not take the chance, not with Alyson's comfort and perhaps even her safety at stake.

Neither, however, could he take her home. St. John's Town of Perth lay forty-five miles up the Firth of Tay from St. Andrews. Although the wind would be with them, the tide would not. In any event, his sworn duty was to report Jamie's capture to Wardlaw as swiftly as he could.

That meant he could not bypass St. Andrews even on Alyson's account.

He remembered then that although St. Andrews Castle was an all-male establishment, it *had* briefly housed noblewomen before. He also recalled that such women had always had a maidservant, an attire woman, or a husband with them.

Through the open door, he looked down the length of the ship to the bench where Alyson liked to sit. She was enjoying her hot meal, presenting her beautiful profile as she talked to Will. When she smiled, Jake gritted his teeth.

He set his empty mug and spoon on the nearby wee table.

Will was describing the days after his father's death, living with the tanner of Doune, when Alyson saw Jake striding toward them on the gangway and lost the thread of what Will was saying. She failed to notice that she had done so, however, until Will said indignantly, "Did ye stop listening, me lady? Ye didna ought tae ask a chappie questions if ye're no a-going tae listen tae his answers."

She looked at him ruefully and said, "You are right, Will. I did ask you what you'd meant by calling the tanner a grugous molligrumph. But I..." She paused, not wanting to admit that she'd stopped listening because of Jake.

Will stood, saying, "I just meant he were quick tae tak' leather tae a lad. But I can see why ye stopped heeding me. Cap'n Jake's looking peevish, and a body needs only good sense tae ken that *that* be time tae get out o' his way."

"Nay, Will, stay here. I don't think he's angry."

"Aye, well, I ha' me doots he'll want *me* about, any road."

Proving that Will's instincts were good, Jake said, "I left my mug and spoon on the table in my cabin, lad. Stow them for me, will you?"

"Aye, sure," Will said, giving Alyson a sage look. "I kent fine that ye'd ha' summat for me tae do."

"You're a wise lad."

"Aye, I ha' a proper head on me shoulders. Ye said so yourself."

"Go," Jake said.

Will ran off, and Alyson scooted over on her bench to make room for Jake. As she did, she said, "Will said you were looking peevish. That's why he thought you'd send him away."

"He was right. We must have a talk, lass, before we reach St. Andrews."

"Now is a good time then, is it not?"

He nodded. "Sithee, I had meant to leave you on the *Sea Wolf* whilst I talked with Wardlaw. But we'll arrive after dark, and Albany might send a night patrol through town. He does so often, and they are always curious about vessels in the harbor. I failed to consider that because I'd hoped to arrive earlier, report to Wardlaw, and take you on home afterward."

"I doubt that Albany's men would trouble me, sir. If you leave Mace and mayhap one or two of the others—"

"Sakes, lass, I'll leave lads to guard the *Sea Wolf* in any event. I'm more concerned about Albany's men being disrespectful to you or blathering to others that I keep a woman aboard. Without another female to lend you countenance, we'd be wise to keep your identity to ourselves."

She understood him at once. The situation aboard the *Sea Wolf* had not troubled her in the least, because she trusted him and his men. However, his bluntness stirred thoughts of how her family might view her return on a ship full of men, without Niall or Ciara to protect her.

"In troth, sir, if you worry about what my parents might say, you need not. Some of my kinsmen—"

"I ken two of your kinsmen fine," he said dryly. "Ivor will have things to say and will say them, come what may. Fin will let Ivor do the talking and will agree with much of it. But they will both know that you've been safe with me."

"For the most part," she said softly.

He smiled a little. "Aye, for the most part. I don't mean to apologize for the other part, either. I enjoyed it too much to make a sincere apology. But I should warn you that Wardlaw is likely to take a dimmer view of it."

"I don't see why he should," she said, raising her chin. "Since I have never met the man, he can have no cause to think ill of me."

"Not of you, nor of me, I hope," Jake said. "But he's unlikely to approve of your having been the sole female on my ship. Few people would approve of that."

"But you rescued me! Had you not, I'd have drowned on the *Maryenknyght*."

"Even so, lass. I tell you this, because I must ask him to house you in the castle overnight, to be safe. Doubtless he'll know a respectable townswoman who can bear you company whilst we are there. However, I don't know him as well as I knew Bishop Traill, and when he hears my report, his thoughts will be for Jamie and Orkney. I wanted to prepare you lest I've misjudged his most likely reaction."

Ever practical, she said, "I'll do as you say, sir."

"Good lass. He may insist that we take that respectable woman along when I return you home. If he does, her presence may ease your family's concerns."

"I tell you, sir, the only one who might speak harshly of my coming home with you after such an ordeal as we had would be Great-Aunt Beatha, for she does have a sharp and ready tongue. But she will be more worried about Niall's fate... aye, and mine as his wife, too, if we cannot prove he is dead."

He pressed his lips together, and she wondered why. Although he had expressed skepticism about her dream of Niall in a coffin, she knew that Jake was as certain as she that Niall was dead.

~

A twinge of something that must have been his own conscience warned Jake, despite his belief that Clyne was dead, of the lingering possibility that God had worked a miracle—or Auld Clootie had worked his devilry—and the blasted fool remained alive somewhere.

Blinking at the track his thoughts had taken, Jake wondered at himself for hoping Clyne was dead. Such thoughts could only get a free man in trouble. He cared about Alyson, certainly. How could a man not care about a woman whose life he had saved, especially one as beautiful, as selfless, and as intriguing as she was?

That did *not* mean he wanted to marry her. Forbye, the woman was right about one thing. She could think nowt about another marriage whilst her husband's fate remained uncertain. Without proof of Clyne's death—witnesses, at least—the Holy Kirk would never deem her a widow or allow her to wed again.

But why should *he* care one way or the other? Clyne's fate could remain unknown for months, even years, unless the man turned up alive in Scotland. And, if *that* happened, she'd still be the fool's wife and would have to remain so.

It had long been Jake's opinion that Sir Kentigern "Mungo" Lyle must have some idea, at least, of what had happened to Clyne. But if Mungo was Albany's man, he'd be unlikely to testify under oath to aught that might lead to more public speculation about Jamie's and Orkney's capture than Albany would tolerate.

Whatever Mungo's role was, he'd left the English ship in Bridlington harbor. In the unlikely event that the English *had* kept Clyne alive as hostage for Mungo's actions or any other reason, he could not know now if Clyne was dead or alive. The pirates' known ruthlessness, and Albany's, made it most likely that Clyne was dead.

Since well before they had neared the Firth of Forth and passed within sight of its mouth, they'd kept watch for observers and vessels that might take an interest in the *Sea Wolf.* One or two ships had passed near enough to make out their flag, but none had challenged them or drawn near enough to give Jake pause.

The rest of the day remained peaceful, and St. Andrews Castle came into sight high atop its cliff in the early evening, a half hour before they would pass beneath its walls. Now impregnable thanks to repairs and augmentations made under Bishop Traill's supervision, it was an impressive sight. If Jake's internal clock was operating with its usual accuracy, they would arrive in the bay shortly after the hour of vespers and would reach the castle before the service ended.

One of the Blackfriars or Austen Canons who served the bishop would be watching from the tall sea tower. So word of their arrival would quickly spread, and someone would likely meet them at the harbor.

Jake climbed atop the forecastle cabin to keep watch as they approached.

The sun was dipping below the western horizon, its last orange-gold light gilding the offside of the castle, leaving its seaward side in shadow.

The tide was on the ebb and would remain so for another hour or two. The wind blew steadily from the east. If it continued so overnight, he'd have it at his stern the next day as they sailed up the Firth of Tay to Perth.

Whatever it did tomorrow, they were in time for supper tonight.

"Is that St. Andrews on those cliffs ahead?"

"Aye, it is," he said, turning to smile at Alyson and her shadow, Will.

"Why are they flying two flags?" Will asked.

"They fly only the bishop's, lad. Sithee, he acts as Prelate of Scotland, which means he is first of all bishops in the land. So when he is in residence here or visits other bishoprics, his banner flies to show that he is there."

"Aye, well, I can see two o' them up there now," Will said.

Having heeded only the castle, not its details, Jake looked again and saw that the lad was right. Praying that the second banner would not be the royal one, which Albany customarily flew despite having no right to do so, he kept his eye on both banners until they were near enough to make out their colors.

When he noted the gold and white of the second one, he realized that their visit might prove even more complicated than he'd expected.

Alyson noted Jake's dismay. She noted, too, that he was striving to conceal it when he turned to Will and said, "That, my lad, is the papal banner. The Papal Legate has apparently arrived earlier than I'd expected. Come to think of it, though, Easter *is* just a fortnight away now."

"The consecration," Alyson said quietly. "We ought to have remembered."

"What's a papal legate?" Will asked.

"He acts for the Pope in other countries," Alyson explained.

"Aye," Jake agreed. "He has been visiting England and comes now to install Wardlaw formally as Bishop of St. Andrews and Prelate of Scotland."

"Did ye no ken that he'd ha' a banner o' his own?"

"In troth, I did not think about him at all," Jake admitted.

"You thought that it might be someone else's banner," Alyson said.

"Aye," Jake said.

"Whose?" Will demanded. "I ken fine that most nobles fly banners. Sir Ivor had two o' them... nay, three."

"I have seen only two, Will," Alyson said. "He flies Clan Chattan's banner when he is on confederation business. Otherwise, he flies the Mackintosh banner."

"Aye, sure, but he also flies one wi' a golden hawk on a blue background like the sky," Will said. "I saw it m'self."

When Alyson looked quizzically at Jake, he smiled. "He does fly that one when he prefers that others not identify him as a Mackintosh."

"Sakes, why—"

But Jake was shaking his head. He said, "We'll reach the harbor shortly. You will both want to tidy yourselves."

Will's eyes widened. "Ye'll no be a-leaving me here, will ye?"

"Would you not like to stay, Will?" Alyson asked. "St. Andrews has been your home now for a year, has it not?"

"Aye, sure, but that were when Jamie were here. Till he comes back, I'd liefer stay wi' Cap'n Jake. Ye did say I could," he reminded Jake.

"I remember what I said, and I meant it," Jake assured him. "But you must pay your respects to Bishop Wardlaw. He'll want to talk to you, to hear just what happened on the *Maryenknyght*. I was not there to see it, after all, and you were."

"I dinna mind telling 'im," Will said. "But I'm no a chap as wants tae become a friar or a priest. And if I stay here, them priests will press me hard tae do one or t'other. Sithee, I'm Jamie's man, now and for aye."

"We'll all be Jamie's men one day," Jake said. "But, until then, you're free to make some choices. You'd receive a fine education here, you know. It is where I got mine, and an education is always useful. But no one will force you, lad. If you want to stay with me aboard the *Sea Wolf*, you may."

"Aye, then, if we be agreed on that, I'll tidy m'self and go wi' ye tae talk tae the bishop," Will said. "He's a good chap, and I like him. But I dinna tak' much tae praying or learning Latin. Happen one day I'll change me mind, but for the noo, I'd liefer tak' the freedom o' the sea wi' ye."

Amused, Alyson glanced at Jake and saw a look nearly matching the dismay he'd revealed at seeing the papal banner.

Briefly meeting her gaze, he looked back at Will and said, "I'll expect you to speak respectfully if Bishop Wardlaw urges you to stay."

"Coo, I wouldna back-jaw him," Will said, eyes wider than ever. "But he's no a man tae tak' leather tae a chappie for saying what he thinks."

"Just mind ye dinna gang over the tow, lad, or ye'll no ha' your sorrows tae seek, for I'll visit them on ye m'self," Jake said sternly.

"I ken that fine, sir," Will said, flushing.

"Good, then go to the forecastle cabin and wash your face and hands."

"I understood about seeking his sorrows," Alyson told Jake as Will hastily obeyed him. "But not 'to gang over the tow.' Is that going beyond bounds?"

He grinned. "Aye, and 'tis what my da used to say when it meant I'd be sore for days if I disobeyed him. Da still says it occasionally when he thinks I'm taking too great a risk. And I still mind my tongue after he says it."

"Do you still obey?"

"Usually."

"But not always."

"A man has to do what a man has to do. He cannot be thinking of his father's warnings in the midst of a battle or when taking the risk provides a chance to seize victory from defeat."

"I see," she said dryly. "And what do you say afterward when he asks if you heeded his warning?"

"Victory redeems a multitude of sins, lass. No one thinks then to inquire about earlier warnings or even to recall threats he may have made."

She shook her head at him but with a near smile. "That castle grows ever nearer," she said. "I'd better follow Will's example and wash my face at least."

"Put on your pale green kirtle," he suggested. "I like it better than that blue one, so I'm sure it will find favor with Wardlaw."

She nodded. She had scarcely worn the green kirtle, because it showed dirt more easily than the darker one, so it was cleaner, too. By the time she had tidied herself and changed her dress, the men had brought the *Sea Wolf* to anchor in St. Andrews Bay and were launching the tow-boat to take them ashore.

Will banged on the door. "We be ready tae go, m'lady!"

Taking her cloak from its hook, she draped it over her shoulders and went with him to meet Jake.

Although the sun had gone down, enough dusky light remained to give Jake some concern about Alyson's walking beside him from the harbor, through the east end of town, to the castle. He said naught to her, though, assuring himself that no one was likely to recognize him or her. If anyone did recognize him, the person would likely assume that Alyson was his wife.

After tying the towboat to a jetty and telling the two oarsmen to come with them, he looked up to see a man in the familiar white surplice and black hooded cowl of the Austen Canons hurrying down the steep pathway from town. Jake recognized him as one of the priests who served at the cathedral.

"Welcome back to St. Andrews, sir," the priest said. "Bishop Wardlaw will be pleased to see ye. Forbye, ye've returned earlier than he'd expected ye."

"I have, Father Matthias," Jake said. "Thank you for meeting us."

He did not present Alyson, and if Father Matthias recognized Will or saw aught amiss in his being with Jake, the priest did not mention it.

He said only, "I'll lead the way, shall I, sir?"

Nodding, Jake offered an arm to Alyson, and they followed the priest.

"D'ye ken this legger chap yourself, Cap'n Jake?" Will asked a short time later as they approached the gate in the castle's high curtain wall.

"He is a legate, Will," Jake said patiently. "I have never met him, because Scotland has not seen a papal legate in years." He was not about to try to explain to the lad the current chaos of papal politics or Scotland's unique view of the Roman Kirk. So he added only, "If he addresses you, you may call him 'your eminence' when you reply. If you cannot remember that, just say 'sir' as you usually do."

"Dinna some people call the Pope the prince o' the Holy Kirk?"

"Aye, they do," Jake said, surprised that Will would know that.

"Jamie told me," Will explained. "We dinna even call *our* princes, princes. Jamie's nobbut the Earl o' Carrick, for all he does *be* a prince and ought tae be a duke, too, now that his brother Davy be dead. But if the Pope does truly be a prince, and this legate chap acts as Pope in Scotland, should I no call the legate 'm'lord'?"

" 'Sir' or 'eminence' will do unless he tells you otherwise."

"Good, then."

Silence fell as they passed through the wall's deep torchlit archway to the castle entrance, where Father Porter waited in the doorway with a beaming smile.

" 'Tis good to see you again, Sir Jacob, and you, too, Will, my lad. Bishop Wardlaw will receive you in his privy chamber, sir," he added. "As you may have guessed, he is not alone there."

"I did see the papal flag, Father. I will take the lady Alyson in with me, and young Will, as well. I expect you can provide these others with supper. The rest of my lads will see to themselves on the *Sea Wolf*."

"Aye, sure, sir." He glanced expectantly toward Alyson again, but Jake thought he'd said enough. He would speak to Wardlaw before issuing orders or requests on her behalf. However, Father Porter said, "One must suppose that her ladyship will want supper, too, sir."

"She will indeed, Father," Alyson said, smiling.

Abandoning what was doubtless undue caution, Jake said, "In troth, Father, she'll need more than supper. I'm hoping you know a respectable woman who might be willing to stay overnight with her here. The fact is that things are not as we'd hoped, but I must speak with Bishop Wardlaw before I say more."

"I understand, sir," Father Porter said. "I will seek to arrange for a suitable woman before we sup. Now I will take you to the bishop."

They followed him up the shallow steps to the great hall and across it to the adjoining room in the far corner that Wardlaw, like Traill before him, reserved for private matters.

Thrusting the door open after a single rap and preceding them inside, Father Porter stood back and said, "My lord, here is Sir Jacob Maxwell returned to us."

"Come in, Jake," Wardlaw said genially. "I must make you known to the Papal Legate. Father Antonio de la Luna, allow me to present Sir Jacob Maxwell, one of Bishop Traill's former students and a knight of the Scottish Realm."

Politely, Jake greeted the legate, a slender, dark-haired man of middle age dressed informally in his black surplice and a white cap. Wardlaw, too, wore his surplice and was, at present, bareheaded. He was the younger and stouter of the two.

"Father Antonio has been kind enough to come all this way to consecrate me as Bishop of St. Andrews and as Prelate," Wardlaw added.

"I thought ye was already a bishop," Will said. "Be ye *not* one then?"

Jake put a quelling hand on the boy's shoulder, but Wardlaw said, "He asks a good question, Jake. I was already Bishop of Glasgow, Will, and the Pope himself named me Bishop of St. Andrews, so I do serve in that position, too. Consecration here in Scotland will emphasize the power of the position by reminding people that the Bishop of St. Andrews is first bishop of the Scottish Kirk."

To the legate, he said, "Young Will was my student here this past year, but he has been away. I own, I did not expect you back again so soon, lad."

Feeling Will tense under the hand still on the boy's shoulder, Jake said, "We do bring news, sir. First, though, I should present to you both the lady Alyson MacGillivray of Perth. She was a passenger aboard a ship called *Maryenknyght*, as was her husband, Niall Clyne, who served as a secretary to the Earl of Orkney."

"Mercy," Wardlaw said, crossing himself. "I will own that, not having expected your return for a sennight or longer, I feared that something had gone amiss. Lady Alyson, you are welcome here at St. Andrews, although I fear that we are an all-male establishment. You and your woman will—"

"Forgive me, my lord," Jake interjected. "I should explain further, if I may." He glanced pointedly at Father Antonio.

"Aye, sure, Jake," Wardlaw said. "Whatever you say, his eminence should hear. We do not keep secrets from Holy Kirk."

"As you will," Jake said, but his thoughts tumbled over one another, and instinct warned him to tread lightly. The Holy Kirk being well-known for its own secrets and machinations, he would choose his words with care. "See you," he said, "I was on the *Sea Wolf*, and as I mentioned when last we spoke, sir, we headed south through waters some distance off the northern English coast..."

He paused long enough for Wardlaw to interject more information if he chose. When the bishop continued to gaze blandly at him, giving only the slightest of nods, as if acknowledging a previous conversation, Jake went on. "The storms that plagued the whole coastline for a fortnight before then were still fierce when my lads and I came upon a merchantman in difficulty. Pirates patrol that portion of the coast, which is—"

"Pirates!" Father Antonio exclaimed.

"Five ships, your eminence, with cannon," Jake said. "Two had flanked the *Maryenknyght*, and men boarded her and took captives whilst we watched. I should explain that my ship is a small vessel and my men and I carry only swords and dirks as arms. I doubt that, in their eagerness to assail the *Maryenknyght,* the English ships even saw us. When they left her, she was listing badly. Seeing movement aboard, we went closer, boarded her, and found the lady Alyson and young Will. The *Maryenknyght* sank soon after we rescued them."

"Were they the only ones you were able to rescue?" the legate asked.

"Aye, sir. These events occurred a mile off a point called Flamborough Head. I talked with a taverner nearby and learned that the pirates sailed for London the next morning with their captives. Forbye, he also told us they threw everyone overboard who would not fetch a great ransom in return for his release."

Crossing himself again, Wardlaw murmured, "The blessings of God be upon them and remain with them. But how many captives did they take?"

"We *know* of only two, my lord, although the ship's captain may be a third," Jake said. "They apparently threw everyone else overboard. The two that we know they kept are the owner of the *Maryenknyght* and a lad traveling in his charge."

"Prithee, who is this unfortunate owner?" the legate inquired.

"Henry Sinclair, second Earl of Orkney, your eminence."

"That young man is certainly wealthy enough to arrange for ransom," Wardlaw said. Then, forestalling further questions, he added, "We must talk more about all of this after supper. They will be serving it shortly."

The legate said mildly, "Regarding young Lady Alyson, Sir Jacob. You say that she was aboard that ship, but surely she had a duenna to bear her company."

"Her companion was captured whilst helping Lady Alyson hide from the pirates, your eminence, and fell overboard whilst attempting to cross to one of their ships. In the heaving seas, they were unable or unwilling to rescue her. Lady Alyson's husband likewise fell captive and would have fetched little ransom, if any. The English pirates are known by repute to men of that area, who told us that any man lacking wherewithal for ransom would not have made it to shore alive."

"Then you declare that, to the best of your knowledge, this woman is a widow and has been in your sole charge, aboard your ship, for nearly a fortnight. One must understand that her reputation is now at dire risk."

Relieved though Jake was that the legate had fixed his attention on Alyson's plight, rather than on demanding to know more about Orkney and his young charge, those last few words put Jake's internal warning system on full alert.

Chapter 14

Alyson stood quietly beside Jake while he talked with Bishop Wardlaw and the Papal Legate, who, despite a heavy accent, spoke Scots understandably and seemed to understand Jake and Wardlaw, too. Now, although Jake did not say a word or make any discernible movement, she felt his tension in response to the legate's words as surely as if she had been touching him.

Bishop Wardlaw must have sensed his reaction, too, because he smiled at the legate and said, "I think you will agree, Father Antonio, that we should discuss her ladyship's situation later. Forbye, I will order our supper served here. It will be more comfortable for her than our refectory would be."

"Surely, we should discuss her situation with Sir Jacob first," the legate said.

Alyson thought he looked at Jake rather sternly as he spoke. She ached to insist that she be party to any discussion that concerned her, but she knew better than to set herself against two such powerful men of the Kirk.

Jake was another matter, however. She hoped she might find a way to speak privately with him. Things were happening too quickly if his eminence expected to do something about her "situation" as fast as it seemed that he did.

Jake still had his hand on Will's shoulder. He released the boy and said to Wardlaw, "I think Will might be happier to join the men in the refectory, sir."

"He would, aye," Wardlaw said. Picking up a long-handled silver bell from his desk, he rang it, whereupon Father Porter entered, thus informing Alyson that he'd waited outside the door for such a summons.

Wardlaw said to him, "Will can accompany you as far as the lavatory, so he can wash for supper. Then he may join Sir Jacob's men in the refectory to sup. Meantime, prithee have our meal served here in this chamber. We must also make arrangements for Lady Alyson's comfort whilst she stays with us."

"Just so, my lord," Father Porter said. "I took the liberty of sending for Mistress Fenula Hyde and asked that she be prepared to join you here immediately after supper. I also ordered a cot set up for Mistress Hyde in the guest chamber that we reserve for our noble guests."

"Good," Wardlaw said, beaming. "You will like Mistress Hyde, my lady. She is the wife of one of our burghers, a capable woman and kind withal."

"Thank you, my lord," Alyson said, wishing she could demand to know what they planned for her. Did they expect her to keep this Mistress Hyde with her aboard the *Sea Wolf* when she returned to Perth, as Jake had thought might be the case? Whatever they decided, they obviously expected to ordain her fate for her, just as Will had feared they might ordain his.

She believed she could hold her own in a discussion about her future. But, since the men outnumbered her three to one and clearly meant to discuss her fate privately, and since the woman chosen to protect her was one in whom the bishop put his faith and therefore unlikely to support her, the likelihood...

Jake stepped nearer. As he did, his elbow brushed her upper arm just below her shoulder, and it was as if an electric shock went through her. Her disquiet eased, although she could not have said why it had, even to herself. Somehow, that light touch seemed to say that he would protect her or help her protect herself. And she believed in him.

So lost in thought was she that she realized Wardlaw and the legate had been murmuring to each other only when Wardlaw said, "Then that's what we'll do."

Bracing herself, she looked at them.

Wardlaw said with a smile, "His eminence desires to refresh himself before they bring our supper, my lady. If you would like to do likewise..."

"Thank you, my lord; I have no need. Sir Jacob's *Sea Wolf* boasts excellent amenities." Unless Wardlaw ordered her from the room, she would resist letting him plan her future alone with Jake. Nor would she voluntarily give the men a chance to decide that they need only fob her off on this Mistress Hyde by suggesting that the woman take her home as her guest for the night.

Wardlaw merely nodded, and when the legate had gone, the bishop asked Jake to describe more of what had happened, adding, "Keep your ears aprick for Father Antonio's return. I'd not want him to think we've been talking secrets. He may suspect as much, though. I've found most Spaniards of my acquaintance to be both secretive and suspicious that others conspire against them. I have no cause to believe that Father Antonio is of that sort. But I'd liefer learn that he is—*if* he is—without giving him more information about this matter than necessary. So the English have Jamie," he added grimly.

"They do, sir. We could do nowt to stop them."

"Nor did I mean for you to try. Orkney and I, and one or two others, did all we could to protect the lad, and succeeded for a full year. But wickedness such as this goes beyond our control. We must be thankful that Orkney is with the lad."

"Aye," Jake agreed.

As much to see if they'd let her join the discussion as because she wanted the information, Alyson said to Wardlaw, "How long do you think it will be, my lord, before they can be ransomed?"

The two men exchanged a look. As they did, a chill shot up her spine and the air in the room began to quiver. Although she remained aware of the bishop and Jake, other figures—strangers—surrounded them, passing in front of Wardlaw as they crossed either the room she was in or some more distant one. She saw Jamie then as she had last seen him. Before her eyes, he aged and grew taller.

She blinked and the air cleared as Wardlaw said gruffly, "We must hope they return quickly. But it takes time for arrangements and for messages to travel back and forth. Likewise, Albany or his grace must..." Grimacing, he fell silent.

Jake said, "Orkney has bankers in London as well as Paris, Danzig, Rome, and other cities, my lord. He won't depend on messages to and from Scotland."

"Even so," Wardlaw said. "Such an amount as the King of England will demand, especially as he'll doubtless want to reward these pirates..."

"I think someone else rewarded them, too," Jake said. "In troth, sir, I have doubts that they *were* pirates. They failed to protect the *Maryenknyght*, despite a valuable cargo of hides and wool, not to mention valuables that Henry and other passengers carried with them. Only three pirates stayed long enough to seek treasure they'd heard was aboard, and they failed. Otherwise, according to our Will, those so-called pirates took interest only in passengers, specifically in James."

Frowning, Wardlaw said, "How could Will be sure of that?"

"He was with James when the villains boarded. Their captain, according to men we met that night at an alehouse—or tavern, as they call it—near Flamborough, is one Hugh-atte-Fen out of Norfolk. His ships had been prowling the coast for a fortnight, the taverner said. But they seized no other ship."

He briefly explained how the four of them had reached the Blue Boar and the arrangements he had made before then to reunite with the *Sea Wolf.* Alyson noted that he did not mention her mimicry at the tavern but did say that Lizzie had accompanied her on their journey to meet the ship.

Wardlaw nodded and turned to Alyson, saying, " 'Twas a most discomfiting experience for you, my daughter."

"It was an adventure, sir," she said. "I saw things I had never seen before and met people I was delighted to meet. The ship's sinking was horrid, and I thank God that Sir Jacob and the *Sea Wolf* were at hand to aid Will and me."

"Art sure your husband is dead?"

"Everything says he must be, sir. People in Flamborough were sure. And I did see Mungo ride by . . . That is, I saw Orkney's secretary, Sir Kentigern Lyle, who was with us on the ship. Niall had been with him but no longer was."

"I do not know Sir Kentigern," Wardlaw said. "How is it that you saw him without inquiring about your husband?"

Jake said, "I kept her from showing herself, sir. Lyle is Orkney's chief secretary and was thus her husband's superior. He appeared to be acting as a courier. But as I said, Orkney would not require one to arrange for ransom from here. Moreover, the taverner told us that Lyle traveled under a royal safe-conduct, which can only have come from English Harry. Lyle also had an armed English escort. Thus, I believe that Lyle is Albany's man and that Albany is behind this. See you, sir, Will said the captain of that lead ship recognized James straightaway, as if he were expecting to find him aboard the *Maryenknyght*."

"Our Will saw all this?"

"Aye, my lord, he did," Jake said.

"Then I must talk to him. And I'll want to talk more with you later, Jake. We will keep our supper conversation to everyday topics. I can read Father Antonio's thoughts on this, and I do not disagree with them. However—"

"I pray you, sir," Alyson said, unable to restrain herself. She knew that he was talking about her future again. "I would, with respect—"

She broke off when Jake touched her arm.

"Someone comes," he murmured. Then, in his usual tone, he added, "So you see, my lord, our return was slow, due to the wind being against us until we reached Berwick-on-Tweed. Then, as if it knew we were home again and took no more interest in us, it shifted eastward and eased our way."

Halfway through his last sentence, Alyson heard the door behind her open quietly. Wardlaw smiled and said, "Welcome back, Father Antonio. And here is our supper coming right behind you—in good time, I think you will agree."

Jake knew that Alyson must be burning to ask some pointed questions. She was too astute not to have realized that Father Antonio was distressed about her "situation," as the slender Spaniard had called it. Hearing footsteps approaching the chamber had given Jake a chance to interject a warning.

He had faith in Wardlaw and doubted that the bishop would take offense at aught she might say. However, when they did discuss her, he knew that Wardlaw would prefer to do it without her. Jake hoped he would likewise arrange for the legate's absence from that discussion, but he had less faith that that would happen.

Two Blackfriars carried in a round table. Others covered it with a white cloth and set places for the four of them, drawing two stools from near the wall. They also moved to the table the armchairs that the bishop and the legate had occupied.

The meal was pleasant. Jake thought it might have been more so had he not known that Alyson's thoughts were flying hither and yon over what her fate would be. Briefly, after asking Wardlaw how long arranging ransoms might take, she had seemed distant. Her eyes had lost focus, and he was sure that she had trembled. The moment was so brief that he wondered now if he'd imagined it.

Nevertheless, Jake now felt as if his thoughts had

nearly merged with hers. An absurd thought, to be sure. He gave himself a mental shake and attended to the others' conversation.

He soon realized that Father Antonio must have asked Alyson to tell him about her family. She replied politely but briefly that she lived in St. John's Town of Perth with her mother, her father, her younger brother, and (on a note of humor) a host of frequently-visiting kinsmen.

"And your husband?"

"Since our marriage, your eminence, Niall has been away more than he has been home. But when he was in Perth, he stayed with my family."

The legate seemed genuinely interested. He asked if she visited the royal court when its members were resident in Perth.

"Aye, sir, sometimes."

"I understand that your lords of Parliament will meet there soon, to decide a matter of great importance."

"Aye, your eminence, to decide if the Duke of Albany will govern again."

The conversation continued politely. But Jake could see that her heart was not in it, and he did not blame her.

The meal was nearly over when Father Porter thrust open the door after his usual rap and ushered in a thin woman of indeterminate years dressed in a bright yellow gown with colorfully embroidered bands at neck, sleeves, and hem.

"My lord, your eminence, Mistress Hyde has arrived."

Wardlaw rose to greet her with his cheerful smile, and everyone else stood when he did. "It is my pleasure to welcome you, mistress," the bishop said. "As Father Porter explained, Lady Alyson MacGillivray of Perth has come to us unexpectedly and bereft of her attire woman. She will stay the night and depart for her home in the morning."

"'Twill be a pleasure tae bear her ladyship company, m'lord," Mistress Hyde said. Curtsying to Alyson, she added, "It be an honor tae meet ye, m'lady. I ken MacGillivray House in St. John's Town. Be that your home?"

Alyson nodded and smiled as she assured her that it was, giving Jake hope that she and Mistress Hyde would get on well together.

Wardlaw said, "If you have finished your meal, my daughter, you may go with Mistress Hyde and Father Porter now. Sir Jacob's man took your bundle up for you. And Mistress Hyde has doubtless brought what she will need. Sleep well, and we'll see you on your way again in the morning."

Visibly dismayed, Alyson turned to Jake.

"All will be well," he said.

Wardlaw, looking from Alyson to Jake, said, "I must discuss this matter with Father Antonio before he retires, Jake. He is wont to do so much earlier than I. Perhaps you will escort her ladyship and Mistress Hyde upstairs to see that they have all they require. You will doubtless recall your way to the sea tower."

"I do, indeed, sir," Jake said.

"I'll see you when you return," Wardlaw said. "Bring Will with you."

~

Mistress Hyde prattled as they went upstairs from the hall landing, but Alyson listened with only half an ear. She was more aware of Jake ascending the stairs behind them. Mistress Hyde had lived her whole life in St. Andrews and exclaimed enthusiastically over the many improvements that the late Bishop Traill had made to the castle while restoring it.

"The curtain wall were off-putting tae them wha' live nearby, as ye might imagine," she said as she rounded the first curve. "But that wall, along wi' this great tower and the new kitchen one, do much tae block wind off the sea. Our gardens be more welcoming in the spring now. D'ye like tae plant things, m'lady?"

"We get wind off the sea in Perth, too, so we plant flowers where hedges will protect them," Alyson said. Glancing back at Jake, whose eyes were twinkling, she tried to imagine how they might talk privately.

"Here we be," Mistress Hyde said, opening a door at the next landing. "There be me own things and likely yours, as well."

"If you don't mind, Mistress Hyde, I would like a word with Sir Jacob. I won't be a moment, and I'll leave the door ajar."

"Sakes, m'lady, I've nae objection. I ken fine that I be here tae mak' all look well. Also, I expect, because our bishop kens fine that I dinna ha' a tongue hinged in the middle, as ye might say. Even did I hear ye, I'd say nowt of it."

"Thank you," Alyson said, drawing the door to a crack between them. Then, turning to Jake, she found him grinning. "Mercy," she murmured. "She makes me feel guilty when I've done naught to make me feel so."

"She has the gift," Jake murmured back. "Many women have it. I vow, Giff MacLennan's mam has only to look at a chap to make him recall every bit of mischief he has committed in his life."

"Are there so many?"

He chuckled. "What would you say to me, lass? We'd best be quick."

For a moment, she was at a loss. She had wanted to tell him about the odd thing that happened when the air had seemed to quiver and give her a peek at things to come. But she could not talk about that, lest Mistress Hyde be more curious than she had admitted.

So, Alyson said, "I don't know Bishop Wardlaw, sir. And I do not know Father Antonio. I'd liefer that neither one make decisions on my behalf."

"I know, lass, and I'll do all I can to head them off. They are primarily concerned about your reputation, about word somehow getting around to all and sundry that you came home on my ship without a female companion. If I can persuade them that young Will can attest to your innocence with similar integrity and that none of my lads will say aught of you to anyone, it may ease their minds. But now I must go or that blasted legate will send a priest to fetch me."

"Aye, sure," she said. But she felt as if he were abandoning her.

"Behear the lass," Jake muttered. "I tell ye, this be nobbut trittle-trattle and nowt tae curdle your innards. Bide your time, Allie. Things'll sort theirselves out."

She smiled then and relaxed a little. "I just wish I could be there."

"Nay, ye don't. Nor will our Will when I tell him he's wanted. But between us, lass, we'll see you home again. And one way or t'other, all *will* be well."

She nodded, but for once, she did not quite believe him. She could hear Mistress Hyde humming, though, and knew she should linger no longer.

Jake waited until Alyson was inside the room. As he turned to go downstairs, he heard Mistress Hyde say, "I must say, one could wish for a good solid bolt on that door instead o' that slippy latch."

"In a castle full of priests?" Alyson replied. "I think we are safe."

Although he smiled, his thoughts were busy. He'd sensed her reluctance to trust him and knew she had reason. He just hoped he could prove her wrong.

Finding Will in the refectory, facing Mace across a chessboard, Jake was amused to see that the lad was trying to teach Mace the rudiments of dames.

"An ye get tae this piece o' mine, ye jump right over and tak' him, so," Will said as Mace looked up and saw Jake approaching.

"I hope ye've come tae rescue me, Cap'n," the burly oarsman said. "The lad here must think I've got nowt but straw betwixt me ears."

"I think nowt o' the sort," Will said. "If ye'd attend tae me—"

"Never mind that now," Jake said. "The bishop wants to talk with you, Will. I'm to take you to him straightaway."

Paling, Will said, "Nay, then! I tellt ye, I'm no a-going tae be a priest."

"Forbye, you'll come along with me now, because Bishop Wardlaw commanded it. So now do I."

"Aye, well, I'm a-going then," Will said, getting up. "But only 'cause I think ye're a man o' your word."

"I am, aye," Jake said. "And I give you my word that

I'll put you over my knee if I hear more of your back-chat tonight."

Will glanced back at him, just as Jake exchanged a grin with Mace.

The boy relaxed, and Jake said, "Lead on, lad."

Father Matthias sat by the door into the bishop's privy chamber. When he saw them crossing the hall, he stood and beckoned them forward. "His reverence is alone now, Sir Jacob. He said to go right in, ye and the lad."

"Thank you, Father," Jake said. He rapped twice. Hearing Wardlaw's command to enter, he opened the door and gestured for Will to precede him.

The lad squared his shoulders as if he expected to meet trouble. Then he strode into the chamber, bobbed a slight bow, and said, "Ye sent for us, sir."

"I did, Will. I want you to tell me what you saw aboard the *Maryenknyght* when the pirates boarded her. I've seen in the past that you have a noticing eye, so I expect you noted details that may help us understand all that happened."

"What happened were that them devils stole our Jamie," Will said.

"A dreadful thing, aye. So take that stool, laddie, and tell me all you saw."

As Will obeyed, Jake drew another stool up behind the boy and sat down to listen. As far as he could tell, Will described events for the bishop just as he'd described them before. Jake realized he should have asked Mace if he and Will had talked about the pirates after seeing Lizzie Thornwick to her kinsmen. But a second thought assured him that Mace would have reported anything new he'd heard.

Will also described the attack of the three pirates after Jake and Mace had found him and Alyson. Enjoying Wardlaw's barely concealed amusement at the boy's assurances that Jake and Mace had "finished them villains off in a trice," Jake did not amend or correct anything the boy said.

When Will finished, Wardlaw asked him a few questions, then dismissed him, saying, "You were a brave lad to rescue Lady Alyson, Will. I'm proud of you."

"Aye, good, then. I thought ye might be vexed that I let them get our Jamie."

"It was beyond your power to prevent that, Will. Moreover, I'll wager that he feared for your safety as much as you do for his. You were right to obey him when he told you to help her ladyship. You'd have been right to do that in any event."

"What d'ye mean?"

Wardlaw glanced at Jake with a slightly raised eyebrow.

Understanding that he was loath to tell Will the truth if Jake thought it would distress the lad, Jake said, "Do you recall what the pirates did to men who could not fetch a great ransom and to those who did not quickly obey them, Will?"

"Aye, sure," Will said. "We *saw* what they did." He looked at the bishop. "I'd fetch nae ransom at all. Be ye thinking they'd ha' done that tae me?"

Wardlaw said, "If Jamie saw them throw men overboard, I'm thinking that he feared such a thing might happen to you, aye."

"Coo," Will said. "But mayhap Jamie saw the *Sea Wolf* a-coming. He might ha' done, whilst I watched for Lady

Alyson or after I slipped away. Sithee, I dinna think he'd ha' left me tae drown."

"I'm just glad you slipped away," Jake said. "Had you not, Lady Alyson would certainly have drowned. You saved her life, Will."

"Aye, well, ye helped some."

"Only after you freed her from that kist," Jake said. "Had I not seen her at the rail, we'd have turned away when we saw how badly the ship was listing."

"Aye, well, ye might ha' seen them other louts," Will said.

"Perhaps, but I'd have seen three men with a coble on deck. I'd have expected them to launch it and would not have risked boarding the ship."

"You did well, lad," Bishop Wardlaw said. "Do you mean to stay with us here at St. Andrews, or have you another plan?"

With an audible sigh of relief, Will said, "I mean tae stay wi' Cap'n Jake, sir. I take better tae the freedom o' the sea than tae reading and such."

Exchanging another look with Jake, who nodded, Wardlaw said, "Then I wish you well. You will always have a home here if you need one, Will, and will ever be a welcome visitor whilst I remain Bishop of St. Andrews."

Flushing deeply, Will thanked him and made good his escape.

"Draw that stool closer, Jake," Wardlaw said when the boy had shut the door. Reaching for a pitcher, the bishop filled two goblets with what looked like good claret and handed one to Jake.

"We'll drink to your safe return, lad. Traill warned me that, having spent much time with Giff MacLennan, you had a tendency to share his love of risk-taking. I'll admit that concerned me."

"I don't mind taking a risk when it might lead to success, sir," Jake said. "But I'm no fool."

"No, you're not. But you may have landed in the suds, nonetheless."

The internal tickle of warning that had followed Father Antonio's concern for Alyson's reputation stirred again but included a deeper, warmer sensation that Jake could not interpret.

He managed to say calmly, "How so?"

"Lady Alyson has powerful kinsmen, many of whom I know," Wardlaw said. "I met her father years ago in Glasgow, and I assure you that if Lord Farigaig were the same man today, he would demand the honorable course."

"Truly, sir, there can be nowt to demand. I merely rescued her. As the lad's tale surely made clear, she came to no harm."

"Her uncle Shaw is the war leader of Clan Chattan, Jake. His good-father is the Mackintosh himself, Captain of that powerful confederation. The last thing you'd want is to draw *their* ire. But it gets worse, because Shaw's daughter married Sir Finlagh Cameron, whose brother is a chieftain in the great Cameron confederation of Lochaber. Sithee, lad, Father Antonio likely speaks for the MacGillivrays and Camerons when he says you must marry her."

Chapter 15

Mistress Hyde having no objection to Alyson's suggestion that they retire at once, Alyson now lay awake. She listened to the waves crashing below her window and watched as moonlight peeked through spaces between the shutters.

Had she been alone, she would have opened those shutters to admit the moonlight. But when she had opened one earlier to look outside, Mistress Hyde had earnestly exclaimed that the night air might make them ill, so she'd shut it again.

Rising over the sea, the moon was nearly full and had been low enough to be huge and to cast a wide silvery path across the water. The frothy sea surged around two sides of the point from which the castle overlooked the mouth of St. Andrews Bay. The view had been splendid. She would have enjoyed savoring it longer.

Instead, she lay and thought about Jake and what might be happening downstairs in the bishop's chamber. Wardlaw had seemed to be a sensible man and had behaved so while she was in the room, giving her cause to hope that her instinctive impression of him was the correct one.

Remembering the odd hallucination that she had

endured earlier, she decided that it might have been a spell of dizziness. She had not liked to admit it, but her legs had felt strange to her. After being so long on the ship, she had felt as if the land now rolled and tilted just as the ship had.

The feeling had passed before she came upstairs. However, she was not sure of exactly when it had faded. It might still have been in effect when she'd imagined seeing Jamie change from a boy to a young man. She had been worrying about him, after all, wondering how long it would take to bring him home. Most likely, that worry had led her mind to mislead her.

Mistress Hyde began to snore. First, she snuffled gently, almost a kitten's purr. But the noise soon altered to a rumbly sound. Then it was as if the woman stopped breathing. Just as Alyson had been about to leap up to see if something had gone amiss, Mistress Hyde erupted into sound again with a raucous snort.

After that, it settled into the kitten's purr again. Alyson was wondering curiously what would come next when sleep overcame her.

After Wardlaw's observation that the Papal Legate had said Jake must marry Alyson and that the MacGillivray family would agree with him, a speechless Jake had stared in shock at the bishop, wondering if his ears had deceived him.

"*Must* marry her? Is that what he said, my lord? Because if he did, he *and* you have forgotten one important detail. Her ladyship *has* married. Although we do believe that her husband is dead, we have no proof of it.

So a chance does exist, however unlikely, that he may *not* be dead."

"And so I told Father Antonio, aye," Wardlaw said. "Her ladyship may well be a widow, but at present she is ineligible to remarry. Moreover, her kinsmen are unlikely to approve of any hasty marriage. Give the good father credit, though. He seeks to protect her from unkind—even vicious—gossip that would, of a necessity, include your actions as well as hers, Jake. 'Tis an unfortunate situation."

"It will become more than that," Jake muttered. "What a hell she will live in, sir. As a widow without proof of her husband's death, she'll have no rights over her own estates unless her father can alter her marriage settlements without her husband's signature. Moreover, if by some miracle of God, Clyne does still live and is captive in England, he could remain there for decades. At least, when we do hear from Orkney, we may learn something about Clyne's fate."

"It may be some time though before Orkney can send us a message, especially if he can arrange in London to pay his own ransom."

"Aye, *and* if English Harry tells him he's already sent to inform Albany or his grace, or both, of James's capture," Jake said.

"'Tis plain that you care deeply about this matter, my son."

"I do, sir, aye. Anyone would. Jamie is but a lad, yet he is a pawn in a gey dangerous game of 'who shall be King of Scots?' The lady Alyson is in a similar position, trapped by her marriage into a life that no woman should endure."

"Trapped?"

"In widowhood, aye," Jake said. "And, in her case, 'tis doubly bad, because her marriage was—" He broke off, realizing that he had already said too much, that the rest was Alyson's business and no one else's.

"There was something amiss with her marriage?"

Meeting the bishop's expectant gaze and wishing that he had caught himself sooner, Jake said, "I should not have said that. The tale is not mine to tell."

"Is it Lady Alyson's tale, then?"

"Aye, for it concerns her and her alone."

"Art sure, lad?" Wardlaw paused thoughtfully. "Will she tell me her tale?"

Jake shook his head. "Nay, I am sure she would not, which is why I *should* not. In troth, sir, I doubt that she completely understands her situation."

"Then I think you must tell me. You may be doing her more harm than good if you do not. Mayhap the telling will flow more easily if you think of it in terms of confession. I'd wager that it has been some time since your last one."

Jake was trying to collect his wits and finding it strangely hard to do so. Somehow, Father Antonio had got the notion that he, Jake, ought to marry Alyson. And the fact that a priest thought for even a moment that it *might* be possible was stirring feelings, even thoughts, in him that he had not expected to feel or think.

He had not expected the thought of marrying *any*one to stir them at all.

The possibility that he might *have* to marry was terrifying. How could he feel good about a possible marriage to her when he knew that he would fight buckle and thong to retain the freedom he loved so fiercely? Even if he could marry her—

Sakes, just thinking the half-thought had sent enough fire through his loins to stiffen his cock and make him hope that the sharp-eyed Wardlaw would not notice.

Aye, well, that part of him sought attention wherever it might find it. But what a devilish husband he would make for Alyson! She had already suffered a bad one and did not need another. Clyne had been off and about more than he had been in her bed. The only thing Jake knew that *he* could promise was that if he was ever *in* her bed, he would make good use of his time there!

Realizing that Wardlaw was patiently waiting, certainly more patiently than the bristly Traill would have waited, Jake collected his wits and said grimly, "It has been nearly a year since my last confession."

"Would you like more wine, lad? I see no reason to seek out a confessional unless you would be more comfortable inside one than here."

"This is fine, sir."

"Then tell me about Lady Alyson's marriage."

Jake did so, finding it easier than he'd expected to tell Wardlaw what he knew. In fact, when Wardlaw reacted with anger as grim as what Jake had felt—and felt again in the telling—at learning that Clyne had not consummated his marriage, Jake felt a sudden closer kinship with the bishop.

"Clyne was clearly daft, sir," he said when he'd finished.

"He was more than a fool; he was wicked," Wardlaw said tersely. "Any man who fails to consummate his union in three months of marriage is *not* married in the eyes of the Kirk, my son. But tell me, how do you know this to be true? Surely, her ladyship did not tell you! And surely you did not—"

Breaking off, he scowled at Jake long enough to make him feel uneasy. But he met that gimlet gaze steadily until Wardlaw said, "Have you aught else of your own to confess?"

"Nowt except evil thoughts toward Clyne and those pirates, sir, and a few lustful thoughts and two lustful dreams about Lady Alyson," Jake said, grateful that his conscience was clear on that head. "She did not exactly confide to me his failure to consummate. The taverner's daughter I mentioned is a widow, and she took Alyson's likely widowhood as a sign that they had much in common. Lizzie spoke frankly to her, and Alyson did confide things that Lizzie had said. See you, she did not understand them and thought that I might."

"I see."

"Lizzie had also caused her to think that her marriage might not have been as it should be. I admit that I did ask her some blunt questions then."

"Often the best way to get frank answers," Wardlaw said. "I do the same thing myself. More wine now, lad?"

Nodding, Jake held out his goblet as he said, "That is when I learned that she is still a maiden, sir. When I expressed doubt that she completely understands her situation, I meant that she does not realize all that it may mean to her if God *has* worked a miracle and Clyne does come home."

"I have never believed that keeping women in ignorance of such matters is good," the bishop said. "Forbye, my lad, I may see a way out of this now. It would require my sharing with Father Antonio some of what you have confided to me, and I would need your permission to do that. The rules of confession will also bind him, though. You need not worry about any details going farther."

"If the Kirk can help her out of this mess, sir, I can have no objection."

"Aye, well, you might, though. This information will not change his mind about your part in her situation, innocent though it may be. He will continue to see the matter as he did before and will likely demand the same resolution, and at once.

"In any event, you must take word of James's capture to his grace at Rothesay Castle, as soon as possible after you take her ladyship home," he added. "But you must not abandon her to her family's inquisition or displeasure. You must damp down any such reaction before you leave her at MacGillivray House."

Jake fell silent again, digesting Wardlaw's words. The anger he had felt as he'd told Alyson's story remained strong. It edged his voice when he said, "His eminence would not say aught to her about his knowing the truth, would he?"

"He would not. He'll have much to say to you, though. In fact, he will believe his case is stronger when he learns she is still a maiden. You'd be doing a good thing, Jake. Moreover, 'tis plain that you care about Alyson."

"My feelings matter not a whit, sir. See you, Alyson knows as well as I do that she is a married woman, widow or not. She will strongly resist such a solution. In any event, she can do nowt without proof of Clyne's death."

"That is not so," Wardlaw said. "Alyson can request an annulment now. But neither I nor his eminence should ask such a thing of her."

"Then I do not see—"

"You must do it, Jake. In troth, since our good Lord put you in position to rescue her ladyship, your knightly sense of honor and duty must forbid you to abandon her now. We can arrange it all tomorrow, but you must explain the matter to her first thing in the morning and persuade her to request the annulment."

Stunned, Jake swiftly collected his wits to say, "Even if I could persuade her, sir, annulments take months, even years, to acquire."

"Let me explain," Wardlaw said.

Loud snores drew Alyson from another discomfiting dream of Albany, this time facing his grace. Its details faded so swiftly in the din rumbling through the room that she could remember almost none of them. Just as she decided that she had had all the sleep she was going to get that night, the snoring ceased.

Moments later, she was deep in dreamless slumber.

Jake's mind was still reeling at the bishop's plan when he left Wardlaw's privy chamber and headed for the sea tower. He wondered why he had not fought harder against it. Climbing to the top of the stairs, he entered the tower room, a place reserved for meditation and prayer. Unlike most such places, it boasted windows on all sides, overlooking moonlit land- and seascapes.

Opening the easternmost window wide, Jake gazed out at bright moonlight on endless water. For a long, tense moment, he felt his freedom slipping away.

Drawing a deep breath and letting it out, he felt the tension ease. He recalled too that Giff MacLennan's lady wife never objected to his times away but accepted them as Giff's way of life. Alyson had accepted Clyne's absences. So—

Cutting that thought off when a surge of loathing shot through him at the comparison of himself to Niall Clyne, he shut his eyes to the splendid view and looked inward instead. It took but a short look to realize that he'd do better to talk with Alyson before imagining *his* life with or without her.

Decision made, he wanted to get it done. But one could hardly demand audience with a woman who was sound asleep in her bedchamber.

Then, in the back of his mind, the mutterer assumed Giff's familiar voice to say with a touch of wry amusement, "Reck not!"

The large, warm hand covering Alyson's mouth stifled her cry of alarm when she stiffened and opened her eyes. But she relaxed when she recognized Jake's voice murmuring, "Dinna squeak again, lass. 'Tis only me."

In the background, she heard Mistress Hyde snoring.

Enough moonlight slipped through the shutters to let her see Jake's face peering into hers. He took his hand from her mouth, letting her whisper, "What are you *doing* in here?"

Moonlight gleamed on his teeth when he grinned. "I've come to fetch you, lass. We must talk."

"Sakes, where could we go without meeting anyone?"

"I know a place. You'll like it."

"I'm in my shift."

"Where's your cloak?"

"On a hook by the door."

He moved away without a sound and came back with her cloak. With Mistress Hyde's snorts and snuffles filling the air, Alyson thought it was a wonder that she'd been able to hear what Jake had said to her.

He held up her cloak, opened toward her, providing a screen between them.

Sitting up and throwing back the coverlet, she swung her legs out and stood, shoving her feet into the slippers that she had put beside the bed. Then she turned her back to let Jake drape the cloak over her shoulders. Pulling it closed in front, she held it so when she turned to face him.

After a glance at the other bed, he guided her toward the door with a hand to her shoulder. Leaning forward, he opened the door, urged her to the landing, and gestured upward. She nodded but waited for him to shut the door.

As he did, he put a finger to his lips.

Two landings stood between them and Jake's objective.

He did not know who might be sleeping in those rooms, but Father Antonio was likely in one. The thought of the Papal Legate being just a door's thickness away from them stirred Jake's sense of mischief and recalled to his mind several incidents of such foolery that had enlivened his boyhood days at St. Andrews.

They reached the tower room without incident, and when they entered to find it ablaze in moonlight, he knew from her reaction that he had chosen well.

"Oh, it is beautiful here," she said, moving to the window. "May I open it?"

"Aye, sure, if you won't freeze."

"My cloak is warm," she said, unlatching the window and pushing it open.

He had seen enough as he'd held the cloak for her to know that she wore nothing under her loose shift. The renewed image of thin cambric over soft breasts increased his yearning for her. But it was no time to indulge such yearnings. What lay ahead was bound to be difficult. But it was necessary.

"I am glad to have seen this view," she said, turning back to him. "We should not be here, though. It is wrong."

"I promise you, lass, I have no mischief in mind other than what I've already wrought. Wardlaw persuaded me to speak to you."

"Bishop Wardlaw? Nay, then, how can I believe that? He'd never send you to my bedchamber, sir. You should be—"

"—ashamed of myself? Aye, so I should be, but I'm not. Wardlaw did tell me to talk to you. He did say that I should do so in the morning. But with such a conversation awaiting us, I knew I'd never sleep. Moreover, I could not imagine how we could have such a conversation without others either overhearing every word or at least knowing that we'd closeted together to talk privily. Coming here at once seemed better to me. I did not expect it to be so easy to approach you, though. That woman must wake her neighbors at home."

"She does snore, but I fell asleep despite her and had—Faith, I remember now, I dreamed of Albany talking to his grace. Wednesday night I dreamed of him with Mungo, mayhap talking secrets."

"I expect that they *have* met by now," he said, aware that he was dithering and should not be. "Do you think it was the Sight, lass? What did they say?"

"I could not hear them. Both were likely just dreams, though. Incidents of the Sight are more disturbingly memorable. Even if one begins as a dream, I awaken shaking—often with tears streaming down my cheeks, as I did when I saw Davy's death and those of my brothers."

"Did you feel so after you saw me slumped against that wall?"

"I felt shaken; that's all. A more dismaying thing happened today, though."

"Whilst we talked with Wardlaw, aye," he said, remembering. "It felt to me as if you left us for a moment. It was brief, though, no more than an eye-blink."

Alyson stared at him. "Truly? It seemed longer to me. It happened after I asked him how long it would take to ransom Henry and Jamie. The air began to quiver. Then I saw an opulent chamber and Jamie changing from a child to a man."

"You *have* been worried about him and fretting over his capture."

"Aye, and I still felt a bit dizzy, too. I did not say anything to you, but when we stepped onto the shore my legs felt like someone else's. I'd put a foot down, and the land would surge up to meet it. Or else the ground would seem to fall away just as I thought I'd put my foot down far enough to touch it."

He smiled and shook his head. "You had not got your land legs back yet. I feel that way, too, lass. All sailors do, but we recover quickly. Folks who are unaccustomed to boats take longer, just as they take longer to get their sea legs."

"I thought being dizzy might have stirred my imagination to produce that image," she explained. "But it is still clear in my head. Surely, the King of England would not dare to hold Jamie for so long."

"How could he, lass?" Jake asked. "If heads of state take captives but do not honor the customary methods of ransom and return, how could they trust their counterparts to honor them in turn? Moreover, James will be King of Scots long before he is grown. His grace's health has steadily declined since the Queen's death. If he lasts another year, he'll surprise everyone who knows him."

"But it is Albany, not his grace, who will negotiate Jamie's return," she reminded him. "And Albany is unlikely to press hard for it."

"You are right," he said. "He just wants to bring his son Murdoch home. In troth, I become more convinced each day that Jamie's capture was Albany's way of paying English Harry to release Murdoch. If his grace dies, and Harry keeps Jamie, Albany will also expect to continue ruling Scotland as Governor."

Alyson sighed. Sadly, his words reinforced her belief in her "dream." Collecting herself, she said, "You said that Bishop Wardlaw had commanded you to speak to me. Surely, it was not to talk of Jamie, so what were you to say to me?"

"The Papal Legate says I must marry you," he said. "Wardlaw agrees."

She stared again but blindly this time, her emotions suspended.

Jake had been thinking that the way the moonlight touched her eyes made them look like jewels—and like expensive jewels, at that. To forestall further such thoughts, he had spoken more bluntly than he'd intended.

Now her eyes looked glazed, expressionless. But she recovered swiftly.

"You must be teasing, and that is unkind," she said. "You know I cannot marry again unless I can prove that I'm a widow. *They* must know that, as well."

"I thought the same thing, lass. But I did something—revealed something—that I fear will vex you sorely. In troth, that's why I knew I'd not sleep unless I came and talked to you straightaway."

"But what have you done? I don't believe you'd do or say aught to harm me."

"Not harm you, no." He drew a breath, let it out, and said, "I told Wardlaw more than I should have about your marriage to Clyne. By my troth, though, he gave me little choice in the matter and said I should think of it as confession."

A frown disturbed the smoothness of her brow. She said, "My marriage was no secret. So you must mean that you told him of our conversation when I asked you about things Lizzie said to me."

"Aye, and I would *not* have told him. But he had been describing to me how your kinsmen will likely view our journey here together. He even invoked the image of your uncle, Shaw MacGillivray, as war leader of Clan Chattan."

"Uncle Shaw is Ivor's father, so I warrant you've heard

much of him before now. I doubt that he would blame you for rescuing me. Nor would Ivor."

"In troth, lass, they do not worry me. But I do agree with Wardlaw that, as a woman ignorant of whether her husband is dead or alive, your life would be unpleasant. That is not all I said to him, however."

"What else?"

"I told him that Clyne failed to consummate your marriage. To my astonishment, he said that that alone gives you cause to request an annulment."

"Mercy, how can that be? A priest married us. There are marriage settlements, agreements, a proper marriage record!"

"Wardlaw said that no man who fails to consummate his union in three months of marriage *is* married in the eyes of the Kirk."

"But if, by a miracle of God, Niall *is* alive and *does* come back..."

"Even then..." He paused to consider his next words. Then he said gently, "Allie, the fact that he failed to consummate his marriage with you, a beautiful woman he had known from her girlhood, tells me that he... that he was..."

"That I did not appeal to him," she said sadly when he paused. "That he felt none of the feelings for me that Lizzie described or..." Pausing, she looked away.

"That is true, aye," Jake said, forcing away the fury he felt again toward Clyne. "The man was daft. I swear to you, lass, your beauty and spirit would stir feelings in any real man. But tell me this. Did Clyne stir *your* feelings?"

The moonlight was bright enough to reveal the color that flooded her cheeks. She nibbled her lower lip in the way that made Jake want to order her to stop lest she stir his feelings more than was safe for either of them. But he held his tongue and ignored other, more urgent parts of his body, even when she looked away again.

Then she turned back, and to his surprise her gaze revealed wistful humor. "You do not deserve that I should tell you this, sir. But you like candor, so I will be honest. Niall never made me feel what you can make me feel just by looking at me. As for when you smile at me, or tease me, or touch me—"

"Stop, lass, have mercy! You do answer me, but this is serious. Whilst I would be fain to test your words, we must sort this out before that can be."

"There is naught to sort. I *am* married. Even if I wanted an annulment—"

"There *is* a way if you will agree," he interjected. "You have more cause to do so than you may think, too, if you will just let me explain."

"I will listen to whatever you want to say to me."

"Sithee, what I am trying to say is that if a woman marries a man who lacks interest in coupling with her, she risks never becoming a mother. I have seen you with Will, lass, and I've heard how you talk about Jamie. You would be hard pressed to persuade me that you do *not* want bairns of your own."

"But Niall said that he wants them, too."

"Words," Jake said scornfully. "I thought he was daft to leave you alone so much, because if you were my—" He stopped short, amazed at what he had nearly, and so easily, said to her.

Her head came up sharply. "Sakes, *don't* tell me that you would not be away as much as he was, Jake Maxwell!

You've told me too often how much you value your freedom to ply the seas. You would always prefer shipboard life to life ashore, you said. You have said it so often, in fact, that Will now says it, too!"

"I have, aye," he said, wondering why those words tasted like ashes in his mouth as he said them. His sentiments about life ashore were unchanged. Of that he was sure. He would need only a few days away from the *Sea Wolf* to be aching for the sea. Rallying, he said, "Even so, lass, many women spend months at a time without their husbands at home, especially if the men are knights, warriors, or men of the sea. Giff MacLennan's lady wife is one such. You would like her, I trow."

"Mayhap I would," she said evenly. "But..."

Seizing on the pause, he said, "You do want children, don't you?"

"Aye, sure," she said. "But we can think more about this, because—"

"Nay, we cannot," Jake interjected. "Sithee, Father Antonio wants to protect you as much as he can from the gossips. He and Wardlaw both say you have good cause to annul your marriage at once. As soon as it is done, you can marry again."

"At once? But how can that be? One must send all the way to Rome, to gain the Pope's permission for an annulment."

"Not when we have a papal legate right here," Jake said. "Father Antonio wields all of the Pope's powers, including the right to annul marriages and perform them. Wardlaw told me that we can attend to it all in the morning."

Alyson's mouth dropped open, and the color fled from her cheeks.

Chapter 16

Alyson turned back toward the open window. She dared not speak, fearing that anything she might say would break the spell that had engulfed the pair of them in that magical room so ablaze with moonlight.

Looking out, she saw the moon, brightly white, spilling its light not in a pathway but over a vast silvery sea. Waves rolled in wearing crests of white lace. The water glistened and seemed to go on eastward forever.

How that water must beckon to Jake!

Another thought stirred, chilling her. Without turning toward him, she said, "You told me that the legate said we *must* marry. Did you tell him about me, too?"

When he did not answer at once, she bit her lip, remembered what he'd said about biting it, and drew a deep breath. Then she said flatly, "You did tell him."

"Nay, lass. But he will know by morning, because Wardlaw said that he should know and I agreed. The rules of the confessional forbid either priest to repeat what he knows to anyone else."

"So the bishop would not be telling Father Antonio had you not agreed to it."

"He would not. And if you object to his knowing, I'll

sit outside the bishop's door until he emerges in the morning and tell him I've changed my mind."

Somehow, the fact that he could so quickly agree to do that depressed her as much as it reassured her.

"Before I do, though," he added, "I want you to look at me and tell me that you dislike the very notion of a marriage between us."

"It is not what I want that concerns me," she said, turning and looking him in the eye. "It is whether *you* could ever want any marriage at all."

"I know what I've said in the past, Allie. And I know how I feel about you. I cannot promise that I'll make you the best of husbands, but I will promise to try. Forbye, I'm sure that I'll be a better one than Clyne. By my troth, lass, I *can* tell you that I want you... more, I think, than I have ever wanted anything in my life."

With that, he put gentle hands to her shoulders, drew her closer, and when she continued to gaze at him, he kissed her softly on the lips.

Heat rushed through her, and her arms slid around him, drawing him tightly to her. She felt his body stir against hers. Then one of his hands clutched her hair, lacing fingers through it and cradling her head while he kissed her thoroughly.

Without thought on her part, her mouth opened to his, although Niall had never kissed her so. When Jake's tongue darted inside, hers welcomed it, delighting her and sending shockwaves of pleasure through her.

His free hand moved confidently over her body, exploring its curves and cupping her bottom cheeks, pressing her closer, letting her feel again the urgent movement of his body against hers.

Her hands had moved, too, although she was unaware of that at first. She placed one daringly on his backside to see if he'd allow it. When he made a sound deep in his throat, she pressed harder and smiled against his mouth.

He stopped kissing to look at her. Then he smiled, too. "That is enough of that," he said. "If we continue much longer, you will not be able to look Father Antonio in the eye and declare yourself a maiden. But when you return to bed, lass, think about what I've said to you. I do want to marry you if you'll agree to it, and I'll do my best to make you a good husband."

She could ask no more of him than that. She was as sure as she could be, though, that he would not give up his beloved freedom for any wife. If she saw him more than a few weeks out of a year, she supposed she would be lucky.

That disagreed with her new belief in what a marriage should be and with her desire for his caresses. But it *would* be better than what she'd had with Niall. A few weeks of the year with Jake would be more interesting—and more exciting—than a lifetime with Niall would have been.

She continued to feel sorrow for Niall's death. She also knew, despite Jake's assurances, that she was more willing to marry him than he was to marry her. Where, she wondered, might such disparity of feelings lead, especially if a man felt free to roam? Would he feel free to do other things, too?

She had looked away to think. Now, she looked back and saw that he was watching her closely.

"You're having second thoughts," he said.

"I have not told you what my first thoughts are."

"Aye, but I could see them, lass—and feel them, too, in

your kisses and in the way your body responded to mine. You wanted me as much as I want you. But now you sense a conflict, doubtless in my love of freedom."

Solemnly, she said, "I won't seek to confine you against your will, sir. In troth, though, I am uncertain of my feelings in the face of yours."

"How is that?"

"Sithee, I married Niall so I'd have a home of my own where I could escape my family's incessant demands. I had always liked him. So when he expressed his desire to marry me, I decided that marriage to someone I liked would be better than one to a stranger that my father or brother might choose for me."

"I expect it would be," he said doubtfully.

"Aye, but now I fear that I might accept you for the same reason or to satisfy the bishop and his eminence. You said they'd anticipated my family's reaction, and I must say that the thought of telling my great-aunt Beatha, in particular, that I've annulled my marriage to Niall to marry you without even knowing for sure that he's dead..." She shuddered. "Moreover, if gossips would talk of our *journey*, sir, would they not say worse of our marrying?"

"How long do you think that such people or your family would expect you to wait for Niall?" he asked quietly.

She considered her answer carefully. "I think most of them would expect me to wait as long as it takes," she said at last. "That has been my own expectation. Practically speaking, I think it would depend on how soon my brother Ranald marries. Since I own estates to which I might remove, I doubt that his wife, when he has one, will welcome my presence at MacGillivray House. But my kinsmen would all object to my living on those estates without a husband to protect me, just as they did before, when they realized that Niall would often be away."

"They will eventually realize that, even if he is still alive, he's likely to remain captive for years," Jake said. "An annulment would be the most proper course to follow if that *were* the case, would it not?"

"Do you think so? I doubt the Holy Kirk would agree with you, were it not for the other matter," she said, grimacing. "But if you think I want to tell my family that Niall did not want me, that I failed to please him and was unattractive to—"

"It can have nowt to do with your attractiveness, lass, believe me. Some men are just less attracted to women than others are, that's all. In troth, some men are not attracted to women at all. It has nowt to do with the women."

She heard that edge in his voice again and wondered at it. He seemed to have taken a strong aversion to poor Niall. But instinct warned her not to ask Jake much more about that, lest she hear more than she wanted to hear.

So she said, "'Tis true that I don't know his reasons. But 'twas plain enough since our marriage—mayhap even before it—that he did prefer Mungo's company to mine." She sighed. "What Great-Aunt Beatha will say to all that has happened since Christmas does not bear thinking about."

"Then don't think about it."

"But how can I be sure of my feelings?"

"Like this," he said softly, kissing her again and holding her close.

Sighing again, this time with pleasure, she realized that with such methods he could persuade her to do whatever he wanted her to do. Resolutely, she put her hands to his chest and gently pushed him away. "Don't you see, Jake? You are appealing to my emotions. And my emotions are what urged me to marry Niall."

"Then I'll return you to your bedchamber and let you think about all that has happened and what we'd like you to do—what *I want* you to do. If by morning you find that you cannot stand the thought of marrying me, I'll take you home and stand by you whilst we explain to your family just what happened."

Again, such ready agreement stirred her annoyance. But, telling herself she was being unreasonable, she let him take her to the door. Before he opened it, he said, "If Mistress Hyde awakens, tell her you were seeking the garderobe."

"There is a pail," she said.

"Aye, well, sometimes a pail is insufficient or one fears that its contents might offend the other party in one's chamber."

A gurgle of laughter bubbled up, surprising her. Nevertheless, she was delighted to see him grinning back at her.

"Come now," he said, opening the door and preceding her down the stairs.

At her room, he brushed her lips with his, opened the door more silently than she could ever have done, and urged her inside.

Mistress Hyde was snuffling with reassuring regularity. So Alyson crossed the room to her own cot and slipped quietly beneath the covers.

It was long, though, before she slept.

Jake reached into his wee pouch and took out the circle stone, idly rubbing its smooth surface as he sought his bedchamber. Alyson's uncertainty matched his own, because he questioned his feelings as much as she was questioning hers.

His liege, the Lord of the Isles, also commanded most of the western coast of Scotland. MacGillivray House and at least one of Alyson's estates lay in Perth. To be sure, she had mentioned an estate near the Moray Firth, doubtless in Clan Chattan territory and thus near his friends Ivor Mackintosh and Fin Cameron.

Remembering days at St. Andrews, when the three of them would confer before making decisions, he wished that one or both men were at hand now. Both would visit Perth when Parliament met and be at Scone Abbey for Wardlaw's consecration in a fortnight. But that was not soon enough.

Remembering that his first reaction to Wardlaw's declaration that he should marry Alyson had been a sense of dismay at having stepped into a trap, he realized that his dismay had eased even before she'd said she had no wish to confine him.

Perhaps thoughts of honor and duty had eased it. Perhaps it was his strong desire for the lass. He slept at last without drawing any conclusion, and the next morning when he met Alyson on the stairway, he was just glad to see her.

Bidding her good day, he added, "Where is your respectable companion?"

Smiling, she said, "She takes longer to dress and agreed that there could be naught amiss in my awaiting her downstairs in the bishop's privy chamber."

"I doubt you'll come to harm there. Forbye, I thought it was her duty to lend you respectability. Mayhap you ought to have waited for her."

She looked mischievously at him. "In troth, sir, I think that as a burgher's wife, she is unaccustomed to noblewomen. I offered to aid her, because she did not bring her woman. But my offer put her in a flutter, and she shooed me out."

"In troth, I'm glad she did," Jake said. "It gives us a chance to talk, although we should not speak more than pleasantries on this stairway."

"As you wish," she said amiably.

Jake gave her a searching look as they continued down the stairs, trying to discern what she was thinking. When he could not, he decided he could at least ask her one question: "Have you made up your mind yet?"

"Almost," she said.

He stifled a near growl in his throat.

Alyson followed silently as Jake continued down the stairs. She could sense his frustration as if it had wafted through the air to engulf her.

At the great hall entrance, he paused long enough to say, "What impedes your decision, Allie?"

"It is all so sudden, happening so fast," she murmured. "I ken fine that my prospects are dim if I don't do this. I know, too, that if Niall *should* still be alive and will not couple with me, we'll have no children. I know people will blame me for that, too. But even wanting it with all my heart, knowing that you agree, and with two priests telling me that annulment is the right thing to do, it still *feels* wrong. I cannot help it, Jake. I feel as if I'm betraying *my* promise to Niall."

"Since he broke his vows to you, to the Kirk, and to God Himself, I believe it is the other way round," Jake said grimly as he urged her into the hall.

Several priests sat at a table near the fire, talking in low voices. So Alyson and Jake crossed in silence to the bishop's chamber. At the door, Jake stopped her and said with that strange edge in his tone that meant he was thinking about Niall, "Tell me something, lass."

"Aye?"

"Do you think that *I* would abandon you if you were in danger?"

Without hesitation, she shook her head. "Nay, I have seen that you would not. But why do you ask such a thing?"

"Because that is the chief reason that you must agree to this annulment even if you do not marry me afterward—although I hope with all my heart that you will," he added. Putting his face close to hers and speaking urgently, he said, "Don't you see? You could *not* depend on Clyne if he *does* live. He has proven to you by his actions or, rather, by the sorry lack of them, that you could never *trust* him again."

"But he must have thought—"

"Don't make excuses for him! You heard Will just as I did. And that lad has given neither of us cause to think him a liar. He said Niall called out for you but turned away as soon as Mungo said he'd sent someone to fetch you. He did that even though everyone knew by then that the *Maryenknyght* was sinking."

"But Niall would have *believed* Mungo."

"Whom would Mungo have sent to find you?"

"I...I don't know. One of the men, I suppose."

"But all was chaos, Will said. Men were hurrying to board the pirate ships, abandoning the *Maryenknyght*, terrified of going down with her. Sakes, Niall and Mungo were amongst them. According to Will, when Mungo beckoned, Niall went unhesitatingly. Do you think I'd let someone lead me away by the nose if you were in danger? Sakes, do you think *I'd* believe that *you* would leave me?"

Jake saw the truth dawning in Alyson's eyes as she stared into his. "Even if someone had tried to persuade me that *Niall* was safe," she said, "I would not have left the *Maryenknyght* until I'd seen him with my own eyes. Nor would I have let that ship sail away without him, had I had any means to stop it."

"Niall cannot have believed you were safe unless he wanted to believe it. From what I've heard of him, I can easily believe that *he* persuaded himself. And, if he did, he was not only a bad husband; he was a damnably bad friend. This is no longer about Niall Clyne and whether he lives or is dead."

She eyed him bleakly. "Is it not?"

"Nay, 'tis about you, Allie, and whether you're willing to accept a future with me in place of the dismal one you'd have had with Clyne. Had this not happened, you might easily have muddled away the rest of your life without *knowing* that your marriage was a pretense that the Kirk could undo."

Tears filled her eyes, but she dashed them away and

said, “Very well, sir. However, you might as well know now as later that I am an abject coward.”

“Ye’re nowt o’ the sort,” he said gruffly.

“I am, aye. I shrink at what my family will say about this.”

“You let me worry about your family. I’ll see to them.”

“Even Ivor?”

“Especially Ivor. In troth, he will give me less trouble than some others may. I do not know this Great-Aunt Beatha of yours, or your parents. They might present more difficulty than you’ve suggested in describing them to me.”

“Ranald, too, can be difficult,” she said. “He sees difficulties even where there are none. ’Tis his nature.”

“I will attend to Ranald, too.”

She put a hand to his cheek. “You sound gey fierce, sir.”

“I feel fierce when I think of how that scoundrel Clyne treated you. Your kinsmen had better come round quickly. That is all I will say about them.”

“Is that door locked, or were you two meaning to break your fast in the hall?”

Wardlaw’s hearty voice startled them both. When they turned toward him, they saw the Papal Legate at his side.

“Father Antonio has drawn up the annulment document, Lady Alyson,” Wardlaw said as Jake opened the chamber door for him. “You may sign it at my table yonder, along with the fair copy that Father Matthias prepared for you to take with you. Once you have signed them and Father Antonio attaches the papal seal, your unfortunate marriage to Niall Clyne will be as if it had never been. By my troth, my lady, it never *was*, due to his failure. Do you understand that?

“I do, my lord.”

“And do you agree to this annulment of your own free will?”

Alyson drew a deep breath, and Jake realized that he was holding his.

"I do agree to it, sir," she said quietly but firmly.

"Do you likewise agree to marry Jake Maxwell when you are free to do so?"

"I do."

"And you, Sir Jacob Maxwell, do you agree of *your* own free will to enter into marriage with the lady Alyson MacGillivray?"

"I do," Jake said without hesitation. As he did, a warm and pleasurable feeling swept through him unlike any other that he could recall.

Father Antonio murmured something in Latin, and Wardlaw smiled. "He says we should get on with it. Then you will receive communion, break your fast, and get on with your consummation."

Alyson gasped, and Jake experienced another surge of warmth altogether different from the first one and more easily recognizable. He wanted her badly.

His hands ached to touch her, his arms to hold her, and his cock to conquer her. All in all, he decided that he'd better hold his tongue until he was sure that she would go through with this outrageous wedding of theirs.

Alyson could not breathe. She had told the priests that she was ready, that she acted of her own free will. In truth, she wanted nothing so much as to be married to Jake. How that could be possible when she had known him for such a short time, and how she could be so sure of herself, she did not know.

She had nearly choked on her own indrawn breath

when the bishop mentioned consummation. Now that she had more knowledge about such things, the thought of coupling with Jake stirred feelings she had never even imagined feeling for Niall. Nor, she was certain, had Niall felt such things for her.

Before and after her wedding to Niall, when she had imagined their future together, she had imagined benign things such as discussing what needed doing on her estates, how many children they might have, how many tenants and servants they might need, and other such ordinary matters. Even sleeping beside him, she had never felt the stirrings she felt whenever she saw or thought about Jake.

Her feelings for Jake had seemed sinful before, as if she ought not to be feeling them. But he had shown her that they were natural, normal, and inevitable when two people loved each other. Moreover, he shared those feelings, so when they touched, the effect was magical.

Imagining marriage to Jake made her body tingle with anticipation.

Wardlaw and Father Antonio were businesslike. Urging her to sit at the table, the bishop examined his quill, sharpened it with a wee knife, and tested the ink from the pot. Then, dipping the quill and giving it a brisk shake, he gave it to her and showed her where to sign her name.

"Pray, tell me what the Latin means, sir. My cousin said that I should never sign a document without knowing what it says."

Explaining that it formally annulled her marriage and any other agreements that may have alluded to her erstwhile husband, he translated the exact words.

When he finished, she had only one question: "What

about agreements that pertained only to me and preceded our marriage?"

"Such agreements will remain in effect under most conditions unless they designated you and your husband as one, naming you together as a married couple. In that instance, the designator must issue a new document."

"There are none like that," she said, signing her name without hesitation.

Wardlaw took the quill from her and wiped it with the cloth kept for that purpose. Then he said, "I ought to have asked earlier, my lady, but what have you done with Mistress Hyde?"

"She will be along shortly, sir. In troth, she made no objection when I suggested preceding her. However, I am glad I was able to talk freely with Jake and with you before she arrived."

The legate said quietly then, "Art ready for the ceremony, my lady?"

"Aye, but—" She broke off when a loud rap announced Father Porter, who ushered Mistress Hyde into the room.

"Be there aught else I might do for you, your reverence?" the porter asked.

"Tell them to serve our breakfast here if you've not already done so," Wardlaw said. "And see that Sir Jacob's room is made ready."

"I took the liberty of seeing to that as soon as I received word that he was up," Father Porter said, smiling at Jake. "I also ordered your breakfast served here."

"Excellent," Wardlaw said. "You may stay if you like. Father Antonio is about to marry this pair."

Mistress Hyde beamed at Alyson. "It be an honor tae attend ye, m'lady."

"I know that we can rely on your discretion, Mistress Hyde, as always," Wardlaw said with his charming smile.

"Och, aye, your reverence. I dinna talk o' nowt I see here, even tae me man, unless ye say I may. Which ye never do," she added conscientiously.

"You are a rare woman, Mistress Hyde," he said. "Shall we begin, Father?"

"We shall," Father Antonio said. "As to asking if anyone here knows just cause to object to this wedding..."

"We can dispense with that," Wardlaw said easily. "Jake, if you will stand beside Lady Alyson..."

Jake did so, and five minutes later, Alyson had married him. The ceremony seemed to go much faster than she remembered.

When Father Antonio declared them husband and wife and Jake had given her a chaste kiss, Wardlaw rubbed his hands together and said, "Prithee, see if our food is forthcoming, Father Porter. New beginnings give me an appetite."

Conscious only of Jake standing beside her with his hand at her elbow, Alyson could not seem to think about food.

"Don't be nervous, lass," he murmured when Wardlaw turned away to seat Mistress Hyde at the table they'd used the previous night.

"I'm not nervous," she said. "I'm curious."

Alyson's frank statement stirred Jake's libido so strongly that his appetite for food vanished. Knowing he would need all his energy to get through the day, especially since he'd not slept much during the night, he forced himself to focus on the ale, bread, and soft-boiled eggs that constituted his breakfast.

Father Matthias was one of their servers. Jake nodded at him and smiled, although he knew that the priest would not speak or respond in any other way while seeing to his duties unless Wardlaw or Father Antonio addressed him.

They ate silently and finished their meal quickly. Meantime, Jake mentally calculated how long it would likely take the *Sea Wolf* to reach the harbor at Perth from St. Andrews Bay.

Having seen when he awoke that the tide was low but on the turn, he knew it would flow with them for hours but would turn against them at midday. During the afternoon, it would flow hard against them until low tide, soon after dark.

Allowing for the vagaries of the wind and the tides, it would take ten to twelve hours, *after* they got going. The *Sea Wolf* would go nowhere until he had consummated his marriage, but he did not object.

He would *not* make the same mistake that that dafty Clyne had made.

Chapter 17

The view from Jake's bedchamber was as splendid as the view from the tower room. But when he shut the door, Alyson's interest in the panorama fled.

The room suddenly seemed much smaller.

Jake stood with his back against the door, gazing at her as if the sight of her gave him deep pleasure. That look stirred the sensations she felt whenever her gaze met his but stronger than ever. She wondered if her parents felt so when they'd first married. She was sure Lizzie and her Jeb had.

"How curious are you, lass?" Jake asked softly.

A jolt of fire blazed at her core, as if her body burned for him to touch her there. Surprised to feel such a sensation before he had touched her, she knew she was blushing and could think of nothing to say.

"Speak, Allie. You don't usually hesitate to tell me what you think."

When his eyes began to gleam wickedly, she realized she had drawn her lower lip between her teeth again. Faith, she was chewing it!

"I've warned you about that," he murmured. He straightened like a stretching cat and moved toward her purposefully.

Licking her lips, she said, "Is it better if you *tell* me things or show me?"

He grinned. "We must try both to find out. We'll begin, I think, with the showing. I want to see you, lass, all of you. Let me help you unclothe yourself."

His words increased the flow of heat through her body. When he looked into her eyes as he reached for her bodice lacing, a hunger for him filled her that was unlike anything she had ever known. He wore his usual leather vest, white shirt, deerskin breeks, and rawhide boots, and she was about to suggest that he, too, was overdressed when he reached into the pouch attached to his belt and took out the circle stone that he'd found on the cliffs.

"Remember this?"

"Aye, sure."

"I looked through it again after we boarded the *Sea Wolf.* Guess what I saw."

"What?"

"This," he said, pulling her close and kissing her. Her clothes were quickly gone, and although he made no move hastily, she was soon in his bed, where he began at once to teach her what other married couples did in their beds.

First, he stroked her bare skin gently, as if he feared he might bruise her if he pressed too hard. The sensations astonished her, making her moan and her body writhe as if every nerve and muscle urged him to do more. Then he began to kiss her again, not just her lips but all over, even her legs, her thighs, and…

Feeling his breath where no one's breath had caressed her, she exclaimed, "What are you doing?"

"Shhh," he murmured, stroking her there and bringing

an echo of Lizzie's words to her mind when he said, "Let me pleasure you as you should be pleasured."

Moving upward to kiss her belly and lave her breasts, he left his hand where it lay and slid a finger inside her as he captured her lips again.

When she gasped, he took it as an invitation to explore her mouth with his tongue. An extraordinary feeling below, where he rubbed, made her jump.

Jake murmured, "Easy, lass, just feel. Relax as much as you can, and it will be easier. I don't want to hurt you."

"They are waiting for us, are they not?"

"Forget about them. We'll leave as soon as we've finished here. Next time, we'll enjoy ourselves more. 'Tis good reason to take care now."

He eased over her as he spoke. She felt him at her opening. Then, although he eased himself in, the ache was nearly more than she could bear. Remembering his advice, she did her best to relax. He slipped in and then seemed to reach a barrier. When he penetrated it, she cried out.

"Shhh," he murmured. "That was your maidenhead, sweetheart. You are a wife now, for better or worse. And you're mine."

She was so beautiful. Her skin was so warm and softly silken that afterward he wanted just to hold her. She fit into his embrace as if God had created her for that purpose. Never before had he felt as if he knew what a woman was thinking, let alone understood her thoughts. But Alyson's face was so expressive that her mind seemed as open to him as her body was.

The thought was a potent one. It made him *feel* powerful. At the same time, he knew that he'd never felt so protective of anyone. Sakes, he had never thought he would *want* to feel so. Offering protection created burdens, did it not, responsibilities that chained a man as much as land and a wife chained him?

Had he not believed that for years? Had he not also thought he understood himself and knew exactly how he wanted to live his life?

"What are you thinking?"

His racing thoughts banged together in a disordered clump. "About you," he said. "And about me."

"And about freedom," she said.

"Nay, or not entirely. I was thinking about how I thought I knew myself and coming to the conclusion that I was a bit owf, as one might say."

"Do you regret marrying me, Jake?"

"Nay, sweetheart. In troth, I've rarely regretted anything. Everything we do teaches us something helpful."

"Even bad decisions?"

"Especially bad ones," he said, grinning at certain memories although he knew she had not meant to amuse him. "This is not a bad one."

"I don't think so, either. We do have to go soon, though, do we not?"

He agreed, so they tidied themselves and dressed. Downstairs, as they said their farewells, he knew despite her air of calm dignity that she felt vulnerable. She was thinking that the priests, although celibate, probably knew all about life and lovers and exactly what the two of them had done. She was probably right.

~

As Alyson ascended the *Sea Wolf*'s gangplank, she felt as if the sleek little ship offered more sanctuary than St. Andrews had. The thought seemed odd when one was leaving a place that had safely harbored young Jamie Stewart, but it flitted through her mind nevertheless.

Her body still tingled and ached from the consummation, but the *Sea Wolf* seemed to welcome her. Coll and the oarsmen were all smiling. The ship, its wood strakes and planks newly polished and gleaming in the sun, seemed to smile, too.

While Will and Mace helped their oarsmen stow the towboat, Jake escorted Alyson to her cabin.

"How long will it take to get to Perth?" she asked as he pushed the door open and set the bundle she had taken with her to the castle on the alcove table.

"We should arrive around dusk," he said. "We'll have the tide against us this afternoon, so I want to make speed whilst we have the wind and tide at our back."

"Must I stay inside?"

"I see no need to lock up so bonnie a wife," he said, putting a finger under her chin and tilting it up to kiss her. "We'll pass some fine scenery, but keep your cloak handy unless you're sheltered from the wind."

She smiled. "I'm hardy, sir. I like to feel the wind."

Her answer clearly delighted him, because he kissed her again and grinned as he said, "Please yourself. Nae one will pay us heed."

For much of their journey from England, until they neared the Scottish border, they'd kept well off the coast, and the unending seas had grown tedious. But this day's journey delighted her.

The sun shone, albeit disappearing behind one scudding cloud or another to reappear shortly afterward. The air was crisp but not cold, making it pleasant to watch the shoreline pass on either side. The northern shore was distant at first, drawing closer as the firth narrowed to meet the outflowing river Tay.

She watched monks from Lindores Abbey, on the south shore, piling fresh-cut squares of peat in neat, monk-high stacks to dry near their woods. The sight reminded her of the awful dream she'd had of Niall's coffin in the forest of pikes and lances, when men had charged her on flying horses, bellowing that she had no right to be there, while their mounts kicked up peat squares as they flew.

With the tide ebbing, the river rushing out with it, and the wind easing as the sun dropped behind western hills, the oarsmen worked harder. She sat on the bench by the cabin, where their rhythmic movement, emphasized by the low *boom-boom* of the helmsman's drum, lulled her thoughts so that occasionally she dozed.

Whenever she awoke, she saw Jake smiling. The sight warmed her, whether he was looking at her or elsewhere.

Approaching the harbor, she saw Perth's stone bridge ahead. For seventy-five years, people had used it to cross the river Tay. Although it stood where the original one had, at the first place narrow enough to bridge the firth, townsmen had lost track of how many bridges they'd lost since. But the stone one ought to last.

The sun had set when they entered the harbor, as Jake had said was likely. The emotion that swept over her at the familiar sight was nearer trepidation than delight at her homecoming.

She watched as Jake dropped the sail and oarsmen

maneuvered the ship to anchorage and prepared the towboat to take them ashore. Remembering that Jake had said he would handle her family, she tried to imagine how he would do that.

He had said they'd take only Will and a pair of armed oarsmen with them to the house. Mace and Coll would take charge of the *Sea Wolf* and the other men.

Soon, too soon, she and Jake were walking briskly through town with their escort. Because of the increasing darkness, he had opted for four men rather than two. One man ahead and one behind carried torches to light their way.

Alyson guided them from the harbor past St. John's Kirk, from which the walled town had taken its name. They proceeded along the Skinnergate and Castle Gable almost to North Port, the northernmost gate in the wall.

Jake said, "Did not the ancient castle stand nearby?"

"Aye, across the common. The Blackfriars Monastery lies just beyond. 'Tis where Albany and his grace stay when they come to Perth if they don't stay at Scone Abbey. The way we've come used to be a direct route from the castle to St. John's Kirk. The next turning is ours, sir. The gate to the close will still be open."

When they entered the close, MacGillivray House stood directly ahead. Alyson's stomach clenched at the sight but relaxed when Jake touched her elbow.

"Courage, sweetheart," he murmured.

Squaring her shoulders, she went up the steps. Since darkness had fallen, she plied the knocker, because they bolted the door at dusk. Hearing muffled sounds on the other side, she looked at the squint and smiled.

The door opened swiftly.

"M'lady!" exclaimed her father's ancient porter as his

gaze swept her escort and came to rest on Jake. "What be this, then?"

Alyson said, "You need not announce us, Malcolm. Sir Jacob, this is our porter, Malcolm Milroy. Is the family in the great chamber or the solar, Malcolm?"

"Ye ken fine that the laird likes tae sit doon tae his supper afore dark, m'lady. They be still on the da—"

"Allie! What the devil? Where's Niall? And who are these men?"

"Good evening, Ranald. Malcolm, please see that our men and this laddie, Will, get a good supper straightaway. Sir Jacob and I require supper, too, so we'll join the others. Nay, Ranald," she said when her brother strode purposefully forward. "I must speak with Mother and Father, and there is no need for me to tell my tale twice. We'll go into the great chamber, if you please."

"Well, I do not please," Ranald said testily. "Everyone is in there, because Great-Aunt Beatha and Sinead have not gone home yet, and others have arrived to await the sitting of Parliament and Bishop Wardlaw's consecration. I don't think it is wise to inflict all these visitors on our father and mother, in any event."

"Is that not for your lord father to decide, lad?" Jake said with an easy smile. "Surely, your parents will want to see for themselves that Lady Alyson has got home safely after ruthless pirates attacked her ship."

"Pirates!"

Keeping her patience with difficulty, Alyson said, "Aye, pirates. So prithee, move, Ranald. I grow cold standing here."

"We'll go, then. But you must first tell me who this officious fellow is."

"Certainly," she said. Without looking away from Ranald, she said, "As you doubtless have guessed, Sir Jacob, this is my brother Ranald." Then, savoring the moment, she added, "Ranald, this is Sir Jacob Maxwell, my husband."

Jake thought Alyson's timing was rather abrupt, but her brother's slack-jawed reaction almost made him laugh. The younger man's mouth gaped, and his eyes grew big, revealing utter shock.

"But you cannot be married to him," Ranald said. "You married Niall."

Stepping forward with his hand out, Jake said as Ranald automatically responded to the gesture, "We'll explain it all, lad, but to everyone at once. As we are brothers now, prithee, call me Jake."

"This is madness," Ranald said. "You may lead the way, Alyson. I trow, I do not know what everyone will say to you."

"But how could you know that before they speak?" she said, resting her left hand on Jake's proffered right forearm.

He put his left hand over hers and gave it a squeeze. Hers trembled briefly. Then, her serenity apparently restored, she guided him through an arched opening into the great chamber. Though not lavishly appointed, it seemed comfortable. The fire in the hooded fireplace emitted a pleasant odor of peat and burned cheerfully. It was, as far as Jake could see, the only cheerful thing in the room.

Eight people sat at the dais table, facing them, and all

eight looked up at their entrance. Their combined reactions were much as Ranald's had been.

Ranald must have thought so, too, because he said, "As you see, Allie has come home. What you do not immediately perceive is that she has brought with her a new husband, although I cannot tell you how *that* has come to pass."

He had everyone's attention, Jake thought, surveying them.

Ranald's seat clearly had been the empty space to the right of Lord Farigaig, whom Jake had met on his previous visit and who sat in a two-armed chair beside his lady. The person next to Lady Farigaig was a skinny, elderly woman whose gimlet gaze threatened to pierce Jake through. She sat rigidly upright, her eating knife poised over her trencher. Her white veil began inches back from her brow, revealing hair of so light a gray as to be nearly white itself. Her face was long and wrinkled, but she was far from decrepit. He was sure she must be Lady Beatha.

Alyson stopped at the foot of the dais, facing her parents. "My lord, my lady," she said. "May I present Sir Jacob Maxwell of Duncraig in Kintail, and other places. You may recall that he visited us last year with Ivor." To Jake, she said, "Next to my lady mother, sir, is my great-aunt, the lady Beatha MacGillivray. And before you demand to know, Aunt Beatha, Ranald is right, although he ought to have let me tell you all myself. Sir Jacob is indeed my husband now."

"That canna be but a wheen o' blethers, Alyson," Lady Beatha said in high-pitched but noble accents. "I witnessed your marriage tae that fool, Niall Clyne, at Christmastide. I dinna say that this chap, wi' his good looks and fine physique, doesna outshine Niall. But ye canna just doff one husband and don another like a new kirtle, lass. Ye've created a scandal, and we shall *all* be caught up in it."

The older of the other two men at the table, a stout chap with red cheeks, said in bewilderment, "What ha' ye done wi' Niall, lass?"

Alyson gripped Jake's forearm as she said, "That is my mother's cousin, Patair MacNiven of Inverness, who spoke, sir. English pirates attacked and sank our ship off the English coast, Cousin Patair. They captured Niall, and we fear—nay, we believe—they threw him overboard."

Testily, Lord Farigaig said, "Ye *fear*? Ye *believe*? Sakes, daughter, ha' ye lost your wits? Ye canna marry again without *knowing* that the lad be dead."

"With respect, my lord," Jake said then, "it would be wiser if you and I, and Ranald—and mayhap these other two gentlemen—discuss the matter fully after supper, and elsewhere. You have my word that all is in order. I will make everything plain to you, whilst Alyson explains it to her mother and these other ladies."

When her father did not agree at once, Alyson said, "The other man at the table, sir, is Patair's brother, Donal, also of Inverness. The other women are my great-aunt's woman, Sinead; Cousin Patair's wife, Elsa; and Donal's wife, Mairi."

As she introduced them, Jake nodded to each. When the silence continued, Alyson scarcely dared to breathe or to look again at any of them, least of all her father or great-aunt. Even Jake's presence failed to reassure her.

"I'll speak wi' ye after supper, lad, and Ranald may

come with us," Farigaig said at last. "But come now, the pair o' ye, and take supper with us. We'll, *none* of us"—he shot a look at Lady Beatha—"discuss this at the table."

Alyson felt her tension ease. Her father had not spoken so curtly to anyone in years. She hoped it would prove to be a good omen, not a bad one.

Jake readily accepted Farigaig's invitation. Not only was he hungry, but he also wanted to learn more about Alyson's family before he talked with her kinsmen.

Despite his host's stricture regarding conversation, it went on apace in Scots and Gaelic, often at once. However, although Ranald twice wondered aloud if Niall could really be dead, Farigaig stifled every attempt to quiz Alyson or Jake. Recalling her description of her father, Jake watched him. Farigaig did not otherwise join the discussion but clearly kept track of it all.

After eating all he wanted, the laird declared that as his son was likewise finished, the two of them could now talk with Jake. "Patair," Farigaig added as he got awkwardly to his feet and reached for the cane hooked over the back of his armchair, "ye and Donal will liefer stay and finish your supper, aye?"

Aware that the MacNiven men's presence would make it harder for Alyson to tell her tale, Jake was about to object when Patair MacNiven said amiably, "I'm for me bed soon, Farigaig. Donal and our ladies will go up with me. Our Alyson is a woman grown and, tae my mind, must do as she pleases. She can tell us whatever she wants tae tell us later, if she likes. I dinna speak for Beatha, o' course."

Farigaig nodded. Signing to Jake and Ranald to follow

him and leaning heavily on his cane, he led the way into a room off the dais that Jake thought must be Lady Farigaig's solar. A fire burned on the hearth there, too.

"Everyone will leave us be, in here," Farigaig said, drawing a back-stool near the fire. "Sit, Ranald, and stop scowling until ye ha' cause tae scowl."

Clearly astonished, either by his father's words or by his crisp tone, Ranald glanced at Jake, then drew two stools from the wall by the fireplace.

Without waiting for them to sit, Farigaig added, "I want tae ken summat more about ye, Sir Jacob. But afore ye start, d'ye truly think our Niall be dead?"

"I do, my lord," Jake said, setting his stool so that he faced Farigaig with Ranald between them at Jake's left. "Before I say aught else, I should tell you that Father Antonio de la Luna, the Papal Legate, married us. He is in Scotland, as you must know, to consecrate Bishop Wardlaw in a fortnight's time at Scone. You will also know that a legate wields all of the Pope's powers whilst he is here. It was he who annulled Alyson's marriage to Niall Clyne, sir... for cause."

Farigaig seemed to freeze and then, mentally, to wrestle with himself.

Content to let him do so, Jake saw Ranald open his mouth as if to speak and then shut it. So the lad either had sense or simply knew not what to say.

Fixing his attention on Farigaig, Jake noted lines of worry or grief etched into his face. It was likewise nearer gray than any healthy color. What remained of his hair was darker than Alyson's but lighter than Ivor's tawny locks. His eyes were the same light gray as his daughter's, but he wore black, so Jake could not tell if their color was as changeable as Alyson's eyes were.

"Ye said the annulment were for cause, lad," Farigaig said tersely.

"I did, sir." He did not elaborate. Knowing little about Ranald, he was reluctant to be more explicit and would take his cues from his host.

"I did think she was making a mistake," Farigaig said. "I ought tae have stopped it then, but I lacked the vigor. See you, Niall Clyne were a younger son wi' next tae nowt of his own and made nae secret of wanting her estates. But Allie thought he'd suit her as a husband, and she kens her own mind. Forbye..." He paused, glancing at Ranald. Then he said, "I feared that Niall would have let her rule the roost. I dinna think that be good for any woman."

"Clyne was not home often enough to rule it himself," Jake reminded him, feeling a sense of irony as he said it and equal determination *not* to be like Clyne if he could just figure out a way to have his freedom and still look after his wife.

"And why was Niall never at home?" Farigaig demanded. "Mungo Lyle is why. He had only tae crook a finger, and off our Niall would go."

"Of course, he did," Ranald said indignantly. "Mungo serves Orkney, and so did Niall. When Orkney beckoned, they both *had* to go."

Farigaig looked at his son again and back at Jake. "I thought Niall were nobbut a prickmedainty and worth nowt as a husband."

"You should not say such a thing," Ranald said. "The man is dead!"

With a flickering glance at his son, Farigaig said to Jake, "Whenever Niall's family would visit, he'd follow our Allie about. Despite her being the younger by three years, Niall always looked tae her tae decide what they should do."

"So what?" Ranald said. "They were bairns."

"Will ye say then that Niall took the lead after they grew up?"

"Nay, but Alyson has a habit of telling *everyone* what to do."

"D'ye think so, lad?" Jake asked, quirking an eyebrow.

Ranald looked sourly at him. "Are you saying she does *not*?"

"I rarely discuss any lady when she is not present," Jake said gently. "But, you *are* Alyson's brother. You must know that her nature is charmingly serene."

"I have rarely found it so," Ranald said.

"Then I would suggest that henceforth you regard her more carefully," Jake said. "And speak of her more cautiously, withal."

Ranald met his gaze directly this time, seemed to study it, and then looked away without attempting a reply.

Jake turned back to Farigaig and saw a near smile on the older man's face.

"Methinks she will not rule your roost, Sir Jacob," Farigaig said. "I begin to feel hopeful again. I do recall your visit last year. I fear I was a bad host, but Ivor was here, and he is competent in the role. Forbye, I wish I'd heeded ye more. If ye be a Maxwell, ye canna hail from Duncraig, though, as Allie said. More likely ye hail from Nithsdale, east o' the Borders, aye?"

"I was born there," Jake said. "My father has property near Dumfries. But we're men of the sea, so a cousin manages the estate. I studied at St. Andrews with Ivor and also with Fin Cameron, who married your niece Catriona."

"I do recall that now, aye," Farigaig said.

He asked more questions about Jake's connections. Then they talked of people they knew in common. Such discussions were inevitable when Highlanders got acquainted, but Ranald soon began shifting on his stool in evident frustration.

Farigaig noticed but let it continue for a time before saying, "I see that ye find all this chat tiresome, lad. Ye needna stay."

"I want tae know more about our Allie and Niall."

"Aye, well, I ken all that I need tae ken. We'll discuss it another time."

"But—"

"Goodnight, Ranald," Farigaig said. "Dinna trouble the womenfolk in the hall but get off tae bed or tae some better amusement. I trow, ye do ha' some."

Ranald got up and turned away. When Farigaig cleared his throat, Ranald turned and bade him goodnight. Farigaig glanced toward Jake.

Although Ranald's lips tightened, he said, "Goodnight, Sir Jacob."

"Goodnight," Jake said. "Prithee, do not pester Alyson for more details."

"I suppose I can ask my own sister whatever I like."

"You can, but I *am* her husband, lad. If you do trouble her, you will answer to me. Forbye, I'll discuss anything you want to discuss. I must leave in the morning for Stirling, but I'd welcome your company."

That he would ride to Stirling was true, although he would pass through the royal burgh and on to Rothesay Castle, to deliver his news to the King.

Clearly startled by the invitation, Ranald recovered

to say with disdain, "I have no wish to accompany you anywhere."

"As you wish," Jake said. "If you change your mind, I mean to leave soon after I break my fast."

Ranald replied with a look that matched his earlier tone.

Chapter 18

To Alyson's relief, after Jake, Farigaig, and Ranald had gone into the solar, her great-aunt sent Sinead away with the MacNivens, leaving Alyson at the dais table with only her mother and Lady Beatha.

The latter said, "Give us the round tale, lass. We'll see what we make of it."

Thinking of Jake and what he faced with Ranald and her father, Alyson found it easier than expected to say, "It is as it should be, Aunt Beatha."

"This wheen o' blethers about Niall being dead and ye already married again? I dinna mind telling ye, I canna get my mind round it."

"Nor can I, Alyson," her mother said fretfully. "If you do not *know* that Niall is dead—"

"I *saw* Niall in his coffin, Mam," Alyson interjected.

Both women stared at her and then at each other. She knew that the two of them accepted her Sight more readily than the rest of her family.

Lady Beatha, for once, did not assert herself but nodded when Lady Farigaig said, "Even so, Allie, this marriage you've made with Sir Jacob cannot be lawful."

"But it is, aye, Mam," Alyson said. "Sithee, the Papal

Legate annulled my marriage to Niall, because…" Meeting her never-wed great-aunt's piercing gaze, she faltered, drew breath, and said, "That is, Niall…we never consummated our union. Mayhap you do not like to hear me say such a thing, Aunt—"

"Pish tush, Allie. I'm neither blind nor stupid. Come tae that, I've helped wi' many a birthing, so I ken what's what about such things. I can guess that *ye'd* had little ken o' such, though. So if yon fool, Niall, didna show ye…"

After that, it was easy to explain what had happened. She did have to explain to her mother about the powers of a papal legate. But Lady Farigaig acknowledged then that she thought Jake might make Alyson a good husband.

"Aye, sure, he will," Lady Beatha said. "Wi' a pair o' shoulders like his…sakes, I'd fall for the man m'self."

The image those words brought to Alyson's mind forced her to suppress a smile, and she wondered what Jake would say when she told him. That she looked forward to telling him pleased her. That he had to leave in the morning to tell the King the English had captured Jamie did not.

After Ranald left, Farigaig said, "I was right about Niall, aye?"

"Aye, sir. Your daughter remained a maiden. I learned as much—"

"Never mind how ye learned it, lad," Farigaig said. "That ye be Ivor's friend and studied under Bishop Traill tells me I can trust your sense of honor. Had I retained more o' mine after my sons died, I'd have stopped that wedding afore it began. But I be good for nowt these days.

I couldna make m'self care enough. In troth, with Eamon and Artan gone, leaving only Ranald..."

A twinge of something stirred in Jake when Farigaig paused. Impulsively, he said, "Sakes, sir, do you fear that Ranald may be *like* Niall?"

The bleak expression on Farigaig's face gave Jake his answer.

Jake shook his head. "Ye ken more o' your son than I do. But what I see is a lad whose family turned him into what we from the Borders call a mammie-keekie or a dandilly with too much cosseting. From what Alyson has said of him, I'd expect that he needs only firmer guidance and a purpose in life."

Farigaig grimaced. "He shows nae interest in such."

"With respect, sir...Is it possible that when your sons died, your grief led Ranald—who was likely also grieving—to fear that you cared more for Eamon and Artan than you do for him? If members of your family had petted and pampered him before and he came then to believe that he's a great disappointment to you..."

He paused, aware that Farigaig was frowning, digesting his words.

At last, Farigaig said, "We'll discuss that further anon if ye will. I would likewise discuss other matters with ye after ye return from Stirling."

"In troth, sir, I go to Rothesay Castle," Jake said. "I did not tell Ranald, because I'd liefer keep my business private for now. Alyson knows where I go and why, and you should know that the journey may take some time and that it would be unsuitable for her to accompany me."

"Ye'll see tae your affairs as ye must, lad, and I'll tend tae mine here. Just thinking o' ye and our Ivor studying with Traill makes me ponder what the man would ha' said o' my behavior these past years, had he had ken of it. I've much for which tae atone, as ye'd doubtless agree."

"In troth, sir," Jake said, smiling, "I have a few such things on my plate, too. Does that jug on yonder table contain summat we might drink?"

"A fine claret, aye," Farigaig said. "Ye'll find goblets in the wooden kist behind the jug. I own, I've more questions I'd like tae ask ye."

Alyson escaped from the great chamber as soon as she civilly could. Then, asking her father's steward to direct Sir Jacob to her bedchamber, she managed to do so in her usual manner, without concerning herself with what he might think of her new marriage. When he agreed in his own usual way, she hurried upstairs, calling for a maidservant as she went.

The necessity to summon the maid reminded her of Ciara's fate and stirred both remorse and guilt. Common sense reminded her that she could not alter Fate, so she returned her thoughts to what she must do before Jake came upstairs.

Ordering a tub and hot water, she bathed hastily but thoroughly by candlelight with the maidservant's help and let the lass brush her hair and plait it. By the time Jake came upstairs Alyson had tidied up, ordered more hot water for him, and donned her most becoming robe, of pale green silk.

Hearing the latch rattle, she said to the girl, "Thank you; you may go."

Jake held the door open for the girl but fixed his gaze

on Alyson. "I like that robe," he said, shutting the door and moving nearer.

He had not yet touched her, but the familiar tingling had begun the moment he'd opened the door.

He reached for her, but she eluded him, saying, "If you touch me, you'll get no bath before you leave tomorrow. And your water will get cold."

"Is it hot now?" When she nodded, he said, "Almost you tempt me, lass, but to bathe properly I'll require assistance."

She smiled, feeling daring. "I thought you might."

"You'll ruin that robe if you get it wet," he said with a mischievous look.

"Get in the tub. I'll fetch another—"

"Nay, Allie. We'll take it off and put it aside. I want to look at you."

He touched her sash. Heat rushed to her cheeks and spread elsewhere.

Jake saw the color suffuse her cheeks and neck. But, to his delight, she did not object when he removed her robe and cast it over a stool. She had plaited her hair, and he wanted to see it unbound. But that could wait. Hastily and without awaiting assistance, he got out of his clothes and stepped into the tub.

She scrubbed his back but refused when he suggested that she should scrub him all over. "You'll do that faster yourself. Warm or not, this room is not cozy enough to be long without clothing, sir. If you mean to wash your hair, I'll pour the rinse water for you. But I must put on another robe first or get into bed."

"Nay, put on the green one again. I like it, the silk will keep you warm, and I can pour my own water whilst we talk. I like your father, lass."

"Do you? I think he likes you, too. I fear that he'll expect you to take over here, though," she added, slipping into the robe. "He wearies quickly, and although he did seem more himself tonight, such vigor may vanish when he learns that you will not stay. He has missed having me to run things."

"I think you are too quick to submit to your family's demands, lass, and I own, I don't understand that. You disagree easily enough with me. Why do you not tell them to stop expecting you to be always at their beck and bay?"

"You discuss things with me, Jake. When I disagree with you, you don't make me feel guilty for doing so."

"Is that what they do? Sakes, if I *were* to run things, I'd send all save your parents to perdition. At least you'll be free of such demands when we do leave."

"You don't know them. They'll visit *us* at the first opportunity."

"I'll forbid it, for now at least. They'll expect you to obey your husband."

"You will not forbid it," she said. "One does not turn even an enemy from a Highland door, as you must know. I'll welcome my family wherever I live. Faith, but I shall *need* them, because you will be off tending to your duties and savoring your freedom. I wager I'll see less of *you* than I saw of Niall."

With mock ferocity, he said, "Mind your tongue, lass. I dislike back-chat."

"Do you, sir? You are ill-equipped just now to do much about it."

"Mayhap I am," he said. "But I dry quickly. And then, lassie mine..."

When he paused, Alyson's nipples hardened and muscles contracted elsewhere, as the rest of her body tensed in its eagerness to test his challenge.

She could find no words. So she gazed at him silently, thinking that most tall men would look silly folded up in a tin tub. Jake did not, not at all.

When he stood, he looked magnificent.

"Hand me a towel, wench," he said.

"Aye, Cap'n," she replied without a blink.

His wonderful grin flashed then, and he laughed. He was still laughing when she tossed him the towel. Drying most of himself as he watched her, he stepped out of the tub, wrapped the towel round his waist, and took her in his arms.

She raised her face, inviting his kiss. Instead, he scooped her into his arms and carried her to the bed.

"Now," he said, laying her down against the pillows and dropping the towel, "you will learn to do as I say."

She smiled invitingly. "Will I?"

"You will, or you'll pay the consequences." With that, leaving all the candles in the room alight, he slid into bed beside her and began to stroke her silk robe... all over, until she squirmed and begged him to do other things.

"Other things?" He quirked an eyebrow. "Tell me where you want me to touch you, sweetheart."

"Kiss me."

Slipping a hand under her robe, easing the silk off her

body inches at a time, he kissed places as he bared them, working his way down to the fork in her legs.

She grabbed him by the ears. “I want to kiss *you* now.”

~

Grinning, Jake let her have her way and was delighted when she moved over him, following paths similar to those he had taken in kissing her, clearly enjoying herself and doing much to satisfy her feminine curiosity. As she explored his body with her soft hands, fingers, lips, and tongue, he savored the scent and taste of her all over again and soon slid a hand down to cup her silken mound.

Encouraging her to do as she pleased, he employed his skills to heighten her passions, and his own. Slipping a finger inside her, then two, he soon discovered that she felt only pleasure and no lingering pain from their consummation. When she gripped his cock a bit too hard, he moved his free hand to show her how better to excite it. Hearing her chuckle low in her throat, he grinned again.

“Art pleased with yourself, lass?” he murmured.

“I was not sure what to do, but this seems to work well.”

It was working too well. He did not want to finish before showing her what she could feel, so he took command until she moaned and whimpered her pleasure. Then he eased inside and brought her to her climax before pounding to his own. When his cock exhausted itself, he rolled so that she lay atop him.

“Mercy,” she said, looking into his eyes. “I had no idea.”

“Sweetheart, there is much more to discover, and we’ll explore every possibility together. But now, we must sleep.”

He awoke once during the night, heard her breathing

softly beside him, and fell back asleep in contentment. When he awoke the next morning, recalling her insistence that her family would visit whenever they liked, he wondered if she had bewitched him. Perhaps their marriage was a mistake, but even if it was, he was in it for a lifetime and would feel his way. He smiled then at the thought of how *she* had felt and had made him feel the night before.

Getting out of bed, he glanced back and saw her smiling wistfully.

Enticed again to kiss her, he did so and said, "Go back to sleep, love. I'll leave after breakfast."

"We still have matters to discuss."

"We do, aye, but we'll discuss them when I return." He kissed her again, lingering to savor her taste.

Downstairs, he found Will awaiting him in the great chamber.

"Them other men said ye'd told 'em tae go back tae town, sir. But they didna ken what tae do wi' me. So I thought I'd watch for ye and ask could I go with ye tae see his grace. I'd like tae tell him—"

"Ye'll ha' to stay here, laddie," Jake interjected gently. "I trow ye've said nowt to anyone about where I go." Will shook his head dismally, so Jake added, "I need ye here to keep your eyes on m'lady for me. Can ye do that?"

"I can, aye. I'll keep a good watch over her whilst ye're gone."

"Good lad."

The feelings Jake had had, of having put himself in the trap he'd sworn would never snare him, vanished only to reappear when he found a sleek, well-muscled black horse awaiting him at the stable, along with Ranald MacGillivray.

Alyson did not go back to sleep after Jake left but lay in bed for a time, pondering a strong sense of ill usage. The thought of facing alone the members of her family downstairs, as well as those arriving from the Highlands for Parliament and the bishop's consecration, made her wish that Jake had wakened her earlier.

Then they might have had time to talk. She'd have liked to tell him what she thought of him for abandoning her so soon. Clearly, he had not wanted to discuss that. Nor had he wanted to talk of such matters as how long they would stay at MacGillivray House or where they'd go when they left.

He'd distracted her from conversation the previous night—admittedly in a delightful way. But his sense of relief at having reason to leave that morning had been nearly palpable. Doubtless, she had annoyed him by saying he'd be away from her more than Niall had been, but she was sure that that was true.

Memory stirred then of her relief and the heady sense of freedom that she had felt as she and Niall had ridden away from MacGillivray House to meet the *Maryenknyght*. She suspected that Jake harbored similar feelings of freedom now from her parents, her brother, and other kinsmen whom he doubtless viewed as chains binding her, and thus now binding him, too.

However, memory of the freedom she had felt, leaving with Niall, also made her wonder what impulse had led her to defend her kinsmen's habit of visiting—often for long periods. Even Highland hospitality did not demand that one allow leechlike kinsmen to stay indefinitely.

"What if he doesn't come back?"

Shutting her eyes in astonished annoyance at even muttering such a thought about a man who had proven himself honorable, she got up and poured water into the basin to wash her face and clear her mind. Jake *would* come back.

She smiled then, realizing that whatever he thought of her kinsmen, he'd come back because Ivor, Fin Cameron, and their families were coming to Perth. Jake would return as soon as possible if only to keep Ivor from fetching him.

She was still smiling when she went downstairs to break her fast and see to her customary duties. Her great-aunt's voice welcomed her.

"There you are, Alyson," she said. "You are late this morning, and I arose early. Sithee, I've taken certain liberties here that I must explain to you."

Having met Ranald in the stableyard and noted that, besides the black horse, he'd tied a good-looking bay to a rail behind him, Jake realized that the lad meant to go with him after all. When Ranald avoided his gaze, Jake supposed he was sulking and wished he'd never expressed willingness to accept his company. He hoped Farigaig had not ordered him to go.

When Jake greeted him and extended a hand, Ranald shook it, looking wary.

Understanding then that Ranald feared he might have changed his mind, Jake said, "'Tis a fine mount you're lending me, lad. Art ready to ride?"

"Aye, for you said you wanted to be away early. Are you sure you dinna mind if I go?"

"I say what I mean," Jake said, mounting the black.

Untying the bay and flinging himself onto it, Ranald said, "I didna ken if you'd want an armed escort. We have few men-at-arms here, because my da keeps those we have in Perth at Braehead, our hunting tower. 'Tis nobbut three miles or so from here if ye want a proper tail."

"If I'd wanted a tail, I'd have summoned my lads," Jake said. "I've two score of them at the harbor. Forbye, I'd liefer go quietly. I see you brought your sword and dirk. D'ye ken how to use them?"

Ranald grimaced and said, "I'm not as good as my brothers were, if that's what you mean."

"It would mean nowt to me if you'd said you *were* as good," Jake said. "I've nae ken of your brothers, lad. Just answer my question, and don't be putting thoughts in my head. Like as not, they won't match the ones I've got."

"I know how to use my weapons," Ranald said.

"Good, then."

They rode in silence for nearly half an hour, long enough to pass through the town and two miles along the Stirling Road.

Having confirmed his notion that Ranald compared himself unfavorably to his brothers, and aware that Farigaig had, too, Jake decided to let the lad choose when next to talk. He always enjoyed good conversation, but the day was fine and their pace would get them to Stirling in five hours or so.

The sensible thing would be to spend the night there and leave at dawn for Rothesay. But he knew the Glasgow road and decided he'd press on to Dunipace, a village seven miles beyond the river Forth bridge in Stirling.

It boasted a fine alehouse with excellent food and good

beds. If they stayed there, they'd make it to Rothesay Castle before noon the next day.

Alyson had listened to Lady Beatha's description of her "improvements," seen naught amiss that could not be mended after her great-aunt left, and thanked her sincerely for taking such interest in the household. Then, leaving her to her stitchery with Lady Farigaig, Alyson sought her father's steward to learn what remained to do before their guests arrived. She was deep in conversation with him when Will came running to tell her that the porter had sent him to fetch her.

"I dinna ken why," he replied when she asked. "I'd heard riders, and when I got downstairs, someone were a-knocking. Malcolm were watching 'em through the squint and said tae hie m'self and tell ye ye'd better come."

Shaking out her skirts and hoping that if unexpected guests had arrived, she would not greet them with smudges on her face, Alyson hurried upstairs from the kitchen area toward the entry. She stopped with a gasp several steps below the landing when she saw who awaited her. Both men had their backs to her, facing the main stairway to the upper floors, but she recognized them easily.

Behind her, she heard a soft, "Coo, that be them, the *pair* o' them."

Feeling faint and putting one shaking hand behind her to wave Will away, she collected herself and continued to the entry at a dignified pace.

Certain that Malcolm would never offer information about the family other than answers to specific questions from someone entitled to ask them, and certain that the men watching the upper stairway had *not* asked for her, she watched them as she said, "I see we have more visitors, Malcolm."

Both men whirled to face her, and she could not decide which one looked more astonished or paler of face. Mungo's color returned in a flush, but Niall recovered his voice first. "Allie! Thank the Fates! We thought you were dead."

"It is no thanks to you that I'm not, Niall," she said. "The two of you left me to drown." She heard Malcolm gasp but kept her eyes on Niall.

He reddened and glanced at Mungo, clearly seeking assistance.

Mungo looked sternly back at him but said only, "That was through no fault of ours, my lady, I assure you."

"Don't take me for a dafty," she retorted. "You fled that ship without sparing a thought for me."

"Now, Allie, that is *not* true," Niall said. Flicking a glance at Mungo, who nodded, he added coaxingly, "You don't understand, lass. Those pirates captured us. To escape them, we had to fling ourselves off their ship and swim for shore. We could do nowt for the *Maryenknyght* or anyone on her. She'd already sunk."

As dismayed by the obvious lies as by Niall's return, Alyson said, "Malcolm, do not disturb my lord father or mother. These gentlemen will not stay, because we have too many visitors arriving to house them as well. Doubtless, the Blackfriars will have room. Do show Sir Kentigern to a room where he can tidy himself. Whilst he does, I'll talk with Master Clyne in your sitting room."

"Now see here," Mungo said, but Alyson cut him off without hesitation.

"I *will* have privy speech with Niall," she said. "Do not try to interfere."

Clearly irked, Mungo replied with a curt nod.

"Niall, come with me," Alyson said as Malcolm led Mungo to the stairs. She entered the porter's room left of the front door and gestured Niall toward its center.

"What is this about?" he demanded without turning when she shut the door.

She moved to look him in the face and said bluntly, "It is about the pair of you lying to me, Niall. I know exactly what you and Mungo did. You boarded that pirate ship like lambs when they told you to and left me to drown. Mungo had only to crook his finger for you to leave me there."

"That is not so!"

"It is, aye. And *don't* tell me that Mungo said he'd sent someone for me."

"But he did say that!"

"He did not *send* anyone. Even if he had, you should have made sure I was aboard that ship before it left without me. You did nowt o' the sort." Hearing Jake's voice in those last words made it seem almost as if he stood beside her.

"But you are *here*, Allie," Niall said. "And, I'm delighted to see you. But you must not talk to Mungo as you did. You'll anger him."

"I don't care if I do."

"But *I* do, and I am your husband, lass. My friends—"

"You are *not*."

"Not what?"

"You are no longer my husband, Niall. I had our marriage annulled."

"You cannot possibly—"

"By my troth, sir, I'm already married to someone else."

"Who?"

"No one," Mungo snapped from the doorway, startling them. "She lies, Niall. You must teach her not to do so."

Alyson turned back to Niall. "You know I do not lie, Niall, so you should believe me when I tell you that the Papal Legate, here to consecrate Bishop Wardlaw, annulled our marriage and married me to the knight who rescued—"

She stopped when Mungo clapped a hand across her mouth and wrapped his other arm around her torso so tightly that she feared he would break ribs.

He said to Niall, "I got the porter out of the way. Look and see that no one else is there. We'll take her out the way we came in and through the North Port to your tower. I'll sort her out there."

Struggling, Alyson tried to free her mouth long enough to tell him that Niall had no tower. But she could not. Nor could she manage to bite Mungo's hand, although she tried, fiercely.

Niall's eyes widened. But he did nothing to stop his so-called friend.

Jake judged that they were nearly halfway to Stirling when Ranald said in a surly tone, "You said you'd discuss whatever I want to discuss."

"I did, aye."

"Did you mean it?"

"I told you, lad, I mean what I say."

"Well, I don't see how Allie can have married you when she is plainly married to Niall. What cause could anyone have to annul *their* marriage?"

"I'll explain," Jake said. He did so bluntly, explaining the influence he believed Mungo exerted over Niall. Ranald continued to express skepticism until Jake described just as bluntly Niall's departure from the pirate ship. The younger man's face paled then, revealing shock and dismay.

"They left her to drown? *Niall* did?"

When Jake just looked at him, Ranald said grimly, "I see. By my troth, sir, although my brothers never liked Niall, I did. I don't say you're right about him and Mungo, but I'd never have believed Niall could be capable of such betrayal."

"Believe it," Jake said.

Chapter 19

Furious that Niall had allowed Mungo to carry her off without objection, Alyson felt more helpless than she had aboard the sinking *Maryenknyght*.

Mungo kept a hand over her mouth until they were outside in the close, where she was shocked to see a crowd of men and horses. She had not known that Mungo had men of his own, but they were clearly his, because they merely watched while he used his neck scarf to gag her and Niall's to tie her hands behind her.

She recalled that Will had said he'd heard horses, but no one had said how many there were. However, Malcolm would not expect MacGillivray people to look after so many, especially after she'd said they would not be staying. Doubtless, he had been as shocked as she was to see Niall and had simply let her put first things first. To him, Niall and Mungo must have seemed harmless.

When Mungo mounted and told Niall to help set her on the saddle before him, Niall obeyed without question. Then he mounted his horse while Mungo draped his own long cloak over her and arranged it and her so that she could barely see. No passerby would notice her gag or bindings.

"If you try to scream or do aught to draw attention, lass, I will make you gey sorry," Mungo muttered in a tone that chilled her.

She told herself that she was not afraid of him. Despite the armed escort and Niall's traitorous behavior, she did not believe he would let Mungo harm her.

They rode out of the close, turned toward the North Port, and were soon outside the city wall, crossing the North Inch, where the great Clan Battle of Perth had taken place when she was twelve. Her own confederation, Clan Chattan, had won. Her uncle Shaw, as their war leader, had fought there, and Ivor had, too.

If only Jake, Ivor, or Shaw were there now! But they were not, so she would have to take herself in hand and decide what she could do.

Less than an hour later, Braehead Tower came into view, high on its lofty hilltop overlooking the river Almond two miles before it flowed into the Tay.

"There it is, Allie," Niall said. Then, glancing at her, he said, "You must remove her gag, Mungo. The men-at-arms there ken her fine."

"How many?"

"As I recall, nobbut a dozen or so."

Mungo undid her gag. As she worked her mouth to ease its dryness, he grabbed her chin and made her look at him. "How long have you been home?"

"Since yesterday," she replied, seeing no reason to anger him.

"Then these people ken nowt of the lies you told about your marriage." Her silence apparently being answer enough, he added, "You'll do as I say, or your husband—and they'll believe Niall, not you, about who that is—will punish you severely. I'll watch, too, to be sure he does a thorough job of it." Giving her chin a squeeze that would leave bruises, he said, "D'ye understand me?"

She could see Niall, but he did not look at her.

When she could talk, she said, "I don't understand what you hope to achieve by bringing me here. You called it Niall's tower, but it's my land."

"Blethers to that," Mungo said. "You have marriage settlements, deeding this estate and another one to Niall as your husband. And he *is* your husband. Sakes, you should already be carrying his bairn."

"Nay, I could not be. He never consummated our union."

She'd kept her voice down so her words would carry to no one else except perhaps Niall. But she saw that she had stunned Mungo.

He recovered swiftly. "Did anyone examine you to prove the lack of union?"

"Nay, why should they? I told you, I do not lie."

He smiled. "It matters, lass." Lowering his voice, he added, "I'll not deny I was sorry to find you alive, because Niall and I have plans for this Glen Almond land. We're going to train men-at-arms here for the Crown. We can do it with or without you. I'd liefer it be without. But if you behave…"

A chill swept over her again, and she was glad Jake was not there. The image she'd seen of him that moonlit night, slumped against a wall in darkness, and of herself cradling what was left of him, filled her mind and made her shudder.

"Good lass," Mungo murmured. "Clearly, you understand me."

Steadying herself, she said, "I understand that you

mean to have your way, but you misstated the facts. My father deeded Braehead and Ardloch to me, not to Niall. Were he still married to me, he *would* collect the rents. He'd also control the estates during my lifetime. But he cannot inherit them."

"We'll fix that when we explain that he did consummate your union."

"But he did not. Faith, he'll admit that himself," she added, raising her voice enough for Niall to hear. "Moreover, my true husband will tell—"

"Niall *is* your true husband," Mungo snapped. "Nae one else need enter into it. If anyone does, d'ye think I cannot defeat him?"

"You are gey sure of your skill," she said.

"I am sure, lass. I'm also sure that Niall and I will own those estates. Sithee, the Duke of Albany has... has taken interest in our plans. As Royal Chamberlain, he controls all charters and can take them away or award them as he chooses. He has promised to see that our plans succeed."

"King David awarded our charter over a century ago, so only the King—"

"The King is old. We'll wait for him to die if need be. I doubt we'll wait long."

Sorrow nearly overcame her. His grace *could* die at any moment, and when he did, Jamie would be King of Scots. But with Jamie in England, no one would be able to keep Albany from doing as he pleased.

~

Finding Ranald more amenable after their little chat, Jake had encouraged him to talk about himself. When he mentioned that his father was glad Allie had come home to manage things again, Jake said, "That is not her responsibility, lad. You're the one who will inherit your father's large estates. You should be doing all you can now to learn from him how to manage them yourself. 'Tis the only way you'll know how to go on when the time comes."

"I doubt he thinks me capable," Ranald said, sighing.

"Why should he?" Jake retorted. "Thinking you capable would not make you so, would it? One must seek capability for oneself, Ranald. Show him you *want* to learn and I ha' nae doots the man will welcome the opportunity to teach you."

They continued to discuss such things, and Jake described more of what had happened on the *Maryenknyght* and during their return. He did not mention Jamie or Orkney, having no idea how trustworthy Ranald might be. But he did describe Lizzie Thornwick and got a laugh from the lad when he did.

They were some five miles from Stirling when Jake recognized an alehouse that had won his favor on a previous visit.

"We'll have a bite and a sip and see what news we glean," he said.

Ranald agreed, but the result was not what Jake wanted to hear.

Seeing how swiftly and easily Mungo's men-at-arms disarmed hers and locked them in the tower dungeon, Alyson decided that compliance might provide her only defense. Pretending she yielded not to Mungo but to Niall's persuasions, she promised to stay in her bedchamber while the men gathered in her great hall.

Mungo looked skeptical, but Niall reassured him. "Allie never lies, sir. If she says she'll stay in her room, she will."

"She'd better," Mungo said. "Can this place accommodate my men?"

"Not without notice," Alyson said. "They can camp in our woods by the river, but they must look after their horses and cook their own food. The kitchen *can* feed up to a score, if you want to feed your commanders. But it will take time to produce even a light supper for that many." Without another word, she went upstairs, cudgeling her mind for a plan.

She had been alone for a quarter hour when she heard the latch softly click. As she looked up, the door opened to reveal Will at the threshold.

Putting a finger to his lips, he stepped in and shut the door. "I feared ye might ha' bolted it," he confided, grinning.

"Mungo would break it down if I did. How did you find me here?"

"I hung about after ye flapped your hand at me, so I saw Mungo go into the room wi' Malcolm and come out without him is how. I found Malcolm on the floor and thought he were dead. But he moved, so I ran down tae the kitchen and told 'em he were hurt. Then I got me a horse from the stable and followed ye. Sithee, it were easy tae follow so many horses."

"I'm glad you did, because you can help me," she said. "I want you to go down to the kitchen. Are the men still in the hall?"

"Aye, sure. There be a score o' them a-talking in there and more outside."

"Well, don't let them see you. The kitchen is below the hall. Tell the cook that I'm here against my will and to send for our people hereabouts to meet in the yard as soon as they can with as many men and weapons as they can bring. And tell Cook to send a pair of mounted men to the road leading into the Highlands. I have kinsmen coming, who may be near enough to help us. I don't have a plan yet, Will, but I'm thinking. Sakes, if our people can help me get away..."

"I'll tell 'em, aye. I told Malcolm and them at the house that them villains took ye. And I tellt 'em, too, tae send some'un straightaway for Cap'n Jake."

Alyson's heart sang, and the calm Jake could instill in her with a touch enveloped her like a warm blanket. Too soon, though, common sense and memory of his slumped body warned her that Will might draw Jake right into a deathtrap.

A steady buzz of solemn masculine conversation greeted Jake and Ranald when they entered the alehouse. The ale-master bustled to greet them.

"I've nae table for ye," he said. "But ye be gey welcome tae me ale. I'll warn ye, though, 'tis a sad day for Scotland."

"What has happened?" Jake asked.

"His grace is dead."

Although he'd half-expected the news, Jake felt a rush of sorrow, for Jamie as much as for his sire.

"When?" he asked.

"Yestereve or this morning, depending who tells it. They say the Duke o' Albany ha' sent men tae Perth and be gathering more tae take there wi' him. The chaps he sent tae warn the Blackfriars tae expect him stopped in for a dram. They said the King signed a letter tae Parliament two days ago, recommending Albany as Governor again. 'Tis likely they'll name him tae govern for Jamie now."

"How soon does Albany leave?"

"Sakes, he could be on his horse whiles we talk," the alemaster said.

Jake said, "We'll have ale and cheese, and be on our way."

When the man left, Ranald said, "Sakes, the King is dead? Does that mean Albany will become King of Scots?"

"Not yet, it doesn't," Jake said. "Jamie is King now."

"He's nobbut a lad," Ranald said. "He cannot rule the country."

"Nay, and you heard the man. Albany has a letter from his grace, so doubtless Parliament will name him to rule for James."

"I never thought to ask you why we're going to Stirling," Ranald said.

"It is not important now. We're going back."

"But—"

"If you must know, I was going to Rothesay from Stirling. I said nowt of that because I'm not sure how much to trust you. I was to see his grace."

"Sakes, have you *met* him?"

"Nay, but I had a message for him."

"What was it?"

"It does not matter anymore, because things are as they are. We're turning back. If we go at once, I can be with my lass when she goes to bed."

"Sakes, we've come at least twenty miles on these horses," Ranald protested. "They'll be weary by now, as am I."

"We haven't pushed them, and we won't. If you don't want to go back, ask the alemaster to put you up here for the night."

In the tower stableyard, with dusk approaching, Alyson studied the expectant faces of MacGillivray men that the cook's lads had collected, and tried to think. She could not get to her men in the dungeon, and too few stood before her. She feared that if Mungo strode into their midst and began issuing orders, they'd obey him.

They stood silent, wary. With two exceptions, they looked eager to support her, but she knew she could lose them all if she misspoke.

Beside her, Will shuffled his feet but, wisely, did not speak.

Seeking inspiration, her gaze alit on a small stack of peat with two shovels stuck into it. It reminded her of peat squares flying from horses' hooves, and the forest of pikes and lances in her nightmare. When she recalled next the monk-high stacks she'd seen at Lindores Abbey, a possibility suggested itself. Numerous tall stacks of drying peat, future fuel for the tower's fires, stood nearby.

"I need your help," she said at last, hoping her voice would carry to her men without drawing attention from inside the tower. "Braehead Tower is mine," she added. "I think you know how much you all mean to me and my family, but a man has come who would seize Braehead for himself. I want to stop him. I must tell you, though; he is a close friend of Niall Clyne's. You all ken fine by now that I married Niall. So, doubtless, you also know, thanks to the speed at which such news travels, that we were sailing to France when English pirates sank our ship."

She paused, saw nodding heads, and continued. "They captured Niall and others but left me to drown. A knight named Jacob Maxwell, who saw us sinking from his much smaller ship, rescued me and this lad beside me. When we learned that the pirates had thrown most of our men overboard, keeping only those who could pay ransom, we believed Niall had drowned." Briefly, even glibly, she explained that the Papal Legate had deemed her marriage false, annulled it, and married her to Jake to protect her estates and reputation.

"I won't try to persuade you to think aught about what I've told you save what your conscience dictates," she added. "Forbye, Niall and Sir Kentigern want to seize control of Braehead because they choose to believe that my marriage settlements granted this estate and Ardloch to Niall."

"But that canna be," one man said. "The laird wouldna put our land out o' the family, nor awa' from Clan MacGillivray. He'll tell them so."

"He would, Gibby, but they'd ignore him," Alyson said. "I told them that the estates form the principal part of my tocher and never belonged to Niall. But Sir Kentigern says that by Crown authority my estates will *become* Niall's and that they plan to train men-at-arms here for the Crown."

"For the Crown, eh?" Gibby said. "But his grace be at Rothesay and wouldna thrust hisself betwixt his people and their lands. Forbye, the men wha' came wi' them thieves today said *they'd* come from Stirling."

Another man said, "We ken fine who *does* seize lands. Sakes, he makes a habit o' stealing 'em from women when he can, and he *is* in Stirling. I'd wager me best bull the villain claiming such authority be yon wicked duke, Albany."

Muttered assent came from others in her audience.

Alyson said, "What matters now is that we're too few to muster a strong defense. Sir Jacob is away, but we've sent for him, and he will bring more men. Also, kinsmen, including Shaw MacGillivray, war leader of Clan Chattan, will—"

"*How* was your marriage tae Clyne a false one?" a man shouted. She recognized the voice.

"Those details, Rab Barty, don't concern you," she said. "The Papal Legate has authority to undo an improper marriage and perform a proper one. By Kirk law, it is as if the Pope himself unmarried me from Niall and married me to Sir Jacob. Now, all of you," she said when no one else spoke up. "The villains are at supper in the woods and in the hall, but if they get warning of approaching riders, they'll swiftly arm themselves. I need your help and advice to prevent them from doing so or at least to give them pause until help arrives. Let me tell you what I propose."

The men remained silent.

"Regard that peat pile yonder," she said, gesturing. "To me, those two shovel handles sticking up might, in poor light, be mistaken for pikes or lances."

"They may look so, mistress, but we've few men tae speak of, and that wee pile o' peat doesna look like one man, let alone a host o' armed ones," Gibby said.

"Aye, but the peat stacks yonder by the woods *are* tall

enough," she replied, gesturing again. "If we shift them into woodland shadows and stick every tool we have with a long handle into them, can we not make them look as if we have a small army of men poorly concealed there? After all, we need fool only Mungo, Niall, and the men-at-arms they brought with them."

"We heard that they expect more tae come," Gibby said.

"Sir Kentigern lies, so if he said he *expects* more, it is likely an empty threat, and we need keep him at bay only until help arrives. If he and his men take over tonight and their reinforcements come before ours do, Braehead is lost."

Gibby said doubtfully, "We might make it work, m'lady, but just for the night. And only if the moon be late rising or them clouds can hide it. Also, if they see what we be a-doing afore we get set and full darkness comes… Sithee—"

"I know," she said. "But if it *might* work…"

"It willna serve past dawn," he warned.

"I ha' me doots it'll serve at all," pessimist Rab Barty declared.

"Aye, well, ye'll shut your gob and do as ye're bid, Rab," Gibby warned, "or ye'll answer tae me."

"That's tellin' 'im," Will muttered.

"Shhh," Alyson murmured back. Aloud, she said, "I'll leave it to you to make those stacks look like our army, because I must get back inside before they miss me. Will, you may stay and help them or come with me, as you choose."

"I'd best go wi' ye," Will said. "Sir Jake said I should watch over ye, and I dinna trust them two deevils inside as far as I could spit 'em."

As they crossed the inner yard to approach the tower entrance, she saw men emerging. Enough light lingered for her to see Will slip a hand under his jerkin.

"If you've hidden a dirk, don't touch it," she said. "Niall is with them. He won't let anyone hurt us."

"I dinna trust him any more than t'other 'un," Will said darkly.

"Well, I do," Alyson said, hoping she *could* trust Niall and wondering if she'd ever really known him.

~

Jake was keeping an eye on the sky, as was his habit wherever he was. Clouds had gathered in the afternoon but only enough to provide a good sunset. The sun touched the western hills, so it would be dusk before long.

Ranald had been quiet, clearly thinking. He said, "Why do you think Albany is coming to Perth?"

"I wish I knew," Jake replied. "He should be arranging his grace's funeral."

He wondered about the men Albany had sent ahead and wished he'd thought to ask *when* and if the alemaster had seen them go by or had only heard about them. Jake had a bad feeling about it, but if the duke was on their heels and were to overcome them, the meeting might offer a chance to renew his acquaintance with Albany. The duke would likely recall his obligation to him, and reminding him of that debt now might prove useful in future.

He noted that he'd increased his pace, and slowed. Impatience to see Alyson was no reason to punish his horse. His thoughts returned to their last discussion.

He was not a man to put his foot down where women were concerned. He'd never before had one for whom he felt responsible, although he did keep an eye on Giff's wife, Sidony, when Giff was away. She sometimes sought Jake's advice, but he could not imagine himself commanding her to obey him. Giff frequently did, sometimes successfully.

But Alyson was *his* wife, and there were things he had to clarify with her if they were not to be often at odds. Her relationship with her demanding family was one such thing. Her father was still man enough to look after his own if he'd take the trouble. That he had abdicated his responsibilities was not Allie's fault. But her willingness to assume them let both MacGillivray and Ranald take unseemly advantage of her. Although Ranald seemed to take Jake's advice to heart, if Allie felt obliged to stay home and run things, Ranald would let her.

The obvious solution was for Jake to insist that he and Allie live on that second estate of hers, near the Moray Firth. It would be accessible for the *Sea Wolf*, and if things went well, he could harbor her nearby and arrange to acquire another vessel for the Isles. These images pleased him more than his earlier thoughts, and he had decided just to tell her what they would do, when Ranald said, "That lad yonder's in a gey great hurry."

Jake was making way for the rider pounding toward them, when Ranald exclaimed, "Sakes, that's one of our kitchen lads, sir. Hey, Tam!"

"What is it, Tam?" Jake demanded when the rider yanked his horse to a plunging halt. "Is aught amiss with Lady Alyson?"

"Aye, but no as ye mean it . . . or no as bad . . ."

"Just spit it out, lad. What's amiss?"

"Her husband came back from the dead."

"*What!*" Jake and Ranald exclaimed as one voice.

"Aye, and Sir Kentigern be wi' him, Master Ranald. So he's no dead neither. They say Lady Alyson's lands dinna belong tae her but be Niall Clyne's, on account o' their marriage. They didna ask the laird aboot that."

"How do you know this, Tam?" Jake asked.

"That Will Fletcher what came wi' ye told us, sir. He said they took her ladyship away. He sent me tae tell ye. And Malcolm Milroy and the laird sent a lad off, too, tae try tae find kinsmen what be coming from the Highlands. The laird said they might be near enough tae fetch quick."

"Mayhap they will be," Jake said. "But what do you mean, they took her? Surely, her father and the others—"

"Did nowt, sir. Nobbut there were nowt they *could* do. Sir Kentigern had dunamany men wi' him, Will said, and they slipped away. See you, Sir Kentigern knocked Malcolm down. Had Will no found him—"

"Where have they gone?"

"Tae the hunting tower," Tam said. "Will heard 'em and said I should hie me tae find ye. I near killed this pony a-getting here."

"You did well," Jake said. "We must get back to—" He had another thought. "The hunting tower, Ranald, did you not say it lies three miles northwest of town?"

Ranald said, "Aye, atop a hill near the river Almond. We get prime hunting in Glen Almond in springtime and fall."

Jake's thoughts raced. "How many men do those villains have, Tam?"

"Will said three score or more. He didna count 'em. Also, Sir Kentigern said the Crown will protect Niall's rights. We all ken fine that means Albany—"

"Albany is on his way," Jake said. "We may be less than an hour ahead of him. He means to stay with the Blackfriars tonight."

He did not mention the King's death or that Albany could now be certain that, with his grace's letter to present, he'd easily reclaim the Governorship. Moreover, with the new King of Scots captive in England, Albany had good reason to get to Perth and take control as the lords of Parliament arrived, rather than wait and make a grand entrance after they'd gathered, as had been his habit.

Ranald said, "We can reach the tower from here, sir. A turning just ahead will take us there. 'Tis nobbut six miles from here."

"How hard would it be for me to find the tower alone?"

"Sakes, you cannot miss it. The road from town runs along the river Tay, and the Almond flows into the Tay. Sithee, the Tay road crosses the Almond within sight of the tower. At night you'll see its lights easily. But I'll go with you."

"Nay, for I want you and Tam to ride to town as fast as you can. My men from the *Sea Wolf* are at the harbor. Find my man Mace, and get my lads mounted. I'll take that turning ahead and meet you at the tower. Send Tam here to the house to arrange for horses. They'll have enough there for thirty men?"

"Aye," Ranald said. "I'll *find* enough."

Jake heard him but was already riding for the turn.

Chapter 20

Alyson was determined to hold her own with Niall. She knew he not could see her men in the outer yard and hoped to keep him from going farther.

"What are you doing here, Allie?"

"This is my home, Niall. I go where I like."

"You know you promised Mungo you'd stay in your room."

"No one need keep a promise to dishonorable men, Niall. I don't answer to Mungo, or to you. You left me to die. You know you did."

"I did not know you were still on the ship!"

Beside her, Will snorted.

"How can I believe you when you lied about the rest, Niall?" she demanded, ignoring Will. "You boarded that ship willingly, and you did *not* jump overboard. For all I know, you are as complicit in Jamie's capture as Mungo is."

"We had nowt to do with the bairn!"

She stared at him. "Is *that* how you manage your conscience? Do you pretend that Jamie, although heir to the crown, is just a bairn rather than a noble and thoughtful prince betrayed by his greedy uncle's wicked schemes?"

Niall had the grace to look ashamed, but he made no apology.

She knew she'd do better to keep silent and was sure that Jake would recommend it, but she had been silent about too many things for too long. She said, "I thought I knew you, but I do not."

"Then how can you *know* we did not save ourselves by jumping overboard?"

Will made another sound, this one a sibilant huff of disgust.

"Because I ken fine that you cannot swim," she retorted. "When I think how desperately worried I was about you when we learned that they had *thrown* so many overboard, I feel sick."

"We should not have lied, Allie. I don't know why we did."

"*You* lied because Mungo did or because he told you to. Does his good opinion of you matter so much more than anyone else's?"

"I suppose it may," he admitted. "But we should not have lied. I should have remembered that you know I can't swim."

He avoided her eye, and she wanted him to look at her.

"Niall." She waited until, reluctantly, he met her gaze. "Saying that you forgot I know the truth just means you are sorry that you got caught," she said. "Frankly, I think you did remember but decided that my knowing was irrelevant. The one thing you've said that I do believe is that *you* thought I'd drowned. A dead woman could not call you a liar, could she?"

"Allie, don't... you mustn't. You'll upset yourself to no avail. You heard what Mungo said. Albany promised that your estates will be lawfully mine. And Albany will keep his word."

"I'd wager that when he said that, he believed you were my husband. But you are not."

"As I'm not dead, lass, Mungo says Albany will direct Wardlaw and your legate to put things back as they should be. Albany did say that the land is mine as your husband, and after we brought him word so quickly of the disaster at Flamborough Head, he promised to make sure that it remained so."

"Certes, but you are a fool, and stupid withal," Alyson said. "Or do you merely pretend not to *know* that your odious Mungo betrayed us all?"

"What a thing to say!"

"But true, aye," Will muttered.

His mutter drew a look from Niall. It was only a look, but Niall's anger was plain, increasing Alyson's doubt that he'd known about Mungo's true mission.

"Think, Niall," she said. "How do you imagine that you and Mungo acquired an armed English escort to see you to the Scottish border?"

"I don't understand how you can know so much, Allie, and not recall that our two countries are at peace."

"Yet Will heard the pirate captain say that the reason they stopped our ship was that it lacked English Harry's permission to be in his waters. Truce or none, you *must* know that Harry regards Scotland as an errant English possession."

"But the fact that Mungo and I did travel safely, with English men-at-arms willing to keep us safe, proves the truce."

"For mercy's sake! That pirate captain *knew* his

prizes—Jamie and Orkney. Neither Mungo nor you could fetch much ransom, Niall, and every *Maryenknyght* man except you two went into the sea. Why did you not? I saw Mungo the next day at the Blue Boar. He told the taverner that he carried a royal safe-conduct to get him home to Scotland."

Niall glowered. "You cannot know any such thing."

"But I do, because the taverner told Sir Jacob. And Mungo certainly did not get a royal safe-conduct from the King of Scots to cross England. The only one who could issue such a document is English Harry. If you can think of any reason for his doing so, other than Mungo's having betrayed Jamie's presence on our ship, so the English could capture him, prithee tell me what it is."

Niall looked mulish. "Do *not* be such a fool as to fling that wild accusation at Mungo," he said sternly.

Calmly, Alyson said, "It is no mere accusation, Niall. It is the unpalatable truth. Now, stand aside. I'm going in."

He hesitated. But when she moved, he did step aside, and she swept past him with a blessedly silent Will at her heels.

Only as they neared the entrance did Will mutter, "Hoots, but that man's a feardie! Ye'll be gey happier wi' Cap'n Jake as your man than *him*."

Alyson's lips parted to call him to order before realization struck that she agreed completely. She was more than happier. She was in love with Jake.

An hour later, Jake crested a rise and saw the tower looming out of the darkness. Lights shone in four windows, and pale moonlight through occluding clouds turned the tower walls a ghostly gray. Leaving his horse in woods below the tower, he skirted the hill to explore. The first thing he saw was a clearing below with campfires, men around them, and snuffling horses grazing nearby.

He slipped by and came to a stable and stableyard. The yard was large and dark, and men moved in it like shadows. Woodland beyond it looked occupied, too. He saw no sign of Alyson and no way to enter the tower or pass safely across the outer yard to what looked like a courtyard leading into the tower. So he returned to the hillside to await his men, and saw riders soon afterward.

They carried no torches but traveled by the pale, hazy glow of the moon, reassuring him that they weren't Albany's. When the moon peeked between clouds, brightening, he recognized Mace in the lead with Ranald riding beside him.

They slowed when he neared them, and he heard Ranald say, "If they're keeping watch, they'll see us coming."

Knowing his men would be alert for trouble, Jake said, "I saw many camped on the hillside above the river and others in woods east of the yard, so beware. None will recognize us, so we'll approach quietly as if we ken nowt o' them."

Turning his mount, he led the way up and around through woodland west of the tower. When they rounded the hilltop and the stableyard came into view, he saw many more men gathered there.

Tension filled the air, stirring him to reach back and adjust his sword.

Mace and Ranald had brought him thirty-four men. But if Will had judged aright when he'd seen them in town, Lyle commanded half again as many.

To the two riding behind him, Jake said, "Pass word

back that every man must keep his head and do nowt without my command."

He could see in the brighter moonlight that things had reached some sort of standoff in the yard. Men who looked like farmers holding rakes, hoes, shovels, and the occasional lance, axe, or pike faced many more men-at-arms. No one moved.

"That's Mungo... Sir Kentigern," Ranald murmured. "The one wearing the French breastplate, with his long cloak flung back to show it off."

The man's breastplate gleamed like polished silver, an absurdity against farmers, Jake thought. Urging his mount on slowly, he wondered if Mungo's sword was as well-maintained as his plate and if he would challenge him.

Jake hoped he would.

The man-at-arms who seemed most likely to do so was the only visible man of Mungo's on horseback. Mungo remained as he was. A younger chap stood beside him, whom Ranald identified as Clyne. Either both men were trying to appear indifferent to Jake and his men or they had mistaken them for someone else's.

The mounted man, likely Mungo's captain of arms, rode up to them, saying, "This be private land, sirs. Ye've missed your road a half mile back."

"Sakes," Ranald said, "who do you think you are?"

Just then, Jake's sweeping gaze alit on Alyson, nearly out of sight behind Mungo. Two other men flanked her... nay, dared to restrain her.

Aware that Ranald was still speaking, Jake interrupted to say firmly to the captain, "You are the one who errs, sirrah. I am Sir Jacob Maxwell. The lady Alyson is my wife, and this is our land."

"Seize him," Mungo said, but the men afoot hesitated.

"You are in the wrong, sir," Jake said, shifting his gaze to Mungo.

"Dinna come closer, sir, or ye'll regret it," the mounted captain said, drawing Jake's attention swiftly back to assess him.

"I dinna think *I'll* be the one to regret it," Jake said softly, challengingly.

The captain whipped out his sword, but Jake was faster. He parried it with a clang, feinted high, and when the captain began to raise his to deflect it, Jake reversed with a twist and sent the other weapon up and away. A farmer, holding a shovel in one hand, snatched the sword out of the air by its hilt with his free hand.

"Dismount and return to your men," Jake said to the stunned captain, who looked over his shoulder as if trying to understand what had happened.

Turning back to eye Jake defiantly, the man said, "Unless there be more wi' ye than I see, we outnumber ye by many."

"We have support," Jake said, gesturing toward the farmers he assumed to be Alyson's tenants.

The captain snorted. "A worthless lot. Tried tae pretend tae be an army by sticking shovel handles and such up from yon peat stacks. I'll admit they looked summat like a company o' lancers till the moon peeked out o' the clouds. It turned them right quick from armed men tae peat stacks."

"We'd give you fierce battle," Jake said. "But you should hear me out first." Looking at Mungo, he said, "You are a knight of the realm, sir. So I'll do you the honor to explain why attacking us would be a grave mistake."

" 'Tis yourself be making the mistake," Mungo snarled. "I act for the Duke of Albany. *He* promised me this land."

"I heard it a bit differently, but as you are a fellow knight, I'll accept your version of what he may have said. Forbye, since you claim him for a friend, you should know that he is likewise a friend of mine."

"Aye, sure, he is," Mungo retorted with a sneer.

"I've known him since my childhood," Jake said calmly. "Moreover, he believes he is deeply indebted to me. So, I assure you, he will disapprove of your plan to take *any* land from my lady wife."

"Albany holds himself indebted to nae one. He keeps his word, too. Sakes, I'll let ye face him for yourself when he comes, as he will shortly. In troth, I'd expected him afore now."

"He suffered a delay, thanks to news he received this morning," Jake said. "But he did say he would stay with the Blackfriars, so I suggest you send someone to meet him in town and guide him here. Your man can also take a message from me. Then Albany can decide who is friend and who is not."

Mungo looked shaken at hearing such news of Albany's intentions coming from Jake but said staunchly, "I'll do nae such daft thing. Seize them, lads!"

The swordless captain reached for his dirk, but a gesture of Jake's weapon persuaded him to hesitate. He glanced at his master.

Jake, too, looked at Mungo, aware of a nervous stirring of men in the yard and those behind him. His own men had put hands to their weapons but would not draw them without his command.

He thought Mungo would see the folly of engaging a

mounted troop with most of his men afoot. Then, hearing noises from the track near the tower, he glanced that way. Mounted men appeared there.

"They are also mine," Mungo said grimly.

Jake met his gaze. "We should talk privily."

"Ye'd do better tae surrender. Tell your men tae throw down their arms."

"I think not," Jake said.

Reaching behind him, Mungo grabbed Alyson and jerked her forward, drawing his dirk as he did and aiming the point of its blade low between her breasts.

"Do as ye're bid, sir, or I'll split her. Then we'll hang ye as a welcome tae your good friend Albany, who doubtless finds ye as great a nuisance as I do. None will be left then tae debate Niall's claim tae this land and *mine*."

Alyson had managed to move enough to see past Mungo. Because she was watching Jake, Mungo's swift move to grab her had caught her off guard. She'd tried to wrench away, but he was too strong, and now his dirk pricked her just below the joining of her ribs, forcing her back against him out of fear that he might, even inadvertently, pierce through.

Niall shouted at Mungo to let her go, but the point pressed harder.

Mungo shifted away from Niall, still holding her tightly, but Niall grabbed the hand gripping the dirk. Certain that he would not be strong enough to hold it for long, she was terrified that in the struggle, Mungo might kill her.

His left arm was a bar across her upper chest. As they wrestled for control, that arm shifted up nearer her throat.

Sensing that he'd fixed his concentration on Niall, she eased her upper arm free of his fingertips. She heard Jake shout but paid no heed.

The pressure of the dirk's point eased.

Her right arm slipped free, and the point shifted away. Alyson ducked, jabbed her elbow into Mungo's midsection as hard as she could, wrenched free, and shot out under his arm. Tripping over his feet—or her own—she fell headlong, and scrambled up in time to see Niall collapse.

"Niall!" Rushing to his side, she shouted at Mungo, "What have you *done*?"

Mungo stood frozen. Then he dropped to a knee beside her. "Niall, lad, look at me," he begged. "Och, laddie, why did ye interfere?"

"Get away from him, you villain," Alyson cried as she probed gently but swiftly to find where Niall was wounded.

"Don't, Allie," he murmured. "That devilish blade"—he paused, gasping—"it drove straight... into my chest. I'm done."

"Nay, you're not!" she cried, slipping an arm under his shoulders and drawing him close, as if she might keep him from dying by force of will.

He gazed at Mungo. "Not your fault, m' lad," he muttered. "But... you should not... have threatened... Allie." On that last word, his voice broke in a rattling sob, and he grew heavier in her arms. Shocked, she recalled her vision, when she had thought the man she held was Jake.

Firm hands gripped her shoulders, and she heard Jake's voice from a great distance, saying, "He's gone, love. We'll look after him now."

"Nay!" The word exploded from Mungo in a bellow of fury that snapped her back into the moment, in time to see his body fly toward her.

Before she realized that he was leaping at Jake, Jake straightened and his hands left her shoulders, apparently to defend himself against Mungo.

Bending protectively over Niall, she did not see what Jake did. But she heard a sort of thump. Collecting her wits enough to realize that he had done something to send Mungo soaring up and over himself as well as over Niall and her, she looked back to see Mungo crash hard to the ground.

In seconds, Mungo was on his feet, charging Jake again. Trusting Jake's abilities, Alyson watched confidently as Mungo's own fury carried him chin-first into Jake's fist and senseless to the ground.

"Mace, see to him," Jake said, wincing and cradling his right hand in his left.

Alyson returned her attention to Niall, but Jake had been right.

Niall was dead.

~

Jake's hand hurt enough to make him fear he might have damaged it badly. But seeing tears on Alyson's cheeks banished his physical pain and stirred something new inside.

The image of Mungo holding a dagger to her breast had evoked fear in him unlike any he'd known. That he might have lost her had been bad enough. Seeing her weep over Clyne stirred something that made him feel murderous again until she looked up, her eyes still full of tears but with a new, soft look on her face that Jake knew she meant for him.

That look sent a glow of warmth through him. But he had no time to savor it.

Shouting for two of his men, he went to her. "Let my lads take him now, love," he said gently.

"Aye," she said, letting him help her up. "He tried to protect me, Jake, and it cost him..." Her voice broke.

"I'm grateful to him, sweetheart. 'Tis Lyle who should be dead. In troth, he should be glad he's unconscious. If he weren't, I'd kill him."

She looked at him, her lashes damp and heavy. He knew that she was recalling the night on the *Sea Wolf* when she had thought she'd seen his death.

His own emotions still unstable, he greeted with relief the two men he had summoned. "Take care of him, lads. He may have saved my lady's life tonight."

"Will we bury him in the graveyard here?" one of them asked.

Alyson said, "Find my steward and tell him to ask some of our women to prepare Master Niall for burial. They'll know what to do. We must summon a priest, too, to say words over him."

"This 'un be coming round, Cap'n," Mace said of Mungo.

Jake turned and knew that Mungo would make no more trouble.

Getting unsteadily to his feet, the man stared at Niall.

"Niall's dead then," he muttered.

"He is, aye," Jake replied. "Your dirk..."

"I ken fine it was mine," Mungo said. "I never meant..." He paused and then seemed unable or unwilling to continue.

Watching him, Jake saw that he was truly shaken, even grief stricken.

Glancing at Alyson, he saw similar awareness in her eyes.

Nevertheless, the situation remained precarious.

Mungo said to one of his men, "Fetch my cloak." When the man handed it to him, he draped it carefully, tenderly, over Niall's body.

"Jake," Alyson said, looking beyond him.

He turned and saw that Mungo's other men had dismounted.

One stepped forward but kept his distance as he said, "If ye've got summat tae say tae the Duke o' Albany, ye'll soon ha' the pleasure. The man be a-riding up the hill yonder wi' a long tail o' followers."

"Good sakes, he cannot want to stay here!" Alyson exclaimed.

"He won't," Jake said. "I'd wager that he came with a force of men to ensure that Lyle and Clyne would succeed in claiming the land he'd promised them. But he'll stay with the Blackfriars tonight."

"You seem sure of that, sir."

"I am, but it will gain them nowt," Jake said. Turning to Mungo and seeing him still gazing blindly at Niall's cloak-covered body, he said to Mungo's captain, "Send one of your lads to meet Albany: Tell him the captain of the *Serpent Royal* desires speech with him here at his earliest convenience."

The captain nodded to one of his men, who darted off. To Jake, the captain said, "I'll tell the others tae stand down, sir. That might anger the master, but I'm thinking we'll see nae more fighting tonight."

Eyeing Mungo, Jake agreed. "I'll keep my men as they are, though, until we know what Albany means to do."

The captain nodded. "The master thought much o' Master Niall. The lad were like his shadow, always following where he led. Ye could ha' knocked me down wi' a quill when he tried tae interfere wi' him as he did."

"Lady Alyson *was* Master Niall's wife for a time," Jake said dryly. "One might expect he'd take exception to anyone threatening her with a dirk."

"Aye, perhaps," the other said doubtfully.

The runner returned soon afterward, bobbed in Jake's direction, and said, "He says he'll see ye and hear ye oot, sir, if only tae hang ye straightaway."

Jake nodded. To Alyson, he said, "You go on inside, love. You won't want to see him, so slip on upstairs. I won't be long."

Hesitating, she reached out a hand to him. "Prithee, sir, aid me so I do not fall again," she said. "Niall was heavy, and my leg went to sleep."

"Aye, sure," he said. Extending a forearm, he murmured in the same dry tone he'd used to supply Niall's reason for protecting her, "Can you walk thus supported, madam, or shall I carry you?"

"I'll manage, although it still feels as if pins and needles are shooting up my right leg." To the messenger, who gaped at them, she said, "You did mean that the duke will be coming round here, did you not?"

"Aye, d'ye no hear their horses a-coming . . . m'lady?" he added hastily when Jake caught his eye.

"Then, prithee," she said, turning to Mungo's captain, "leave Sir Kentigern to grieve and take your lads and horses into the woods, where you may prepare for departure whilst Sir Jacob and I make Albany welcome." To one of the farmers, she said, "Gibby, prithee..." She gestured toward the peat stacks.

Nodding, he signaled his men and melted into the shadows with them.

Deducing that she wanted to speak privately with him, Jake dismissed the two waiting to tend Niall's body. As they strode to join Mace and the others near the stable, leaving Mungo to a lone vigil, Jake said, "Sweetheart, I think—"

"We will see Albany together, sir."

"In troth, I do think it wiser—"

"I ken fine what you think, sir. If we discover that my presence prevents needful discourse, I shall go in. Meantime, I'll wait with you to greet the duke, if only to remind him whose property this is."

Involuntarily, Jake's mouth quirked when he realized whom she was really reminding, but he managed not to grin. It would not do to let the lass rule the roost entirely—not when he was at home—although it would be fun sometimes to let her try. She was eminently capable of managing any household. But he knew, just as she did, that he would have his say in theirs.

He said, "We'll wait then and trust that he takes no offense at the lack of a formal welcome. One wonders if he expected to ride into a battle."

"In troth, I think Mungo's men are glad you avoided one. They must have seen that this land belongs to me. Faith, Mungo may still insist that it's his."

"He'd do better to accept disappointment," Jake said.

Although Alyson hoped that Albany would validate Jake's trust in him, she could not be as confident of the duke's acceptance of her unusual annulment and marriage to Jake as Jake seemed to be. If Albany had promised her estates to Mungo in return for betraying Jamie, then...

Armed horsemen rounded the tower. The first two carried the royal banner and Albany's personal one. They drew rein just inside the yard.

"Identify yourself," the one on the right commanded, looking at Jake.

Alyson stiffened at the man's tone and opened her mouth to explain that they were on her land. Slight pressure of Jake's fingers against her hand stilled the words on her tongue.

He said calmly, "If ye'll rein your horse aside, I'll identify myself to your master. Ye'll find that his grace, the duke, kens me well."

"Do I?" Albany said coolly, urging his horse forward as the leaders made way. The duke wore all black, as usual, and rode a richly caparisoned black horse. Looking at Jake, he added, "I approve of the royal manner in which you address me, sir. But you are either too arrogant for your own good or a regrettable liar. You do not look at all familiar to me."

"Aye, well, when ye clap your keekers on me in brighter light, I'm thinking ye'll ken me fine, m'lord duke," Jake said in a much stronger, much commoner accent than any Alyson had yet heard from him. "I'd be that same wretched bairn wha' saved ye from them wicked assassins years back. Though I've growed since then, d'ye still say ye dinna ken me the noo?"

A brief but pregnant silence ensued.

"I do recall you, Jake Maxwell," Albany said. "Step nearer, lad."

Alyson could not tell what the duke was thinking. He gave nothing away by demeanor or tone.

When Jake did not immediately obey him, Albany made a slight beckoning gesture. Jake squeezed her hand, urging her forward with him.

She wondered if he had dared to give Albany the same look he gave her when he expected her to understand what he was asking of her. In any event, he'd interpreted Albany's gesture to mean that they might approach him together.

Chapter 21

Albany said, "You identified yourself as the captain of the *Serpent Royal*, Jake Maxwell. I'll wager you no longer call the ship so."

"I call her *Sea Wolf*, my lord, which was what my fellow students at St. Andrews called me because of my skills on the water."

"You studied with Bishop Traill, then."

"I did, for my sins."

A gleam touched Albany's eyes but whether of humor or something else, Jake could not determine. The duke said, "The *Serpent* is still on the water?"

"She is, aye, and will be for years to come," Jake said. "In troth, although I am most grateful to you, sir, loving her as I do, I think you were right daft to leave her for me to claim at my coming of age."

"As I recall the matter, despite a regrettable impudence in your manner then, which I see that you've failed to overcome, you *had* rendered me a signal service. But how is it that we find ourselves together now? I came here to meet Sir Kentigern Lyle. Is he indisposed?"

"You might say so, sir," Jake said. "He ran into my fist.

Perhaps, before I explain, I should present the lady Alyson MacGillivray to you."

"I do recall her ladyship from events at the royal court," Albany said with a nod to Alyson. "She married Master Niall Clyne, did she not?"

"Aye, she did, but the Papal Legate annulled their marriage."

"You interest me, lad. How came *that* about?"

"The matter is personal to her ladyship, sir. 'Tis sufficient to say that the legate deemed their marriage null and married her to me."

"Two estates were included in her marriage settlement to Clyne."

"Not only does the annulment render that settlement moot, my lord, but her father deeded this estate and the other one to Lady Alyson as part of her tocher."

"You are *certain* that Farigaig deeded the land solely to her?"

"I am. More to the purpose," Jake went on, "Niall Clyne is dead by Sir Kentigern's hand. It was an accident, witnessed by many. As you see, Sir Kentigern remains distraught," he added with a gesture toward Mungo, ten yards away, his body revealing grief in every line as he kept vigil over Niall's body.

Albany's lips pressed together. "I do see that Clyne's death must have been unintentional," he said. "However, your marriage to her ladyship seems most extraordinary. If it should be deemed unlawful..."

Jake needed no interpretation of his meaning and nor, by the way she gripped his arm, did Alyson. When women owned land that the acquisitive duke wanted, his behavior was well-established. He made those women royal wards and took their lands under his own control or gifted them to men he sought as allies.

But Jake still had arrows in his quiver, and he let them fly. "By my troth, sir, we present no danger to you," he said. "But by law, the estates must remain her ladyship's. Not only does her father still live and retain the right to dispose of them as he chooses, but Sir Kentigern Lyle can have *no* lawful claim on them. Despite what Lyle may have told you, any claim that her erstwhile husband *thought* he had ended with the annulment of their marriage, not to mention his death. The most pertinent fact, though, is that Niall Clyne, although fond of her ladyship as a friend, was—utterly, completely, and widely known to be—under *his* friend Lyle's thumb."

Silence ensued. Although it lasted long enough to make Jake uneasy and pray that Albany was as swift of mind as he believed him to be, he became aware that the hand Alyson still rested on his forearm had relaxed. His peripheral vision revealed that her expression was again serene. Whatever fears Albany had stirred in her, Jake's words had extinguished, to his relief.

He did not want to have to explain his certainty about Clyne's proclivities, or Lyle's, any more clearly than he had.

Albany, too, glanced at Alyson. Then, after a slight nod to Jake, he awarded him a smile warmer than any he customarily offered anyone. He said, "You have not changed much since last we met, Jake Maxwell. I admired your courage then as I do now. I also respect your way of thinking and expressing your thoughts. By my troth, lad, if you would swear fealty to me, I'd welcome you to my service."

Alyson's hand on Jake's forearm remained motionless.

He said sincerely, "You honor me, my lord duke. But I must decline. Donald of the Isles is still my liege lord. I also owe fealty to my wife and her family. Alyson and I will take some time to ourselves here and then remove to MacGillivray House until Bishop Wardlaw's consecration."

With a half smile of his own, he added, "Afterward, we'll take the *Sea Wolf* into the Moray Firth and have a look at the Ardloch estate."

Alyson's hand twitched on his arm then.

"I see," Albany said. "It occurs to me that in explaining your marriage, you said naught of how the two of you came to meet."

Meeting his gimlet gaze, Jake wondered for the first time if he'd have been wiser to invent a tale to tell instead of the truth. Since he had not, he said, "My lads and I came upon the *Maryenknyght* whilst she was sinking, sir. The pirates who seized her took captives, including Orkney and James, then abandoned the ship. Her ladyship and a young friend of James's remained aboard. I rescued them and brought them back to Scotland."

"To St. Andrews," Albany said.

"Aye, your grace. I thought Wardlaw should know what had happened."

Horns sounded in the distance, and Alyson said, "That din doubtless heralds the arrival of my kinsmen from the Highlands, my lord duke. They will ride on from here to MacGillivray House, but we'll provide supper for them first and would be pleased to have you as our chief guest."

"Thank you, my lady," Albany said. "But my men and I will ride on to the Blackfriars, rather than impose on your hospitality. You'd liefer enjoy your family. Moreover, there is much yet for me to do in town and naught more to do here."

Signing to his men, he reined his horse around, only to pause and look back. "You will not want to house the men who rode here with Lyle, so I'll take them with me... Lyle, as well." Directing two of his men to see to it, he urged his mount forward again. His other men swiftly made way for him before following.

Hearing a sigh from his lady, Jake put an arm around her, drawing her close.

After a short time, she looked up at him and said, "Prithee, sir, what are 'assassins'? You mentioned the word earlier, and I had never heard it before."

"Killers," he said briefly, hugging her again. "I'll tell you all about them one day, but we have other matters to discuss first. Now, we will greet your family."

"That be a good notion," Will said from nearby shadows. "D'ye want me tae help the duke get rid o' all them other louts first, Cap'n Jake?"

Jake looked sharply at the boy. "What the devil are you doing there?"

Will stepped into the torchlight, cocking his head to one side. "Did ye no tell me tae keep me keekers on her ladyship?"

Amused, Alyson shook her head at Will and told him to stay near. "He has been gey helpful to me, Jake. Do not scold him."

"Nay, I'm pleased with the rascal," Jake said, ruffling Will's hair.

A few men still milled in the yard. Mungo was glowering

at one of Albany's men. The man spoke, and Lyle reluctantly went with him.

"I'm glad he's going," she said. "I'd not have known what to do with him."

"I know what I'd like to do," Jake said. "But I warrant Mungo won't make any more mischief."

A note in his voice made Alyson look at him but then decide not to demand an explanation. Albany's ruthlessness, especially toward those who had failed him, was renowned.

The yard was no sooner empty of Albany's men and Mungo's than the Highlanders arrived. The men rode into the yard first, led by Sir Ivor Mackintosh and Fin Cameron.

Dismounting, the tall, tawny-haired Ivor looked at Jake and Alyson and said, "What the devil are you doing with your arm around my cousin, Jake? What have you done with her husband and the troublemakers we heard about?"

"Come inside, *cousin*, and we'll tell you the whole tale," Jake said, grinning.

~

The Highland women arrived with Shaw MacGillivray and others who had remained to protect them. By then, Ivor and Fin—having ridden ahead with armed tails in response to messages from Farigaig and Alyson—had settled their men and beasts and were ready to accompany their wives in to supper.

Dismissing the servants as soon as platters of food, baskets of bread, and jugs of wine were on the table, Jake told his tale with Alyson assisting as necessary until they had related the whole story. Jake remained circumspect in his comments about Niall, so when Fin's wife—Ivor's sister, Catriona—demanded further elucidation, he held his breath and left the reply to her husband to make.

Fin said mildly, "We'll talk about that later, Cat."

Noting Alyson's astonishment at Catriona's nod of agreement, Jake recalled that Ivor had more than once referred to his sister as a wildcat. That Ivor, with his temper, had thought Catriona untamed made Jake eye Fin with even greater respect.

Ivor's wife, auburn-haired Lady Marsaili—or Marsi, as she preferred them to call her—looked thoughtful but asked no questions. Instead, she said with a small sigh, "I am sorry that his grace has died. He was always kind to me, and he loved Aunt Annabella so dearly. As for what happened to poor Jamie after we kept him safe last year, how I'd like to have Albany under *my* thumb just long—"

"Enough, lass," Ivor said. "Recall that castles have ears where one least expects to find them. In troth, Jake," he added, "I hope that you and Allie mean to remove to her Ardloch estate after the consecration. You'll both be safer there. I ken fine that Albany owes his life to you, but I'd not trust him a whit."

"Ivor's right," Shaw said.

"I know that, sir," Jake agreed, glancing at Alyson. "In troth, we'd be fain to travel north with you when you return."

"Then you will," Shaw said with a smile just like Ivor's.

Alyson said, "Well, as to that..." Pausing, she gave Jake a look.

"When and where do they mean to bury his grace?" Marsi asked.

Realizing that she addressed him, Jake said, "I don't

know, my lady. His grace likely made arrangements for a royal tomb somewhere."

"Nay, he did not," she said. "He told Aunt Annabella when she urged him to prepare one for himself that he was a wretched man unworthy of such a proud sepulcher. He told her to bury him in a dunghill with the epitaph, 'Here lies the worst king and the most miserable man in the whole kingdom.' "

A tear spilled down her cheek, and she said no more for a time.

Knowing that she had served as a waiting woman to her aunt, the late Queen, Jake was sure that she spoke the truth. He knew, as most Scots did, that Robert III had not liked being King. But it disturbed him to know that the man, who had tried so hard to protect his younger son, had thought so little of himself.

Alyson eyed Jake several more times while she caught up with details of her cousins' lives. Marsi and Ivor were expecting their first child in the fall; Catriona and Fin related several anecdotes about their two bairns; and Shaw reported that the elderly Mackintosh and his lady were as lively as ever. Shaw's wife, the lady Ealga, had remained with her parents when the others had ridden to Perth.

Although everyone seemed reluctant to part even for the few days remaining before the lords of Parliament would meet, Shaw soon rounded up his party and rode off with them to MacGillivray House, leaving Jake alone at last with Alyson.

She whirled to face him. "Jake, I don't know why you told Uncle Shaw that we'd ride back with them after the consecration. I cannot be ready to leave so soon. I'll have much to do to put MacGillivray House in order again before—"

She'd have gone on, he knew, had he not swept her into his arms, demanded directions to their bed, carried her there despite her protests, and dumped her on it.

As she scrambled up again, he said, "We are going with them, my love, because I have decided that we will. You need no longer see to your father's and Ranald's responsibilities. In troth, I mean to ask Farigaig to look after Braehead Tower for us after we leave, and to teach Ranald what to do here, as well. My hope is that Farigaig will stir himself to teach Ranald *all* that he must know. Your father and your brother both need an object in life. As for you, I mean to be yours."

Sitting on the bed, she cocked her head skeptically. "Do you mean that you'll give up the freedom you love so much to stay home with me?"

"Nay, lass, I won't make a promise I know I cannot keep. As a warrior owing fealty to my liege, I'll often have duties that take me from home. That is especially true now in the Isles, because Albany makes no secret of wanting to control them and the Highlands as well. And Donald of the Isles is determined to stop him."

"Then, I don't see how you expect to be my object in life," she said. "Even if Father agrees to look after things here... and with Catriona and Marsi nearby when you're away... Jake, I don't want to spend my life waiting for you to come home."

"Forbye, lass, you did say that you like the wind in your face. And I saw how much you enjoyed being on the *Sea Wolf*. I'm hoping that you will often travel with me, if that would please you. Much of my duty lies in carrying messages or supplies from one isle to another, and womenfolk abound on most of them who would be fain to welcome you. Moreover, today I almost lost you, Allie. It made me think hard."

"It made me think, too, and recall what I 'saw' on the *Sea Wolf* that night, when I thought I was feeling you die in my arms. It wasn't you but Niall."

"What I think is that you have much to learn about your gift and should question it always. It was right about Mungo meeting with Albany, and other things. But what I learned today, love, is that you've become more important to me than the *Sea Wolf*, and far more important than trying to enjoy my freedom without you. When I say that duty will often take me away, I know that I will always return to your side as quickly as I can. And there I will stay until duty calls again. I want bairns with you, sweetheart, lots of them, and I want to grow old with you. Sakes, I'd even like to bring my father to stay with us if he'd like to do so, and take you to Nithsdale to see where I was born. Now, lass, what do you say?"

She gazed into his eyes searchingly but only for a moment or two. Then, smiling, she said, "I say this, Jake, my beloved. Come here to me and show me that you mean that as much as I hope you do."

Needing no further invitation, he stripped off his clothes, noting with delight that she managed to rid herself of hers almost as swiftly.

Once he was in bed with her, the urge to take her quickly was strong. But he took his time, teasing her senses until she writhed in her pleasure and pleaded for release. Using hands, fingers, and lips, she stirred him until he could wait no longer.

Easing himself over her, he smiled when an impatient hand closed around his cock to help it find its way inside. Her velvety sheath pulsed hotly around it, melting away his last few grains of control.

With a groan, he gave himself up to his passions, letting her moans and small cries of pleasure fuel his efforts and carry them together to climax.

When they lay back against the pillows, sated, Alyson's head on Jake's shoulder, his arm around her, holding her close, she murmured, "You have a most enjoyable way of showing your feelings, my love."

Grinning, he murmured back, "Want me to show you again?"

Dear Reader,

I hope you enjoyed *Highland Lover* as well as the two other books of the Scottish Knights trilogy, *Highland Master* and *Highland Hero.*

Some of you will have recognized Jake Maxwell from *King of Storms.* Those of you who did not might enjoy reading it to see what Jake was like as a child.

As always, I know that some of you may have questions about the historical background, so here are a few facts that may clarify certain points:

Jamie Stewart was an English captive for more than eighteen years. Henry V of England sent him home in 1424. Both English Harry (Henry IV) and Albany had died before then, and Albany's son Murdoch Stewart became Governor of an ever more lawless Scotland. One of Jamie's first official acts was to hang Murdoch.

As mathematicians among you will note, I took an unusual (for me) liberty with this plot. I set the date of James's capture three years before its most likely date. Historical sources do exist that put it as early as the spring of 1403. James himself said it was 1404. But it is more likely that took place in March 1406. King Robert III died April 4, 1406, and at the time, folks blamed it on Jamie's capture.

The *Dictionary of National Biography* is one source acknowledging the earliest date but points out that Jamie's capture then would have been "in most flagrant defiance of a truce agreed to by Henry (King of England) till Easter 1405." That very English publication makes the statement as if it proves a date later than 1405. In fact, though, King Henry IV was well known for breaking truces. From the entry on him, in the same above source, "Before Easter 1405 an English ship had captured the heir to the Scottish throne, who... became James I."

My primary reason for putting Jamie's capture in 1403 was to keep the flow of the trilogy going without having to explain plausibly and at necessary length why it took so long for the King to realize after Davy Stewart's murder (March 17, 1402) that Jamie needed protection and decided to send him to France.

The "pirates" blamed for his capture are as suspect in reality as they are in *Highland Lover.* Not that they weren't pirates. At least, Hugh-atte-Fen (Hugh of the Fens), from Cley on the Norfolk coast, was a known pirate. However, he apparently did know that James was aboard the *Maryenknyght* and identified him at once on seeing him. Someone did betray Jamie, and Albany is the most likely one.

The city of Perth in Perthshire was originally St. John's Town of Perth, named for its Kirk of St. John. St. John's Town was the walled town. Perth was the shire containing it. That remained so until the late eighteenth century.

It was one of only two walled cities in Scotland before the sixteenth century. St. Andrews had a "west port," so there was a barrier of sorts there, but the English occupied Berwick-on-Tweed and St. John's Town of Perth in the thirteenth and early fourteenth centuries, and *they* walled both towns. The Scots saw little reason to wall their towns and did not do so before 1500.

Taverns (from the Latin *tabernae*) were English public houses that offered a night's lodging, along with various forms of entertainment. They date from the days of the Romans, who occupied Britain for four hundred years (from AD 55 to about 350) and brought the idea with them from Italy, where taverns were common. Inns and alehouses date from Saxon days (AD 728 on), and the equivalent of taverns in England were generally called alehouses in Scotland (Frederick W. Hackwood, *Inns, Ales, and Drinking Customs of Old England*, London, 1985).

Forms of chess were available from the Roman period onward.

Marsi's description, near the end of *Highland Lover*, of the conversation between Robert III and Queen Annabella, when Annabella urged him to follow the example of his ancestors and the custom of the age by preparing a royal tomb for himself, is accurate and his only recorded speech. However, he lies interred before the high altar at Paisley Abbey near Glasgow.

I extend a special thank-you to Andrew Mead, bookseller, of Filey, England, for his generous assistance with certain details about the area around Filey Bay.

As always, I also thank my wonderful agents, Lucy Childs and Aaron Priest, my editor Frances Jalet-Miller, Senior Editor Selina McLemore, my publicist Nick Small, Senior Managing Editor Bob Castillo, master copyeditor Sean Devlin, Art Director Diane Luger, Cover Artist Claire Brown, Editorial Director Amy Pierpont, Vice President and Editor in Chief Beth de Guzman, and everyone else at Hachette Book Group's Grand Central Publishing/Forever who contributed to this book.

If you enjoyed the Scottish Knights trilogy, please

look for the first book in the upcoming Lairds of the Loch series at your favorite bookstore in January 2013. Meantime, *Suas Alba!*

Sincerely,

Amanda Scott

http://www.amandascottauthor.com

Don't miss Amanda Scott's
next Highland romance!

Please turn this page for a
preview of the first book in the
new **Lairds of the Loch** series,

The Laird's Choice

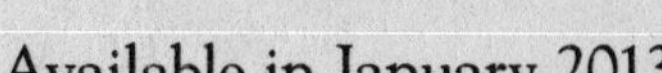

Available in January 2013

Chapter 1

Scotland, East Coast of Loch Long, 1425

Dree, what's amiss?" sixteen-year-old Lady Muriella MacFarlan demanded as she stopped her spinning wheel and pushed a strand of flaxen hair out of her face.

Her nineteen-year-old sister, tawny-haired Andrena, had stiffened on her stool near the fireplace in the ladies' solar at Tùr Meiloach. Now, eyes narrowed, head atilt, listening, but with every sense alert, Andrena set aside the mending that she loathed, remaining silent.

"Dree?"

Standing, holding a finger up to command silence, Andrena moved with her usual athletic grace to the south-facing window, its shutters open to let in the fresh, sun-warmed afternoon air, which was particularly welcome after the previous night's fierce storm. She could see over the barmkin wall to the steep, forested hillside below and other hills rolling beyond it to the declivity through which the river marking their south boundary plunged into the Loch of the Long Boats and on to the sea.

When Muriella drew breath to speak again, the third person in the room, their eighteen-year-old sister,

Lachina, said quietly, "Murie, dearling, contain your curiosity in silence for once. When Dree knows what is amiss, she will tell us." After the briefest of pauses, and not much to Andrena's surprise, Lachina added, "*Is* someone approaching the tower, Dree?"

"Perhaps not approaching," Andrena said. "But the birds seem distressed. I think someone has entered our south woods—a stranger—nay, more than one."

"Can you see who they are?" Muriella demanded, resting her spindle in its cradle and moving to stand beside Andrena at the window.

"I cannot see through the trees," Andrena said. "But it must be more than one person and likely fewer than four. You can see for yourself that the hawks are soaring in a tight circle yonder in the distance. And, if you look higher, you'll see an osprey soaring above them. I'm going outside to have a closer look."

In the same quiet way that she had spoken to Muriella, Lachina said, "Mayhap you should tell our lord father, Dree, or Malcolm."

"What would you have me tell them?" Andrena said with a slight smile. "Do you think either of them would send men out to search for intruders merely because I say the birds are unsettled?"

Lachina grimaced. They had had such discussions before, and both of them knew the answer to her question. Andrew Dubh MacFarlan would trust his men to stop intruders, and Andrew's steward, Malcolm Wily, would look long-suffering and declare that no one was there. By the time he decided, for the sake of peace, to send men out to look, there would *be* no one. Andrena had suggested once that perhaps their men had made more noise than the intruders did, but her father had said only that if that was so, her intruders had fled, which was the most desirable outcome.

"I'm going out," Andrena said again.

"Surely, men on the wall will see anyone coming," Muriella said as she peered into the distance. "Our boundary rivers are still in full spate, Dree. No one can cross them. And if anyone were approaching elsewhere, our lads would ring the bells. I think those birds are soaring just as they usually do."

"They are perturbed," Andrena said. "I shan't be long."

Her sisters exchanged a look, but although she noted the exchange, she did not comment. She knew that neither one would insist on accompanying her.

An instinct that she rarely ignored urged her to make what speed she could without drawing undue attention to herself. Therefore, she hurried down the service stairs, deciding not to change from her green tunic and skirt into the deerskin breeks and jack that she usually favored for her rambles. It occurred to her that she would have no excuse, having announced that strangers had entered the woods, to say that she had not thought anyone outside the family would see her in the boyish garb.

Andrew did not care what his daughters wore, but he did care when one of them distressed their mother, who had already deemed the breeks shameful. And her mossy green dress *would* blend well with woodland shrubbery.

From a rack near the postern door, she took her favorite wool cap and twisted her long tawny plaits up inside it. Then she donned the gray woolen shawl hanging next to it and grabbed the dirk that had hung by its belt under the shawl.

Fastening the belt so the weapon lay concealed beneath

the shawl, and leaving her rawhide boots where they lay on the floor, she went outside barefoot and crossed the yard to the narrow postern gate.

Three of the dogs, anticipating a walk, sprang up and ran to meet her.

Catching two by their collars, she said to the wiry red-headed lad eyeing her as he raked wood chips near the gate, "You'll have to keep them in for now, Pluff. If anyone should inquire about me, I'm going for a walk. But I don't want to have to keep the dogs from disturbing the woodland creatures."

"Aye, m'lady," the boy said with a gap-toothed grin. Setting aside the rake, he ordered the dogs back to their naps and unbolted the gate for her, adding, "Just shout when ye get back and I'll let ye in."

Smiling her thanks, she went through the gateway, hearing the heavy gate thud shut and then Pluff shooting the bolts. Looking skyward as she crossed the clearing between the barmkin and the woods, she saw that the circling birds had drawn nearer. Whoever was there was moving uphill toward their tower.

Looking over her shoulder, she saw one of their men on the wall and waved.

He waved back.

Satisfied that her sisters and at least two of the men knew she was outside the wall, she hurried into the woods. She had her dirk and the wee pipe she always carried in a pocket that Lina had cunningly woven for it in the shawl. Thanks to Andrew's teaching, Andrena was skilled with the dirk and, if necessary, could use the pipe to summon aid. Since she did not expect anyone in the woods to see her, she doubted that she would need help.

He was out of breath from running, but he knew that while pelting away from his pursuers he'd left evidence of his flight for a regrettable distance before he'd been far enough ahead of them to take precautions. As it was, he needed to find cover quickly and catch his breath. That his pursuers had lacked dogs to set on his trail was a rare boon from the ever fickle Fates.

He had been both careless and foolhardy, and it irked him. To have scaled the cliff from the stormy loch had been sensible, since he had seen no way in the pitch darkness to get safely away from the loch. The place he had come ashore had provided naught to warn him that he could travel no farther south without fording the damned river, which plunged to the loch in a hurtling waterfall.

To be sure, he had seen the land hereabouts from the water and knew how steep it was. He had seen the high, sharp ridge of peaks beyond it, too. But although the falls were full even then, he had assumed he'd be able to cross the river.

Apparently, one could, if one had the means. But after climbing up from the shore, he had seen how the river raged through its bed, tumbling over boulders and rocks as it went—too deep to ford and too wide and turbulent to swim safely.

He was well away from the river now, deep in ancient woods—a magnificent mixture of tall beeches, oaks, thickly growing conifers, and where it was dampest, spindly birches and willows. The woodsy scents filled him with a heady sense of freedom, but his pursuers were not far enough behind him yet for safety.

Although he had not entered such woodland for nineteen long months, he had hunted from the time he could keep up with his father, and he knew that he had retained his skills, even heightened some of them. Quietly drawing deep breaths and releasing them slowly as he moved, he forced himself to relax and bond with the forest while he listened and waited for the forest creatures to speak to him.

It occurred to him then that although he had moved more carefully and in near silence for the past quarter-hour, the denizens of the forest had remained remarkably still. He had not listened for them earlier, knowing that the roar of the river would conceal them and being more concerned about his pursuers.

A hawk cried above. An osprey responded with its shrill whistle, declaring the woods its territory, although it would have more luck catching fish from the nearby Loch of the Long Boats and ought more sensibly to leave the woodland to the hawks, who were better suited for hunting in them.

Thought ceased when he sensed someone moving as silently as he was through the woods north of him. Had one of the devils got round him? Was one south now and the others north? He had seen only three men earlier on the far side of the devilish river. They had swung across it on a rope tied to a high, stout branch of an ancient beech rooted in what had looked from a distance like solid rock.

The three carried swords and dirks. He had recognized them easily and knew they were searching for him. A soughing of leaves above him drew his glance to a female goshawk on a higher branch. The canopy above her was dense, but he knew that hawks, even big ones like the gos, with two-foot wingspans, were perfectly at home in the Highland woods. He had occasionally delighted in watching one take prey by flying between trees that had left insufficient room for it and at such speed that, to fit through, the bird seemed to fold wings and body into a thinly compressed arrowlike shape and do it without missing a single sweeping beat.

The hawk above him fixed one fierce yellow eye on him. Then, as if that glance were all it required, it opened its wings and swooped down and away.

He eyed the gos's erstwhile perch. It was high, but in the dense canopy above it a man might rest unseen for hours. A rustle of disturbed shrubbery south of him, accompanied by a man's muttered curse, made the decision an easy one.

Andrena heard the curse, too, and froze in place, listening. She had sensed the trespassers' approach more easily with each step. The woods were her true home, their every sound familiar. She had noted the eerie silence, had seen the goshawk as it shot through the trees in front of her at speed and without sound.

The hawk's presence might have frightened nearby small creatures to silence but would not account for the unnatural stillness of the forest at large. It seemed to hold its communal breath, to be waiting just as she was for the intruders to reveal their nature. The air was so still that, far below to her right, she could hear waves of the loch, still unsettled from the storm, hushing against the rockbound shore.

The strangers were much closer.

Sound traveled farther and more easily through the woods than most people realized, and her ears remained deer-sharp as she eased her way. The intruders were a score of yards away, perhaps a bit more, but an effortless bowshot in the open. She would soon be able to see them.

Noting movement near the ground, she saw that at least one creature had followed her from the tower. Lina's orange cat eyed her curiously through slender branches sprouting new leaves. Without a sound, the cat glided off ahead, doubtless prowling for its supper.

Andrena moved on, too. She did not hear noises specific enough to identify but knew there were at least two or three men. Careful to stay hidden but watchful, she also knew that her sweeping gaze would detect movement if there were any.

A large shadow passed between two large-trunked beeches ahead to her left.

Going still, she waited and watched as a stranger stepped between the two trees toward her. Two others followed. All three wore saffron tunics, kilted plaids of dull reds and greens, swords slung across their backs, and dirks at their belts.

So much, Andrena thought, for Muriella's certainty—and their father's—that no one could ford the furious river south of their tower without plunging to the loch and out to sea with the tide. Either the three men had forded it or they'd found other means of trespassing onto Andrew's land without his or his men's knowledge.

The man in the tree suppressed a curse at the sight of the lass below him. Who the devil, he wondered, would be daft enough to let a girl wander out alone in such dangerous times? His eyes narrowed as she carefully shifted her shawl and he saw the dirk in its sheath at her narrow leather girdle.

The louts searching for him would spit her or capture her without heed to the blade she carried. If she had an ounce of wit she would shift her shawl back over it. If they saw it, and they would, they might kill her just to teach her a lesson.

Realizing that he would be wise to recall that they might sense his presence as easily as he had sensed hers and to do what he could to prevent that, he fixed his gaze on a leaf midway between the three men, only five or six yards away now, and the girl moving toward them—ten paces from his tree—and let his mind go blank.

The last thing he wanted was for anyone to sense him watching them.

The men had come more swiftly than Andrena had expected when the birds caught her attention. Irritation with herself stirred at the sight of the three making their unlawful way through her father's woods. She had expected to get her look at them from the next rise and realized that she had taken longer than intended. In truth, she had paid more heed to the creatures' silence than to its most likely cause—that the intruders were moving faster than she had anticipated.

Lachina would say, and rightly, that having formed an image in her mind of what would happen, Dree had let her thoughts wander and, thus, had failed to think through all the possibilities of what *might* happen before coming out to investigate.

Hoping that Lina would not learn what she had done,

Dree considered what she ought to do next. She was close enough to Tùr Meiloach for people on its wall to hear the wee pipe if she blew it, so she slipped it out of its pocket into her hand.

Doubtless, the hawks still lingered nearby, as well.

However, she would not hesitate to offer assistance if the men had been storm-tossed onto the loch shore and simply missed their way. So perhaps if she…

What the devil was she doing now?

He tensed as he watched her step out into the path of his three pursuers but knew that he need worry no longer about their sensing his presence. The louts had seen her, and the Fates knew that she was stunning enough, even with that ridiculous boy's cap covering her hair, to stop most healthy men in their tracks.

She walked with grace on the uneven forest floor and did so without once glancing at her feet. Her posture was regal, and the soft-looking shawl did little to hide a curvaceous, womanly body.

Hearing a scrabbling on the bark below, he glanced down and saw her absurd cat clawing its way up the tree toward him. He could even hear it purr, when it should by rights be flying, claws spread, at the villains approaching its mistress.

"Forgive me, good sirs," the lass said in a clear, confident tone, her voice as warm and smooth as honey. "Doubtless, you have lost your way, but you are wandering in our woods. I fear that my father, the laird, requires that men present themselves at our tower before trespassing hereabouts."

"Does he now?" the tallest of the louts said, leering at her. "What else does your father, the laird, ha' tae say for himself, lassie?"

"We be searching for an escaped prisoner, mistress," the second man, dark-haired, said sternly. "Ye should no be out here on your own like this."

"I'll see her tae safety," the tall one said. "Come along, lassie. I dinna think ye belong tae the laird at all. A laird's daughter wouldna be wandering here all by herself. Doubtless, when we tell him ye've been pretending tae be his daughter, ye'll find yourself in the brambles. But I'll no tell him if ye be kind."

"I will gladly direct you to the tower," she said. "It lies—" Breaking off, when he grabbed her arm, she said icily, "Let go of me."

"Nay, then, I'll ha'—"

Putting two fingers to her lips, she whistled loudly.

"Here now, what the—"

A sparrow hawk flew from a nearby tree right at his face, flapping its wings wildly and shrieking its angry *kek-kek-kek* as it did.

With a cry, the man flung up an arm in defense. Shearing away at the last second, the bird swooped around and struck again. Flinging up both arms this time, the lout released the girl, who stepped away from him.

The cat had reached the branch on which the hunted man lay stretched, and walked up his body to peer over his right shoulder into his face, still purring.

Short of grabbing it and dropping it on one of the men below, he could do nothing useful, so he ignored it.

Had he his sword with him or even the lass's dirk, he might have dropped in on the conversation. As it was, he hoped they would realize from her demeanor that she was as noble as she claimed and would wonder, as he did, why men were not already rushing noisily to her aid, summoned by her whistling.

He had barely finished that thought when three goshawks arrived. Shrieking wildly, and all much larger than the sparrow hawk, they frightened the men badly. The first man, already intimidated by the small hawk, took off running back the way he had come. The others tried to shoo the goshawks away, but they screamed as if they were new parents and the men had disturbed their young.

"Our birds are exceedingly territorial, I fear," the lass said matter-of-factly.

"Call them off, ye devilish witch!" the dark-haired man yelled at Andrena while flapping his arms. Since he was also trying to protect his eyes with his hands, his flailing elbows had little effect.

"They are scarcely my birds, sir," she replied, elevating him with that single word far above his deserved station in life. "They simply know that I belong here and you do not. Had I brought my dogs, they would act in a similar way, as I am sure your dogs do when someone threatens you. I cannot call them off, but if you follow your friend back the way you came, they *may* stop attacking you."

The hawks, acting more helpfully than hawks usually did, continued flying at the two men despite their furious waving and shouts. One reached for his sword.

"Don't touch that weapon if you value your life," she said, raising the wee pipe near her lips. "If I blow this pipe, our men will come, so you should know that my father wields the power of the pit and gallows. Our hanging tree stands just outside our gate, and he will not hesitate to hang you for harassing me. If the men on our wall have not already heard the birds shrieking, they will hear my—"

The man was staring beyond her. Glancing over her shoulder, she saw that in the racket the three hawks had made, she had failed to hear the osprey's arrival. The huge bird perched on a nearby branch, looking even more immense when it puffed up its feathers and glowered at the intruder.

"She has much worse manners than the others, so do not challenge her," Andrena said. "Truly, the birds hereabouts do *not* like strangers in their territory."

"We're a-going, then. But ye'd best tell that father o' yours that if he finds our prisoner wandering about, he must send him back to the laird in irons."

"I will give him your message, but you must tell me who your laird is. I am unable to glean such information from your mind."

"Aye, well, I thought ye'd ken well enough who we be. The missing chap be one o' Parlan Pharlain's galley slaves, taken in fair capture whilst raiding."

"Then doubtless my father will do as you wish," Andrena said mendaciously. Andrew would more likely help the man on his way.

The osprey, balefully eyeing the intruders, spread its wings and twitched its talons menacingly.

Abruptly, the men turned and followed their erstwhile companion. The goshawks, being one of the few hawks that will hunt together and now a veritable flock, swooped after the intruders.

Andrena stood for a time, listening, to be sure they

were well on their way. Then, hearing a loud purr at her feet, she looked down and saw the orange cat. It walked right across her bare feet, rubbing against her shins.

"Where did you spring from this time?" she asked it.

The cat blinked at her, then continued around her and back toward the tower. Turning to follow it, Andrena found herself face-to–broad chest with a very tall, broad-shouldered, muscular, half-naked stranger.

Startled nearly out of her wits, she snapped, "Where did you…that is, who are…How did you get so close behind me? I never—"

"Hush, lass, they may still be near enough to hear." His voice was deeper than her father's, and mellow, unlike any she could imagine coming from a villain.

"They are halfway down the hill to the river by now," she said.

"They may be, aye, but I want to be sure."

"Then follow them. But how did you get so close to me, especially as big as you are? Faith, you're a giant, and I can nearly always—" Breaking off, aware that she was talking too much, she said, "You must be their missing prisoner, aye?"

His twinkling gaze met her curious one. "They would identify me as their prisoner, aye. But I disapprove of slavery, so I don't see the matter as they do."

"I suppose not. But—" Breaking off again when she saw that he still gazed steadily at her, she eyed him askance. "Are you *not* going to follow them, then?"

"Nay, for I canna leave a wee lassock like yourself out here alone. I'll see ye safely tae your gate first."

"Thank you, but I don't want or need your escort," she said firmly.

"Aye, well, ye need not look so displeased by the notion," he said with a wistful-looking smile. "Unless ye fear that he'll hang me for escaping..."

"Nay, he will not do that. He has nae love for Parlan Pharlain."

"Then why do you hesitate, lass? Art afraid he'll punish you for coming out all alone and learning how dangerous that can be?"

"Nay, for he won't do that, either. In troth, although he will not hang you, you *are* the one who should be leery of him."

"And why is that?"

"Because, since you managed to escape from Parlan Pharlain and must therefore be his enemy, Father *will* almost certainly insist that you marry me."

THE DISH

Where authors give you the inside scoop!

From the desk of Vicky Dreiling

Dear Reader,

HOW TO RAVISH A RAKE stars shy wallflower Amy Hardwick and charming rake William Darcett, better known as "the Devil." I thought it would be great fun to feature two characters who seem so wrong for one another on the surface but who would find love and happiness, despite their differences.

Miss Amy Hardwick is a shy belle who made her first appearance in my debut historical romance, *How to Marry a Duke.* When I first envisioned Amy, I realized that she was representative of so many young women who struggle to overcome low self-esteem. Amy doesn't fit the ideal image of the English rose in Regency Society, and, as a result, she's often overlooked by others. But as I thought back to my days in high school and college, I remembered how much it helped to have girlfriends who liked and supported you, even though you didn't have the flawless skin and perfect bodies airbrushed on the covers of teen magazines. That recollection convinced me that having friends would help Amy to grow into the woman I knew she was destined to become.

Now, during her sixth and quite possibly last London Season, Amy is determined to shed her wallflower image forever. A newfound interest in fashion leads Amy to draw designs for unique gowns that make her the fashion darling of the *ton*. All of her dreams seem to be coming true, but there's one man who could deter her from the road to transformation: Mr. William "the Devil" Darcett.

Ah, Will...*sigh*. I confess I had a penchant for charming bad boys when I was in high school and college. There's a certain mystique about them. And I'm certain that the first historical romance I ever read featured a charming bad boy. They really are my favorite type of heroes. So naturally, I decided to create the worst bad boy in the *ton* and throw him in sweet Amy's path.

William Darcett is a younger son with a passion for traveling. He's not one to put down roots—just the occupation for a bona fide rake. But Will's latest plans for another journey to the Continent go awry when he discovers his meddling family wants to curb his traveling days. Will refuses to let his family interfere with his carousing and rambling, but a chance encounter with Amy in a wine cellar leads the wallflower and the rake into more trouble than they're prepared to handle.

This very unlikely pair comes to realize that laughter, family, and honesty are the most important ingredients for everlasting love. I hope you will enjoy the adventures of Amy and Will on their journey to discover that even the unlikeliest of couples can fall madly, deeply in love.

My heartfelt thanks to all the readers who wrote to let me know they couldn't wait to read HOW TO RAVISH A RAKE. I hope you will enjoy the fun and games that finally lead to Happily Ever After for Amy and Will.

Cheers!

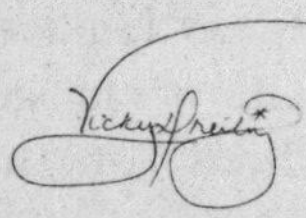

♥ ♥ ♥ ♥ ♥ ♥ ♥ ♥ ♥ ♥ ♥ ♥ ♥ ♥ ♥

From the desk of Amanda Scott

Dear Reader,

What happens when a freedom-loving Scotsman who's spent much of his life on the open sea meets an enticing heiress determined to make her home with a husband who will stay put and run her Highland estates? And what happens when something that they have just witnessed endangers the plans of a ruthless and powerful man who is fiercely determined to keep the details of that event secret?

HIGHLAND LOVER, the third title in my Scottish Knights trilogy, stars the fiercely independent Sir Jacob "Jake" Maxwell, who was a nine-year-old boy in *King of Storms*, the last of a six-book series beginning with *Highland Princess*. Lifting a fictional child from a series I wrote years ago to be a hero in a current trilogy is new for me.

However, the three heroes of Scottish Knights are friends who met as teenage students under Bishop Traill of St. Andrews and later accepted his invitation to join a brotherhood of highly skilled knights that he (fictionally) formed to help him protect the Scottish Crown. I realized straightaway that the grown-up Jake would be the right age in 1403 and would easily fit my requirements, for several reasons:

First, Jake has met the ruthless Duke of Albany, who was a villainous presence in Scotland for thirty-one years (in all) and is now second in line for the throne. Determined to become King of Scots, Albany habitually eliminates anyone who gets in his way. Second, Albany owes his life to Jake, a relationship that provides interesting twists in any tale. Third, Jake is captain of the *Sea Wolf*, a ship he owns because of Albany; and the initiating event in HIGHLAND LOVER takes place at sea. So Jake seemed to be a perfect choice. The cheeky youngster in *King of Storms* had stirred (and still stirs) letters from readers suggesting that an adult Jake Maxwell would make a great hero. Doubtless that also had something to do with it.

Jake's heroine in HIGHLAND LOVER is Lady Alyson MacGillivray of Perth, a beautiful cousin of Sir Ivor "Hawk" Mackintosh of *Highland Hero*. Alyson is blessed (or cursed) with a bevy of clinging relatives and the gift of Second Sight. The latter "gift" has caused as many problems for her as have her intrusive kinsmen.

Alyson also has another problem—a husband of just a few months whom she has scarcely seen and who so far seems more interested in his noble patron's affairs than in Alyson's Highland estates or Alyson herself. But Alyson is trapped in this wee wrinkle, is she not? It is, after all, 1403.

In any event, Jake sets out on a mission for the Bishop of St. Andrews, encounters a storm, and ends up plucking Alyson and an unknown lad from a ship sinking off the English coast two hundred miles from her home in Perth. The ship also happened to be carrying the young heir to Scotland's throne and Alyson's husband, who may or may not now be captive in England.

So, the fun begins. I hope you enjoy HIGHLAND LOVER.

Meantime, *Suas Alba!*

Amanda Scott

www.amandascottauthor.com

♥ ♥ ♥ ♥ ♥ ♥ ♥ ♥ ♥ ♥ ♥ ♥ ♥ ♥ ♥

From the desk of Dee Davis

Dear Reader,

I've been a storyteller all of my life. When I was a kid, my dad and I used to sit in the mall or a restaurant and make up stories about the people walking by or sitting around us. So it really wasn't much of a leap to find myself a novelist. But what was interesting to me was that no matter what kind of story I was telling, the characters all seemed to know each other.

Sometimes people from other novels were simply mentioned in another of my books in passing. Sometimes they actually had cameo appearances. And several times now, a character I had created to be a secondary figure in one story has demanded his or her own book. Such was the case with Harrison Blake of DEADLY DANCE. Harrison first showed up in my Last Chance series, working as that team's computer forensic expert. It even turned out he'd also worked for *Midnight Rain*'s John Brighton at his Phoenix organization, even though the company was created at the end of the book and never actually appeared on paper.

Interestingly enough, Harrison, although never a hero, has received more mail than any of my other characters. And almost all of those letters are from readers asking when he's going to have his day. So when A-Tac found itself in need of a technical guru, it was a no-brainer for me to bring Harrison into the fold. As he became an integral part of the team, I knew the time had come for him to have his own book.

And of course, as his story developed, he needed help from his old friends. So enter Madison Roarke and Tracy Braxton. Madison was the heroine of the first Last Chance book, *Endgame*. And like Harrison, Tracy had been placed in the role of supporting character, as a world-class forensic pathologist.

What can I say? It's a small world, and they all know and help each other. And finally, we add to the mix our heroine, Hannah Marshall. Hannah has been at the heart of all the A-Tac books. A long-time team member, she's always there with the answers when needed. And like Harrison, she made it more than clear to me that she deserved her own story. With her quirky way of expressing herself (eyeglasses and streaked hair) and her well-developed intellect, Hannah seemed perfect for Harrison. The two of them just didn't know it yet.

So I threw them together, and, as they say, the plot thickened, and DEADLY DANCE was born.

Hopefully you'll enjoy reading Harrison and Hannah's story as much as I did writing it.

For insight into both Harrison and Hannah, here are some songs I listened to while writing DEADLY DANCE:

Riverside, by Agnes Obel

Set Fire to the Rain, by Adele

Everlong, by Foo Fighters

And as always, check out www.deedavis.com for more inside info about my writing and my books.

Happy Reading!

♥ ♥ ♥ ♥ ♥ ♥ ♥ ♥ ♥ ♥ ♥ ♥ ♥ ♥ ♥

From the desk of Katie Lane

Dear Reader,

Before I plot out the storyline and flesh out my characters, my books start with one basic idea. Or maybe I should say they start with one nagging, persistent thought that won't leave me alone until I put it down on paper.

Going Cowboy Crazy started with the concept of long-lost twins and what would happen if one twin took over the other twin's life and no one—save the hot football coach—was the wiser.

Make Mine a Bad Boy was the other side of that premise: What would happen if your twin, whom you didn't even know you had, married your boyfriend and left you with a good-for-nothing, low-down bad boy?

And CATCH ME A COWBOY started with a melodrama. You know the kind I'm talking about, the story of a dastardly villain taking advantage of a poor, helpless woman by tying her to the railroad tracks, or placing her on a conveyor belt headed toward the jagged blade of a saw, or evicting her from her home when she has no money to pay the rent. Of course, before any of these things happen, the hero arrives to save the day with a smile so big and bright it rivals the sun.

For days, I couldn't get the melodrama out of my mind. But no matter how much the idea stuck with me, I just didn't see it fitting into my new book. My heroine had already been chosen: a favorite secondary character from the previous novels. Shirlene is a sassy, voluptuous west Texas gal who could no more play the damsel in distress than Mae West could play the Singing Nun. If someone tied Shirlene to the train tracks, she wouldn't scream, faint, or hold the back of her hand dramatically to her forehead. She'd just ask if she had enough time for a margarita.

The more I thought of my sassy heroine dealing with a Snidely Whiplash–type, the more I laughed. The more I laughed, the more I wrote. And suddenly I had my melodrama. Except a funny thing happened on the way to Shirlene's Happily Ever After: My villain and my hero got a little mixed up. And before I knew it, Shirlene had so charmed the would-be villain that he stopped the train. Shut off the saw. Paid the rent.

And how does the hero with the bright smile fit into all of this? you might ask.

Well, let's just say I don't think you'll be disappointed.

CATCH ME A COWBOY is available now.

Enjoy, y'all!

Katie Lane

Find out more about Forever Romance!

Visit us at
www.hachettebookgroup.com/publishing_forever.aspx

Find us on Facebook
http://www.facebook.com/ForeverRomance

Follow us on Twitter
http://twitter.com/ForeverRomance

NEW AND UPCOMING TITLES

Each month we feature our new titles
and reader favorites.

CONTESTS AND GIVEAWAYS

We give away galleys, autographed copies,
and all kinds of exclusive items.

AUTHOR INFO

You'll find bios, articles, and links to personal websites
for all your favorite authors—and so much more.

GET SOCIAL

Connect with your favorite authors, editors, and
other Forever fans, and share what's important to you.

THE BUZZ

Sign up for our monthly romance newsletter,
and be the first to read all about it.